What the critics are saying…

BEST NEW AUTHOR ROMANCE EROTIC CAPA 2004

GOLD STAR "If you think an erotic romance can't surprise you, think again. There were moments in the story that were utterly unexpected and all the more erotic for that fact....The romance between Jessica and Mac was bumpy, but if there was ever a GREAT, realistic HEA, this one was it...Sarah McCarty managed to stick great characterization, bits of humor, amazing sex, and an incredibly believable HEA into her book, and I'm glad I've read it. If there is just one book you pick up from Ellora's Cave this week, grab Unchained: Mac's Law without hesitation!" ~ *Dani JERR*

GOLD STAR "Mac's Law has the WOW factor. This book is impressive, multi-layered, with three-dimensional characters that jump off the pages and make you wish you were visiting with them in the small Texas town of Round the Bend. Mac's Law is steamy, memorable, and unforgettable in its raw depiction of small town America and the complex relationship that develops between Mac and Jessie....Sarah McCarty has managed to impress me again with her marvelous, heart-wrenching, and addictive writing. Mac and Jessie sparkle when they lock horns, and their sexual banter pulls the reader further into their story. The dialogue is fresh, the characterization is believable and the plot unfolds realistically... Mac's Law definitely belongs on my keeper shelf." ~ *Aggie JERR*

5 BLUE RIBBON AWARD "MAC'S LAW... is HOT, HOT, HOT!!! Ms. McCarty has created two characters whose sexual tension is palpable and whose chemistry singes the pages. Their emotions grip the reader and hold their attention throughout. MAC'S LAW is not to be missed." ~ *Ansley Romance Junkies*

5 STARS! "Sarah McCarty is certainly making a name for herself. She's got sexy alpha heroes, strong and feisty women and a plot that will grab your emotions and not let go. All of those and more are in this latest release. UNCHAINED: MAC'S LAW is an exceptionally wonderful story that is full of lust, laughter, and lots of love... MAC'S LAW is phenomenal!... It is the emotions that are invoked that make this a top-notch read. You feel for these characters and can't wait to see how they work everything out. Now go grab a glass of ice and a significant other and prepare to be blown away by this intense story!" ~ *Nicole eCataRomance*

RECOMMENDED READ- "Sarah McCarty's contemporary erotic romance, Mac's Law seduces and holds a reader captive to the sexual tension, chemistry and emotions of the characters... The heart and strength of Mac is powerful and a reader can't help but fall in love with him. Jessie is electrifying. She is a feisty, strong, yet vulnerable and very endearing... she is an amazing heroine who readers won't soon forget. The secondary characters in this tale were a wonderful and delightful addition to this story, they made me laugh out loud and appreciate the bond of friendship. Mac's Law is 100% seductive, hot and realistic..... Mac's Law is a fantastic start to this new series." ~ *Tracey Road to Romance*

SARAH McCARTY

UNCHAINED
MAC'S LAW

An Ellora's Cave Romantica Publication

www.ellorascave.com

Unchained: Mac's Law

ISBN #141995170X

Edited by: Pamela Campbell
Cover art by: Syneca

Electronic book Publication: September, 2004
Trade paperback Publication: May, 2005

Warning:

The following material contains graphic sexual content meant for mature readers. *Mac's Law* has been rated *E-rotic* by a minimum of three independent reviewers.

Ellora's Cave Publishing offers three levels of Romantica™ reading entertainment: S (S-ensuous), E (E-rotic), and X (X-treme).

S-*ensuous* love scenes are explicit and leave nothing to the imagination.

E-*rotic* love scenes are explicit, leave nothing to the imagination, and are high in volume per the overall word count. In addition, some E-rated titles might contain fantasy material that some readers find objectionable, such as bondage, submission, same sex encounters, forced seductions, etc. E-rated titles are the most graphic titles we carry; it is common, for instance, for an author to use words such as "fucking", "cock", "pussy", etc., within their work of literature.

X-*treme* titles differ from E-rated titles only in plot premise and storyline execution. Unlike E-rated titles, stories designated with the letter X tend to contain controversial subject matter not for the faint of heart.

Also by Sarah McCarty:

Promises Linger
Promises Keep

Mac's Law

Dedication

For Joy: A woman who generously shares her gift of laughter with us all. Joy, may you always laugh, always find pleasure in the moment, and most of all, may you find that special man who delights in you, the way you've always dreamed.

Chapter One

Oh Hell! Homer Lone Tree was at it again.

Mac sat on the bar stool in the local bar and grill, pinched the bridge of his nose between his thumb and forefinger, and willed his headaches to go away—the one throbbing behind his eyes, and the one walking down the street with the purpose of a man bent on proving a point.

He sighed. His day only needed this. It wasn't enough the cook he'd hired through some fancy employment agency in Dallas had pulled a no-show. Now he had to watch Homer make a fool of himself with the only person who had gotten off the late afternoon bus—a delicate, citified woman with blonde hair. With one hand, he rubbed the ache from behind his eyes while motioning to the bartender with the other.

Bull stopped his perpetual wiping down of the orange Formica counter. "Tough day, huh?"

"It's only going to get tougher," he answered grimly. "That new cook that was supposed to turn up on the six p.m. bus?"

"Yeah?"

"He pulled a no-show."

"That's the third one this month!" Bull whisked away the beer and supplanted it with two fingers of whiskey. Mac looked at the glass, looked at Bull, and cast a longing glance at his beer.

Bull intercepted the latter. "Forget that namby-pamby stuff." He pushed the glass an inch closer. "You're going to need every drop of this, if not for courage, then for anesthesia."

Mac grimaced. "The men will understand."

Bull emitted a noise that crossed the line from laughter to hoot. "You made a promise, Mac."

His fingers curled around the glass. "Yes, I did, and I've done my best to fulfill it."

"I see," The older man resumed wiping the counter. "And I assume you're expecting the men to be satisfied with that, to continue to do their best work, even though you keep slopping them like hogs?"

"The beans weren't that bad. Just a little scorched."

"A little light in the description, aren't we?"

"What do you mean?"

"I mean I heard about what you tried to feed the men last night."

Mac winced. A cook he was not. "What do you mean, 'heard'?"

"I mean exactly that. The men are fed up, son. For two months you've been shoveling them garbage like that."

"It hasn't been all garbage. Granny Ortiz sent over some stuff."

"Well, it couldn't have been frequently enough then, because the men have been wandering around town all day garnering sympathy for their plight."

"I'm a rancher, not a cook."

"Well, you'd better learn to tie an apron quick," Bull countered. "Because the men are talking strike and no one in town is against it."

"Damn." That was not good news. Mac took a sip of his whiskey, forgetting what a kick Bull's favorite brand possessed. He smothered the sound of his cough with a squeak of his vinyl-topped stool. God, he hated whiskey.

The bell over the door rang. Bull looked up and smiled in anticipation. "I guess it's just not your lucky day. Here comes Homer."

Mac sighed. "I don't know why you keep insisting he's my problem. I'm the Justice of the Peace. I'm supposed to be marrying people, not arresting them."

Bull shrugged, obviously unconcerned with such trivial hairsplitting. "A Justice of the Peace is as close as we get to law around here."

"We could call in the county sheriff," he countered dryly.

"Ah hell. No one wants to see Homer arrested. He'll work it out of his system soon enough."

"He's either got to get it out of his system, or that theme park has got to hire him," Mac said as he turned his stool around. "He can't go around harassing our female visitors forever. Too few of them stray our way in the first place."

"Ain't that the truth?" Bull agreed, scrubbing at an imaginary spot. "But for the life of me, I can't see what they expect to find in Dallas that they can't find here."

"A night life?"

"Hell, we've got night life. We've got Homer."

Mac laughed. "I'm not sure that qualifies as a life. More like a nuisance."

"That's no way to be talking about your own."

"I'm best friends with his brother, Bull. We're not blood."

"Same difference."

Yeah, he supposed it was. In a town as small as Round the Bend, Texas, playmates were hard for a kid to rustle up. Once a playmate was discovered, he or she tended to become part of the extended family. "Well, kin or not, I wish Homer would pick something less embarrassing to do with his Saturdays."

And stop expecting him to step in at the crucial moment to save his ass.

"Personally, I hope he keeps it up for at least another month," Bull countered. "Saturday afternoons used to be slow, but with all this extra money, I might just make enough to get my son that fancy bike he wants for his birthday."

"Uh-huh."

Pushing his battered black Stetson off his brow, Mac watched Homer zero in on his unsuspecting prey. And sighed.

Ever since that theme park had refused to hire Homer for one of their shows, claiming he didn't look "Indian" enough, Homer had been staging his own impromptu shows, bent on proving them wrong.

Mac redirected his gaze to the woman. She looked the type to scream at a mouse. Lord knows what kind of ruckus she was going to throw when Homer got near. She'd probably bring down the roof, just as the last victim of Homer's temper had. Then everyone would deem it his responsibility to save the hysterical damsel in distress.

He'd rather be nibbled to death by ducks.

He glared through the plate glass window. If he focused his gaze dead center between the "Bull" and "Bar" of Bull's Bar and Grill, he could see Zach, standing in front of his law office, grinning from ear to ear, no doubt anticipating the show he'd be able to see through the window. He flipped Zach an obscene response to his grin. He just shrugged and shook his head.

If not him, then who?

Mac pulled his hat back over his brow, ducked his chin, and from beneath the protective shadow of his Stetson, studied Homer's approach from a different slant. He wondered if maybe Grandma Ortiz, the town's matchmaker, had been the one to put the wild hair in Homer's pants. If this was another of her efforts at getting him married, at least her taste in victims had improved. This woman was a far cry from the pretty, brassy redhead she'd tossed his way last Christmas. Not only had that woman had a mouth that would have done a sailor proud, but she hadn't had one smidgeon of humor in her fully stacked body.

He took a more cautious sip of his whiskey. The woman Homer was closing in on, however, was a lady from head to toe. Her streaky blonde hair was in place despite what had to have been a long bus ride. Her makeup was perfect, enhancing her sun-kissed complexion right down to the deep pink lipstick that outlined a full, totally kissable mouth. He shifted uneasily in his chair. There was a certain lift to the corners of that mouth that told him it was used to laughing. There was nothing that turned him on faster than a laughing woman. He wondered who she was in town to visit. If her sense of humor was as well turned out as her appearance, it might be worth looking her up and seeing if she was interested in a no-strings western fling.

He pushed his glass aside when Homer stopped just short of the woman. Ah, hell he really was going through with this. Again.

As Homer straightened his buckskin shirt and arranged the feathers on his shield, the patrons of the grill did something Mac hadn't thought possible. They shut up. With a deep sigh of resignation, he settled back on his stool. The show was about to begin.

Homer stepped in front of the woman's booth. This was the first of several well-rehearsed, predictable moves. If he called out right now, Mac knew, he could put an end to this foolishness. He was halfway to committing social suicide when Bull flicked him with the bar towel.

"Don't be spoiling things, now," Bull whispered. "Homer's entertaining, but harmless." He shook the bar towel to reinforce his point. "And you know it."

"Yeah, right. He may be harmless to the women, but not to me. I damned near lost an eardrum the last time he pulled this stunt." He pointed his finger at Bull. "If this one's a screamer, I'm quitting."

"Twenty dollars says she's not a screamer."

Mac redirected his gaze to the woman. She had screamer written all over her. "You're on."

"No," Bull corrected as Homer stepped in front of the woman's booth. "I'd say you are."

"Nice woman," Homer said loud enough to carry. Mac winced. He had spoken to Homer before about his dialogue. If the kid was going to create these scenes and expect him to charge to the rescue at the appropriate time, he felt he was within his rights to demand a little attention be paid to the script. He noticed the woman had also winced, and wondered if it was Homer's breath or choice of words she found offensive.

"Thank you," the woman said coolly, accompanying the reply with a slight incline of her head.

"Must be her mom taught her manners carried the day," Bull whispered.

"Yeah." Despite himself, Mac was impressed. It wasn't every woman who could maintain her cool when a nineteen-year-old Comanche Indian in full war paint and slightly moth-eaten regalia popped up at her elbow. Impressed enough that he handed over the twenty, not taking his eyes off the unfolding drama. Not only because he didn't want to miss his cue but also because the more he watched the woman the more interesting she became.

Homer thumped his closed fist against his chest. "Me great warrior."

"I could tell that from the feathers attached to your shield."

Titters of laughter ebbed and flowed around the room.

"This ought to be good," Bull whispered. "Nothing gets Homer going faster than being humored."

That's what Mac was afraid of.

And rightly so, because in the next second, Homer attempted to catch the woman's hand in his and succeeded in knocking over her cup instead. It tumbled off the table and onto the worn linoleum where its contents formed a puddle. The woman jumped up from the seat, and tried to stop the flood with her paper napkin.

"Better get a mop and another cup of coffee ready," Mac whispered over his shoulder.

"She's drinking tea."

As if he needed anymore reminding that she was city. "That figures."

He returned his attention to the scene. He could tell from Homer's scowl that he was embarrassed. The woman wasn't so easy to read. The expression on her face could be either pained or amused, probably the former from the way all ten fingers were flattened on the top of her purse.

"If this is some kind of Western pickup, I'll have to decline." Her voice was all prim and proper. Definitely Eastern. She shrugged. "It's not that I don't find your approach…unique. I'm just not in the market."

Homer wasn't having any of that. He scowled so hard, his war paint cracked. Mac couldn't blame him. If Homer succeeded in dragging this blonde home, his girlfriend Molly definitely would sit up and take notice. Probably just long enough to load Homer's ass with buckshot.

The woman grabbed more napkins as the first turned to mush and dabbed at the spill on the table. Homer, out to impress, captured her hand in his. With muscles honed through years of construction work, he pulled her away from the booth and up against his buckskin-clad chest. She promptly sneezed.

Mac rubbed his hand across his mouth to hide his amusement at Homer's astonishment.

Homer whipped out a rubber tomahawk and raised it threateningly. "You now my woman."

"I don't think so." The dismissal was coolly to the point. Homer was having none of it.

Mac sighed. It was probably time to do his hero to the rescue routine. He slid off his stool.

Homer wrapped the woman's fat braid around his wrist. "Come, woman."

"Look, big guy," the woman said, with a twitch of her lips. "I already told you this caveman approach is wasted on me, so why don't you find someone else to harass and let me get back to my tea?"

"Come now."

"You're pulling my hair."

Homer switched his grip to her arm. "Come."

"I'm warning you," she said. "I'm going to hurt you if you don't let me go."

Homer, of course, did nothing of the sort. What was one delicate city woman against a big strapping country boy?

The woman sighed. Then on a "Have it your way," she turned in his grip. Mac marveled that she could still appear delicate and fragile as she dropped the six-foot-two-inch teen with a hard jerk of her knee.

Mac very slowly backed off until his legs hit the stool he'd just vacated. He ran his eyes over the woman from the top of her head, with its elegant French braid, to the tips of her pretty pink toenails peeking out from her open-toed pumps. He watched as she gingerly stepped over Homer's prostrate form, slung her purse over her shoulder and walked up to the counter.

"Do any of you know where I might find Mac Hollister?" she asked, coming around the counter and scooping ice into a large dishtowel. Silence greeted her question. The woman pulled herself up to all of her five-foot-nothing height. Mac figured they were supposed to be impressed.

"Well?"

Not a single man let his eyes stray toward him. Mac, in turn, watched the woman as she harrumphed "Figures" and strolled across the worn gray linoleum to shove the ice pack into Homer's hands.

"Try to remember in the future that manhandling a woman is not the safest course to choose in these troubled times."

Homer just stared incredulously at her, his hands automatically clutching the ice pack to his groin.

Mac glanced around and was relieved to see that he wasn't the only one who was gaping like an idiot. Bull cleared his throat meaningfully. Mac turned to the redheaded man and got the message loud and clear. Someone had to deal with this crazy woman, and from the looks he was getting, it appeared he was elected. Sliding off the stool, he settled his hat. It might just be his pleasure.

"I don't think Homer's likely to forget that in the near future, ma'am."

*****

Jessica slowly straightened and looked at the man before her. She'd noticed him the moment she'd walked into the grill. What red-blooded woman wouldn't? The man practically oozed testosterone, drawing the eye whether a woman wanted it drawn or not. His indolent posture, easy confidence and raw masculinity just screamed "bad boy". Top that off with the way he was attired—worn, blue denim shirt that hugged his broad shoulders, jeans so broken in they clung to his lean hips and muscular thighs—and the man was a fantasy come to life. The battered black Stetson he wore slightly forward and to the side was just icing on the cake.

And he was now standing before her. All six feet, two hundred mouthwatering pounds of him. This close, she could see his hair was thick and chocolate-brown with a tendency to curl where it brushed his collar. He was around thirty. His eyes were deep blue with faint lines at the corners. The laughter lurking behind the politeness in his gaze told her those lines were created as much by a sense of humor as by long hours in the sun. A sense of humor was high on her list of qualities in a potential lover, and this man definitely had potential. She gave him a small smile and nodded toward the teen on the floor. "Does he do this often?"

He blinked twice before answering. "Only when he and his girlfriend fight, and he decides it's time to make a few points."

"With whom?"

"With his girlfriend, for starters," he said. In the face of her stare, he shrugged. "He feels a periodic need to make her jealous."

"Right." He said that as if it made perfect sense.

"And secondly?" she asked trying to keep her smile down to casual when it wanted to kick up to laughter at the sheer absurdity of what she was hearing.

"And to the hiring officials at the local theme park." The man's gaze narrowed its focus to just south of her eyes. "Seems they didn't think Homer looked Indian enough."

He was staring at her mouth, she realized. Did she have lipstick on her teeth? She switched her smile to the closed-lip variety. The last thing she wanted to do was to scare off the first "possible" of the last twelve months before she'd had a chance to adequately explore his…possibilities.

"Have they seen him lately?" she asked with an arch of her brow.

"Nope." He pushed his Stetson back further. His chin jerked in Homer's direction. "Who taught you that little trick?"

"A friend." It was her turn to shrug. "He guaranteed it as the most effective method of taking the starch out of a man."

"Everyone knows Homer is harmless," the man said. If she wasn't mistaken there was a touch of reproach in his tone.

"Everyone except the poor defenseless visitors who come to this town."

He shrugged. "We don't have a movie theater," he explained and added as if to make it more acceptable, "and it's only the female visitors."

The man squatted next to Homer. The muscles in his thighs strained the worn material of his jeans as he slid an arm behind the other man's back.

"Damn, she's got a sharp knee," Homer groaned as he leaned on the other man.

"I warned you this could happen, Homer." The first man shifted his arm around the other man's waist and took his weight against him. "Not everyone gets your sense of humor."

"What's not to get?" Homer grunted as he lurched to a crouch.

Both men flashed her a glance, and for no valid reason whatsoever she felt guilty. She slipped her shoulder under Homer's free arm. "I'm sorry."

With Homer's arm draped across her shoulders, the ice pack he was holding bumped her collarbone. The weight of all that muscle almost dropped her to her knees. She couldn't see his face, but his fingers curled around her upper arm as he said, "You should be." They tightened slightly as he added, "Just about ruined my whole act."

Ridiculously, she found herself apologizing again.

The first man looked pointedly down at her before mentioning, "You're a little bit short to be a prop."

"Consider me moral support then," Jessie said, reaching for the ice pack as the other man stood, taking Homer with him. By the time they reached their full height, the only part of Homer touching her was his hand.

"Do they grow everyone in this neck of the woods this big?" she asked, looking up, way up, at both men.

The first man shifted two steps to the left and then nothing of Homer touched her. Homer glanced at the other man, laughed, shrugged and chucked her chin with his finger. "Everything's bigger and better in Texas."

She pulled her face away. "Even the fools, it seems," she observed as they deposited Homer into an empty booth.

The first man stood and cut the teen a disgusted glare. "That's been the walking truth lately."

As his deep blue eyes met hers, a shiver of excitement snaked down Jessie's spine. The intensity in his gaze told her that this man didn't do anything by half measures, and indicated a strength that whispered he could be trusted. Oh damn. As slim as the chance was that a man this masculine and this sexy was unattached, she offered up a little prayer of thanksgiving that he'd stumbled into her path. She couldn't think of anyone more perfectly suited for her first ever fling than this man. And to think she'd wasted a year looking for him in bars and meat markets that masqueraded as gyms!

He put his right hand in his pocket. His biceps bulged enticingly against his sleeve, making her mouth water with the urge to sink her teeth into it, and his weight relaxed into his hips in a way that just screamed sex. Oh wow, she caught her breath, trying not to eat him up too obviously with her eyes. Mystery man was so much more than perfect. He was a fantasy come to life. All she had to do was convince him that she was perfect for him and her longstanding to-do list would become a thing of the past. That is, if she didn't totally freak him out first by gawking at him rather than holding up her end of the conversation.

"What? No more defending the tradition?" she asked after she handed the ice pack back to Homer.

"You struck me with the truth."

If she wasn't mistaken, that was a smile ghosting the corners of his mouth.

"That happens."

That ghost of a smile became a sensual reality. "Does nothing get you flustered?"

A smile like that would do it any day. She clamped down on her body's response, crossing her arms over her chest to hide her tingling nipples. "Not much anymore."

"Why not anymore?" he asked as Homer slumped back in the booth, closed his eyes, and clutched the ice pack to his groin, clearly concerned with nothing but alleviating the effects of her knee.

Jessie contemplated the last four years of her life. There was nothing like working at a school full of adolescent boys determined to see who could make her scream first to keep a woman on her toes. "Combat training."

"Uh-huh." His smile faded to a glimmer. The rest of his expression settled into lines of pure male interest as his gaze traveled a leisurely path from her head to her toes.

There was no doubt he liked what he saw, and the knowledge struck her with the force of lightning, electrifying every nerve ending into a state of eager anticipation. Her knees wavered as he did an even slower perusal on the way back up, pausing to check out the rapid pulse in her throat before taking that last little trip up over her face. By the time his gaze met hers, that smile had deepened at the corners and her breath was coming in halting stutters.

"Are you going to be in town long?" he asked.

She couldn't even begrudge him his knowing smile as she was reacting so very visibly to his interest, but she'd kill him if he was married or had a girlfriend. She'd made out with men for a good twenty minutes and never been as remotely turned on as this man made her feel with just a look. She really, really wanted to know how good he could make her feel if he set his mind to it.

"I suspect I'll be in the area for a while."

"Maybe I could show you the highlights sometime?"

Oh please let that invite mean he was free and available for plucking.

She kept her thoughts to herself and feigned shock. "You mean this wasn't it?"

His amusement was slow and leisurely, starting in his eyes, moving to his lips before spreading outward, infusing his face with a heavy sensuality that had her breath catching in her throat. "Not quite."

"Is there something around here that could top it?"

His gaze flicked to the front of her blouse and his smile broadened. "Oh yeah."

Jessie gripped her arms with her fingers to keep from dissolving into the floor. She couldn't help it. She had to know. "Are you married or otherwise attached?"

His right eyebrow cocked at her. No doubt he was surprised by her aggressiveness. Truth be told, she was a little surprised herself, but she'd been waiting so long for someone like him.

"No."

She closed her eyes on a silent "Thank God".

When she opened them he was still staring at her. He might have wanted to say more, but the bartender chose that moment to call out, "Would you like another cup of tea?"

Her walking fantasy closed his sexy mouth. Rats!

"Yes," she answered, biting back a sigh. Tea and a little distance might just keep her from acting the total fool. "Thank you."

She gave Homer a last pat on the shoulder, fetched her tea and headed back toward her booth. She held her breath as she waited to see if her man would follow.

He did. She released her breath on a long steadying exhale as he poured himself a cup of coffee and strolled toward her. "I get the impression you weren't too scared by Homer."

"Was I supposed to be?" she asked, snagging some sugar from another booth since her bowl was empty. As she stood, she caught those blue eyes appraising her ass. From the curve of his lips, she knew he liked what he saw. She took a little longer straightening than she needed to, teasing him, feeling a little drunk on her daring.

He took a sip of his coffee. "I'd think that when a strange man in full Comanche paint waves a tomahawk over your head, it would be prudent to at least be alarmed."

She sighed. "I have a problem with that."

His eyebrows rose as he waited for the woman to seat herself. "You have a problem with being alarmed?"

She bit her lip and smiled. "I have a problem with being prudent."

Especially lately. She'd discovered the bubbling sense of freedom that had taken her in the wake of her mother's death was harder to control than the resentment she'd felt at Alzheimer's slow destruction of the person her mother had been. It kept sneaking past her guard when she least expected, encouraging her to make up for lost time. Lost opportunities. She looked at the big man in front of her, from the tip of his worn boots to the top of his equally battered hat. And, man, this was one hell of an opportunity.

"Uh-huh. Care to explain?"

She slid into the opposite seat. "I have an inappropriate funny bone."

He grabbed a packet of cream off the table and added it to his coffee. "Homer?"

"I found it impossible to quake in fear of a man who reeks of mothballs."

That he'd been expecting some other response was evidenced by the way his laughter caused him to choke on his coffee. While he wiped his mouth with a napkin, she asked, "I'm kind of in a pickle here. Seeing as how you were a bit delayed in your chivalrous impulses, and therefore owe me, do you think you could help me find Mac Hollister? I don't know what's up with the guy, but every time I mention his name, people either break into laughter or get all quiet and wary."

The man swore under his breath as every eye in the place pointedly skirted his direction.

It took Jessie two heartbeats before realization dawned. "You're Mac Hollister?"

He grimaced. "Yeah."

"The Mac Hollister who owns the Circle H?"

"The only one around these parts."

"Well, hell!" Disappointment slammed into her hopes. "You're not sixty, squinty-eyed and choking on a wad of chewing tobacco."

He carefully lowered his cup to the table, eyeing her as if she'd just slipped a screw.

"You have a problem with the way I look?" he asked.

She shook her head sadly, and sighed. It just figured her first walking invitation to her first affair would come with a hitch.

"I do, and so will you."

She rose and stepped out of the booth. Mac stood also, in a display of manners she liked. With a sad thought to what might have been, she stuck out her hand. "How do you do, Mr. Hollister. I'm J. C. Sterns, your new cook."

Chapter Two

Mac slapped his hat against his thigh. Thoughts of lawsuits danced through his head. "You're the big, strapping cook I asked that damned agency for?"

"No," J. C. Sterns countered, her voice laced with enough sweetness to set his back teeth to aching. "I'm the cook capable of creating 'mouthwatering meals in quantities to keep all of Texas in heaven for a week' that you demanded." She arched a brow at him. "I believe that's a quote."

"I recognize my own words when I hear them," he growled, frustration eating at his gut. He dropped into the opposite side of the booth. The hard plastic creaked in protest. Running his hands through his hair, he felt like throwing things. He needed a cook who could wield huge pots and pans with ease, a cook who knew the ins and outs of cooking from the barnyard up. He did not need a slender bit of femininity fluttering around his ranch dropping handkerchiefs while she got her fill of the Wild West. No matter how drop-dead sexy she was. "Look, obviously some kind of misunderstanding has occurred—"

"I don't think so. I've been hired for a job, and I intend to do it."

What little patience he had was gone before she completed the statement. He never did take well to being told what to do. "Not on the Circle H, you're not."

She reached into her purse, pulled out a folded paper. As she spread it flat on the table between them, the pink of her nails very bright and very feminine against the stark white paper, he recognized the contract he'd signed with the employment agency. She pointed to his boldly scrawled signature at the bottom with one long finger. "Is that your signature?"

He slapped his hat against the side of the seat. "You know damned well it is."

"Are you prepared to pay me the six month severance since you're not going to give me the trial period?"

Damn! He'd forgotten about that clause. "Not likely."

The woman, J. C.—damn, she didn't look like a cool impersonal J. C.—refolded the contract. "Then I suggest we get going."

He slammed his hand down on that escaping bit of paper. "*We* are not going anywhere."

Her chin came up and out. Just figured that she'd have a stubborn side.

"Yes, we are." She took a deep breath that thrust those full breasts up against her shirt. Through the thin silk he could make out the shape of her nipples. They were as small and as neatly feminine as the rest of her. His cock tingled with interest. "I'll be honest with you, Mr. Hollister. I came to Texas without any job prospects. My credentials are excellent, and I didn't foresee any difficulties."

He could hear it coming. "But…?"

"But I land every job until the people get a look at me. One woman actually told me she didn't want me around because her husband had a tendency to wander."

"I could see where that would be a problem." She was a very tempting woman, the kind a man wanted to toss onto the nearest bed and take a month or two to sate himself in. The kind of woman who just reeked trouble the same way she reeked city.

"Yes. Well…" She cut him a glare from under her thick lashes. "I was just as glad not to land that job, but that was the only one. Four other employers turned me down simply because I am a woman."

"You haven't been on too many ranches, or you'd realize just how much of a problem being a woman presents."

Especially when the woman in question was a walking pot of simmering sexuality he'd love to immerse himself in.

"This contract states I have a two-week period during which I intend to prove myself." She folded up the contract with efficient movements. She shoved it back into her purse. "Until those two weeks are up, you're stuck with me."

Too bad for her he didn't agree. "Well, honey, as pretty as you are, there are some circumstances I'd have no trouble being stuck in with you, but..." She glanced up from zipping her purse as he stood, "working as a cook on my ranch simply isn't one of them."

Mac settled his hat on his head, watching J. C. Stearns' expression go from disbelief to anger, her eyes from light to dark green with the intensity of emotion she banked. *Damn!* He bet she'd be a live wire in bed, all snap and sizzle beneath his touch. He was tempted to let her come to the ranch for the trial period just to find out, but then he thought of the chaos all that dainty feminine beauty would cause among his men, and he booted the temptation aside.

While she stood there, working up an argument to his decision, he tipped his hat in farewell and headed for the door. Bull shot him an incredulous look. He probably was insane, but he needed solutions not more hassle. Bright sunshine struck his eyes as he opened the glass door.

"See you next week, Bull, Homer," he called over the clatter of the attached cowbell.

He adjusted his hat against the glare as the door swung shut behind him. He wasn't even halfway to his truck before he heard the cowbell jangle and the rapid tattoo of high heels coming up fast. He pulled his hat low over his brow and pretended the steps weren't coming two for his one, and getting louder by the second.

"Mr. Hollister!"

Damn, he even liked the sound of her voice when she screeched. Tucking his chin deeper, he walked faster. The staccato tattoo picked up its beat.

Curtains began to flutter as she yelled his name again. The knowledge that he was providing the town with its entertainment this Saturday evening brought him to a halt.

His sudden stop caused the woman to crash into him. Her nose hit the middle of his back, and she stumbled. Mac spun and caught her before she could fall to the dusty sidewalk. She felt good in his arms. Dainty. Lush. Tempting. He released her faster than he would a bouquet of poison ivy.

"What part of the word 'no' don't you understand?" he asked as she straightened her suit jacket with one hand while rubbing her nose with the other.

She checked her palm for blood, looking at him over her fingers. "The part that doesn't fit in with my plans."

Now why didn't that surprise him? "Woman, what do you want from me?"

She smoothed the front of her skirt, and shifted her purse strap higher on her shoulder. "A ride out to my job, for starters."

He wanted to throw up his hands. He settled for frowning. "Don't you ever give up?"

Her answer was short and to the point. "Not when it's important to me."

Mac whipped off his Stetson and slapped it against his thigh. Conscious of windows opening, he made an effort to lower his voice.

"And what makes this job so damned important to you? It's only an average ranch on an average amount of land with an average crew."

"You mean despite the principle that you're reneging on the contract simply because I'm a woman?"

"Yeah."

"You can't do that, Mac." The comment came from his right.

Hell, luck really wasn't on his side, Mac decided, realizing he'd pulled up short in front of his best friend's office. Zach leaned against the doorjamb, looking big and all Indian with that long black hair blowing around his face. Hair he refused to cut despite the way it angered the local judge. Hell, probably precisely because it angered the local judge. Zach was funny that way. "It's against the law," Zach continued with pseudo helpfulness, knowing damned well the hornet's nest he was stirring.

Before Mac could flip him off, a splat of tobacco juice landed within two inches of his brown leather boots. Mac looked up.

"Didn't you have a woman cook out at the Circle H last year?" Henry Morgan, Zach's grandfather asked as he strolled closer.

That bit of information had the Sterns woman pulling herself to her full height, and the light of battle entering her eyes. "Well?" she prompted when he didn't answer immediately.

Mac was beginning to feel like Custer at his last stand. "Sort of."

She folded her arms across her chest. "There are only two sexes; male or female, so which was it?"

"You wouldn't say that if you'd seen the McGillicutty woman." Another voice jumped into the fray. Mac almost groaned out loud when he recognized Arnie Miller, the town handyman and former mechanic. There was nothing Arnie liked better than to stir the pot. As if to prove that point, Arnie offered up, "The woman was as old as the hills and built like them, too."

"I gather your last employee was female, then?"

Mac slapped his hat harder against his thigh "She was old," he said as if that explained everything. Dust flew as his hat assaulted his thigh again. "Dammit woman, can't you just take no for an answer?"

The woman's gaze dropped to the hat, and then back to his face. The smallest of smiles touched her lips. "No."

"Well, why the hell not?"

"For the simple reason I can't afford to."

Mac blinked. He looked J. C. Sterns up and down, from one expensive end to another. "You can't afford to?"

"You needn't look so skeptical. You know from my résumé that I left my last job three months ago."

"Why, Mac Hollister!" a quavery voice called from two doors down. "I am disappointed in you! It's bad enough you're reneging on an honest deal, but to leave this poor thing penniless as a result, well it's too much." Grandma Ortiz raised her bullhorn to her mouth again. "I bet your dear Mamma is turning over in her grave, God rest her soul."

His ears were turning red. Mac just knew it, and that hadn't happened since he was thirteen and got caught by his father with a girl up in the hayloft. It was on the tip of his tongue to tell Grandma Ortiz that his mother would be even more shocked if he ended up seducing a woman under his protection, but he bit his tongue. Grandma Ortiz was a respected fixture in Round the Bend. Smart-mouthing her would likely get him tarred and feathered.

Henry spat again, this time in the direction of two doors down. "A body can't get any privacy since that woman went and ordered that fancy listening device from that electronics catalogue."

"I heard that Henry Morgan!"

"Then pay attention and turn that damned thing off!"

Grandma Ortiz rapped the porch railing with her cane. "If that's the way you feel Mister Morgan, don't you come around here with any invented excuses this Thursday when I set to making my peach tarts."

Henry visibly paled. "I'd better get over there right away and make my peace," he muttered before excusing himself all around. As he stomped down the steps, he continued to mutter,

"She could have at least warned me before I opened my mouth that she was going to make those tarts Thursday!"

Jessie looked around at the small crowd fencing her and Mac in. On all sides, complete strangers picked up their argument and ran with it. She raised her gaze to Mac's.

"When did I lose control of this conversation?"

He snorted in disgust, grabbed her arm and shouldered their way clear. "About the time you stepped off the bus. Welcome to Round the Bend."

Jessie looked back over her shoulder as Mac hustled her along. She shook her head as no one noticed their leaving, too caught up in continuing the discussion to care.

"I wonder who's going to win the argument, you or me?"

An answering grin tugged at the corners of his mouth. It took his face from rugged to sexy with one quirk. If he hadn't put his hand under her arm in preparation of helping her in, she would have made a fool of herself staring. Damn! The man had a face she could stare at forever. As it was, she had to worry about remembering to breathe as his finger on the inside of her arm teased all sorts of interesting nerve endings to life.

He opened the door of a dusty blue pickup and handed her up. "No doubt we'll find out in church."

"Church?" Did she look the religious type?

Mac ambled over to his own side of the truck. As he swung around the front she had a nice view of his broad shoulders in their denim shirt tapering down to the tight butt blocked from her view by the hood of the truck. Damn! What fun was ogling if she missed the good parts? The man was a tease, pure and simple.

The driver's door creaked as he opened it and swung in. "It's either show up in one of the town's two churches or be forever branded a sinner."

The door clunked shut and the hot interior was suddenly filled with his scent. He smelled like spring looked. Clean, earthy, and full of promise. She savored another breath and asked, "Would that be so bad?"

He started the engine. "Not if you don't mind being the town's only cause."

She shuddered at the thought. "I'm a Methodist."

"Thought you might find religion." The truck pulled out from the curve.

"I've always had religion," she clarified. "I just have a problem doing what I'm told."

"So I noticed," he muttered under his breath. As he shifted to second gear, he shot her a sideways glance. "Are you really broke?"

His eyes were bright blue against the tan of his face. Full of intelligence and life. She couldn't have handpicked a more perfect man for her first affair. But, he was her boss. Jessie sighed before answering honestly. "Close enough."

She was broke, scared, and hopeful, a strange combination of emotions that bubbled through her system like sparkling wine. Because she was also free. For the first time in her adult life, and she was so going to make the most of it.

"And that's why you took the bus rather than driving? You don't own a car?"

"I didn't need one in the city."

Jessie looked out the window and saw the town was already behind them. "My bags!"

With a thrust of his chin, Mac indicated the back of the pickup. "Larry must have put them in the back when you told him where you were going."

"Larry?"

"He runs the general store and bus depot."

"Oh yes. I did ask about the Circle H there. He's the one who told me to wait over at the Bar and Grill for you." Jessie saw the way her reluctant employer's face fell from good humor to anger. It wasn't hard to guess what he was thinking about. "I really am an excellent cook."

"Your cooking abilities aren't the problem here."

"Then just what is?"

"You're the problem."

Her hand clenched on her purse. She was not losing this job. "I'm sure we can work out any personality conflicts between us."

Mac pulled over to the side of the road, applying the brakes so hard, if it hadn't been for her seat belt, she would have flown through the windshield. He unfastened his seat belt and ran his arm across the back of the seat as a cloud of brown dust rose around them. Jessie suddenly became conscious of their isolation. Flat brown nothingness, periodically broken up by a scraggly tree, spread out on either side of the vehicle for as far as the eye could see. And in front of her seethed an angry man.

"Just how old are you?"

Not angry, she corrected herself. Frustrated. "I'm twenty-nine, but my age has nothing to do with my qualifications for this job."

Mac snapped the rearview mirror around until she could see her reflection. Her hair was coming loose at the temples.

"That's the problem, honey."

She assumed he meant her appearance.

"I have fourteen women-hungry men working my ranch. Their ages run from twenty-two to forty-eight, and not one of those men is going to miss the opportunity to try to get you into his bed."

"I can handle men, *darling*."

He ignored her jab.

"Because you spent the last four years working at a boy's academy, you think you can take on my ranch hands?" He swore and slapped the wheel with his palm. "You're kidding yourself. We're talking men here, not boys."

Jessie opened her hands on her lap. She thought of everything she'd gone through in the last four years, not only her mother's last incoherent years, but also as the prime outlet for a hundred high-spirited boys. There were teen crushes, frogs in her bed, hot spices in her food, and fledgling seduction attempts. The last made her smile.

"I never kid myself. I can handle your men." Of that she had no doubt. "And unless you're prepared to write a sizable check right now, you don't have any choice but to sit back and let me prove it."

She wasn't going to back down, Mac realized. For probably more reasons than she was revealing, the woman was determined to keep this job. Which meant there was no point in continuing the argument because he sure as shit didn't have the money to buy her off, which meant they were both going to have to make the best of what was, no doubt, going to be a bad situation. Son of a bitch, his luck was running badly. Tipping his hat lower over his eyes, he turned the ignition and spun back onto the blacktop.

"Let's hope you can," he said resignedly, "because for the next two weeks, you're going to have to."

She looked up from checking her seat belt. "You mean it? I've got the job?"

"You've got the trial period." He did some quick mental calculations. "With that plus some severance pay, you should have enough to tide you over until your next job."

"You're so sure I'm going to fail."

Mac kept his eyes firmly glued to the road. "Honey, something as fancy and as delicate as you, just wasn't meant to live out here."

Her soft "You're going to eat those words" filled the cab with the snap of a gauntlet being thrown down. Everything masculine inside him surged to the fore at the feminine challenge, eager for the chance to spar with her, to find a venue in which to assert himself. He tamped down the aggressive reaction, knowing she had no idea what her challenge did to him. Had no idea of the kind of man he was. What kind of lover he was.

He cut her a glance only to find her looking out the window. It didn't matter. She'd soon find out that he wasn't like the men she was probably used to. Gentlemen who asked before touching, and took orders in bed rather than giving them. Men who were his complete opposite.

He'd been brought up to make hard decisions in the blink of an eye, to wrestle with nature and come out the winner. To face the impossible and through sheer force of will, twist it into a done deal. He wasn't soft, and he wasn't a pushover. This was his domain and he was master of all he surveyed, which would include her as soon as she set foot on his land, something she hadn't yet figured out. His lips twitched as he envisioned her reaction when that reality kicked in. No doubt she'd go off like a rocket, and kick up a fuss the men would be talking about for years. And when she was done with that, well then he had no doubt, she'd start slinging orders.

He shook his head. He bet she was damned good at giving orders, too. J. C. Sterns was a damned competent woman who exuded self-confidence, but while he'd do just about anything to keep his woman happy, he didn't take orders from anyone.

His knuckles whitened as he clenched his hands around the steering wheel. Ah hell, when had he started thinking of her in terms of his?

He cut her another glance, taking in the thickness of her hair, the clean lines of her profile, the stubborn set of her mouth, and shook his head as his cock, oblivious to common sense, swelled and fought for space in his tight jeans. J. C. Sterns wasn't his woman, was never going to be his woman, and the sooner he and his penis accepted that reality, the better they all would be.

As if to challenge his silent declaration, the woman ran her pink tongue over her full lips, pausing only to deliver a teasing flick to the corner nearest him. His pulse, his cock and his interest all spiked to attention. He forced his gaze back to the road and swallowed a hungry curse. Oh yeah, the next two weeks were going to be a real pleasure trip. One long fucking excursion in blue-balls hell.

* * * * *

"What does J. C. stand for anyway?" Mac asked as he helped her down from the cab.

"Nothing much," Jessie replied. No way was she telling anyone her middle name. He stepped back to reach over the side for her two suitcases.

"What's your real name?" The question ended on a grunt as he hauled the big one out.

"Jessica."

"What do your friends call you?"

"J. C."

He stared at her a minute. Long enough to make her wonder if her shirt had come unbuttoned. Then, as if he'd reached a decision, he nodded and swung her other suitcase over the side. Holding both at his side, he said, "I think I'll call you Jessie."

He turned on his heel and headed for the house.

Jessie stared at his broad back as he strode across the lawn with her belongings. She had a feeling it wouldn't do much good to protest his adaptation of her name. The man swung those hips in a purely masculine way that boasted an arrogant confidence. As he strode onto the wraparound porch of the two-story farmhouse with its twin oak sentinels, she remembered to protest. "You can call me Ms. Sterns or J. C."

"I like Jessie better," he called back as he vanished into the dark interior of the house.

"And that settles that," Jessie muttered as she picked her way across the soft lawn in her high heels.

He popped back out the front door just as she reached the bottom of the stairs, frowning as she pulled her heel out of the grass. "I hope you brought some sensible clothes with you."

She smoothed a crease from the jacket of her linen suit. It was her best outfit. "I wore this today in the hopes of impressing my new boss."

He hovered as she climbed the uneven, wooden steps. "Your boss would have been a heck of a lot more impressed if you'd worn a pair of jeans and running shoes."

"How was I supposed to know my boss was going to be so easy to impress?" She stepped into the foyer ahead of him, silently cursing her impulsive tongue. They'd just reached a truce and now she was heating things up again. What was it about the man that just made her itch to make him sit up and take notice? She glanced over her shoulder, took in the breadth of his shoulders, the flash of humor in his blue eyes and the intelligence in his rugged face. Okay. So she knew why. She just needed to learn to handle it better.

The same way she needed to learn to handle how he could make a look trace over her skin with the impact of a touch, leaving goose bumps springing to attention, her breasts swelling and her nipples perking with availability.

For heaven's sake, the man was a walking pheromone. She folded her arms across her chest in self-defense, forcing strength to her knees and looked right back at him. With no visible effect. Darn it. First chance she got to go to town, she was getting a book on how to reduce a man to a puddle of mush with a look. She definitely wanted tit-for-tat in that department.

Her boss noted the crossing of her arms with a lift of one dark brow, his mouth quirking up at the corner. She so did not want to know what he was thinking. She stared back at him and waited. The other side of his mouth turned up before he motioned to the right of the center staircase.

"The kitchen and pantry are through the dining area there. There is a separate eating area for the hands. We reserve this room for company."

Jessie took in the room with its old fashioned floor-to-ceiling windows and the lace panels filtering out the late evening sun. More lace covered the table and the mahogany sideboards. There was an aura of family in this room that didn't only come from the collection of pictures covering the mantel of the brick fireplace. A sense of continuity. "Has your family owned this house long?"

There was no mistaking the pride in his voice when he answered. "My great-great-great grandfather settled this land back in 1855. It took some doing, and we almost lost it once or twice, but a Hollister has always lived here."

She smiled wistfully. "It must be nice to have such a strong sense of where you come from."

He hesitated as he hefted the suitcases again. "Nobody in your family kept records?"

"Not that I know of." Her family had been small, just consisting of her mother and herself. Now, it was just her.

"I'll show you to your room." With a wave of the smaller suitcase, Mac motioned her to go ahead of him up the stairs. "Third on the left," he instructed when she reached the landing before reverting to the discussion at hand. "If you really want to trace your roots, I've got a friend who does it professionally."

She shook her head and forced smile. "That's not necessary." She really didn't want to know how many people she could have met, should have met, and never would meet.

He shifted his grip on the suitcases, the muscles in his upper arms straining his shirt deliciously. She'd never been turned on by muscles before, but on this man each bulge and flex was enticing. Almost an invitation for her hands to wander.

"If you change your mind, let me know."

"There's not much point. My parents are both dead."

"I'm sorry."

So was she. Some days. "Thank you."

She opened the door and stopped dead. Her bedroom was a beautiful light-filled study of yellow and white. Here and there bright touches of blue caught the eye.

"This is wonderful!" She turned to Mac and reached for the larger suitcase, attempting to take it from him. "It'll be a pleasure to stay here." She tugged.

He didn't let go. He did step further into the room, forcing her to step backward. "I'll tell my sister you like it."

"This is your sister's?" she asked, reaching for the smaller suitcase. He arched his brow at her and shook his head. She frowned at him. He smiled back. She gave up trying to take the suitcases from him.

"Won't she need it?"

"No."

"Should I be staying in it?"

"Yes. I've got you staying two doors down from me for a reason."

"I hope it's a good one."

That sharp comment earned her an impatient look. Jessie didn't really care. Niggling, uncomfortable bits of suspicion were creeping up her backbone. After all, beyond the fact that the man had great buns, just what did she know of Mac Hollister?

His eyes narrowed as he realized what she was thinking. "I have no intention of paying you any late night visits."

"That's a relief." And wasn't she just the biggest liar to come down the pike this year?

Mac removed his Stetson and slapped it gently against his thigh. Something she was beginning to realize the man did when he was bothered.

"The truth is," he admitted gruffly, "I can't say the same for all of the hands. I've got a couple of new men this year that I don't want to find out about the hard way." The battered Stetson slapped against his hard thigh a couple of more times as he weighed the dilemma in his mind.

"I understand." And she did. She even appreciated the concern.

"Dammit," he ground out, "I was expecting a man."

"I told you it's all right." And then because curiosity always sat on her shoulder, she asked, "What about your sister? Will she mind?"

Mac looked up from the spot he'd been studying on the floor. "What? Oh, Amanda. She just got married. God willing, we won't have to put up with each other for a long time."

"You don't get along?"

He shrugged and tossed her biggest suitcase—the one with all her cookbooks in it—up on the bed as if it were a feather pillow. The mattress croaked a protest.

"We get along fine. We're just too much alike, and there can only be one boss to an outfit."

"And you're it."

"And I'm it." He glanced at the door, his words revealing his mind had never left the previous subject. All the delicious possibilities of why that was sent her hormones into ecstatic cartwheels. "If you're nervous about staying in the house with me, I can get you a more substantial lock for your door."

"It's not necessary."

He stopped, frowned and thumped his hat against his thigh. "Maybe I should get you one anyway."

Jessie placed her hand on his forearm as he swung the smaller suitcase up on the bed. The muscles beneath were hard and jerked at her touch. "There's no need. I trust you."

He studied her hand as it rested on his arm for a full five seconds before his blue eyes locked with hers. "Maybe you shouldn't."

She knew what he was telling her. He was interested in her. She also knew a man that could be so loved by an entire town to the point that they saw his life as theirs to worry over, wasn't going to rape her. "I'm going with my instincts on this one."

The hat came to an immediate standstill. "And your instincts say to trust me."

"Yup."

"Damn." With precise movements, he placed his hat on his head and adjusted the angle. His smile was slow and easy as he grazed her cheek with his callused fingers, then turned and walked away, without another word, leaving her to wonder about that "damn" and all its possible ramifications.

Chapter Three

At four o'clock the next morning, Jessie was in the kitchen gathering her ingredients for Sunday breakfast. Mac had said the previous evening that it wasn't necessary to cook this morning. Most of the hands had Saturday night off and probably wouldn't show for breakfast anyway, but Jessie knew differently. Hungry men who had been surviving on the remains of the meal she'd cleaned up last night would be lining up outside the door with optimistic faces to see what the new cook could do. And she had no intention of disappointing them. The way she figured it, if a threatened revolt had landed her this job, another one could allow her to keep it.

She grabbed a colander and started scooping the dried apples out of the water in which they'd been soaking. She gave them a shake and frowned. Assuming she wanted to keep it. She dumped the apples in the large stockpot on the stove. As she went back for more apples, she acknowledged that was a pretty big assumption considering the temptation she had tossed and turned with half the night.

She sighed and wiped her hands on her apron. More than she needed this job, she needed to live. To experience the things other women her age had long since tucked into memories. She dumped the last of the apples into the pot. For the last ten years she'd been taking care of her mother as she'd battled Alzheimer's. That hadn't left much time for dating, let alone deeper relationships. As a result, she was way behind in life experience. And quite frankly, she was eager to catch up. The problem was, despite her determination, this last year, she hadn't met a man who could get her hormones to flutter let alone get them into an uproar. Or a man who didn't run when she exposed her real desires.

Until Mac. She poured the sugar and cinnamon mixture over the apples, dropped the cover on the pot and turned the heat to low. Mac was her fantasy come to life. Everything she'd ever wanted. He had that edge to him that told her he could handle her dark side. Might even enjoy it. She sighed. It just figured she'd have to choose between employment and satisfaction. Seems no matter what she did, she leaned toward the hard way. Her mom always said it was because she loved the challenge, but she was wondering if maybe she just had a penchant for bad luck.

She hefted the batter bowl to the chair seat so she'd have some leverage. Grabbing the large slotted spoon, she whipped the batter for apple pancakes. Convincing Mac she was worth the trouble might be her second biggest stumbling block. She blew a tendril of hair off her face. A man of his looks and age no doubt had tons of experience. Educating a woman of her well-read but limited practical experience might not be his idea of fun. She grabbed a precooked ham and cut off thick slices in preparation for frying. Reluctance on his part would definitely put a crimp in her plans, but it wasn't going to stop her. More than anything in the world she wanted to know what he could do with the sexual energy that throbbed through her when he was around.

A glance at the clock revealed it was almost five a.m. She put the coffee on. As with everything she'd made that morning, she estimated the amount she would require to feed teenaged boys and doubled it.

Turning back to the stove, she checked the temperature on the lard she had heating. Three hundred seventy-five degrees. Perfect. She dropped the first round of doughnuts in. Before the second batch had been pulled from the softly hissing oil, she heard the first set of boots hit the back porch. She turned with a smile. "Good morning."

"Ma'am."

He stood there after the introduction, doing nothing but breathing deep, and scoping out the kitchen. And her.

She took the opportunity to stare back between doughnut loads. The cowboy had obviously taken great care with his appearance. His face was smoothly shaven and scrubbed clean, handsome in a rugged outdoorsy way. His clothes were too good to be working clothes, and his boots were the fancy kind a man wore into town. She judged him to be in his forties. His hair was a dirty blond cut short and his eyes were a friendly grey. And he was making her uncomfortable with his staring. The way all men did. It wasn't that she didn't want to be found attractive. She just didn't know what to do with it. After she gave the apples a quick stir, she did what she always did with male attention. She redirected it to an area in which she was comfortable. Her cooking. She dropped two doughnuts into a paper towel and held it out.

"Want to be the official taste tester?"

"It'd be my pleasure." The way he smiled at her made her wonder if he thought she was flirting.

"Damn—I mean darn, this is good," he managed through the second bite.

"Thank you." The bliss in his expression was familiar ground. "The coffee's ready if you'd like some."

"The name's Will, ma'am, and I'd love a cup of coffee if it comes with another one of those." His gaze fell to the plate Jessie was filling with the next batch of doughnuts.

Jessie laughed. "The name is J. C., and help yourself."

Will proceeded to do just that, but at his first sip of the coffee, her confidence took a hit. Obviously she'd screwed that up. "What did I do wrong?" she asked. Will took another swallow, but his grimace made it obvious the brew wasn't improving with familiarity.

"This stuff's on par with cat p—" He caught himself. "It's pretty weak, Jessie."

She didn't even bother to correct his misunderstanding of her initials as she reached for the pot. Damn, now she'd have to start over and that was going to throw off her timing. "If I start again, do you think you could show me the way it should be done?"

Will got there before she could. "I'd show you, but there's no time for that now." He motioned with his head to the hot grease. "You'd better put some more of those doughnuts in, because as sure as shootin', when I don't come back with my tail tucked between my legs, those boys down at the bunkhouse are going to start believing what their noses are telling them."

Jessie scooped the ham steaks off the grill, slipped on some more and glanced at the wall clock. "Breakfast isn't supposed to be until six a.m. on Sunday," she said as she cut and flipped doughnuts into her hand, before deftly slipping them into the oil.

Will grabbed a couple of handfuls of grounds and threw them into the coffeepot. "Ma'am, we've been listening to you clank around in here for a good hour and a half, and everyone's been saying how nothing you cook up could taste as good as our imaginings."

Jessie turned the doughnuts, allowing herself a small smile. She'd never met a man who could resist a fresh doughnut. "And why is that? I am a cook."

Will shrugged. "When the boss came down to the bunkhouse last night and left his sense of humor at home, we all kind of concluded that you must not be much of one."

Jessie judged the doughnuts ready and started transferring them to the plate to drain. "Mr. Hollister is a bit impulsive in his decisions."

"I've known the man for years and I've never known him to be impulsive."

She flipped the ham steaks over, checked the apple mixture and mentioned, "I've known him for less than one day and found him to be nothing but."

Will rummaged through the cupboards until he found some cheesecloth and some twine. He arranged the cloth over the spout of the pot so it worked as a filter. Pouring himself a cup, he took a sip before responding. "Mac takes his responsibilities seriously. If you got hurt, whether on or off the job, he'd consider himself responsible."

"I'm sure that makes him an admirable boss, but I'm pretty determined I'm getting a fair shot at this job." She noticed Will wasn't grimacing as he took another pull of his coffee.

"How is it now?"

"Not great, but nobody will croak on the stuff."

"Damn," she swore as she added more doughnuts to her growing mountain. "I wanted everything to be perfect."

"Ma'am, you just put this pile of doughnuts in front of the men, and they won't care whether you serve them mud to go with it."

She looked at the thick brew swirling in his cup. "From what I can see from here, there isn't much difference."

He laughed a low, lazy chuckle. "In all my forty-eight years, I haven't yet met a woman who didn't feel that way."

"Glad to say I'm sticking within the norm." The clomping of many boots on wood alerted her that the rest of the crew was here. She put the huge skillet on the stove, and ladled in the pancake batter.

Will watched her for a moment before speaking his mind. "The boss was real explicit last night about your being off-limits."

She glanced over her shoulder. "Off-limits?"

Will shifted his hip against the counter, took a sip of coffee and continued. "Most of the crew are good men."

She put more ham steaks on and turned, "But?"

"But we had to hire two new guys this year. They are excellent with cattle, but I'm not so sure about women."

"Which two are they?" She so did not want to end up the source of amusement for a couple of bad apples.

He studied her face quietly for a moment. "Good to see you're not getting angry at the suggestion that you couldn't take care of yourself."

She checked the oven. The temperature was perfect. "I'm not stupid, Will. I can hold my own in most situations, but I'm not Wonder Woman. If there's danger about, I'd rather be warned. Now, which two are they?"

He grunted in what she assumed was approval. "Jute and his brother Jeremy. You can't miss them. They stand right out. Flaming red hair and more freckles than you can shake a stick at."

"I'll keep my eyes out for them."

He nodded. "You do that. And if they corner you alone anywhere, don't bother trying to talk them down. You just start screaming. We'll be keeping an eye out for you."

"Thank you." Jessie wondered if that "we" included Mac, and then chastised herself for being a fool. Of course it did. He was the boss. She could sue his ass if she got hurt working here. He'd probably sleep with one eye open, alert for all eventualities. Which probably included sexual harassment. Damn. Like she needed another complication to her plan.

Will grabbed another doughnut, and tipped his hat before heading out the door, his "You're welcome" trailing in his wake. He paused when he reached the door. "Boss."

Jessie cut a glance at the door as she ladled more batter into the waiting pan. Mac was just like she remembered, big, well-muscled, with an aura of masculinity that made her breasts tingle and her knees weak. She sucked in her breath and put a rein on the delight skipping through her bloodstream. She would never get anywhere with a man this confident, by gawking like a starstruck teenager. She forced herself to continue cooking breakfast as if his eyes weren't burning a hole in her spine.

His low good morning rumbled over her senses in a welcome caress. She could listen to the man forever.

"Good morning yourself," she tossed the greeting over her shoulder.

Mac came into the kitchen, noting the orderly chaos that reigned. "I thought I told you it wasn't necessary to cook this morning?"

She shrugged. "You did, but I'm used to waking early. Since I was up, I didn't see any reason not to whip something up."

His brow rose. "You call homemade doughnuts, apple pancakes, fried ham and—" He spotted several cartons on the counter, "—eggs, whipping something up?"

He had an excellent view of her back as she answered, "Yes."

She held herself a little too carefully to be telling the truth.

"Uh-huh." Mac admired the trim line of her figure as he poured himself a cup of coffee. She was small and dainty, but with a lushness to her curves that drew him. His eyes lingered on the perfect heart shape of her ass beneath the faded material of her jeans. Definitely squeezable. He took a sip of the coffee. The smell warned him before his taste buds could chime in. He winced. "I taste Will's influence in this."

Jessie turned halfway around and noted the cup. She shrugged and slid ham onto the pile on the platter. "He said it was too weak the way I made it."

He took another cautious sip. "I've no doubt it was, but the way Will likes to repair the damage is worse."

She paused before turning back to the stove. "I was going to make a new pot," she admitted. "But then Will produced his remedy and I needed a shortcut."

"Some shortcuts just aren't worth the trip."

"So I'm finding out." She flipped a switch off on the stove. The soft click punctuated her turn. "But seeing as the doughnuts are ready and I've only got four minutes until the first pancake is done, the men will just have to make do with orange juice while you make another pot."

"I'm making a pot?"

"If you expect me to hold back some of these doughnuts for you, you are."

He guessed he'd be making coffee then. She grabbed a huge pitcher of orange juice out of the fridge. She placed it on the table before hefting the mountainous platter of doughnuts up onto her shoulder.

He straightened. "You want me to carry that for you?" She looked like she'd overbalance any second.

"I've got it. Thanks."

He put his cup down, intending to insist, but before he could say a word, she had the pitcher tucked onto her hip and scooted past him out the door into the dining room.

There was an immediate roar for coffee and some ribald remarks. Most stayed within the realm of good taste, but Mac noted Jute and Jeremy stepped way over the line more than once. He waited by the door, ready to intercede if necessary both for the comments and for the lack of coffee.

Denying a cowboy coffee was practically a hanging offense. He may not want the woman here, but he wasn't going to let her be abused while she was under his roof. He half expected to hear Will jump in, but there was only the soft murmur of Jessie's voice and then as one, all the complaints dropped off. Then there was no sound at all except Jessie's cheerful "Be right back". Mac poured the coffee into the sink and refilled the pot with water.

She came sailing back into the kitchen without a hair out of place, wearing a little smile on her lips that had his cock perking up and giving his libido a nudge. The woman was a menace.

He turned the coffee grinder on. The unexpected noise knocked that too tempting smile off her lips. She nodded in his direction and opened the oven. The smile was back, replete with satisfaction, as she pulled a twenty-four inch cast-iron pan out of the oven. The scent of apples and cinnamon intensified in the room, wrapping around his senses as he stared at her mouth and that sexy smile.

He bet she wore that exact smile when she was damp and exhausted after her man pleased her in bed. The image wouldn't leave his head, Jessie naked on his bed, the sheets bunched around her feet, her body flushed with the pleasure he'd given her, the taste of her on his tongue, her body sweetly limp in his arms. Damn, he wanted to place his lips against hers and taste that soft sighing emotion for himself.

He spun around and dumped the ground coffee into the receptacle with a disgusted flick of his wrist. Hell, he was having sexual fantasies over a smile, for God's sake. That just clinched it. The woman had to go, or he was going to be in court for sure. Kissing the cook had to violate some law, and he'd spent all the free cash he had on that new bull. Otherwise, he would have paid the severance and sent her on her way yesterday. And what a poor justification that would be for spending money. He put the top on the electric percolator and turned it on. Hell, he was a thirty-one-year-old man, not a fifteen-year-old boy. He ought to be able to keep his cock in his pants for two damned weeks.

Jessie cut the pancake into twelve portions before transferring them to another platter. Nothing in her manner even indicated she was aware that he was in the room. That rankled even more than the fact that she had this effect on him. He leaned back against the counter and folded his arms across his chest. "So how'd you get past the hollering?"

She glanced up from where she was pouring more batter into the pan. "What?" She added apples to the mix.

He waited until after she'd loaded it into the oven to ask, "How'd you get away without coffee?"

"Oh that." She flashed him a grin that had his cock jerking against his jeans as she reached across the table for the powdered sugar shaker. "That was just a matter of realigning their thinking."

He widened his stance to make room for his growing erection. She could light up a city block with that smile. "Realigned how?"

She shook the sugar over the top of the finished pancakes. "I merely pointed out that ticking off the cook on her first day with a lack of patience would result in peanut butter for lunch and my slopping the hogs with the rest of breakfast." Her breasts jiggled as she worked. His cock expanded down his thigh.

"We don't have any hogs."

She glanced up, her smile fleshed out with laughter. "No one seemed hung up on that point."

In one surge his cock went rock-hard. Standing as he was, she couldn't miss the bulging ridge of hard flesh stretching halfway down his thigh. He knew the exact moment she noted his interest. The shaker jerked to a halt and her green eyes widened. He made no apology or attempt to hide. She stared like that for a few seconds, frozen. Then her tongue came out over her lips and slowly spread tempting moisture across their full curves as her eyes ate him alive.

He bit back a groan. Damn it. He bet if he walked over there and slipped his hands inside her jeans, she'd be wet. His cock throbbed and jerked, straining in its tight confines. She gasped, her gaze flew to his. He had just enough time to register the shock mixed with desire in hers before she scooped up the pancake platter and rushed out of the room.

Good. Let her run. All the way to a new job. Behind him the coffeepot began to gurgle. Any woman her age who fled at the sight of a man's hard-on did not have what it took to be his lover. He grabbed his hat and slammed open the back door. Which, he told himself, was a good thing. His cock, only interested in having those lush lips tucked snug and tight around its sensitive shaft, totally ignored his point. It ached and throbbed with unrelieved anticipation. Mac cursed and headed for the barn. Maybe mucking out some stalls would put some perspective on the situation.

*****

An hour later Jessie sat at the kitchen table staring at Mac in exasperation. Didn't the man ever give up?

"I can't believe we're going through this again." Jessie sighed wearily, plucking a piece of apple off her pancake. She waved it at him before asking, "Didn't we decide yesterday that I had no intention of leaving before my two week trial period was over?"

"Nope," Mac answered, stealing a piece of apple for himself. Since he was straddling a chair across from her, it was within easy reach. She raised her knife threateningly. He calmly licked his fingers as he continued, "We sort of agreed to let the conversation rest."

"While you schemed and concocted your way out of the agreement?"

"I never said I had any intention of reneging on this agreement."

Jessie narrowed her eyes, obviously sensing the trap beneath his logic. "Then what exactly was the point in coming in here and announcing that I should plan on being on the next bus back to Dallas?"

"Lord, you are a suspicious one."

She put the apple in her mouth, chewed deliberately and said, "I'm beginning to believe with you, I have to be."

"I'm an honest man."

She took another piece of apple from the pancake in front of her. "One who is intent on getting his way."

She was right about that.

She chewed and swallowed the small bite, folded her arms across her chest and asked, "So what exactly are you trying to say?"

"I have no doubt that you are a terrific cook," he began as he filched a second piece. She glared at him. He shrugged and popped the piece into his mouth. He was hungry. "Breakfast this morning proved that beyond a shadow of a doubt, but I honestly don't think you're equipped to deal with the realities of life around here."

Jessie cracked his knuckles with the flat blade of the knife before he could remove her last bit of apple. She got to her feet and went to the warming oven. She pulled out a plate heaped with pancakes, eggs and ham. She plopped it down in front of him before resuming her seat and asking, "What 'realities' are we talking about here?"

"Thanks." He poured syrup over the pancakes and ham. As he was cutting up his first bite, he asked, "Where do you think the eggs you used to bake these pancakes came from?"

Jessie took one look at the way he leaned on the back of that ladder-back chair, his eyebrows raised superiorly, and she knew that the supermarket wasn't the right response. Her gaze fell on the window over his shoulder. "I would guess from that chicken coop over there."

He smiled. "Nice guess. Are you beginning to see my point?"

She took a sip of her glass of milk. Milk that came from a carton in the fridge. "Not really. I understand that you are relatively self-sufficient here. Mr. Price at the employment agency was quite explicit about that."

"And?"

She shrugged in the face of his skepticism. "I'll tell you what I told him. I am an intelligent woman. I am not averse to learning new things, and I am quite willing to understand what is involved in—" She paused and raised her eyebrows inquiringly. "How did you phrase that?"

"I did and do need a cook who knows the ins and outs of food from the barnyard up."

Jessie placed her knife and fork precisely on the side of her plate. "Well, neither Mr. Price nor I were exactly sure what that entailed, but faced with my qualifications and confidence, we both agreed I'd be able to adapt."

He laughed outright at that.

"Well, what did you mean?" she demanded, beginning to get angry as he eyed her from head to toe and broke into fresh amusement. "It's not like I have to milk a cow or anything." She held up her glass. "This came from a grocery store and so did a heck of a lot of other stuff in that fridge."

Mac took a bite of his ham and eggs. She had to wait until he finished before he answered. "Honey, you don't have the slightest idea of what you've gotten yourself into, do you?"

"I haven't gotten myself into anything," she denied. She took a last bite of her breakfast before getting to her feet. As she scraped the rest into the trash she said, "And you can just stop trying to scare me away from this job." She put her dishes into the huge dishwasher and turned around, arms folded across her chest. "My contract says I have two weeks in which to prove myself, and that's exactly what I intend to do."

He didn't look the least intimidated by her stand. He just calmly took another bite of food, savored the flavor, swallowed, and then pointed out, "Your contract says I can't fire you for any reason except failure on your part to perform your duties."

"That's 'reasonably' perform my duties," she countered.

He waved that aside like so much trivia. "How about we make a little side wager here?"

"What kind of wager?" she asked suspiciously.

His smile was a pure masculine stretch of his lips. It radiated confidence and so much appeal she pressed her thighs together. At the same time, it made her wary. Only someone with a trick up his sleeve was that cocky.

"Why don't we say the first time you fail in your duties, you pack your bags and catch the next bus home?"

"And if I don't?"

"Then you get to stay the entire two weeks without a word from me."

Jessie shook her head. "Not good enough. I've already got that by virtue of my contract."

He arched an eyebrow at her. It only made him sexier. More drool-worthy. "You've done this kind of thing before?"

Jessie shrugged. "A time or two."

"So what do you want?"

"A six month option." She may have been on the Circle H only a day, but the place seemed to welcome her home. She wasn't above negotiating it into one.

"All right," he agreed. "As long as you agree to a condition of mine."

"Shoot."

"If you lose, you forfeit your pay."

She swallowed hard. She couldn't afford to lose that money.

As if sensing her hesitation, Mac sat up straight and folded his arms across his chest. "What's the matter? Afraid you can't do it?"

She wasn't afraid of anything, least of all someone foolish enough to doubt her abilities in the kitchen. She stuck out her hand. "You're on."

Mac caught her hand in his and stared hard into her eyes. "Then we're agreed. As cook of the Circle H, you agree to provide the meals, and try to supply as many of our needs as possible from resources here at the ranch. And you accept the responsibility of getting that food to the table."

Her eyes narrowed, knowing that he was wording things so carefully because there was something he didn't want her to guess, but unable to find it. She almost backed down, but then that corner of his gorgeous mouth quirked as if he knew what she was thinking and she was pumping his hand before the sense of caution had more than a flicker of life.

"Agreed."

At the satisfied smile that stretched his sexy mouth, she felt a shiver run up her spine. Something told her it was going to be a rough two weeks.

Chapter Four

So this was to be her punishment for refusing to leave. Jessie stood arms akimbo, staring at the poor unsuspecting chickens clucking and scratching around in their comfy, fenced in yard. And she was supposed to invade their private sanctum and commit murder. Her stomach roiled at the thought.

She recalled her dismissal of Mac's concern about her abilities. If this was what he meant about knowing how to cook from the barnyard up, he'd been right to doubt. One white chicken with a tiny speckle of black on its breast, clucked up to the fence and looked her right in the eye. She glared at it and tried to shoo it away, but the bird just stood on the other side of that fence, scratching at the ground, attempting to strike up a friendship, chicken style.

"You're a smart one, aren't you?" she asked. The chicken blinked slowly and gave a little fluff and a tail flutter in return. "You know I've got to wipe out four of your family, and you don't want to be one of the chosen."

The chicken cocked its head to the side almost as if it understood. Involuntarily, she smiled at it. It blinked slowly and gave a purring chirp. She was grinning before she realized what had happened. Oh hell. She'd bonded with the damned thing.

"It's not going to work," she told the softly clucking bird. "If you had the sense God gave a gnat, you'd be running for your life."

"More than likely, she's probably figured out she's not in much danger."

There was no mistaking the laughter in that low drawl. Jessie counted to five before turning around, bracing herself for the confrontation. Mac stood about ten feet away, leaning his broad shoulder against the tree, the muscles of his chest stretching the cotton of his black T-shirt. His hat shadowed his eyes, but his mouth—that wide, totally take-me-now mouth—was completely visible.

She might be a technical virgin, but she was a well-read one and she'd been doing nothing for the last twenty-four hours but fantasizing about what he could do with that mouth. To her. He was fast becoming an obsession. When that right corner of his mouth kicked up in amusement, she had to bite back a moan as her pussy clenched with sharp arousal. The sheer magnetism of the man didn't seem to recognize time of day or appropriateness of victim. He just indiscriminately oozed sexual promise and to hell with the consequences. She didn't know whether to jump him or hit him. He had no right to look so big and sexy this early in the morning. As a matter of fact, it should be outlawed for any man to look that good anytime. Unless he was about two seconds from taking her to bed. Which, her gaze dropped to his crotch, it didn't look like he was ready to do. Just one more thing not going her way today.

She shot the chicken a dirty look. "Oh she's in danger. There's no way in hell I'm losing a job because of a chicken with a good line."

"I could tell from your approach."

"Do you have a problem with a humane approach?"

"Don't you think it's a little cruel getting her hopes up only to take her life later?" He tipped his hat back off his face, revealing the amusement in his eyes before motioning to where the chicken was pecking around her feet through the mesh. "Hell, she thinks she's made a friend."

She looked at the peacefully pecking chicken. Okay. The man was sexy but devious, pointing out how her actions could be misconstrued. She folded her arms across her chest. "Making me feel like an axe murderer isn't going to get me to quit."

"You're the one striking up conversations with your victim."

"She took me by surprise."

"Uh-huh."

Mac almost laughed out loud as Jessie whipped around, her thick braid flying over her shoulder as she faced him. She was fun to get going. The chicken squawked at the sudden movement and flapped its wings.

"I said I could do this and I will." The vehemence in her voice had the chicken clucking again, its feathers as ruffled as Jessie's were, except on Jessie the anger exhibited itself in the strength with which she crossed her arms under her chest and the tight line of her mouth. He liked her mouth relaxed so he could admire the full curves, but when it came to crossing her arms, heck, she could do that all day long. As long as she wore a low scooped "T" like the one she had on today. The gesture had her breasts almost popping up and out from the red cotton. And damned delectable breasts they were, too. Plump and white. A good handful, with the cutest freckle decorating the left one, halfway down. He'd really like to taste that freckle. Test the resilience of that flesh with his lips. His tongue. His teeth.

Her gaze followed his. With an exasperated snort, she slammed her hands on her hips. Her breasts relaxed out of view. Her smile was a wry twist of her lips, but it had a predictable effect on his anatomy. One she obviously didn't miss as her gaze fled the vicinity of his groin with the speed of a jackrabbit.

If he hadn't seen her checking him out, he would have thought she was all business. Her "I really can do this" was that convincing. Too bad for her he'd seen the interest in her eyes. And maybe he didn't have to keep his cock holstered for the next two weeks. Not if she was willing to pass the time with a no-strings affair.

"Face it, honey. You're too soft for this."

She glared at him and then at the chicken. "Like heck I am."

She was. Which is why he'd come up with the idea this morning of having chicken and rice for supper tonight. If McGillicutty had refused to kill a chicken and she'd been raised on a farm, there was no way a woman as soft as Jessie was going to do it. Traditionally, Will had always done the messy job, but Mac wasn't volunteering that information today. A bet was a bet and his attraction to Jessie too strong to leave the situation as it stood.

He wanted her under control before he did something stupid. Hollisters had a family tradition for being stupid when it came to women. Always falling for the wrong ones. He looked Jessie over—from her neatly manicured nails, and expensive-looking clothes, to her highlighted hair. Oh yeah. She definitely fit in the category of wrong, at least for long-term consideration, but she might have short-term possibilities, He was real eager to check into those, just as soon as they got this little point behind them.

"You plan on willing her into the cook pot?" he asked as the chicken wandered back over to feed at her feet. She squared her shoulders and shot him a dirty look. "No."

She was game, he had to give her that. She reached for the chicken but it skittered away, squawking reproachfully as it did. The expression on Jessie's face was priceless. Surprise washed in with exasperation and distaste as the chicken eyed her warily.

"So much for friendship," he heard her mutter as she crouched over, and sidled to the left, obviously planning on cornering the chicken. The short burst of laughter that slipped past his control had her lips setting in a straight line and determination driving all other emotion from her face.

With that intensity of focus, he bet she'd be a force to reckon with in bed. Demanding. One who wouldn't be satisfied unless she found a lover confident enough to meet all of her needs, even those she didn't admit to herself. His cock jerked and stretched at the thought of being the man to introduce her to those needs. To make her ache for the pleasure he could deliver. To hear her cries of surprise and then ultimately, satisfaction. Hell, she could probably burn him up and make him love every minute of the flames. Someone that intense didn't do half measures.

He shifted his stance and adjusted his jeans, enjoying the flow of arousal as he eyed the shift of her buttocks beneath the soft denim. Damn. That ass alone could bring him to his knees.

Jessie glanced back at Mac from the corner of her eye. He still leaned against the tree. She still couldn't see much of his face beyond his chin and mouth, but there was something different about him. A certain awareness in his stance that had her nipples peaking beneath her shirt, and had her exquisitely aware of the view Mac had of her rear as she chased the stupid chicken. She let her gaze drop to his groin. She sucked in a hard, hurting breath. Oh Lord! Her memory wasn't playing tricks on her. He was huge. And hard. For her. She turned away and licked her suddenly dry lips. She looked at the chicken with renewed determination. The bird was going down. And when that was done and this bet behind them, she was getting that man into bed.

In a wild tackle, she dove for the chicken. The pen exploded into chaos. Feathers filled the air as the hens flew to separate corners, squawking harsh warnings as, by luck more than skill, she caught her quarry by its foot. The bird was surprisingly strong for its size, and she pecked like a demon, but after rolling around for what seemed an eternity in the smelly pen, Jessie made it back to vertical. She held the screeching hen upside down by its legs like she'd seen done in a movie. Adorned in more foul-smelling grime than she cared to identify, she emerged from the pen. Tossing her braid over her shoulder, she allowed herself a small grin. Hollister was going to eat that "too soft" comment and she was going to enjoy feeding him every bite.

Mac leaned against the chicken coop watching her approach, one booted foot casually draped over the other, his hips thrust slightly forward. His hard-on mouthwateringly evident. His gaze was aimed too high to be focused on the chicken.

"Do you know how to kill a chicken?" he asked, one rich brown brow arched in inquiry.

"I suppose you're going to fill me in?"

Her mouth. It was her mouth he focused on, she realized when she paused in front of him. Her breath hitched and that delicious weakness flooded her muscles. He was hard and focused on her mouth. The possibilities for that had her breasts tingling and her pussy gushing with delight. When the time came, would he let her take him in her mouth? She'd always wanted to try that. To hold a man helpless that way, his pleasure hers to grant. Oh yeah, that was way up on her fantasy to-do list.

"Do you need me to 'fill you in'?" he asked, bringing her back to the task at hand.

With her arm stretched way out in front of her, Jessie surveyed her victim. She thought of how friendly the hen had been, and how she was contemplating her for dinner. She couldn't begrudge the chicken the few pecks she'd landed from her awkward position. But as much as Jessie wanted to let the chicken go, she couldn't. The gleam in Mac's blue eyes just dared her to wimp out. If she did that, he'd never respect her, and she absolutely refused to have a lover who didn't respect her.

Keeping as much distaste as she could from her expression, she admitted, "I haven't the foggiest idea how one goes about killing a chicken, but I can tell you're just dying to educate me, so go ahead."

"The two most common methods are to wring the chicken's neck or to chop off its head."

She shuddered. From the coldness in her cheeks, she bet she'd just turned whiter than a ghost. From the roiling in the pit of her stomach, she was also willing to bet that white was going to be replaced by an interesting shade of green. "How does one go about wringing the neck?"

"Imagine whipping a noisemaker above your head."

She closed her eyes as the image ran through her mind. In her hand, she felt every pulse of the hen's rapidly beating heart.

She willed her stomach to settle. She started to shift her hold to the bird's neck when his next words froze her cold.

"Of course, if you don't do it right, the poor thing takes forever to die, slowly strangling as it tries to breathe through a crushed throat."

Jessie quickly returned her grasp to the bird's feet. "I want to kill the thing, not torture it."

"I'm glad you intend to be humane." His expression was as bland as his tone, but this close there was no missing the humor darkening his gaze.

"Just cut the sarcasm," she growled. "And point me in the direction of the chopping block."

Mac pushed his hat back off his brow and nodded to the right. Jessie followed the direction of his gaze and saw a huge stump right up next to a weather-beaten shed. Still carrying her squawking cargo, her arm aching from the strain, she grimly marched off to do her grisly chore.

One of the cowboys saw her destination and called to a fellow. By the time she arrived at the stump, four or five men had lined up to watch the spectacle of the city girl beheading supper. She shot each and every one a dirty look.

"You'll need this." One of the hands offered as a hatchet thudded into the scarred surface of the stump. She considered using it on her boss instead, when she saw his lips twitch with laughter. He was so damned sure she was going to fail, the bastard! The hen's survival instincts were top-notch, because as soon as she prepared to switch hands, she started flapping and pecking to beat the band. Jessie finally succeeded in switching the bird to her left hand so she could snatch up the hatchet in her right. For a moment, she just stood there, feeling the morning sun warming her right shoulder, *her killing arm,* she thought morosely as she held the hatchet high and met Mac's gaze dead on.

"I hope you realize I'm going to make you pay for this."

He folded his arms across his chest, laughter making his shoulders shake. "It's all part of the job, honey."

"That's Ms. Sterns to you, buster!"

"So you keep telling me."

Jessie considered throwing the hatchet. A titter of laughter erupted from the men behind her. Never taking her eyes from Mac's, Jessie warned. "The next person who laughs gets beans for supper."

The laughter halted as if cut by a knife.

Mac nodded to the frantically twisting bird. "I thought you said you weren't going to torture that bird?"

"I'm merely granting her a few more precious seconds of life while I wait for you to tell me how I get this whirlwind's neck to stay in place."

Mac removed his battered hat and ran his hand through his hair before readjusting his headgear. "Funny. I would have sworn that you were stalling."

She bared her teeth in a smile that felt more like a snarl. "I wouldn't dream of it."

"In that case, I'd just toss that bird down and swing the hatchet. If you do it clean, the head should pop right off."

Jessie closed her eyes against the nausea that welled with that image. Three deep breaths and she no longer felt that puking was imminent, but she was no closer to the "fling and pop" than she had been five minutes ago. While she stood there lecturing herself on the rightness of the food chain, she heard Mac sigh.

"I've got an appointment in town."

She opened her eyes in time to see him push away from the tree. He motioned to the squawking bird with one hand while fishing in his pocket with the other. His keys jangled as he said, "I'll be expecting chicken and rice when I get back."

"You've got it." Jessie kept her tone as conversational as his.

He stared at her a long moment, and then pulled his hat low over his brow and headed off to his pickup. She waited until he was behind the wheel and had the engine started before she released the breath she'd been holding. She still had the horrendous task before her, but at least she wouldn't have Mac as a witness while she bawled and puked in the aftermath. With a flip of her wrist she flopped the tiring bird onto the stump. She raised the hatchet over her head. A movement out of the corner of her eye caught her attention. She suddenly recalled she still had other witnesses. Four of them to be exact, and they looked as settled as if they were about to view a John Wayne film festival.

Her breathing eased. A beatific, purely wicked feeling of elation took wing inside her as Mac's truck roared out of the yard. She didn't even wait for the dust to settle before she made her offer.

"There's a chocolate torte with walnut butter cream filling for the first man to relieve me of this disgusting duty."

Four pairs of hands reached for the hatchet and the bird. She gladly handed over the hatchet, but she righted the hen and tucked her protectively under her arm, shaking her head. "I think this girl's suffered enough."

One of the men, a skinny hand unimaginatively nicknamed Slim, took the hatchet. He touched the brim of his hat with his fingers in a brief courtesy. "Pardon me, ma'am, but we kind of got the impression that this chicken killing was some kind of personal thing between you and the boss."

She flashed the shy man a wide grin. "Mac certainly thought it was."

"So did you," Slim pointed out while the other men nodded in support.

"Only for as long as I let my anger override my brain," she admitted cheerfully. "But to soothe your worries, killing supper isn't going to make you step over any male lines."

"In other words, when you and the boss laid down these rules, the boss forgot to dot a couple 'i's."

Jessie strolled back to the coop with her conspirators in tow. "You might say that." She deposited Mac J. Jr. back in her home. She turned to the blond man. "I'm sorry, I don't remember your name."

"It's Chuck, ma'am. And this is Jeremy, Slim, and Tim. And if you'll pardon me, ma'am—"

"J. C."

Chuck nodded at the correction. "If you'll pardon me saying so, Jessie, that doesn't much seem like Mac."

She dusted off her hands and wondered if it was a Texas affliction that no one could accept her initials as her name or if it was Mac's influence. "He was rather distracted at the time."

The four men exchanged glances. It wasn't hard to see where their minds were wandering. She hastened to divert them. "Since I need four chickens and there are four of you, I'll consider our deal met if each of you kills one."

Those arrangements didn't suit Chuck at all. "Have you ever plucked a chicken, Jessie?"

"I can thankfully admit to never having had the pleasure."

The men chuckled at that.

"It's a nasty business," Tim, a shy young man, jumped in, his face burning red, obviously seeing where his mentor Chuck was heading.

"I see." Jessie folded her arms across her chest, sensing the groundwork being laid for a bargaining session. "Well, of course I'm taking your word for the distastefulness of chicken plucking, but I could probably see clear to working something out."

Chuck let out the breath he'd been holding. She wondered if he hated killing chickens as much as she did. "There's no need to work anything more out. Jeremy and Slim will kill the birds and Tim and I will clean them."

"Sounds good to me," Jeremy piped in, his eyes lingering on Jessie's breasts long enough to make her uncomfortable. "I've got to be out at the South range with that irrigation pipe pretty quick anyhow."

"Then it's settled?" Jessie asked, shifting away from Jeremy's line of view.

"It's settled."

"Then I'll head back up to the house and get started on those cakes. Just be careful you leave Mac J. Jr. be."

"Jr.? You're naming a chicken after the boss?"

She shrugged, stroking the bird's back. "There's something about the way she strutted so arrogantly up to her death that made me think of the boss."

The men stared at the cocky, ruffled chicken for a second before breaking out in huge guffaws of laughter. Jessie knew it wouldn't be an hour before word got back to her boss a chicken had been named after him.

Halfway back to the house, she heard pandemonium break out in the chicken coop. Looking back, she began to swear viciously. That son-of-a- bitch Mac hadn't bothered to tell her that square little pen on the side of the cage was some sort of chicken catcher. She watched as Slim tossed some corn in the little chicken wire box and the second chicken strolled right on in to be efficiently caught as the trap door dropped.

Jessie looked at her bruise-pecked hands, smelled the chicken droppings on her clothing, and saw red. Mac Hollister was going to pay, and pay big for withholding that little bit of advice, she decided as she threw open the back door and headed for the shower.

*****

Mac entered the house and his nose twitched. Chicken and rice. Damn, he thought as he stepped into the shower. He couldn't believe she'd gone through with it. He called to mind her small, sick face and slammed his hand down on the faucet control in the shower.

"There's no way she killed those birds," he stated aloud ten minutes later as he tried to force clean jeans to slide up his still damp legs.

"She was turning green at the thought," he told his reflection as he combed back his damp hair. He grabbed his blue shirt out of the closet—the one that exactly matched his eyes—and tucked it into his jeans. His thoughts in turmoil, not sure whether he was mad or glad that Jessie wouldn't be leaving in the morning, he went down the back stairs into the eating area. There, along the table, were four fragrant skillets. Of the cook, there was no sign.

His suspicions rose when ten perfectly innocent faces lifted at his entrance and cheerfully greeted him. Something was going on here.

"Jessie?"

Will pointed with a fork toward the kitchen.

He found her whipping cream into a topping. She turned toward him, her brow creased in inquiry.

There it was again, Mac thought. That perfectly bland expression that fairly shrieked trouble. "Did you go into town today?"

Jessie raised her eyebrows. "How could I?" she asked. "You neglected to leave me the keys to the station wagon." Both knew the neglecting had been deliberate.

"You know," he stated conversationally, snagging a chair from the small desk. He turned it around and straddled it backward. "Ever since I came back today, everyone I've met has been giving me that same perfectly innocent expression you are wearing right now."

She turned the hand mixer on high. "That's a problem?"

"Honey, I haven't seen an innocent face in this crew since three years ago when Will substituted a rodeo bronc for the cutting horse I was supposed to be riding."

"I fail to see where that has anything to do with me."

He folded his arms across the back of the chair. From the other room the sound of hearty appetites being appeased could be heard. "Now, how did I know you were going to say that?"

"You're psychic?" she hazarded a guess over her shoulder.

He picked up his chair and moved it so he could see her face. "I don't suspect that's the case."

Jessie added a touch of vanilla and sugar to the topping she was making. She paused expectantly, her face all bland inquiry as she waited for him to continue.

"Where did the chickens come from?"

She pointed out the window with the measuring spoon.

He followed the trajectory of the spoon and saw the chicken coop, now closed up for the night.

"I noticed the old girl you were dangling out on the stump this morning pecking around the yard when I got in."

A drop of whipped cream attached itself to Jessie's finger. She slowly sucked it off.

Mac couldn't pull his eyes from the sight. "It won't do you much good to try and distract me," he warned, his cock hardening. He'd love to have those lips wrapped around his shaft, sucking slow and hard until he couldn't stand it anymore. "Now, what happened after I left?"

She shrugged. She turned the mixer back on. "There was something so mindlessly cocky about the little critter, I decided to spare her."

"I take it that's now Mac J. Jr.?"

"You heard about that, huh?"

"Probably about two minutes after you dubbed her." He fought the urge to smile. It was such a feminine way to get revenge. "What's the J stand for?"

"I can't tell you."

"Why not?"

"Because all the bets aren't in yet."

"Who's the oddsmaker?"

"Will."

"I'll have to look him up."

"Why don't you do that right now?" she suggested helpfully.

He shook his head slowly, a smile tugging at his lips. Damn he enjoyed sparring with her. "Where did the chickens come from?"

"I told you where."

"No, you didn't," he corrected. "You merely referred to the chicken coop."

"Chuck mentioned you had a penchant for dotting 'i's and crossing 't's."

"Comes from living with a sly father and a lazy brother. If you weren't quick enough to spot a loophole, you tended to end up doing all the dirty work."

She dropped the beaters into the sink. Mac rescued one, and scooped the cream off with a fingertip.

"Is this where I'm supposed to sigh in sympathy over your abused childhood?" Jessie asked.

Mac licked his finger clean. Her eyes followed every move of his tongue around his finger.

"Nope," he said. The way she swallowed in conjunction with him brought a smile to his lips, and prompted him to reach for another finger full. He'd never had a woman so aware of him. It was both arousing and fun. "I learned fast."

"Somehow I'm not surprised."

"I haven't forgotten the subject."

She unplugged the mixer and put it away. "What subject?"

He twirled the clean beater in his hand. "I thought that might be your game."

She managed to appear affronted. "I don't play games."

"Like hell." He got up and put the beater in the sink. "Where did you get the chickens, honey?"

"Oh, that subject. I thought we'd already settled that." She walked around him and opened the fridge and pulled out the chocolate tortes with their chocolate leaf decorations.

Mac's taste buds leapt to life. He struggled to remember the conversation. Suddenly it didn't seem all that important when faced with a confirmed chocoholic's dream. "Not quite."

"I got the chickens from the chicken coop here on your ranch. The one you can see through that window to your left."

He didn't bother to look out the window. He searched her face for the truth. No matter how hard he looked, he saw no sign of deceit, but damn it, he knew there was no way she had wielded that hatchet and lopped off those critters' heads.

Jessie just kept on looking innocent. She picked up the first of the cakes. From the diminished sounds out in the dining room, supper was winding down. "Excuse me."

Mac realized he was blocking the door. He got up and returned the chair to the desk. When she passed through the door, he was right on her heels, and not only because she was carrying that dream of a cake, though he would have followed that to hell and back. Something was going on here, and he wanted to know exactly what.

All sound stopped as Jessie entered through the door carrying that cake. Chuck clasped his chest and pretended to faint. "I think I've died and gone to heaven."

Jute reached for the cake as she drew near. "Let me help you with that, gorgeous."

Jessie skirted his hands. Slim kicked him in the shins. "That's not for the likes of you."

"What the hell do you mean?"

Mac shot Jute a glare. "Watch your language."

Jute in turn, glared at Jessie as if the reprimand were all her fault. Jessie placed the cake in front of Chuck.

"Here's my part of the bargain."

"Looks like I got the better part of this deal," he responded, rubbing his hands in glee.

Jessie grinned and shook her head, sucking a smear of chocolate off the side of her hand. "I think that totally depends on your point of view."

"What about ours?" Slim, Tim, and Jeremy piped up as one.

Mac smelled a rat.

Jessie pointed toward the kitchen. Chairs clattered as three sets of boots made a beeline for their prizes.

The seven remaining men at the table began to smell the same rat, Mac noted. "I suppose the rest of us are just going to have to do without?"

Jessie rubbed her palms up and down her thighs, and chewed her lower lip before admitting honestly. "You're going to have to do without the chocolate cake, but I make a mean peach cobbler."

Everyone came to the same conclusion at the same time, but Will was the one who spoke up. "What did those four do to deserve that?" He pointed to the chocolate confection that Chuck was zealously cutting into. He appeared ready to commit murder.

Jessie studiously avoided Mac's gaze. "They were kind enough to help me out with a messy chore."

Chuck took the first bite of the cake. His expression melted into sublime bliss. When he opened his eyes, his gaze bounced off Mac's angry one before meeting her expectant one. "I think you can call us even."

"Good."

Her smile was genuine, lighting her eyes as well as her face. It hit Mac like a sucker punch, stealing his breath and his ability to even think for all of two seconds. When the feeling returned to his body, it all focused in his aching groin. A glance around the table told him he wasn't the only one who'd noticed how

Jessie's smiles took her from sweet to siren. To a man, he wanted to shove their faces in their plates.

He pulled out his chair and sat down, adjusting his jeans as he did so, wincing as the material bit into his aching cock. He grabbed the half-empty skillet nearest his place at the head of the table. Someone had been kind enough to leave him some rice. He scooped it onto his plate, ladling the gravy mixture over the top.

"Looks like I'll be looking for another cook come morning."

Dead silence greeted the announcement. Slim paused in the swinging door that connected kitchen to eating area, his fork halfway to his mouth. Jessie would have laughed at the expression of utter dismay on his face another time, but right now she was gearing up for battle. Every eye in the room turned to her for comfort. Every eye except Mac's. His eyes met hers in pure triumph. She folded her arms across her chest.

"The only way you'll be looking for a new cook tomorrow is over my dead body."

Mac scooped up a forkful of fragrant rice. "I don't see where that will be necessary, since you lost the bet."

"How do you see I lost the bet, Mr. Hollister? You stipulated that the food come from the ranch, and that as cook, it was my place to see the job done. I saw to it."

Mac gave the food a couple of cursory chews and swallowed. Before the food was halfway to his stomach, he knew it had been a mistake. Fire burned over his tongue, seared his throat, and closed off his windpipe. He grabbed for his glass of water, chugging it as tears poured down his face. It felt like his insides were erupting in flames.

"What are you trying to do, kill me?" he rasped when he could catch his breath.

Jessie raised her eyebrows innocently. "I distinctly heard you tell me you liked your chicken and rice spicy." She looked around. "Tim, Jeremy, Slim, Chuck? You all heard him, didn't you?"

The three younger men looked a little hesitant to so obviously go against the boss, but Chuck had no such compunction. "Spicy is what I heard," he confirmed around a mouthful of cake.

If he'd been capable of clear speech, Mac would have blistered his friends' ears for turning traitor, but another surge of heat had him grabbing for his water glass. Around him, men laughed and joked. Across from him, Jessie stood looking as if she were wavering between satisfaction and apology. With a few hacking oaths, he pushed back his chair, and bailed.

Jessie watched as Mac bolted from the room and bit her lip. She might have taken her revenge too far.

Chuck started to laugh so hard, Rafe had to slap him on the back to stop him from choking. "What did you put in that batch to do that to him? Mac's a Texas boy. He's been breathing fire since the cradle."

Jessie turned away from the door, smiling at the men. "Ever heard of Sichuan Peppers?"

"No. You put one of those in there?" Rafe asked.

She shook her head. "No. I put about fifty of them in there. I ground them up real fine and stirred them right in. They looked like pepper."

"Holy sh—I mean cow!" Jeremy swore.

"If that man has a stomach left, it'll be a miracle," Slim interjected.

"I know!" she admitted, still chuckling. "But I can't work up one iota of guilt. I expected him to chew the darn food before he swallowed."

"I expect he will in the future," Slim interjected.

"If he still has a stomach to fill after this," Tim ventured.

"You know he's going to be hell to live with after this," Chuck pointed out.

"At least until he gets even," Slim agreed.

"Which I suspect he's dwelling on right now," Jute added, with a lot less mirth than before.

All eyes fell pointedly on Jessie. She threw up her hands. "Hey. I thought you were on my side."

Chuck shrugged. "We are, but until Mac gets even, he's going to be tough to deal with."

"In other words, I can expect no warning from any of you?" She slowly stood up.

"It's just a matter of self-defense," Slim apologized.

She halted any more such excuses with an upraised palm. From the determination she could read in every eye, she knew better than to appeal to their stomachs. She narrowed her eyes, and settled her hands on her hips. "Before you all go sending me off to OK corral on my own, do you mind telling me just how that particular skillet got half empty? Especially after I warned everyone away?"

Slim and Chuck looked at each other. Both men shifted uneasily in their chairs. "Well, it would have looked funny if there was a platter of untouched food on the table, so we took some out of that one."

"Uh-huh," she said, borrowing one of Mac's favorite expressions. "I suggest you keep that in mind when you catch wind of his plans for revenge."

"Now, Jessie," Chuck interjected placatingly. "You wouldn't tell the boss about that, would you? That wouldn't be fair."

She held her hand up in front of her face, curled her fingers down toward her palm, and did an in-depth study of her nails. "I suppose I could be persuaded to keep my mouth shut if you could be persuaded to keep yours open."

"After the way we helped you this morning," Slim pointed out reasonably, seeing a way out of the middle of this. "There's no guarantee the boss will confide anything in either of us."

"Then it's up to you two to keep the lines of communication open," she declared heartlessly.

The rest of the hands were quick to pick up on an advantage. "I might be persuaded to betray a few secrets for a piece of that cake," Rafe speculated.

Chuck saw the way Rafe's brown eyes coveted his prize and swore. He began to slice off a piece.

"A big piece," Rafe corrected seeing the miniscule slice Chuck was endeavoring to pare off.

"Greedy bastard," Chuck muttered, disgruntled, as more voices promised secrets for cake.

As the noise swelled all around, Jessie headed out into the soft evening twilight. She was going to try to reduce the damage.

"Hey, you never told us what the 'J' in Mac J. Jr. stands for," Will called to her back. "We've got bets to settle here."

Jessie tossed the answer over her shoulder. "Jackass!"

Chapter Five

Jessie found Mac down by the corrals. He was leaning with one booted foot on the lower rail, watching the sorrel in the corral munch on some hay. That he was scheming was obvious by the way a long stem of hay twirled between his lips.

"Are you going to sulk all night?" she asked, drawing close enough to be heard.

Mac turned around. He took the hay out of his mouth and tossed it to the ground. "I might." His right brow cocked up. He jerked his chin in the direction of the house, "Do you think it's such a hot idea for you to be out here with me so soon after that stunt in there?"

"I'm trying to minimize the damage," she confessed.

"By reminding me of how foolish I looked?"

She took the two steps necessary to reach his side. "By reminding you that you deserved it for not telling me about the chicken catcher."

"Uh-huh."

"What exactly does that mean?"

"Whatever your guilty conscience tells you it means."

"I do not have anything to feel guilty for."

He smiled despite his ill humor. Jessie found that an attractive quality in a man. "Not even for deliberately using your initials so I'd think you were a man when I hired you?"

"It's a tough world out there. A body has to use every bit of leverage she can find."

"I'm beginning to believe you're quite talented in leveraging your way around this world," he said as he eyed her.

There was an assessing quality to his gaze that made her think he was debating something.

"I'm not a naïve kid, Mac." She experimented with standing on the bottom rail of the fence. "I can handle myself in most situations."

"I'm beginning to believe that."

"Good." Dangling on the fence was not only awkward—it was uncomfortable. Not at all conducive to the conversation she wanted to have. She stepped down and sighed.

"Something on your mind?" Mac asked as she stared off into the darkened sky where the first stars were putting in an appearance.

"Yes." Jessie held on to the second rail and began to push herself back and forth. She dropped her gaze to the placidly eating sorrel and kept it there. "Why don't you like me?"

There was a rustle, and she knew he was looking at her. "What gave you the idea I don't like you?"

She snorted inelegantly, a habit she'd already picked up from Will. "The fact that you want me gone and are doing everything in your power short of buying me off to ensure I leave."

He pushed his hat back on his head. "I could claim you're imagining things."

"We both know I'm not, so why don't you like me?"

"Are you always this blunt?"

She shrugged. The sorrel was getting full, she noticed. Soon he would move away, and she wouldn't be able to use him as a distraction. Then she'd have to meet Mac's eyes, and she wasn't sure she'd be able to maintain her cool if she had to look into his eyes when he told her he found her annoying. "Call it a character flaw. Am I going to get an answer?"

"Do you really want one?"

"I wouldn't have asked the question if I didn't."

He caught her braid in his big hand, looping it once over his wrist, turning her face to his. "I want you," he stated bluntly. "I've wanted you since the moment you stepped off the bus."

Jessie caught her jaw before it could drop.

"So what's the problem?" she asked.

"You're my employee."

"You're worried I'm going to sue you?"

"I'm worried I'm going to give you enough reason to file a case."

"So you're trying to drive me off?"

His eyes met hers unflinchingly. "Yes."

"By making me stick to the letter of the contract."

"Yes."

She rested her hand on his forearm beside her cheek. Beneath her palm, his muscles were hard, flexing at her touch, vibrating with tension. "Your plan's not going to work," she informed him gently.

His head tilted a fraction.

"Because you hate to lose?"

His grip on her hair remained firm. She screwed her courage to the sticking point. It was now or never. "Because I want you, too."

"You have no idea who I am." His voice had an inflection she couldn't define. His eyes a determined hardness.

She shrugged. "I know enough."

"You don't know what I'll want from you."

Did he think she was a moron? "I've a good idea."

His eyes narrowed. "No, you don't."

She rolled her eyes as she finally put two-and-two together. Good God, he was trying to protect her. From all that gorgeous animal magnetism he exuded. "You are so sweet."

His hand in her hair tugged her head back, pulling her hips into his hips. His cock, hard and thick, pressed into her thigh. "Don't tempt me."

She rubbed her thigh against his erection, smiling when he shook and his blue eyes narrowed to slits. "Why not?"

He'd have to come up with a damned good excuse to discourage her.

"I don't like my sex sweet and neat."

That was supposed to scare her? "I don't think I do either."

"You don't think?"

She took a breath and licked her lips. She wished she had the courage to meet his eyes, but as high as she got was the pulse in his throat. "I've only had one lover and he wasn't the most…apt."

The tanned flesh jumped with his pulse. His hand released her braid and slid to the base of her neck. His fingers stroked gently. His voice as soft as a touch. "He hurt you?"

"Why would you think that?"

His fingers on her neck stilled. "Because you're twenty-nine, as sexy as all get-out, and practically a virgin."

She grimaced. "Not by choice." His fingers on her neck felt good. She arched into them, twisting her hips so her pelvis rubbed against his cock.

"Then what?"

"My mother had Alzheimer's." She arched her hips higher, trying to get closer. Oh God, he felt good. "Between paying the bills and caring for her, there was no time for dating."

"I'm sorry."

"So was I, but at least she's free now." His hips relaxed into hers. His hand behind her neck pulled her chest to his. The heat of his flesh through her clothing burned. Her nipples peaked, straining to be closer. Her muscles stretched, reached, wanting the same thing. Her pussy writhed with dissatisfaction.

His free hand settled on her buttock. She jumped. He used the momentum to pull her up into his groin. The pressure against her clit was both arousing and a relief.

"And so are you."

"Yes." It was an embarrassing, drawn-out sound. He felt so damned good. Hot, hard, and so damned big. She couldn't blame Mac for his smug smile. At least it had a kind edge. She was rather pathetic.

"What you have before you, Mac Hollister, is a sex-starved woman," she admitted on a gasp as he pulled her hips a little higher, and then slid her down an inch. Her insides wrenched on the surge of pleasure that shot through her as his cock burrowed between her legs. Her eyes squeezed shut as she tried to comprehend the sensation. Her whimper was involuntary.

"Oh, I like that little sound," he murmured. With a twist of his wrist he wrapped another coil of her braid around his wrist and pulled her head back. "Look at me."

She opened her eyes. His face was above hers. His expression intent. His smile predatory. "Do you want an affair with me, Jessie?"

"Absolutely."

He blinked. Then laughed. "No question?"

"I've been waiting my whole life for someone like you to come along."

He worked her on his cock. Up and down. One fraction of an inch at a time. "Someone like me?"

She bit her lip against another cry and nodded. "You're the only man my body has wanted up until now."

He jerked her so hard against him it hurt. And even that felt good.

"Damn."

His hand on her ass forced her groin down on his erection with bruising force. She put her arms around his neck and her legs around his hips and let him.

He tugged her braid again. "Look at me."

She forced her eyes open.

"I'm not an easy lover."

"Good."

"I like it rough." As if to prove his point, he ground against her again.

She bit her lip against the cry that welled. He leaned down and nipped her lower lip. "Ow!" She touched her stinging lip. There was no remorse in his expression.

"Don't hide your response from me. I want every cry, every thought you have when I'm touching you. I'll expect you to give me what I want when I want it, no questions asked."

He was annoyed that she'd suppressed a scream? She reached over her shoulder and tugged at her braid. Against her buttock she felt his knuckles press as he tightened, refusing to let go.

"What about what I want?" she asked resentfully.

"All you have to do is ask and it's yours."

She ran her tongue over her lip where he'd nipped her. "I want to be put down."

That fast, she was set away from him. So fast it took a minute for her feet to register that they were on the ground. Her pussy still grasped for his cock as she stared up at him.

"Hell."

He arched that brow at her again. "Not what you wanted?"

She smiled ruefully and admitted. "Now that I have it, no."

His gaze dropped to her lips and he groaned.

"What?"

"You have a great mouth."

Nice, but not enlightening. "Thank you."

He reached out and tucked a strand of hair behind her ear. The calluses on his fingers dragged on her skin. Rough. Masculine. They'd feel great on other parts of her body.

"Your smile turns me on," he clarified.

She smiled so broadly her cheeks hurt. "I'm glad."

His fingers stilled by her ear. "Why?"

She let her gaze linger on his groin. "Because I've got a whole to-do list of sex things for us to try, and it would be really helpful if you were interested."

"Oh, I'm interested." He tweaked her earlobe before sliding his hand around behind her neck and pulling her with him into the deeper shadows cast by the barn.

It was almost too dark to see. His hands slid down her back until they reached the curve of her hips.

"What's your number one fantasy on that list?"

His fingers rubbed over her ass, slid up over the waistband of her jeans and then slipped beneath. She lurched into his chest as his fingers glided over her flesh. He pulled her into his cock. His head bent until his lips brushed her ear.

"Tell."

She couldn't.

"C'mon. What do you want me to do to you?"

"Nothing."

He nipped her ear. "Uh-huh."

"Cut that out." She pulled back from his mouth. The move shoved his hands further down her pants. He spread his fingers over the curve of her buttock pulling her groin up into his. She could've sworn her pussy sighed in relief as the solid weight of his penis pushed against her.

"Did you want me to eat your pussy?" he asked. "Suck your clit until you scream?"

Lord, that did sound nice, but... She cleared her throat, before confessing, "Actually most of my list has to do with the things I'd like to do...to you."

The last came out as a whisper. It didn't matter. It still shocked him. She could tell from the way he froze, sucked in one harshly drawn breath and didn't release it right away. Great. Her first viable sex partner and she might have scared him away by blurting out the truth. All the women's magazines said men found aggressive women scary. Considering how important this was to her, you'd think she would have remembered that.

"I'm sorry," she said, talking fast, petting his chest. "What you suggested sounded great. More than great, actually."

He caught her fingers in one hand, the other pulled her harder against him if that was possible. His chest expanded on a hard breath before he asked, "What exactly is on this list?"

She didn't know if the growl in his tone was a good thing or not. "Well one of the things I'd really, really like to do is…"

"What?"

Now he sounded impatient.

She jerked at her hands. He didn't let go. "It's just not the easiest thing to blurt out."

"Try."

She sighed. There was nothing to do but say it. "I'd really, really like to…masturbate you."

"Damn." His body jerked against her. He yanked his hand out of her pants so fast she stumbled. He caught her by the shoulders.

"Why?"

"Why what?"

"What about jacking me off excites you?"

She wouldn't have answered him at all except that every book and article she'd read said honesty between lovers was critical for a good sexual relationship, and she so wanted this encounter to be different from her last.

"The thought of making a man come…excites me."

"Damn!"

Again with the damn.

"What exactly does that mean?" she asked, exasperation putting an edge to her tone.

"It means you've got me so turned on I'm about to come."

"I haven't even touched you yet!"

She put her hand to her forehead. Oh for God's sake, if she had to blurt out anything, couldn't it have been something more sophisticated?

He pulled her hand away, turned it in his, and kissed the palm, his eyes hot and intent as he stared into hers. "Would you like to?"

She looked around. "Here?"

He brought her hand to his chest. "Yes. And before you ask, now."

She glanced down at his crotch. It was too dark to see. She felt her way down his abdomen, over the ridges of muscles and the slight well of his navel. Her finger caught in a belt loop before navigating the waistband. And then she had him in her hand. She fought the denim as she struggled to judge his girth. He was thick. Very thick. Cupping her palm around him as best she could, she measured his length, smiling at his groan as she inched her way down his thigh. Oh, he liked this. So did she, but this wasn't enough.

"I'll understand if you feel this isn't the time or place, but I'd like to touch you..." She punctuated the statement with a squeeze on the head, "skin to skin."

He shuddered under her hand. "Damn!"

She had the hang of those "damns" now.

"I'll take that as a yes." She had his jeans unsnapped and was working the zipper down before she finished the sentence.

A slight brush on the top of her head had her looking up even as the zipper slid down. His face was just above hers.

"Definitely a yes," he muttered right before his mouth claimed hers.

She'd been kissed before, but they were nothing compared to this. Mac kissed like it mattered. Like she mattered. And he knew what he was doing, too. He slid his tongue over her lips softly when she'd been expecting aggression. Seducing her rather than assuming she was seduced. He paused at the right corner, stroking it softly, coaxing it open before moving to the left and doing the same. Her lips parted. His tongue thrust. Her fingers clenched.

"Easy," he whispered against her mouth. His hand caught hers, easing it away from his cock.

Oh God, she'd practically had a stranglehold on him. She dropped her head to his chest. "You must think I'm a total moron."

The brush came across the top of her head again. It was a kiss, she realized. He was kissing her.

"I think you're hotter than hell." Her hand was still in his. He eased it down the front of his unzipped jeans. The hair on his lower abdomen tickled the back of her hand. "And if you don't get me out of these jeans soon, I'm going to come without you."

She frowned. "Has it been a long time for you?"

He froze again, and she had a sinking feeling she'd once again put her foot in her mouth.

"About eight months, but I don't think that has anything to do with it."

She closed her fingers around his hard shaft. He was so smooth and warm, and the way he pulsed in her hand made her palm tingle.

"You don't?" she asked as she gently tried to work him free.

"Nope. I think it has everything to do with a sexy blonde jumping me behind the barn and telling me she wants to fulfill her fantasies with my body."

His cock was stuck. It was too big to just pull out. This was going to take some thought. "You don't mind?" she asked contemplating the situation.

"Hell no." He slid his jeans down in answer to the question in her glance. "You have to make room."

Oh man, did she ever. She'd never seen a cock this big outside of a porn movie, and she'd assumed those were computer enhanced. She petted her hands along his length, her palm catching on the ridge at the crown.

"I wish I could see." She supported the heavy weight in one hand, tracing the head with the finger of the other. She discovered the tiny wet slit in the tip with her finger. She spread the slippery liquid she found there around the crown, smiling when more immediately appeared. She scooped it up with her fingers. Without thinking, she brought it to her mouth.

Mac caught her hand in his, stopping her finger inches from her mouth.

His voice was gruff. "Don't. Not ever. Unless you're sure the guy's clean."

She closed her eyes. "I knew that."

She'd just been caught up in the moment.

"Damn." He pulled her close, trapping her hand against his chest and slanted his mouth across hers, kissing her hard, deep. Exploring her mouth with his tongue. Stealing her breath with his passion. He separated their lips, his breath mingling with hers as he said, "I'm clean, but I'll get tested again tomorrow so you can be sure."

"And then?" she asked breathlessly.

He dropped his forehead against hers. "Then you can taste me all you want."

His breath was warm and moist on her cheek. The heat from his body reached out to envelop her senses in a leather-scented hug.

"I can't wait." She tugged her hand free and brought it back to his cock.

His laugh was a husky expulsion of sound. "Trust me, honey. Neither can I."

She wrapped both hands around his shaft, marveling that her fingers couldn't meet. "In my fantasy I'm very good at this."

"Lucky me."

She tilted her head sideways to get a better angle to see his eyes. The light was too faint to make out more than a blur.

"This is reality."

"And?"

"I don't know how to make it good for you." It was so much easier to say these things in the intimate darkness where neither of them could clearly see the other, and she could pretend to be a lot braver than she actually felt.

"You want me to show you what I like?" he asked huskily.

"Please?"

"My pleasure." Shifting his body, his hand moved from her hip.

As his large callus-roughened palm cupped the back of her hand, nervousness had her joking. "Literally, I hope."

His cheek slid across hers until his lips rested against her ear. "Oh yeah."

Mac felt Jessie's body start as he curled his hand around hers. For all her bold as brass talk, she was nervous, and he guessed he couldn't blame her. If he waited ten years to act on his fantasies, he'd be pretty nervous, too.

"Just take it nice and slow at first," he told her, his hand schooling hers in the motion he liked. "Let me feel all the textures in your hand. Let me anticipate what's to come."

He leaned back against the wall as she stroked his cock, her soft, smooth palm a lick of flame over his sensitive flesh.

"That's right," he encouraged as she added her second hand to the motion. "Use both your hands to pump me." Damn, she was a natural, seemingly knowing when he needed the pressure increased. But they definitely needed lubrication.

"Wet your hands."

Her fingers stilled on him. Squeezing at the top and bottom of his penis simultaneously, as she considered his suggestion. White-hot sensation shot out from his cock, flaring through his body, gathering energy as it went, rendering him speechless for a moment. His hips jerked. His balls pulled up tight.

"Damn, that's good," he groaned when he could.

She did it again. "You like that?"

His hips bucked helplessly. "Run a hand over the head of my cock and you'll see for yourself," he rasped.

She did, her hand sliding easily with the liberal lubrication of his pre-come. He could barely make out her form in the dark but he thought her head bent, trying to see her hand on his flesh. The knowledge was like a kick in the gut, driving the air from his lungs as lust tore through his body. Damn, he wanted to watch her watching him. She cupped the head of his shaft and rotated her palm over it while the other resumed pumping his shaft. His knees buckled.

Her teeth flashed white in the gloom. "Oh, I like that."

So did he, and when she squeezed him again, he gave her the groan he might have otherwise held back, knowing it increased her pleasure. Her hand left his shaft. She stepped back to make room between them. He knew what she was up to. He caught her hand before she could lick it. The muscles in her forearm trembled beneath his grip. He took a deep breath and caught the faintest hint of feminine arousal. She was as turned on as he was. The knowledge had his balls pulling up tight. He drew her palm to his mouth and first licked and lightly bit the pad of her thumb. She jerked and gasped against him. Her jeans-clad thigh grazed his shaft. He shuddered as pre-release tremors snaked up his spine. Wiping her hand on his shirt quickly, he moved it toward her mouth.

"Get it nice and wet," he ordered as he held her palm against her lips. Her knuckles rhythmically pressed into his fingers as she did. He imagined her pink tongue working over that firm flesh with little flicks and smooth glides and shuddered again.

"Wet it a little more and then do the other one."

She did. When she had both hands around him, he took a steadying breath.

"I'm in the mood to come hard and fast, so you need to do it like this."

With his hands he showed her how to go light on the upstroke, squeeze just under the head on the downstroke, twisting her hands in opposite directions as she did while maintaining the pressure. She didn't immediately start when he removed his hands. He couldn't see, but he could feel her staring at his face. He waited for the question she was contemplating, listening to her irregular breaths, and the first chirps of the crickets.

"If I do this, you promise you'll come?"

His laugh was a harsh burst of sound. Just how inept had her previous lover been?

"Honey, I won't have any choice."

Her hands started to move, lightly, slowly up his shaft. "Really?"

God help him, she sounded intrigued. "Really."

"And it won't hurt if I squeeze hard?"

"In about a minute of you doing that, my only worry will be that you'll stop."

He heard the soft rustle of her braid against her shirt as she shook her head. "I won't do that."

She reached the head of his cock, and gathered the ample pre-come she found at the tip. There was the slightest hesitation and catch in her breath as she did, and he knew, just knew she was itching again to taste him. This time, he didn't know if he'd stop her. He wanted her hot mouth with a vengeance, but then her hands swooped down his cock tightening and twisting as she went, tearing at his control as the hot, tight spiral of desire yanked him in.

"Like that?" she asked.

A one syllable "Yes" was all he could get past the rigid muscles of his throat. He reached for the fastening of her jeans as she started the upward glide again, faster this time. More confident.

The agonizing pleasure of her downstroke had him baring his teeth as he struggled not to tear the jeans from her body, but rather to ease his hand inside. She wasn't just damp. She was wringing wet with sweet cream. He had no trouble finding her clitoris. It was hard and engorged. She was on the verge of a climax just from jacking him off. Oh, he definitely liked that. He stepped closer to improve his angle as he worked his finger deeper into her jeans to trace that hard nubbin. If he timed this right, they could come together.

Instead of leaning into him, she jerked back. His hand in her jeans kept her close, but her hands on his cock stilled as she said, "Don't."

"Why not?" he flicked her clitoris again, smiling when she collapsed into his palm. "You like it."

"That's not the point," she gasped, clutching his cock like a lifeline.

"Then what is the point?"

"I can't concentrate when you do that."

He wasn't quite sure he understood. "And you need to concentrate?"

He felt her body shift and realized she was ducking her head. Like she was embarrassed, but she gamely held to her point.

"Can't you wait until after to touch me?"

He wanted to hear her say it. "Until after what?"

Her response was a thready whisper. "Until after you come."

He pulled his hand from her jeans, being careful to keep his fingers from touching the material.

"Yeah, but it will cost you."

New tension entered her body. "What?"

He brought his hand to his mouth and sucked his fingers clean. Her unique flavor burst on his tongue, making his cock jerk with sheer enjoyment. Damn she was sweet.

"Did you just stick your fingers in your mouth?"

She sounded completely shocked. And this from a woman who'd been tempted to taste him twice. "Yes."

"You said we shouldn't."

"You haven't had a lover in ten years and you were tested last year. I'd say you're safe."

There was another long, pregnant pause and then she asked. "Did you like it?"

"The way you taste?" he asked.

Her "yes" was so strangled, he didn't have to see her to know she was blushing. He ran his hand over her cheek and then around her head until he could wrap her thick braid around his wrist, catching the end in his hand. The other hand he rested along her back.

"Make me come, and I'll answer."

She didn't need any more encouragement than that. Quickly wetting her hand, she went to work on his cock, starting slow before building to a rapid rhythm that had him panting and swearing as he tried to hold back the come boiling in his balls. She was determined and showed no mercy, pumping him hard, pulling him close, chanting soft words of encouragement as she dragged his climax from him. His cock throbbed under her grip as she whispered, "Come for me, Mac." She added a "please" as if sensing he was resisting.

He tried to step aside as the first jets welled, intending to come on the ground but she went with him. Her softly moaned, "Oh, no," was the only warning he had before she tucked his cock up under her shirt, the soft skin of her abdomen burned the underside of his shaft as her hands pressed him close, milking him through her shirt as she whispered, "Give it to me."

The pleasure so intense it was agony, he had no choice. He came, his cock jerking violently against her stomach as he erupted, groan after groan ripped from his throat as she cuddled his cock against her breasts and pumped him dry.

Long moments later, he found his breath. And when he did, he pulled her up and around, using her braid as leverage. When he had her back to the wall, he stripped the jeans and panties from her in one quick move. While she was distracted by her nakedness, he knelt. Her scent enveloped him like a welcome party. She was hot, wild, wet and his. All his. He slid his shoulders between her smooth thighs, lifted her until she sat on them, her back braced against the barn wall, his mouth just a scant inch from her tempting pussy. Her hands tugged at his hair. He looked up. In the faint moonlight, he could just make out the question in her eyes. His answer was to the point.

"My turn."

She blinked at him in the deep shadows, the whites of her eyes disappearing twice before she took a deep breath. The tension in her muscles communicated her doubt before she got the words out. "I'm not sure—"

He smiled. "I am."

He'd never been more sure of anything in his life. Her scent surrounded him. Musky. Spicy. Sweet. Damn, everything about her was going to be sweet, he could just tell.

"You don't have to do this." He nuzzled his way into her curls. Her head clunked back into the barn wall. "Oh my God!"

He laughed against her delicate folds as he lapped along her crease, stopping just short of her clit. He was right after all. She was a screamer. She was also unbelievably sweet, her cream silky against his tongue. Keeping her in place by wrapping his arms over her thighs, he parted her outer lips with his fingers. "You taste like the sweetest honey spiced with pure woman."

"Is that good?" The question was loaded with doubt.

"Oh yeah." How could she not know how incredible she was? How he wanted to drown in her flavor? Her scent? How he wanted to eat her from head to toe and then as soon as he finished, to start all over again?

"You don't have to do this," she repeated, as if he were performing some distasteful chore.

He paused, his tongue a breath from the juicy berry of her clit. Just how awkward and stupid had that boyfriend been? "Anyone ever go down on you before?"

He swore he could feel the heat of her blush reach all the way to her thighs.

"Once."

That one tight, slightly bitter syllable told him all he needed to know about that experience.

"Now that, honey girl, is a damn shame."

"Why?"

"Because I say so."

"And who are you, the reigning authority on oral sex?"

"Before the night's done, I'm going to be the reigning authority on your pussy, so you might as well get that tone out of your voice and sit back and enjoy."

"The night?" Against his cheeks her thighs quivered and tightened. Oh she liked the thought of him feasting on her all night.

"Definitely all night. It's going to take me at least that long to quench my thirst for your taste. And then…"

"And then what?"

He flicked her clit with his tongue, smiling when she squealed and clenched her lush little ass against his chest, her juices trickling onto his collarbone. "And then I'm going to get serious about feeding my appetite."

Another clunk and another "Oh God".

He nuzzled back into her fragrant flesh, swirling his tongue in the thick cream, letting her flavor spill through his mouth. Paying attention to her breaths, he noted that they broke when he circled the shallow valley leading to her vagina but they stopped altogether when he flicked the taut skin just beneath her clit. He did it again simply because it pleased him to please her.

Her fingers sank into his hair. "Mac..."

Damn, he liked hearing his name breathed in that sexy high-pitched little whimper. Hearing it again became a top priority. He laved that sensitive spot over and over, until her thighs trembled and she chanted his name, her hands in his hair pushing him away and them dragging him back. He moved up to her clit, gently resting the pad of his tongue against it, judging her sensitivity. She froze, not moving. Not breathing, her whole body one tight brace of expectancy, her cream spilling in a steady stream from her cunt.

He rubbed back and forth, dragging the rough surface of his tongue along that sensitive bundle of nerves as long as he could, prolonging her pleasure, measuring her reactions until he had her on the edge of what he wanted. With a sharp snap, he lashed her clit, driving her to the response he sought, finding it as she jerked back and sucked in a hard breath. He barely got his hand to her mouth in time as she arched her back and screamed. Her teeth sank into his hand. His cock leapt with delight. He tucked his chin down, getting a better angle to satisfy his hunger as her cream poured from her body.

The soft night was filled with the sounds of her muffled cries and his search for satisfaction. He hadn't indulged in play this innocent in years, couldn't remember the last time, yet he was more turned on than he'd ever been. His cock ached and leaked with each desperate whimper and shudder he pulled from her slender body. And inside, anger roiled, because she wasn't for him. Couldn't be for him, yet he wanted her like hell on fire.

In the distance a door creaked and slammed.

"Mac?"

Dammit! Not now, he thought. *Not when she is so close.* "Yeah?"

"Mac?" The voice got closer. "Lone Tree's on the phone." Mac recognized the deep voice as Will's when he added, "He says there's a problem."

Mac dropped his head against Jessie's quivering abdomen. Will wouldn't give up until he found him and delivered the message. He reluctantly slid her thighs off his shoulder. Jessie collapsed against him. He pressed his mouth into her stomach, steadying her as he fought his own ragged breathing.

Bracing her against the barn, he stood, catching her face in his hands, he slanted his mouth over hers, kissing her hard and deep, aware of Will getting closer. Aware of what he wanted, what he was about to throw away.

"I want you, honey girl, but I'm not a kid, and I'm not the safe little learning experience you're looking for."

"No shit." The little wisp of sound hardly counted as a voice.

"I like my women obedient."

"Wouldn't a dog be less expensive?"

He rested his forehead against hers and laughed. "But not nearly as much fun."

"Mac?" Will called again.

"Coming." Mac called over his shoulder. He smoothed his thumb over her lower lip. "I want a lover in my bed, Jessie. Someone who enjoys taking an order and a spanking. Someone who'll let me take charge, dictate their pleasure. Someone who will trust me to give them what they need. Unconditionally."

She stilled beneath him, catching her lower lip in her teeth. He eased it free with his thumb before placing a regretful kiss on her tempting mouth.

"Somehow, I don't see that being you."

Chapter Six

He was out of his mind. Mac wrapped the barbed wire around the post and reached for the staple gun in his belt. He'd had Jessie in the palm of his hand three nights ago. Right where he'd wanted her. Had her panting and sobbing, limp against him, ready to give him anything he'd wanted, and he'd given her a damned out. He lined the gun up with the wire, and squeezed the handle. The shock of the staple slamming into the wood vibrated up his arm. What in hell was he going for, sainthood? The woman was twenty-nine years old. Old enough to know her own mind. Old enough to know when she wanted an affair and with whom.

So why had he tried to scare her so badly with the truth of the ways he liked to take a woman? He hooked the staple gun back into his belt and grabbed the next string of wire. With other women he'd let them get used to him first then slowly introduced them to the idea, judging from their reactions whether they'd be receptive, and backing off if they weren't.

With Jessie, he'd been cold, matter of fact. Abrupt. Unnecessarily so. Maybe it was because he wasn't sure he'd be able to ease her into anything. Her natural enthusiasm, combined with his natural inclinations, played hell with his restraint. Maybe it was because she scared him. Jessie was a woman a man didn't just glance over. And despite her determination to make up for ten years of sexual deprivation with a white-hot affair, not a woman a man toyed with. She was smart, sweet, giving and way too trusting. If he had a shred of decency in him, he wouldn't have handed her his test results this morning. If he had a single survival instinct, he wouldn't have taken that soft mouth in a hard kiss and left her with an ultimatum. Jessie was too city to take to this life easily, and the years with his mother were a hard lesson in how living in the wrong environment could take its toll on a woman.

He wrapped the wire around the post and grabbed the gun again. Of course, there was a slim chance that Jessie might adjust. And she might come around to his way of thinking in bed. He slammed the gun against the wire and pulled the trigger. Yeah, right. After the way he'd done his best to terrify her, there was no way in hell she would let him near her bed. Nice to know he still had the Hollister talent for shooting himself in the foot.

He put the gun back on his belt and let go of the wire. And sighed when his hand stayed put. *Damn it!* He'd stapled his glove to the post again. He stretched to reach the screwdriver. That was the fourth time today. It took a second to get free, but he didn't reach for the third string. He was too distracted today to be messing with barbed wire.

He pulled off his gloves and wiped his sleeve across his brow. Still there was a chance that Jessie would give him the green light, and if she did, he had to come up with a plan because sure as shootin', he was going to have to keep an eye on her if she did decide to hang around. That woman had a wild streak that wouldn't tolerate the monotony of ranch life. He had only to think of his mother to know that boredom was one emotion he didn't want overtaking Jessie. Boredom led to risk taking, and risk taking led to—

Hell, he definitely didn't want to go where those memories led, he decided as he emptied the staple gun. The staples dropped into their plastic holder with tiny pings of protest. He snapped the lid on the box, dropped the stapler into the toolbox and snapped it shut. It was time for a break. He headed for the pickup, leaving the shade of the trees for the meadow.

The sun beat down on his back and shoulders as he grabbed the red and white cooler out of the cab. He took the cooler back to the shade and sat down under a tree. Before opening the wax paper-wrapped hoagie, he popped the top of an iced tea and drained the can in one long swallow. When he was done, he didn't feel the least refreshed, which only added to his feeling that this day was going to be one long sojourn in Hell. He opened his sandwich with a quick tear, so frustrated he almost missed the piece of notepaper attached.

He reached for it. There was only one person who would leave a note in his food. Taking a breath, he braced himself. There was only one reason Jessie would put a note in his lunch. She was too embarrassed after all her bravado to admit, face-to-face, that she'd made a mistake. He held the note in his hand for a moment, and then, calling himself a fool, opened it. The first piece of paper was easy to see. It was test results. No shock there. Jessie was clean. He slipped it underneath. The second was different. It took a second for him to recognize what he was seeing. It wasn't a note but a list he held in his hand. And from the different colored inks and stains here and there, he'd say a longstanding one. He moved his thumb off the top, revealing the heading.

SEXUAL TO-DO LIST

He scanned the contents and smiled. Son of a bitch, but the woman had a sense of adventure.

* * * * *

Jessie worried her lower lip with her teeth as she put the last of the pots and pans into the sink. Mac hadn't showed up for supper. She didn't know what to make of that. Surely he'd received her message? Had her bluntness scared him off? Had he changed his mind? She'd personally strangle him if he had. After spending all day drowning in sexual tension, there wasn't a woman alive who would blame her.

"I believe this belongs to you?"

Elbow deep in soapsuds, Jessie stiffened at the low drawled question. She knew what she'd find in Mac's hand if she turned around. Heat surged in her cheeks and prickles of cold ran down her arms. Oh damn this was humiliating. What had seemed so appropriate at three a.m. this morning appeared childish and stupid at nine o'clock at night. She scrubbed hard at the spaghetti sauce cooked to the bottom of the cast-iron pan.

"You didn't come in to supper."

"After finding this list wrapped around my lunch, I didn't trust myself within a hundred yards of you. Audience or not."

She knew she should turn around, but all her courage seemed to have deserted her. "I assume that everyone is gone now?"

She couldn't see the smile she heard in his voice, but out of the corner of her eye she could see the piece of folded paper he held in his hand.

"Yup."

Jessie stopped scrubbing the pan. Her breath froze in her lungs as she realized the time she'd been anticipating all day was here.

"Oh."

"Are you going to look at me?"

"No. Yes." She shrugged. "Eventually."

More of his body came into view as he shifted to lean against the doorjamb. "Just how long, exactly, is eventually?"

She grabbed the dishtowel and dried her hands. If he expected her to face him, forever. "I don't suppose we could do this the first time without me having to face you?"

"It's possible." His voice was thick and deep as he added, "But not likely."

"Why not?"

"Because I want to see your face while I take you this first time."

Her fingers clenched so hard on the butcher block cutting board that her nails bent. The note landed beside her right hand. The heat in her cheeks deepened. "I'm sorry," she whispered. "It seemed like a great idea this morning, but I realize now how childish it would appear to you."

From the corner of her eye, she saw him move. Heard him approach, Still, she jumped when his hands slid around her waist. Jumped and shivered when he kissed the nape of her neck. Groaned when she felt him smile against her spine at her reaction.

"I was so hoping to be more sophisticated when it came to this," she admitted on a rush of honesty.

He nuzzled the side of her neck with his lips, but his hold on her softened, became soothing somehow. "Would I be correct in assuming the reason you're standing so stiff in my arms is because you're embarrassed?"

The laugh she meant to sound carefree came out choked and strained. She leaned further into his embrace, seeking the confidence she lacked. "Right the first time."

His hands slipped beneath the sensible cotton of her shirt, and she shivered in anticipation. Would he like what he discovered or would he consider it tacky? There was a pause in his movements as he discovered lace where he expected skin. His breath caught as his lips touched her ear. It came harder as his hands explored further, creeping over her stomach up toward her breasts. He cupped them once, his hips pressing into hers as he rolled her nipples through the lace, abrading the tips deliciously with the rough material, pulling her close when she whimpered, before releasing her breasts and heading lower.

"Put your mind at ease, honey girl," he said as he unsnapped the button of her jeans and slipped his fingers beneath. He paused again when the pads of his fingers slid across her bare flesh. The prick of sharp pleasure sucked her abdomen in and notched her breath. He was so big. So strong, and so damned hot she thought she'd burst into flames. He kissed the taut cord on the side of her neck. Her whole body shuddered in sensation, her knees lost all strength, and she collapsed back against him when he nipped her gently.

"I've never received a more welcome invitation than that to-do list," he rasped as he explored the tiny well of her belly button.

Jessie groaned and dissolved into his embrace. When he deliberately set his teeth to the spot where her shoulder met her neck, she jerked and spun around. Grabbing his shoulders, she tugged. She had to do it twice before the corners of his mouth lifted into a smile, and he obligingly lowered his lips to hers.

"Are we all done being shy?" he asked, the question drifting across her tongue, spicing his warm breath with erotic promise.

"Oh God, yes!" She'd waited a lifetime for this. She'd be damned if she was going to chicken out now that she had her opportunity. She slid her tongue along his lips, teasing the corners as he'd done to her, sucking his lower lip between her teeth for the simple reason that she'd always wanted to. Doing it again because he shuddered and yanked her close.

"Good," he sighed. "Because I'm hotter than a firecracker, and I don't think I have the patience for a slow seduction. Not this time."

"I can tell," she whispered. Her fingers clenched in his mink-brown hair as his lips slid across her cheek in search of the soft skin of her neck. "I can feel the urgency in you."

He pulled back. "Do you mind?" His eyes met hers. "The first time might be a little quick, but I'll make it up to you later."

His evening beard rasped against her palm as she cradled his cheek. With her thumb, she stroked the tension from beneath his eyes. Eyes that measured her response for accuracy.

"No," she said softly. "I don't mind. In case I haven't made myself clear, I want you, too."

He laughed. "I noticed."

"One question?"

"What?"

"Are you protected?" he asked as he slipped those strong hands under her hips and lifted her up onto the counter's edge, so her legs dangled down and she either had to lean back or against Mac for support. She chose Mac.

"Yes." She'd taken care of that a year ago when she'd begun her search for a bed partner.

"Good."

The hard edge cut into her butt as he slid his hands to the zipper of her jeans. She wiggled a bit as she asked, "You don't think I'm too forward?"

"I think you're about perfect." He didn't look like he was lying. He looked intent, eager, hungry. But not like he was trying to spare her feelings. The knot of tension in her stomach eased.

He unzipped her jeans slowly, the metal rasping softly in the silence. He kept his gaze tight to hers, measuring her reaction as he slid his hand over her lower abdomen, tracing the edge of her bustier all the way around her back until his thumbs met and his fingers rested over the curve of her buttocks. She couldn't help rocking into his palms.

"Your hands feel so good."

It was only when his pupils flared and his fingers slipped lower, two pressing into the crease between her cheeks, separating them that she realized she'd said the comment out loud. Oh great. She dropped her head against his shoulder.

"I hope you weren't expecting a quiet lover, because apparently, I'm not going to be good at that."

His fingers wedged deeper, the longest ones hovering just above her anus. Anticipation roared through her like fire. He had to feel the tension in her, the expectant quivering she couldn't control.

"I already told you I wanted to hear what you feel."

"Just making sure you meant it." She'd no sooner finished than he tapped her anus with his fingertip. The pleasure was electric. White-hot. Shocking.

Her body wrenched upright, her cry a high-pitched statement of disbelief. How could such a little thing feel so good? His hand behind her head kept her still while he probed lightly at the sensitive rosette. She couldn't stop shifting with his touch. "Oh my God!"

"You like that." It wasn't a question. And the light probing he was giving her anus was not enough.

"Yes." She bit her lip. And as he tapped her once again, she moaned, "Can't you do it harder?"

His hand wrapped in her braid, pulling her head back, forcing her to arch and look at him while he answered. "Hell, yes."

His middle finger centered on her anus as his gaze centered on her face. With steady pushes he wedged the small opening wider, making it accept the tip. Then he started a rhythmic pulsing. She didn't know whether to grind down or pull away. Without lubrication it hurt, but not enough to overcome the pleasure. And strangely, there was something good about the way the pain and pleasure came together. Something erotically addictive, so she bit her lip and took the small pain, clinging to his gaze, gasping as her pussy ached and clenched around nothing. Hungering. Needing to be filled.

His expression was intent as he watched her. Almost calculating. She arched harder when he pressed in, inviting more of the heady combination. He frowned, and gave her what she asked for. A strong thrust. His finger dragged against the dry tissue as it worked her hungry channel. Even as she cried out she pushed back, straining for more. He stopped and she sobbed. "Oh God, I need more."

Mac forced himself to stop, though everything in him wanted to drive his finger home, to bury it in her hot little ass. Instead, he pulled her face against his shoulder and held her tightly against him. If he kept going she'd tear. Her muscles worked on his fingers, milking him. Begging him.

"Please," she whispered, wiggling enticingly.

"You'll tear if I do anymore," he grunted, battling with his own desire.

"I don't care."

"I do."

As it was, her ass was going to be a little raw, which he suspected, from what he'd seen so far, was going to keep her on the edge of arousal until she recovered. Just the thought of that had his cock jerking in his pants and his muscles gathered to drive his finger home.

"This is on my to-do list," she argued, futilely trying to get more of what she wanted.

"I'm the one calling the shots," he countered, "and I've said no."

"Like hell."

Her teeth sank into his shoulder. He winced and jerked her head back. Her expression was a mixture of desire, frustration and confusion. It was the last that stole his anger. He'd have to be very careful with her until she understood what she was asking for. What her limits were. She was such a baby at this. Incredibly passionate, mind-bogglingly eager, but very much a newbie, and as such it was up to him to set the parameters.

"You might as well settle down," he told her, giving her head a little shake. "I will get around to fucking your ass, and when I do, it'll be as hard and as deep as you can stand." Her whole body shook convulsively at his statement and her lips parted for the hard rasping breaths that echoed in the room. Damn, she was a hot little thing, but before they went any further she needed to understand who was in charge. More importantly to accept it, otherwise she could drive them both into things neither was ready for. "But when I claim your ass, it'll be on my terms. And my way."

That got her attention. "I don't have a say?"

"No."

For a second, he thought she would argue, but she surprised him, coming at him from another angle. Her expression turned amazingly sweet as she cupped his erection in her palm, and rubbed it the way he'd taught her, the impact somewhat lessened by the material between her hand and his flesh, but damned erotic all the same.

"But couldn't you just fuck it a little like you were before? Just for a while longer?" she suggested, all innocence.

He bit back a smile and removed her hand. "It's a damned good thing you've got 'getting spanked' on that list because you sure as shit just earned one."

She fell absolutely still. Her eyes went wide. He didn't know if she was shocked or aroused. He suspected both. Jessie wanted to be mastered, had every intention of enjoying being mastered if her list was to be believed, but he'd bet his last hundred dollars she was in no way prepared for the reality of what that entailed. Though if she kept pushing him, she was about to get a lot closer to understanding it. He kissed her lips gently and hooked his thumbs in the waistband of her jeans. "These have got to come off."

She stared at him, probably still wrestling with the spanking threat.

He tugged. "Lift up."

In slow motion, she lifted her hips. He tugged the pants down, and left them at her knees, using them as restraints. She was wearing a garter belt. It was a sexy red number with lace and cutouts. And no underwear. Not even the tiniest of thongs. Oh yeah. He liked the way she thought.

He cocked an eyebrow at her. "I take it you were expecting a yes to your invitation?"

"I was hoping." She bit her lip, then said, "About the spanking, I really think—"

"If you don't want me adding on to that, I suggest you not mention it at all." He traced the edge of the lace, his finger skirting the dainty cluster of curls topping her pussy. This close he couldn't miss the beads of moisture caught on the inner curls or the sweet scent of her arousal. He leaned forward, wiggling his tongue in between the soft flesh of her inner thighs until he felt the hard bud of her clitoris. He rolled the juicy little nub around beneath his tongue. Her yelp preceded her hands sinking into his hair and pulling his head closer. Reaching up, he removed her fingers from his hair, and stood.

"These," he squeezed her wrists lightly for emphasis before putting her palms on the counter beside her, "stay here."

"But—"

He cut her off. "No buts. I told you I give the orders. If you want something, you ask for it, but do not try to take over. If you do, I'll have to punish you."

She looked frustrated enough to spit bullets. And also intrigued. Oh yeah, she was going to be hell on wheels in bed.

"You're not turning out to be as much fun as I thought you'd be," she muttered.

He smiled and kissed her lips. "That's because you're fighting me."

"I'm not."

He arched an eyebrow at her.

She had the grace to blush. "Well, maybe just a little."

"Uh-huh." He bent back toward her groin, wondering how long she'd hold out before testing his resolve.

She'd made it all of two seconds, before letting loose with a snide, "But I don't see why you have to have it all your way."

"Because we agreed on it," he said on a sigh, scooping her off the counter. He probably should be shocked that she'd lasted that long. She was an impetuous little thing, he thought with an inner smile as he carried her across room. By the time she thought to struggle, he was seated in one of the kitchen chairs, and she was face down over his lap, her jeans bunched at her thighs, her hands pushing futilely at the floor, trying to get leverage. Her bare ass thrust at him with every wiggle. She was throwing threats before he got to the first slap.

"Mac Hollister, don't you dare."

He shook his head and smiled as he brought his hand down gently across both cheeks. She really was one for pushing. She gasped and froze. He left his hand where it landed.

"I'm going to dare a hell of a lot more than this," he warned her as she shifted beneath his touch. She had the most delectable butt. Plump and firm, very white against the tan of his hand. Very tempting.

"You are?" She didn't sound like she knew how to take that.

"Oh yeah." He spanked her again for emphasis, keeping it light, letting her get used to the idea, watching as her ass jiggled under his touch.

"Oh God."

"Did that feel good?" It sure as hell felt good to him.

The muscles of her abdomen dragged on his thighs as she spiked her body higher, positioning herself better. He rubbed his fingers over her left cheek. "Not good enough, Jessie. You have to ask me for what you want."

She wiggled her butt from side to side.

He shook his head at her antics, and gave her a quick pinch in reprimand. "With words, Jessie. With words."

She flopped down on his thighs. "You are so bossy."

"Which you like, so what's the problem?"

"It feels weird."

"To ask for what you want?" He stroked his hand from the base of her spine to the back of her knees, enjoying the different textures on the way, smiling anew as goose bumps sprang up in the wake of his hand.

"To give up control," she said with surprising honesty.

"Ah, honey girl, you gave that up the minute you sent me that to-do list. This is just accepting the reality of it."

"Oh."

"Just 'oh'?"

Her chest flexed on the side of his thigh, and he realized she was nodding.

He wanted to kiss her right then so badly his gut ached. He settled for working his fingers between her legs and stroking her clit with the delicacy of a kiss. The muscles in her spine pulled taut with each pass of his fingers until she was braced across his thighs, her torso parallel to the floor. On the final pass, the muscles over her shoulder blades snapped into delineation and a fine sheen of sweat had her skin glistening. "So honey girl, did that little spank feel good?"

Her "Yes" was a gasp of sound.

He kept stroking her as he asked, "Do you want to feel a whole lot better?"

"Uh-huh."

"Was that little grunt supposed to be an answer?"

Her head arched back as he pinched her sensitive bud lightly.

"Yes."

Mac did it again simply because there was something addictive about pleasing Jessie.

Her gasping "Yes!" let him know he was pleasing her very well. But not in the way she'd requested.

He reluctantly pulled his hand from her sweet flesh, letting his fingers drag up her body's natural path, making sure to connect with everything on the way. His reward was that sexy little whimper of Jessie's that could turn him rock-hard in a second. His cock made its own little whimper in the form of a jerk and a pulse, hungry for her.

Damn, she was potent.

"Then relax across my thighs." Pressure between her shoulder blades had her collapsing against him. "Now just stay like that, honey girl, and let me make you feel good."

Immediately, every muscle in her body pulled tight.

"There's nothing to brace for, Jessie. I'm going to make this very, very good for you. Relax."

He felt her internal struggle to do as he asked in the way her body tensed and shifted on his.

"Very, very good," he drawled as his finger trailed from the base of her neck down her spine to tuck into the crease between her buttocks. He got another one of those high-pitched whimpers and the slow relaxation of her body into his.

"That's right, just relax and let me make you feel good."

His first smack was just a ghost of sensation, just a little teaser to prick her interest. She jerked as if he'd landed a full blow. He shook his head at the reaction even as he ghosted her again. She had a lot to learn about him, one of the things being he would never ever break her trust by hurting her. This time she didn't jerk, just froze.

With the next slap he gave her enough to feel, to arch into, but not enough for pleasure. Her immediate protest and wiggle earned her a little more force on the next blow, and the next. Her butt began to blush pink, her breath began to come faster and every time he pulled his hand back she was pushing up in anticipation.

Damn, she was a hot little thing.

"Do you want more, Jessie?"

He didn't have to ask her twice. "Yes!"

He gave it to her, this time shifting his focus a little lower down and doubling the force. She yelped and bucked, but when his hand came down again she was arching into it, her body reaching for what it wanted as her mind struggled to accept it. He gave her time, keeping the intensity even, the smacks regular until she lay acceptingly across his thighs, no longer fighting, taking her pleasure easily, her rhythmic pants of "Oh yes, oh yes" keeping his cock hard and aching.

Mac spanked her one last time and left his hand where it landed, feeling the heat from her skin, the shivers of ecstasy quivering beneath the firm flesh. She was so into the moment that it took her a few seconds to figure out he'd stopped. And when she did, her response was a shuddering, despairing moan as she held herself absolutely still on his lap, barely breathing. Waiting. Every muscle tense with eager anticipation.

Her butt was a delightful rose. He slipped a finger between her thighs. Her pussy was gushing juice. Slipping his finger between the satiny labia, he followed the natural groove until he found the hard nub of her clitoris, and rubbed slow circles around it until she sobbed and thrust back.

"Was that as good as your fantasies, Jessie?" he asked. "Do you want more?"

Her thighs pressed into his as she arched up in a silent invitation.

He shook his head. "Oh no, that's not good enough. You have to tell me what you want. Whatever it is you want." Her response was a sexy little whine followed by an equally sexy wiggle that had his cock wrenching for space within his jeans.

The press of his palm teased across her butt. "Do you want me to spank this sweet ass some more, honey girl?"

He had to wait through five heartbeats before Jessie gave him what he wanted.

"Please!"

That had been five seconds too long for him. He was throbbing with the need to give the type of spanking that hot little ass was begging for, and now that he could, he wasn't hesitating. He immediately resumed his rhythm, the force the same as before, at least initially, but then he followed her body's signals, adding more, giving her more, watching her ass turn pinker and her hands fist and release against the green ceramic tile.

After eight rapid slaps, he paused, his breath coming as harshly as hers, his excitement matching hers. His control only a little better. Again he reached between her legs, working down to her clitoris, finding it harder, more engorged. He circled it with his finger, making sure the calluses glided over the silken nub. She sobbed and squealed and shook, but she didn't try to make him do what she wanted, which he approved. But she also didn't tell him what she wanted. What she needed.

He sighed and shook his head. Stubborn little witch. He resumed her spanking, a little harder this time, covering one cheek and then the other. Her juices spilled onto his pants, soaking the material. And still he kept it up—watching, waiting. When her upper body was flushed red, her braid whipping across the floor as she begged and sobbed, he stopped. And waited. This time she didn't need to be coaxed.

"Oh God, don't stop. Please don't stop."

"What do you want?" he asked, caressing her hot flesh. Her breath caught as he slipped his finger into the crease between her cheeks, following the pull of gravity down to her core. Her thick cream poured over his hand, a luxurious invitation for more. Mac gave it to her, dipping his finger in the copious fluid before centering it on her anus.

He could see how badly she wanted to move, force his hand. Her body shook with the effort to hold still. He rubbed the tender rosette.

"What do you want, Jessie?" he repeated, his voice harsh with his own need.

He waited for her answer, taunting the tightly clenched hole with a circular massage as he waited. She'd written that she wanted to be spanked until she came, and that was one fantasy he knew how to fulfill, but it would definitely be on his terms.

She finally whispered, "I need to come."

He rewarded her honesty by pushing his finger into her tight channel to the first knuckle. Her high-pitched cry of satisfaction filled the room and was just as quickly followed by her moan of disappointment when he pulled out just as fast.

"How do you want to come?" he asked struggling to stay in control.

This time she didn't answer. He didn't repeat the question, just resumed spanking her, each blow a little harder than the last. His shredded control demanded the game come to an end soon. Finally, finally, she screamed, "Harder. I need it harder. Oh God. Spank me harder."

He did, giving her two hard smacks. She went wild, writhing and screaming for more. And then she grabbed his ankle and tried to bite his calf through his jeans and boots.

"Oh yeah, honey girl, that's it. Go wild. Bite me. Scream for me."

She did, the sound and sensation muffled by his leg as she struggle to connect with him.

He shared her desire and her frustration. He wanted to feel those little teeth sinking into his skin. Feel her screams against his flesh. He slapped her buttocks harder than before, harder than he had planned on probably, a little of his control slipping away as her passion drove him past any place he'd been before.

Instead of protesting, she bit deeper, screamed louder. He grabbed her shoulders and pulled her upright. With one hand he held her in place, taking in how passion darkened her gaze, flushed her cheeks and had her teeth sinking into her lower lip. With the other he tore his shirt open and pulled her mouth against his chest.

"Bite me, honey girl. Let me feel those teeth. Let me feel how good I'm making you feel."

She hesitated. He didn't want her hesitant. He wanted her totally involved in her pleasure, mindlessly enjoying every primitive nuance, reveling in her naturally passionate nature. His palm connected with her buttock and thigh once, twice, three times, pressing her mouth against him, searching for the spot she needed, the force she needed, knowing he'd found it when she gasped against his chest, her breath an incendiary promise he couldn't wait to collect on.

He stroked that spot over and over, groaning as her groin rubbed against his shaft in an unrelenting caress, increasing his determination. He tortured that sweet little spot with erotic stings of sensation until she wailed and went where he led, sinking her teeth into his chest, just above his nipple. A primitive growl of satisfaction rose up from his toes, riding the brutal sweep of lust that raced over his body as his flesh absorbed her scream and took her bite. Son of a bitch, that was good. Too good.

He wrapped both arms around her and held her tightly, his cock pulsing and straining with tremors of pre-release. Oh shit, he wasn't going to come like this. Not this first time. Not yet. He wanted more. For both of them. Against his chest her pants turned to sobs as her thighs ground down on his. Goddamn, she was perfect. Perfect. He rubbed her spine soothingly, easing her down, knowing the trip back up would be that much faster, that much more intense for the delay.

Her jaw muscles eventually relaxed. With a soft moue of apology, her teeth left his flesh. He tipped her head back, kissing her mouth with all the passion driving him, letting her know they weren't done yet. Not by a long shot.

"Why did you stop?" she moaned into his mouth.

He gave her the truth. "Because I needed to."

"That was so good. So good," she sighed.

"Very, very good and now it's time to try some other things that will feel good."

Jessie licked the bite marks on his chest, her tongue lingering in the indentations, "Can't they wait for another day?"

Mac kissed the top of her head and pushed her off his lap with a smile as she stood there and swayed, still dazed. "No."

"Turn around. Let me see your ass." She stood there and blinked at him a couple times, but then she turned with an entrancing shyness that flooded him with tenderness. His gaze dropped to her rear. The plump cheeks were red and quivering. He touched the right one. Jessie gasped and her whole body shuddered. The woman was nearly on the brink of an orgasm. And not shy about going for it he realized as her arm reached around the front of her body. She jumped guiltily when he touched her shoulder, confirming what he knew she'd been planning on doing.

"Don't touch yourself. I'll get you off when you're ready."

"Trust me, I am so ready."

The spark of dry humor pulled a smile past the tight grasp of desire. And also warned him he needed to get back into the command seat. "Good, now bend over and take off those shoes."

She hesitated.

"Yes," he answered her unspoken concern. "If you do that I'm going to be able to see every damn beautiful inch of you." And he was looking forward to it. He unzipped his jeans. By the time she had the first shoe off, he had his cock in his hand and was stroking along its length. She peeked at him from between her legs. Any doubts he had that he was taking her too fast down this road were wiped out by her slow, satisfied smile. Damn, she had a killer smile. His cock pulsed and a bead of pre-come dripped over the top. Her smile broadened as the second shoe hit the floor.

More come welled. He grasped the shaft just beneath the head and squeezed. "If you wiggle that ass enough as you step the rest of the way out of those pants, I'll let you have a taste."

Her eyebrows rose, and she laughed. More fluid spilled onto his hand. Guess he wasn't fooling anybody with that comment. They both know he'd been dying to have her mouth on him since the other night. Still, she didn't let the knowledge diminish her performance. She wiggled that ass back and forth like a pro as she slid the jeans the rest of the way down her thighs. When they were off, she tossed her braid over her shoulder and sent him a questioning glance. She stood there, the garter belt showcasing the soft flesh of her thighs bulging temptingly over the top of her thigh-high stockings, her recently spanked ass glowing beautifully beneath the hem of her waist-length T-shirt.

"Put the heels back on."

She did, with the confidence of a woman sure of her appeal in every move.

"Come over here."

She did, just not in the way he expected. Slowly, one step at a time, she backed toward him, swaying her hips with each, until she was between his thighs. Then she was sitting back, way back, her buttocks settling over his lower abdomen, his cock poking out between her thighs. Her juices immediately soaked his shirt. He instinctively scooted down, making room for her and as he did, she leaned forward and took the wide head of his cock into her mouth.

"Son of a bitch!"

Her tongue swirled over the circumference, lapping at the slit, wiggling between his fingers and the shaft, searching out all the silky fluid she could find. When she'd lapped him clean, she pursed her lips over the slit and sucked. Hard. Pleasure so intense as to be agony shot up his spine. His vision blurred. His balls drew tight. He pushed her off before he could come, anchoring her beside him with his hold on her wrist. As soon as he caught his breath, he realized she'd done it again. She'd taken control. He shook his head at her smug smile.

"You still want to come?" he asked.

"Oh yes."

He patted his jeans-covered thighs. "Then come here."

She went to sit and he shook his head. She hesitated. No doubt now that the excitement was fading she was having second thoughts about picking up where they'd left off. With those heels, all it took was a simple yank to have her off balance. She tumbled down. He caught her, shifting her forward so most of her body was beyond his lap, and she had to support her weight on her hands. He lifted her thigh so his cock rested against her pussy, her thighs and mound were dripping wet. He spread her labia around his cock, pulling the flesh back so that her clit pressed firmly against the base of his shaft.

He then dipped two fingers into the copious fluids leaking from her pussy and spread them around her anus before tucking one finger inside. It was easier this time he noted as the powerful little muscles welcomed him. He left his right hand on her buttock.

"This time you're going to get us both off," he told her.

"How?" The word was an airy, breathless exclamation of anticipation.

"I'm going to spank these sweet cheeks, and you're going to squeeze those thighs and pump that ass in time with me until we both come."

Her muscles tensed. "I'm not sure—"

He didn't let her finish. He made the first slap sharp, ensuring she jerked, up and then down, dragging her clit along his shaft and driving his finger deeper into her ass. Her moan echoed his. He slapped her again. Lighter, this time. Enough to tease and let her catch the rhythm, which she did with ease. Her thighs locked him to her with such force, if she hadn't been so wet, she would have hurt them both.

She wiggled and pumped. He slapped and teased. When her neck flushed again and her breath started breaking into sporadic gasps he got serious. He added another finger to the one tucked into her ass. He gave her a moment to adjust to the stretching and then started fucking her hard, alternating blows with pushes of his fingers, each time going deeper, taking her further, judging what she needed from the way she thrust back against him her breathless cries mingling with his low moans.

"C'mon, honey girl, take what you need," he coaxed. "C'mon, squeeze my cock. Fuck my fingers with that tight ass. Harder, baby. Harder."

She was wild now, bucking on him, her hands locked on the rung of the chair, pushing back into his blows so it was the tip of his cock that slid across her clit, his cock leaking come on every pass, bathing the turgid nub with soft silky liquid. Her butt swung eagerly into every spank. Sweat dripped off both of them as he tried to hold back, and she struggled to come. With every blow, every thrust, she kept chanting "More" alternating it with a moaned "Please." As her clitoris ground furiously down on his cock again, he added a third finger to her ass, working all three deeper as she cried "More."

He gritted his teeth as the pressure in his balls grew too painful to contain. Shoving his fingers to the hilt in her tight channel, he came, his seed wrenching from his body in an agonizing burst. As the first hot splash hit her clitoris, Jessie screamed, her body bucked violently and she orgasmed, one hand whipping between them, holding his cock so that every spurt, every drop struck her hungry clit.

He dropped his head back against the chair and groaned with understanding through the intensity of his release. All she'd needed to come was for him to.

With a final jerk, he gave her the last of his seed. In one smooth move he withdrew his fingers and turned her over, tumbling them both to the floor, catching his weight on his elbow, his palm under her head protecting her from the hard tile. She stared at him, her eyes dreamy and replete. She reached between them and touched her pussy. Her eyes drifted closed.

"I can feel your seed."

He just bet she could. It felt like she'd dragged a gallon out of him. He nudged her knees apart with his. He knelt between her thighs. He dipped his fingers in the wet curls surrounding her womanhood. She was swollen and hot. Wide open and ready. He swirled his finger around her distended clit and then brought it to her mouth.

"Taste."

As she sucked his finger into her mouth, lapping from his flesh the remnants of their release, he lined his cock up with her vagina, nestling the sensitive head into the tiny well, applying enough pressure to keep it there. He pulled his finger from her mouth. She let it go with a regretful pop. Walking his hands up her body, pausing only to nip the hard poke of her nipples through her shirt, he brought his face level with hers. He kissed her mouth, enjoying the feel of her smile against his lips before whispering, "Open your eyes."

"Why?"

"Because it's time to get serious."

Chapter Seven

He nudged his cock against her. Her eyes stayed closed. A dreamy smile curved her lips. She draped her arms lazily across his shoulder as she shifted her hips in greeting. His shaft jerked. Her pussy twitched again, kissing the head with a dainty flex of inner muscles. She felt small and delicate against him like this. Far too delicate to have romped with him like they'd just done. But she had. And he had. And as that dreamy smile spread, her tongue came out to stroke over her lips, leaving them wet and shining, and he was ready to go again.

He cocked an eyebrow at her. "Are you paying attention?"

"Um-hum."

He sighed, making it sound like he was disappointed. "Don't tell me you're going to be one of those women who once they come, just rolls over and falls asleep."

She cracked her right eye. "I'm considering it."

"And here I thought we had all night."

Her left eyelid lifted enough that he could glimpse the glimmer of green through her thick lashes.

"All night?"

He brought his right hand to her breast, and teased her nipple through her shirt. "That was my plan."

Her torso lifted, bringing her breast fully into his palm. "I thought men needed recovery time?"

"Depends on the partner."

"And with me?"

"I'm pretty much continually cocked and ready to go."

He could tell that pleased her from the way her smile stretched wide open.

"I like that."

"So do I." He traced her smile with his tongue, pausing here and there to dip into the moist interior of her mouth, tempting himself with her unique flavor.

She opened her eyes fully. "So what do you have planned next?"

He brushed a hair off her temple with the tips of his fingers. Her skin was so soft and smooth, so he did it again just for the pleasure of feeling their differences. She was so intensely feminine that she put him on testosterone overload.

"I thought I'd see how you like the more conventional approach."

He pressed down with his hips, a gentle hint for her to relax.

She shifted beneath him as the floor pressed into her buttocks.

"Problem?"

"Certain parts of me are a little sensitive," she admitted with a slight flinch.

"Hmmm, then I guess you'll have to accommodate."

"*I'll* have to accommodate?"

"Uh-huh." He was unfazed by her frown. He knew the physical reminder of what they'd shared excited her. The proof covered the crown of his cock. "You just push up when I push down and it'll work out just fine."

"What if I don't want to?" she pouted at him.

"Then you'll take a little pain with your pleasure." Her pussy clenched against him, and her breath caught. "Just the way you like," he added with a smile.

Her lower lip slipped between her teeth.

"Is there a problem?"

She frowned and flicked a worried glance at him. "I wasn't sure about how I should feel about liking that."

"But now?"

"I'm just not sure how you feel about it."

"In case you didn't notice, I wasn't exactly hesitant about spanking that gorgeous ass of yours."

The frown disappeared. "You think my ass is gorgeous?"

"Not to mention eminently spankable."

Her smile chased away the last of her uncertainty. "So you might want to spank me again?"

"I think you can pretty much plan on it." He tugged on her shirt.

As she pulled it over her head she asked, "When?"

"Whenever the spirit moves me." He slipped a finger under the thin strap of the sheer lace bustier. "I like this."

"I was hoping you'd like the way it pushes my breasts up."

He smiled, sliding his finger down the strap, along the lace demi-cups until he could snuggle it into the deep well of her cleavage.

"Have I mentioned I like the way you think?"

"But you like me for my body first, right?"

He slid his finger over to her left nipple. It was a small, hard pink pebble in the midst of a lace rosette. She shivered when he scraped it with his knuckle.

"Why your body first?"

"Well, as my goal is a white-hot affair, I don't want you getting bogged down in mental gymnastics."

"But I can get into all the physical ones I want?"

Her hips shifted on the hard floor. "Oh yeah."

"Good." He skimmed his hand over her stomach, across her hipbone and around her hip. She lifted instinctively, shoving her pussy at his cock, teasing him with the slightest of entries. He curved his palm over her buttock. Her ass was still hot to the touch from her spanking. Her flesh molded to his palm as eagerly as her gaze sought his.

"It's time to get serious," he said again, answering the question he could see in her eyes.

"How?"

He curled his fingers into the firm muscle of her cheek and squeezed. She gasped. Her pussy clenched and then warm cream bathed his cock. He smiled. He had a feeling she'd like that.

"Bring your knees up." He helped her with the right one, sliding his hand down her thigh, drawing her leg up and out as he did. "Higher," he ordered, when she stopped too soon. Sitting back on his heels, he removed her right shoe and then her left.

"Wider," he ordered when she tried to keep her knees discreetly closed. When her heels were practically even with her hips, but out to the side, he said, "Good."

With her heels that close to her body, she couldn't keep her hips on the floor. They hovered suspended from the bridge of her feet and shoulders.

"This isn't comfortable," she informed him a little shakily.

Mac didn't imagine it was, but it was damned arousing to see her like that. Open and displayed for his pleasure. "Consider it a bit of those gymnastics I've got license to indulge in."

Her pussy was in clear view, the inner lips swollen and distended, their color a hungry, eager red. The curls covering her mound were wet with their combined releases. Her inner thighs soaked with fresh cream. The line from her vagina to her anus was hidden from his view at this angle. Her feet shifted. She was getting uncomfortable with his perusal. He met her gaze through the frame of her splayed thighs. Hers shifted away. He sighed.

"Look at me."

She did, but it was the most hesitant of flicks.

"Again and hold it."

She did with obvious difficulty. He touched her thigh gently as he said, "This is another thing you'll have to get used to."

"What?"

"Showing yourself to me whenever I want."

Her eyebrows shot up. "Says who?"

He met her challenge with calm, trailing his hand up her thigh. "Says me."

"Whenever you want?"

"Whenever I want." He curved his hand over the flex of her knee.

"And how am I supposed to know when you want?"

"Whenever I say 'show me' you bend over, flip up your skirt, and let me look my fill."

"Is this one of your rules?"

He glanced down at her pretty little pussy and noted the fresh cream welling. At the top of her folds, he could just make out the nub of her clitoris. He smiled. She definitely liked this.

"Consider it a law."

She snorted, but kept her legs open and her gaze on his. "There's one problem with your law."

"What's that?"

"I don't wear skirts."

"You will from now on."

"Another one of your laws?"

He met her slightly defiant gaze. "Yes."

"And if I don't?"

He skated his fingers down the satin-smooth inside of her thigh. "You'll be punished."

"Some threat that is," she muttered.

He touched the very edge of her left labia with the tip of his nail. "Not all punishments, honey girl, make you come."

The flare of alarm in her green eyes as he scraped his nail along the sensitive tissue was exactly what he was looking for. There'd be no pleasure for her if she was absolutely sure this was all a game.

"You wouldn't hurt me."

"I wouldn't suggest pushing me hard enough for either of us to find out." He worked his finger into her weeping vagina. Damn, she was tight. He ignored her shivery high-pitched squeal as he hooked it against her pelvic bone. He tugged gently.

"Lift up." She did, but not far enough. "Higher."

When she was at the right angle, her back just shy of being arched, he slid his finger free and leaned back. "Now, balance your weight on your shoulders and spread your cheeks so I can see your ass."

She froze. "You've got to be kidding."

He looked at her steadily. Their pleasure depended on his ability to win these little battles of will. "What part did you think was a joke?"

She held his gaze for half a minute before she decided he was serious. A bright red flush spread up her chest and over her cheeks as she reached behind her thighs and clasped the globes in her fingers, and hesitantly spread her cheeks.

The flexing of her fingers warned him before she let go. "Keep yourself open and your eyes on me," he snapped.

She did.

"Good girl."

"I'm not a child," she groused.

"I'm aware of that." Her little rosette was red and slightly swollen, shining with the juice that leaked from her pussy. It twitched beneath his gaze, as if inviting his touch. He stroked the back of his fingers down her labia before turning his hand so the tips of his fingers could graze the glistening portal below. She gasped, and her hips dropped.

"I told you to hold it."

"I'm sorry."

She didn't sound sorry. She sounded breathlessly eager. Of the two, he much preferred the latter. He wanted her burning for him. He placed a finger at her anus. "C'mon Jess, get those hips back up."

She started to but the minute she realized what that meant she froze again. "I can't without..."

"You can't without fucking my finger," he finished, arching his brow at her. "What's the problem, honey girl, don't you want my finger in your ass?"

She blushed and ducked his gaze. He didn't like her uncertainty. He liked her better when she was bold as brass, propositioning him.

"It's awkward."

"Then maybe you should get it over with quickly," he suggested deliberately, feeding that spark of defiance that would fuel the anger that would carry her past her shyness.

It worked. She lay there with her legs splayed, her cheeks pulled wide, and challenged him. "No."

He cocked his head to the side as if considering her response. "You sure you want to say no?"

Her chin set at that stubborn angle that kick-started his desire. "Yes."

She was testing him, trying to see if she could take control from him again. She didn't have to worry. He was man enough to match her. Strong enough that she could safely trust her pleasure to his care.

He spread his big hand over her pubic bone and pressed down, pinning her hips as he pressed two fingers against her anus. She gasped and flinched as he eased them relentlessly deeper, despite her inner tensing. Holding her gaze, he pulled them all the way back, keeping them wider on the way out, making his point while stretching those deliciously hungry muscles, before tunneling back in. He did it again. And again. Each time faster, each time harder, holding her gaze the whole while, greeting challenge with pure determination. Watching as resentment became arousal, until her breath broke into choppy inhalations, until she accepted he would do whatever it took to stay in charge.

Oh yes, his little Jessie was looking for a man to master her. He didn't think she was even aware that she was still in position, still holding her cheeks spread, still holding his gaze, her pussy gushing juice. He kept fucking her ass, knowing it had to burn as much as it pleasured, but he'd be damned if he'd stop until she capitulated completely. And that had to come from her.

It seemed an eternity before her hips pushed against his hand. An eternity in which his cock swelled and ached and he fought back his own impulse. If she pushed him much harder, her ass would be filled with more than his fingers, and it wouldn't be an enjoyable experience. He was too on edge to take her carefully. He sighed in relief when, her eyes damp with frustrated tears, she slowly, slowly, brought those luscious hips up into the surge of his hand. A little more with each thrust until she was back in position.

"Are you done fighting me now?" he asked, moving more slowly in her.

Her "Yes" was hissed out between clenched teeth. Her ass pulsed against his hand, out of rhythm with his movements.

"Is that an angry yes or a hungry yes?"

Her eyes started to close before she yanked them open and back to his.

"Hungry."

He didn't really need to hear the words. From her darkened eyes to her flushed cheeks she was the image of a woman in pursuit of an orgasm.

"Suppose we do something about that, hmm?" He eased his fingers from her rectum. The tender tissue clung and dragged, resisting his departure, holding him to her until, with the most regretful of pops, it let him go.

"No!" she moaned when she realized his fingers weren't immediately coming back.

"Shhh." He rested his hand on her abdomen and dropped his thumb to her clit, circling it gently as he said, "Just trust me and let your hips drop to the floor."

She did, initially panicking that he'd take his thumb away too, squirming slightly when he followed her down, keeping the pressure steady.

"Do you want to come, honey girl?"

She jerked beneath the flick of his thumb. "God, yes!"

"How?"

She frowned at him. He let the edge of his thumbnail scrape her clit. He had to wait for her answer as she jackknifed up and yelped. She clutched his arms, holding on tightly until he shook his head. With a frown, she sank back.

"I'm going to get even with you for this," she groaned.

"I'll look forward to it." He circled her clit again, watching her pussy pulse. Beg. "But right now, how do you want to come? Like this?" He grazed her glistening folds with the back of his finger on the way to her ass, circling the sensitive opening with his fingertips before asking, "With my fingers up your ass?" She shivered and lurched. Her nipples were hard pink points stabbing at the ceiling as her back arched. He brought his fingers back up. "Or buried in your cunt?"

"Or maybe," He grabbed his cock and stroked it as he aligned it with her pussy and leaned forward, catching his weight on his right hand. "—You would prefer something bigger?" He rubbed the swollen head in her wet folds, against her engorged clitoris.

"Harder?" He pressed against the well of her vagina.

"Hotter?" The slick flesh parted the slightest bit cupping him.

"Would you prefer my cock, Jessie?" He nudged deeper. The ring of muscle engulfed the crown. Squeezing like a fist. He ground his teeth as she sank her nails into his forearm, as if she had the muscle to drag him harder against her.

"I want your cock, Mac." Her voice was tight and high, quivering with shyness and something he couldn't quite place. "All of it."

"Are you sure?" He gave her the tiniest fraction more. Just enough to let her get used to the idea. Then he pulled back. Teasing her, entering her again, laughing low in his throat when she gasped and wiggled beneath him. "Maybe you'd like something else?"

"Please don't." To his surprise, her big green eyes filled with tears.

Damn. He couldn't be hurting her. He was barely in her. He dropped to his elbows and stroked a tear from the corner of her eye with his thumb.

"Don't what, honey girl?" he whispered.

"Don't tease me," she whispered back, pride doing little to shield her vulnerability from his gaze. "I've waited so long for this. You. Please don't make this into a game."

His heart clenched. Ah damn. He was an insensitive ass to not have recognized that little something in her voice as insecurity. This was close enough to her first time to call it kin. No matter how hot the foreplay, she'd want some tenderness, some meaning to the moment. And he had her on the kitchen floor giving her orders, testing her limits.

He kissed her eyes closed, gently wiped away the lingering tear that squeezed out and pulled her into his arms. Rolling onto his back, he took her with him.

"This is not a game, Jessie."

She propped herself up on her elbows against his chest, looking down at him, her lip between her teeth. "I'm sorry."

"Don't be." His cock snuggled between them, caught in the crease between her thigh and hip. Still hard, still aching, but its demands were not nearly as important as Jessie feeling good about this. Them. Herself.

"I'm not usually this needy." She blinked rapidly. "I'm sorry."

She was obviously embarrassed.

"I'm not."

This should be perfect for her. He touched the corner of her mouth, that soft sweet, betrayingly vulnerable mouth. Sitting up, he shifted her legs so they wrapped around his waist. He stood, taking her with him, smiling when she gasped first with fear and then with wonder. As he set her on the counter, she touched his biceps lightly. He tipped her head back, and kissed her hard. Hot. Lingeringly.

Her gaze dropped to his penis. She wrapped her hand around it. He caught her wrist before she could seduce him. Bringing her palm to his lips, he pressed a kiss into the center. He closed her fingers around his kiss, and said, "Hold that thought."

Scooping up her shoes and pants and the to-do list, he thrust the bundle into her hands. When she merely stared at him, he swung her up into his arms.

"Where are we going?" She linked her free arm around his neck.

"Off to do this right," he answered. Leaning down, he waited for her to locate the doorknob and passed through to the main living quarters.

From the way she snuggled into his embrace, Mac assumed that she had no objections.

"Have I mentioned that having a strong, handsome man who sets my blood afire, carry me up the stairs with the intent to ravage my willing body has always been the number one beginning to all my fantasies?" she mentioned as they got to the landing.

"Just carrying you up the stairs?"

Her fingers played with the receptive flesh behind his ear as he shifted her high and climbed. "Of course, he has to follow up that particular feat with more serious action."

"I'm glad I'm doing this right then."

She didn't answer right away. He glanced down. She was chewing her lip again. As he reached the top of the stairs, she said, "I'm really sorry about what happened in the kitchen."

"Why?"

"I promised you free and easy."

"I don't remember that conversation."

She shrugged, her shoulder rising against his chest. "I implied it. And I meant to keep it that way. I loved what you were doing, it's just..."

They were outside his bedroom door. He released her knees and controlled the descent of her body so her torso caressed his in one long movement until her feet hit the floor. The heel of one of the shoes she was holding poked him in the stomach as he tipped her chin up.

"You need a little tenderness right now." He rubbed his thumb over her lower lip, pulling it free of her teeth. "I don't have any problem being tender with you, honey girl. You can have anything you want from me." He reached behind her and opened his door as he backed her into the room, taking a half step for each of hers to accommodate their height difference. "I don't have any problem at all giving you whatever you need. You just let me know what it is, and I'll give it to you."

Meeting the deep blue of his eyes, Jessie believed it. She thought he'd be upset that she'd suddenly found what he could make her feel to be overwhelming. Hell, he was overwhelming, period. But he hadn't been upset by her tears in the kitchen. He'd simply understood and given her...exactly what she'd needed.

She took a breath, took in his scent, took in reality. He was still giving her what she needed she realized as she took another step back, his gaze, his hands all reading her mood, assessing her wants. How amazing. His hand in the middle of her back pulled her up short. Mac reached back, and the door clicked closed behind them.

He smiled, that slow, lazy bad boy you-can-trust-me-smile he'd given her the first time they'd met. Her womb tingled and her knees went weak. She relaxed against him, giving him her weight. Mac accepted it with a deepening of his smile. His hand stroked her hair back from her temple as if they had all the time in the world, while against her stomach, his cock thrust impatiently. Oh, she could definitely get into a man like this.

She tossed the clothes in her hand onto a chair to the right of the door. One of the shoes bounced to the smooth wooden floor with a clunk. She slipped her arms up his chest, curving her right hand over his well-muscled shoulder while the other paused at the rapidly beating pulse in his throat. His heart beat against her fingertips as she whispered, "Thank you."

He cocked his right eyebrow. She loved it when he did that.

"For what?"

"For not giving up on me."

"Not a chance in hell." He started backing her across the room.

"Why?"

He took two steps to answer. "Why what?"

"Why not a chance in hell?"

Her knees hit the back of the bed. He gave her a little push. As she tumbled back, he reached for the buttons on his shirt. "I'm not a fool, and you are a treat not to be missed."

She waited until he had his shirt half-unbuttoned before answering. "Good."

She smiled then, letting her pleasure at being someone's treat spread across her face. His breath caught as she had anticipated it would. While he watched her smile, she shifted onto her elbows and brought her heels up onto the bed. His gaze dropped lower. When it reached her knees, she slowly, slowly, spread them, revealing everything between.

"A very sweet treat," he growled, his gaze a burning lick of appreciation. He tore his shirt off—buttons flew through the air and skittered across the floor.

It was her turn to catch her breath. She knew he was strong, and she'd figured he'd have plenty of muscle, but nothing prepared her for the sheer male beauty of him. Broad shoulders topped well-developed pectorals that flowed into washboard abs a workout company would kill to have advertising their products. A fine pelt of dark brown hair accented the "V" between his pecs, arrowing down past his navel, pointing straight and true at that cock. That gorgeous, top-heavy cock currently jutting out from the fly of his jeans, straining for her, but weighed down by its sheer size so that it stretched out and down his thigh. She ran her tongue over her lips. Oh my, he was a tasty feast. And he was all hers. She raised her gaze to his. "This is going to be fun."

He laughed and cupped his shaft in his hand, easing it upward with three gradual pumps of his fist. "I agree." He jerked his chin toward her. "Show me."

Her breath caught at the sensual order. Anticipation and desire combined in a debilitating surge down her arms, rendering her weak. She lifted her hips, reached under and spread her cheeks, struggling to manage a steady breath as his gaze roved over her with the intensity of a touch.

He walked forward, that cock pointed at her like a promise. Clear fluid wet the tip, sliding over the wide head and down the thick shaft. He wanted to come. For her. She held to position and let the knowledge flow over her, increasing her anticipation. She loved it when he came. She loved making him come.

His cock reached her first, slowly, deliberately, pressing onto her clitoris, pushing it in, cuddling it against the slit, forcing it into the small groove. The sensation was so intense, she almost dropped. When she caught herself, he whispered, "Perfect."

She looked down between her breasts. His cock seemed to stretch forever, from his body to hers, ending at where they joined. She closed her eyes and whimpered as sharp pangs of lust shot out from her groin, making her want to squeeze her thighs together to ease the ache. To catch him close and grind herself against that turgid shaft, knowing she couldn't, and almost beside herself with the agony of holding still, staying exposed. Waiting.

A drop of his pre-come slid down her cleft in a trickling caress.

"Ahh!" The cry was ripped from her. She couldn't help it. She shoved against him, her clit rode his slit before springing free with a quick slide across the smooth head. She jerked around on the bed, flipping to her side, catching his cock in her mouth before he could step back. He'd probably punish her for this, but she needed to have him in her mouth. To taste him. She loved the taste of him. He held his cock still for her mouth, stroking her hair as she savored the sweet salty spread of his come.

Mac pulled back as she would have taken more of his cock. "No. Just the head for now. Suck nice and sweet, honey girl. Just enough to satisfy your need, but not enough to make me come."

She wasn't sure she knew how to do that. Or if she even wanted to. She pursed her lips over the slit and sucked. Hard. His hips bucked against her. His cry echoed above her, and his hand fisted in her hair, pulling at the stands caught in her braid. A satisfying stream of ejaculate pulsed into her mouth.

He pulled back, panting. She licked her lips. Frowning, he shook his head at her and tapped her cheek in warning. "Do that again and I won't let you taste me at all."

He looked serious enough to mean it. His taste already fading from her mouth, she weighed her options. Finally, she nodded. What choice did she really have? He angled his cock back toward her mouth, her lips parted, and he eased forward. She opened her mouth as wide as she could and he maneuvered that massive crown back inside, working it up and then down to get it past her teeth. As soon as he was resting against her tongue, she sealed her lips on his shaft. A pulse of salty, hot fluid was her reward. She closed her eyes and smiled around his shaft. This was good. Slow. Gentle. Reciprocal. And just too damned delicious.

Mac groaned. Another pulse of fluid leaked over her tongue. His eyes were glued to her mouth as she smiled around his shaft. Happiness wove through passion. He hadn't been lying. He really did love her smile.

He leaned over her. The mattress shifted as his weight came down on his hands behind her. His cock jerked irregularly in her mouth. It took her a minute to realize he was kicking off his boots. The left one hit the floor with a solid thump as the head hit the back of her throat. He was too big. Too much. She gagged, the involuntary reflex sucking him deeper into her mouth.

"Easy, Jess." He stroked her hair soothingly through the next lingering reflex. His shaft jerked at the strong suction and he filled her mouth with pre-come. She held it on her tongue, reluctant to swallow if he was going to follow through on his threat. When he stepped back she shook her head, pulling her lips back. If he pulled out now it was going to hurt. Unbelievably, he laughed as he felt the edge of her teeth.

"I was just going to take the other boot off."

She wasn't sure whether to believe him. He cupped his palm under her chin. "Another time, when I'm ready to come, you can let me feel those teeth, but not now." His gaze lingered on her bulging cheeks. He stroked the taut skin, caressing her and himself.

"Do you like this?"

She nodded as she sheathed her teeth.

He smiled. "So do I. Do you want me to pull out while I take the other boot off?" She could only manage a small shake of her head.

He traced the stretch of her lips around his cock, his gaze intent. She shivered with sensation as he said, "If it happens again, just relax your throat and swallow fast."

She didn't see how that would help, but nodded anyway, content.

His other boot came off without incident. Then only his jeans were left. His cock shimmied in her mouth as he worked those off. He almost slipped her grip once, but she held him with a strong suction.

Then he was naked. Gloriously naked. From where she lay she had a perfect view of his rock-hard thighs and the full sacs swinging between. She reached out and cupped them in her hand. Beneath the soft outer skin his balls rolled like hard walnuts across her fingers. She admired the long, lean muscles in his thighs. He was just as beautifully made down here as he was above. She took a deep breath, inhaling his clean musky scent before letting it out through her nose in a satisfied sigh. He'd been well worth waiting for.

His hand was back on her hair again. There was a determination in his stroke that told her he was ready to move on. She sighed again for a different reason and opened her mouth. His cock worked out. She moaned when he pulled free. She pushed her tongue against the roof of her mouth, not liking the empty feeling. He shook his head at her and smiled.

"I want my time, too."

"I thought all men loved oral sex," she groused as he turned her so her hips were at the edge of the bed and her legs dangled.

"They do." He knelt in front of her. Over the spring of dark blonde curls covering her mound, his blue eyes met hers. "But I happen to be addicted to the taste of this sweet pussy." His breath blew across her clit. Her internal muscles pulled up tight in quivering anticipation as he draped her thighs over his shoulders. "And I'm hungry."

She expected him to go straight for her clit. Instead, his teeth sank into the soft flesh of her inner thigh. He sucked until she was soaked with cream and burning with longing. He then lapped at the bruise, moving inward until she felt his tongue glide through the juices collected in the crease of her thigh. She was unbearably sensitive there and as soon as he discovered that, he was relentless, lapping and nibbling until she grabbed his hair and pulled his head away. He laughed against her curls, flicked her clit with his tongue, on the way to the other side which he tormented with the same lack of mercy.

Oh God, she couldn't stand this. The pleasure, the hunger was pulsing through her body in a horrendous ache. Sharp and high, demanding satisfaction, promising retribution if it wasn't delivered. An exquisite, ragged-edged agony ripping her apart but not letting her go.

She just needed him to touch her clit. Her aching, swollen to bursting clit, and she'd come.

She tugged on his hair. Mac pretended not to understand and went back to lapping at the open well of her vagina. Sucking as the juices welled, swallowing, working his mouth against her, eating his fill, ignoring her orders. She tugged harder. He smiled and slipped a finger into her shuddering cunt. The sensation pierced her like a knife. But it wasn't enough. Not nearly enough.

She dug her heels into the small of his back and thrust her hips at him. He put his hand over her abdomen and pushed down. The pressure felt good, almost soothing, but then it too joined the storm gathering in strength, and she sobbed his name. Shamelessly begging. "Mac. Please."

He lapped at her with short, tormenting licks from her sensitive anus up to just short of her slit before asking, "What do you want, honey girl?"

"I need you."

He gave the gentlest nip just below her clit. God, she wanted him to sink his teeth into her. If he wasn't going to release her then she wanted him to hurt her. Anything to make this torture end. She couldn't survive this. It had to stop.

"For what?" he asked.

"I need to come. Please make me come."

His eyes widened, darkened. Then narrowed. His finger pulled out and then shoved back in. "Hard or soft?" he asked.

She struggled to catch her breath. To comprehend. What difference did it make?

"Anything. Just make it stop. Please make it stop." Her voice broke on the last as he took her higher with another thrust of his finger.

Between her legs, he paused. This time when he glanced up, his expression was softer. He stroked the inside of her thighs from hip to knee. "It's okay, Jessie."

She shook her head. No it wasn't. This wasn't like before. This was much more powerful. She didn't know herself like this. This was scary.

He removed his finger from her pussy and kissed her thigh. "Jessie. I won't let anything happen to you. Just relax and let go."

She couldn't. She couldn't.

He slid his palms under her hips. As if he understood how sensitive she was, as if he knew the slightest touch was akin to pain, he opened his mouth over her clitoris, but he didn't touch her. He didn't need to. The wet heat of his mouth seared like a brand. Oh, she was close. So close. His lips flexed. There was the barest shifting of pressure and then the moist heat of his tongue rested against her. Her whole body recoiled into his palms. Her mind rejected the sensation. She tried to wiggle away. He held her still for the light movement of his tongue. She screamed and fought. He groaned and held.

"Jessie, trust me, honey girl," Mac ordered, glancing up her heaving body. She was close. So close to orgasm. And so damned afraid to take it.

He pushed his shoulders forward, forcing her thighs wider, her hips higher. She beat at him with her hands, her head tossing on the bed, her chest and cheeks flushed and sweaty.

"Let it go, Jessie," he ordered, taking her clit in his mouth and sucking lightly.

Her response was a long drawn out "Nooooo," as she arched high. He sucked again and she screamed in frustration, the sound dropping off to a moaning sob. "I can't. I can't." When she fell back on the bed, her fingers dug into the bedspread as she glanced at him helplessly. "I can't."

Mac remembered that look from before. "Yes, you can."

He kept his tongue on her clit, and reached between his legs. He was in about as bad a shape as she. He coated his fingers well and then, as he sucked harder on her clit, smoothed them against her lips. Her mouth opened. She took his fingers inside, and as his taste spread through her mouth, she came, bucking hard.

"That's it," he whispered against her fragrant flesh. "Come for me, honey girl."

She bit down on his fingers and his cock jerked. Her fragrance was all around him. Hot and enticing. Her muffled screams filled the room. Her pussy grasped, begging to be filled. He couldn't hold back anymore. He walked his hands up the outside of her body. Forcing her knees back to her shoulders, he glanced down. She was naked and vulnerable beneath him. The tiny opening to her vagina looking too small to accept the broad head of his cock. As if to dispute his thought, her pussy clenched again, sucking inward, tempting him. Inviting him.

She was still sobbing and shuddering as he placed the mushroom-shaped crown at the opening. Her breath hissed in at the contact. He pushed. Her eyes rolled back and her lashes fluttered. Another shudder took her body, vibrating against the sensitive head. His control broke. On the next gasping shudder, he threw his hips forward. The tight outer ring of muscle parted and he was inside the slick convulsing clasp of her channel, forging deep through an unexpected resistance to the searing heat beyond.

He dropped to his elbows. "God Jessie, why didn't you tell me?" he asked, kissing her cheeks, her eyes, her lips, overwhelmed. "Why didn't you tell me, honey girl?"

She was a virgin. His hottest lover ever, and she was a virgin. The knowledge beat at his control. No man had ever been in her incredibly tight cunt. No other man had felt those tiny little muscles flutter along his length. No other man had ever heard her sweet gasps as her muscles parted to let him in.

He was her first. Something wild and restless came to life with the knowledge. His hips flexed involuntarily. She gasped, and winced. He pushed again, wedging himself deeper, catching her airy little pants in his mouth, caressing her cheeks with soothing strokes of his fingers even as he pushed harder. He was her only.

He wasn't prepared for the primal swell of emotion that rolled over him with the knowledge. He wanted to fuck her hard, pound into her, bury his cock so deep she'd never be able to look at another man. He kept it under control with the thinnest of threads as he looked into her deep green eyes, dark with passion and distress.

"Why, Jessie?"

She cupped his face in her hands, her gentleness a balm to the wild emotion ripping at his restraint, "Because I've only ever wanted you."

At that, the deeply primitive part of him that he kept carefully under wraps threw back its head and roared to life.

Chapter Eight

Beneath her fingers Jessie felt the muscles in Mac's jaw tighten. Was he mad? She waited for him to look down, watching him carefully, but he didn't. She couldn't even see his expression since he had his head back. All she could see was the arch of his throat, and the tremors that overtook the long rope of muscle on either side as they locked as tight as his jaw.

"Mac?"

"Don't." It was little more than a grunt.

"What?" Oh God, had she totally messed this up?

"Don't talk. Don't move. Don't even twitch." His drawl was guttural. A primitive expulsion of sound that reached deep into the heart of her and triggered the twitch he'd forbidden.

"Dammit, Jessie!"

She couldn't help it. The low growl had pleasure arcing through her groin again, like chain lightning it leapt from nerve ending to nerve ending, swamping the discomfort of his possession with need, imperiously commanding she move, that she feed its demand for more. More pressure. More friction. More Mac. She couldn't hold still, but she couldn't move, pinioned as she was beneath his big body, his huge penis painfully wedged in her delicate flesh, searing her with its incredible heat.

"I can't help it," she whispered, licking her lips as she rocked her pelvis a fraction of an inch.

"Try." He dropped down over her, pinning her with his torso. "I need a minute, honey girl, or I'm going to be all over you like a wild animal."

She licked her lips again. His gaze dropped to her mouth as she bit her lip.

"God damn!"

"You're in me," she whispered, the reality sinking in. She wasn't a virgin anymore. She had a man inside her. And not just any man. Mac.

"Just a little," he grunted.

A little? She was stretched to her limit. He had to be in to the hilt. She tucked her chin, trying to see. She couldn't see anything except the top of his massive shoulders.

"How little is a little?" she asked, dropping back.

"A little more than the crown."

"Oh my God!" He'd never fit.

"Exactly. I need you to be very still for just a minute." He inched up her body. He was being very careful not to jostle her. Them. They were connected now. One for this brief moment in time.

"And then what?" She didn't think she wanted to hear his answer.

His back bowed as he brought his forehead to hers. "And then we're going to make the sweetest love."

Or maybe she did. "How sweet?"

The soft brush of his lips across the tips of her lashes was a hint. "The sweetest imaginable."

"Oh."

His lips stretched against her forehead with his smile. "Just relax and trust me, honey girl."

She closed her eyes and did, the rest of her senses heightening as she lay there, listening to the sound of his breathing, feeling the warmth of his body above her, the coolness of the comforter below her, the tingling fullness of his possession inside her.

He shifted position, his weight coming down on his elbows just beside and above her shoulders. His torso pressed into hers. The earthy, musky scent of his flesh calling to her. Saliva filled her mouth as she opened her eyes and surveyed the tanned expanse of muscle so temptingly near. This close, she could see the marks of her previous bite. She blushed at the reminder of how wild he'd made her.

His fingers caught in her hair as he attempted to wedge them under her head. She lifted the slightest bit, giving him room. Her lips brushed his chest, directly over her mark, before she dropped back onto the pillow of his big palm.

His weight shifted again as he moved to the side. His cock moved, too, and the resulting flash fire of pleasure made her cry out.

He froze as she panted in rigid hope. He pulled back, searching her face.

"Honey girl, was that a good cry or a bad cry?"

She bit her lips, so hungry for the sensation again that she couldn't find breath. "Good," she squeaked, not meeting his eyes.

"Damn." He relaxed into her. "Let's see if we can make some more of those good cries."

Despite the fact that she could feel the savage tension in him humming just beneath his skin, he didn't drive into her like she expected. Instead, he fondled her breasts, playing softly with the nipples as he rocked his hips on hers, using his big cock to stroke her inner tissues with the briefest of caresses. Teasing and flirting with them until they screamed with frustration and nipped and pressed him for more. He responded with a slightly deeper rhythm, never forcing the issue, never overwhelming her as he so easily could. Just giving her as much as she could take comfortably, nurturing her passion along, giving her time to experience every sensation, every nuance, and then showing her with a flex of his hips, a graze of his lips, just how much more pleasure waited for her.

Just there. Just out of her grasp. And when she was twisting beneath him, unable to bear the agonizing whip of desire, only then did he teach her how to reach for it. To flow with the hunger rather than fight it, to stretch and arch just that much more until she had it all. All of him, his strength, his passion.

On a hoarse shout, his cock jerked within her, and his seed spilled high against her womb. She wrapped her legs around his waist and her arms around his chest as he shuddered uncontrollably with every spurt, pulling him close, as if she could shelter him from the violence of his release, her own orgasm washing over her as he thrust into her one last time, the sound of her name on his lips almost as sweet as his loving.

Mac collapsed over Jessie, catching his weight on his elbows so he wouldn't crush her. He was never letting her go. The knowledge squeezed through the aftermath with the same relentless throb of her orgasm. No matter what he had to do to keep her happy, he wasn't letting her go. His hips still pulsed against her, almost helplessly, his passion spent but needing to feel her muscles pulling at him, demanding more from him. Needing the connection.

His breath sawed in and out of his lungs. Beneath him she panted. The air was rich with the scent of their lovemaking. A bead of sweat trickled down the side of her neck. He caught it with his tongue, savoring the touch of salt mixed with the hint of woman.

She "hmmmed" and curved into his mouth. He pressed his lips against the side of her neck.

"Are you okay?" he asked, feeling her jerk against him on the next pulse of his hips.

Her hair tickled his ear as she nodded. "Better than okay."

He brushed her hair and the strand caught on his finger. He pulled back, the hair stuck, and he wound it around his finger as he looked into her sleepy eyes. "Fading out on me again?"

"Apparently mind-blowing orgasms have that effect on me."

She looked completely comfortable with the realization.

He released the strand of hair. It fell against her cheek in a honey-blonde swirl. Cupping her hips and the back of her head in his hand, he rolled them over, keeping her body against his, his cock in her.

Her thighs fell on either side of his hips. Her pussy wiggled on his softening flesh. He stilled her hips with his hand. "Don't move."

She propped herself up on his chest. "Why?"

"I'm comfortable where I am."

She blew a hair off her face and frowned at him. He could tell she was dying to ask but wouldn't. "I'm big enough to stay in you when I'm soft," he explained, "but not if you squirm."

The blush started at the top of her plump white breasts and climbed. He smiled. When it reached her cheeks he asked, "Unless you'd care to make me hard again?"

She went from pink to red in the blink of an eye.

"Again?" she sounded impressed.

He was a little impressed himself. Considering how hard he'd come, he should be down for at least an hour, but there was something about her that turned him on. Something more than the physical. Something that made him…hunger.

"Yeah." He stroked his finger up her spine, riding the ridges, smiling at the goose bumps that sprang up. Jessie trailed her nail around his nipple and smiled back when it hardened.

"Unless you'd rather talk," he added as her eyes crinkled at the corners.

Her smile slipped. "Men are not supposed to want to talk after sex," she informed him. "Entire books have been written on the subject." She tapped his nipple with her nail, making her point, trying to distract him from that betraying expression. "Talk show hosts have made careers of it."

Mac could have told her it was no use. He noticed everything about her. Wanted to know everything about her. "Lucky for you, I'm enlightened."

She rolled her eyes. "This from the man who just spanked my butt."

"Yup. Enlightened and flexible." His fingers reached the base of her neck, his hand slid over the smooth curve of her shoulder. "What more could a woman want?"

She didn't answer him immediately. Just stared at him, those green eyes dark with emotion. As he cupped her cheek in his palm, an expression flitted across her face. One that made his heart clench and his thumb stroke her face comfortingly. She was uncertain. Nervous.

"No answer?"

Jessie sighed. "None that sounds right."

He liked her honesty. And he liked the way she kept flexing her pussy around him as if she, too, hungered.

"How about I pose a question then?"

"How about you just tell me how I can make you hard again?"

"Too late. That moment's passed."

She raised her eyebrows and squeezed deliciously with her inner muscles. The resulting massage of the smooth inner flesh along his shaft had a predictable effect. His cock tingled and stretched.

She wiggled her hips happily and grinned at him. "I don't think so."

His cock stretched further at the enticement of her smile. Mac shook his head at her. She was like a kid with a new toy, and as soon as they got this matter of her virginity off the table, he'd be happy to romp, but right now he wanted answers. He stopped her antics with a palm on her thigh. "How does it come about that you're a twenty-nine-year-old virgin?"

Delicate muscles squeezed him again. "Not any longer."

No one could resist that satisfied smile, least of all him. He dragged her mouth to his, kissing her hard, possessively. She kissed him with equal ferocity, nipping his lip when he would have pulled back, holding on. Her nipples pebbled against his chest and she gasped as he grew inside her, stretching up into her channel, parting the smooth muscles with a slow expansion.

He gave her what she wanted. His tongue thrust into her mouth, tangling with hers. He teased. And played. And lured. When her tongue made a tentative foray past his lips, he caught it with his teeth, biting down just hard enough to prevent her escape. And then he sucked, lightly at first but building the pressure as she squirmed against him, building the pleasure as he drew out the arousal.

He let her go. As she leaned back and sucked air into her lungs, he put his hands on her shoulders and eased her back until she was sitting fully upright, his penis her anchor.

He trailed his fingers down her shoulders, over the bump of her collarbones to the soft sides of her breasts. She shivered. His cock swelled. Her eyes flew wide as he went deeper.

"Oh!"

He soothed her with a soft glide of his fingers. "Easy, honey girl." He cupped her breasts in his hands, weighing them. "I'll be deeper this way, that's all."

She bit her lip and leaned into his palms. "I'm not sure that's possible."

He stroked her engorged nipples with his thumbs, pressing the dark pink tips into the surrounding flesh, using the pressure to guide her back into position. Damn, if she didn't have the prettiest breasts—soft and white—just enough to fill his hands with an underlying firmness that begged a squeeze. The freckle on the left one beckoned. He rubbed it with his thumb. "If it gets to be too much," he told her, backing his thumbs off, letting the nipple roll over the tip, "you let me know and we'll deal with it."

He brought his forefingers down over the swollen buds and twisted lightly. His cock continued its slow steady push into her ultra-tight channel. Every inch a hard-pressed gain through the slick heat. She jerked and pulled away. He caught her hips in his hands and pulled her back down. "Don't move. Keep that delectable pussy pressed tight against me. So tight there isn't a breath of air separating us."

"But—"

"No buts."

She frowned, but most of her attention was focused inward on the steadily increasing presence of his shaft in her snug heat. He stroked his thumbs in the crease between her thigh and hip. "Was there ever another lover, Jessie?"

It took Jessie a second to process the question. When the implication wormed its way through the thickening haze of desire, she snapped taut with indignation. "Of course."

Mac arched an eyebrow at her, his big body shuddering under the lash of her sudden movement, his erection thickening with a surge that had her wincing. He was much deeper this way, touching parts of her she didn't even know existed. His thumbs stroked over her hips again, the gesture soothing. His blue eyes narrowed. Assessing.

"Okay?"

The pressure eased as her body stretched to accommodate. "I'm fine, but you're not getting out of trouble by pretending concern."

It was his turn to frown. A sexy frown that was probably supposed to intimidate her but just had her tightening around him harder. "There's no pretense."

"Of course there is. We've already done this once. We know you fit."

He started to say something and then decided against it. His thumbs stretched across her lower abdomen, pressing just above the pubic bone. "So what happened to the other lover?"

She bit her lip as he pressed a little harder, setting off a tiny compulsion to press against his hands, to rub her clitoris over the rough hair of his groin, but he'd told her to hold still. It was hard, though. "As you might have guessed, he wasn't much of a lover."

Holding still got harder as his thumbs glided down to rest at the top of her pubic mound.

"How not much?"

Jessie gasped and looked down. His expression was hard, tight, as he watched his thumb press between the folds of the thick outer lips of her pussy. "We dated through high school and college."

"And he kept his hands off you?"

The level of sheer disbelief in his low drawl was a balm to her pride. "He didn't find it that hard."

The sentence ended in a mewling cry as he pressed just under the lip of her vulva, pushing into the base of her clitoris, sending shuddering shockwaves of sensation deep into her vagina. He did it again and she jerked forward, catching herself with her hands on his chest. "Oh God!"

Beneath her hands the heavy muscles shifted, and the sheets rustled as his big shoulders tensed. Pressure on her hips told her he wanted her back upright. His thumb, pressed where it was, made movement impossible.

"Did you try to seduce him, honey girl?"

Jessie just loved the way he said that nickname. As if she was something intimately sweet and tempting that he couldn't resist. Didn't want to resist. "Yes."

The backward pressure on her hips increased. "Sit up."

She took a deep breath, gathering strength. Air entered her lungs in sporadic bursts. She sat up and immediately hunched forward as his cock pierced deep. Bracing her palms on his stomach, she took slow breaths as her muscles strained under the pressure of his girth. His size. At the same time, her pussy caressed him in ecstatic ripples, thrilled with his presence. Wanting, impossibly, more.

His hand left her hip to cup her cheek, bringing her gaze to his. "Okay?"

She bit her lip as his cock responded to the entreaties of her inner muscles and gave her more. "Yes."

It was a strained, harsh syllable, and she couldn't blame him when he didn't look reassured.

His grip shifted to her chin, keeping her gaze on his. "Does it hurt?"

She shrugged, striving for nonchalance, totally missing it because of the incredible feelings washing out from her core. God, she could come from just the way he filled her. So hard, so tight, to the point of pain, just short of unbearable. "Just pinches."

"A little?"

She nodded, pressing her clit against the prickly hairs on his groin, whimpering when he stretched deeper, pressing high inside, the sudden sharp, erotic pain catching her by surprise.

"Dammit!"

Mac pulled her against his chest. His hands stroked down her back, soothing her. Arousing her. Denying her. "Don't do that again."

"Do what?" She pushed against his chest. He resisted for a moment, his hands on her shoulder blades easily keeping her in place, before he relented. He let her put four inches of space between them.

His expression was serious, "Don't try to take more than you're ready for."

God, she didn't think she was ready for what she had. It felt like a thick log was buried between her legs. Her muscles burned with the effort to accommodate his width, and twitched with the desire to feel him move. Just the thought of all that thick male flesh pulling and tugging at her as he fucked in and out, in and out… She squeezed her eyes shut as flashes of yearning made her buck on him. He'd fuck her raw before he'd come. She'd be so sensitive she'd be able to feel every hot spurt as he emptied his balls into her. Over and over, filling her deliciously full. Her whole body shuddered convulsively, and she whimpered in her throat.

Mac swore and arched under her, forcing his cock deeper. "Tell me what you're thinking."

She opened her eyes to find him watching her. His eyes lit with the same desire eating her alive.

"What thought just had you whimpering so sexily, and your little pussy quivering so desperately."

She couldn't say it out loud. She just couldn't.

He smiled as if he knew, trailed his hand down her back and whispered outrageously. "I'll slide my finger in your ass if you tell me."

She shuddered again. Her ass clenched and ached in mournful emptiness. Heat climbed her cheeks, whether from embarrassment or passion, she had no idea. "Which one?"

"What?"

"Which finger?"

His teeth flashed white in a grin. "Which would you prefer?"

More heat washed into her face. This time she knew it was from embarrassment, but she knew from Mac's grin and the way his cock throbbed that he liked her this way, so she pressed on. "The middle finger."

"Why?" His fingertips slipped between the cheeks of her ass.

If she hadn't been holding his gaze, she would have missed the flare of sensual satisfaction as she admitted, "Because it's bigger."

His finger slid around the spasming rosette. "Feeling neglected?"

His finger nudged the tiniest bit in the well-lubed opening. She couldn't hold his gaze any longer. Her forehead dropped to his chest as she admitted, "Yes."

It snapped back up as he thrust his finger in. The burning culmination as her anus stretched over his second knuckle before clamping down on the base arched her back against his hand. He gave her the pressure she needed against her shoulders and her ass as he asked, "Better?"

"Oh yes."

His expression was knowing as he thrust again, and she winced before pushing back, taking a fraction of an inch more.

"Burns?" he asked.

She nodded and bit her lip. With his cock stretching her pussy, his finger felt huge, but at the same time it was good. So very, very good.

"You wrote on that list that you wanted your ass fucked."

He punctuated the statement by pulling his finger out and thrusting back in.

That hadn't been her exact wording, but yes. Oh yes, She wanted that. Hot shivers shot out from her rectum. Her muscles went weak. Her head fell forward as she shook from head to toe. She nodded against his collarbone, her "Yes" a breathless entreaty. Taking his flesh between her teeth, she bit down as the incredible sensation washed over her, making her feel cold and tingly, yet hot and burning.

"Honey girl, I'm a bit bigger than you might have been planning on when you wrote down that fantasy."

Jessie looked up, his skin still between her teeth. She slowly let it slide free as she realized what he was saying. Dismayed acceptance stole some of her languor. "You don't want to do that with me."

It figures she'd get the only other man in the world who didn't have a taste for anal sex.

"Oh honey girl, you should be afraid, I want to do that so much with you. But..." His eyes were soft, tender, she realized as he pushed a tendril of hair out of her eyes. "I was thinking you might want to reconsider."

"Why would I do that? I've spent the last twel—" She caught herself before she could blurt out the truth of how many years she'd been dreaming of that particular fantasy. She didn't need to present herself as being anymore pathetic than she was.

She looked down at him as he lay across the white sheets, his hair a rich chocolate-brown, his face relaxed, darkly sexy. And lower, where his broad muscular shoulders flexed as he played with her hair, the left one stretched down, the muscles elongated and delineated as he slid his finger in and out of her eager rectum. She squeezed her pussy around his thick penis, shivered and mentally shook her head. The man had to be insane to think she'd forgo one single sexual minute with him. He may plan on booting her out in the next week, but right now he was hers. All hers. And she was going to milk this experience for all she could get. "Let me put it this way, no way in hell I'm reconsidering."

The blue of his eyes deepened as his expression went from tender to considering. He tucked the strand of hair behind her ear. "You ever taken a man like that?"

She couldn't hold his gaze. "No."

His thumb tipped her chin up. "You ever try?"

"Yes." And made a mess of it. She remembered Jim's shock. Horror. Ultimate refusal.

The fingers against the side of her head paused, tensed, and then relaxed as he asked, "Did your partner?"

She focused her gaze on the pulse in Mac's throat. "What?"

"Did your partner try?"

She ignored the question. She ignored the quick push of his fingers under her chin. She couldn't ignore the sharp slap on her ass or the wrench in her pussy when she jerked on his shaft. His hand came down on the area he'd just spanked, rubbing the smarting flesh, his small smile telling her he'd enjoyed himself and the way her pussy quivered in reaction, her juices wetting them both. The set of his chin, however, told her that he wouldn't let her hide from him when he repeated his question.

"Did your partner try?"

This was so humiliating. She bit the inside of her cheek to keep the tears at bay.

His hand fastened in her braid and tugged. "Answer me, Jessie."

"No, all right?" She ripped her braid out of his hand with a yank of her head. She blamed the sting of her pulled hair for the tear that spilled over. "He didn't want anything to do with that."

His expression of disbelief was like a slap in the face.

"It's not like I didn't try." Jessie swiped at the tear on her cheek. Her hand collided with his wrist as he caught the tear on his pinkie finger before she could wipe it away. The expression on his face could only be described one way. She didn't need his damned pity. Mac could take it and his big cock, and shove it where the sun didn't shine. Except she'd just invited him to do that to her and he'd refused. Damn it! What was so wrong with her that men turned away?

"I just didn't have whatever it took to turn him on, all right?" she shouted, pushing herself up, struggling against his hold to get up. "Is that what you want to hear? That I wasn't woman enough to even bring a teenage boy to orgasm? Does that make you feel good? Superior?"

She couldn't go anywhere. Between his cock, his finger and the hand he slid around her head, she was trapped right where she was. A stupid, undesirable, horny twenty-nine-year-old virgin who probably only got this man to fuck her because of the novelty of a list.

She went with his tug on her head because if she was trapped here she did not want to see his face as it dawned on him what a poor excuse for anything she was.

He didn't say a word until he had her face tucked into the curve of his neck. His arm slid down to her back and he held her against him, his hand stroking her side so softly. "Ahh, honey girl, the son of a bitch was gay."

He said it with such assurance. She wasn't dumb. The thought had occurred to her too. "He's married with two kids."

His chin rubbed against the top of her head as he shook his head. "He's just gotten better at hiding it then, because no red-blooded man presented with this incredible ass would be able to do anything but fuck himself raw in it."

"You don't seem too eager." Great. Now she sounded like a petulant little kid.

His short laugh had her bouncing, sending all sorts of shivery sensations from her pussy outward. "In case you haven't noticed, I've had my fingers buried palm deep in it since I stripped off your jeans." A slight pressure against her cheek alerted her to his smile. "Still do as a matter of fact."

"That's just foreplay."

Mac tipped her chin up. Sheer hope had her cooperating. "Honey girl, that's more along the line of seducing you into the idea."

She didn't know what to say to that. "Oh." And then she added. "You don't need to seduce me."

His smile spread. "But I enjoy it."

So did she. "In that case, why did you say you didn't want to…have anal sex with me?"

"I didn't say it. You did."

"You implied it."

He rolled his eyes, took a breath. And shook his head. "You have got to be the most contrary woman. I'm lying here with my cock buried in your cunt and my finger up your ass, and you're hell bent on arguing with me?"

Not really. "I'm sorry. I get a little analytical when I'm nervous."

"I'll keep that in mind. What are you nervous about?"

"You'll think it's stupid."

"Jessie girl, when you have a man like you do me right now, I guarantee you anything you do is the sexiest thing he's ever seen."

She laughed and smiled. "So my arguing is turning you on."

He flexed his cock inside her. "You tell me."

"Still hard." The realization had her grinning from ear-to-ear as she propped herself on his chest, the solid muscle making a hard cushion.

"Glad to see you approve."

"I'm sorry. It's just it's so new and you're so...damned good."

He touched a finger to her smile. "Good enough you'll let me finish our conversation?"

Some of her joy evaporated. "If you have to."

His sigh, lifted her up before dropping her back down. "I'm a big man, Jessie, and you've never taken anyone back there..."

"So?"

"I'm just trying to let you know it'll hurt at first. Maybe more than you're expecting."

"You don't have to make excuses. If you don't want to do it."

"Honey girl, I can get you off with a vibr—"

She was shaking her head before he finished the sentence. "It wouldn't be the same."

"I can make it very good for you that way. All the sensations without—"

Again she cut him off. Determination made mincemeat of her modesty. "No. I want you. In me. All the way."

His eyes narrowed. His fingers stilled on her cheek as he said slowly, "You want to feel me come in you."

She clenched on him. An involuntary, shivery motion. "Oh yes."

His hips jerked under her. His cock jerked within her. His fingers dug into her ass cheek as he drove deeper. "You want me to fuck this tight ass, no matter what?"

She nodded as he added another finger to the one in her and began a steady rhythm.

By now she knew what he wanted. "I want you to fuck it until I'm raw and can't imagine a moment without you in me."

"Son of a bitch." His chest heaved beneath her and his fingers slammed hard into her before they came to a halt. He tipped her chin to meet his gaze. "It'll hurt like hell at first, no matter how well I prepare you."

She imagined it would. "I don't care."

"Bad enough you'll scream."

"But I'll like it?"

She just knew she would. His eyes narrowed and then one corner of his mouth curved up.

"Oh, yeah. You'll like it. I'll make sure of it."

He pulled his fingers free, and motioned for her to turn around. With a downward pressure he let her know she was to keep his cock as deep in her as she could while she did it. It was awkward, but she managed it. As she settled back on him, she had a thought. "You're not turned off by…it…are you?"

She'd just die if he was creeped-out by the thought of taking her there. His cock slid back up into her pussy, hitting a whole new set of nerves, the shaft rubbing her clit as the head scraped along the wall separating her rectum from her vagina.

The pat on her ass was reassuring as she heard the nightstand drawer slide open. "Honey girl, that's one worry you don't need to add to your plate."

"You won't mind?" She looked over her shoulder in time to see him pulling out a white tube and a smooth purple vibrator with a fat base. He held her gaze as he greased the vibrator.

"I'll enjoy every second."

"What are you going to do with that?"

"Make you feel good."

"That had better be a new toy if you're thinking of getting it anywhere near me."

He smiled. "Brand spanking new and ready to go."

"Where?" As if she didn't already know. He stroked her buttock. "Here."

She braced her hands on his knees and shook, unable to look away, knowing what was coming.

His lips spread on a slow, sensual smile that had her heart rate tripping over with anticipation. He lubed his fingers and spread the cool cream in her ass, adding more and more until it melted and dripped out of her. He placed his free hand at the small of her back. "Now lean forward. That's right. Take my cock a little deeper." He placed the smooth head of the vibrator against her anus. It felt much bigger than his fingers. "Now push back, honey girl."

It was hard to focus with his cock pulling her muscles so tight. Movement felt distorted. The pressure outside matched the pressure inside as he pressed the device against her.

"C'mon, Jessie girl, you can take this. Just relax and let me slide it in. You'll feel so full." He pressed harder. The familiar burn joined the pressure. She felt herself opening that first tiny bit. "Don't you want that? All those deep, dark places stuffed full?"

Jessie pushed back but the immediate jolt of unfamiliar pain had her gasping and freezing. She was afraid to move. The vibrator stayed where it was. Mac's hand stroked her ass, but he didn't back off, didn't stop, he just held that damned purple thing pressed against her, not giving her a breath.

"It's too much." She didn't know if she meant too big, or too arousing.

"Shhh, honey girl. Don't tighten up." He pressed it harder against her. She cried out with the sensation, almost missing his moan.

"You're almost there, Jessie. God, you're pretty like this. Your sweet pussy stretched around my cock, your little ass opening for me. C'mon baby, just a little more and we can both come. Think of it, honey girl, my cock in your pussy, pumping deep. The vibrator in your tight ass, striving to go as deep. You'd be able to feel them both, rubbing against each other. Both of them pumping, working those sweet nerves. Stretching you, rubbing you. Loving you."

He took a breath, and the hand on her back touched her right shoulder. His breath came in harsh pants as he ordered. "Touch yourself. Put your fingers on your clitoris, honey girl. Stroke it soft and sweet. Swirl them around and get it all hot and swollen for me."

She did. Caught up in his voice. In the moment. In the potential. Desire, sharp and sweet whipped out from her fingers. Her body jerked on his, pulling away and then coming back to land on the hard shaft of his cock and the harder pressure of the vibrator.

"Does it feel good?"

It did. Violently so. She nodded, unable to speak. The discomfort of the vibrator became secondary to the need to move to satisfy the pulsing desire surging outward from her fingers.

"Pinch it now, honey girl, nice and soft, give it a little squeeze. Ah, such a sweet little shudder. I felt that all the way up my cock, but your ass, your poor little ass, it missed all the fun." He worked the base of the vibrator in a small circle causing the head to press against different nerves in her anus. "So empty. So hungry. We can't have that."

His palm pressed harder on her back. "Take a deep breath, Jessie girl and before you let it out, squeeze that little clit hard.

Rake it with your nail as you let out your breath and push back. Really push back."

She tried but getting a deep breath was hard. On the third try, she pulled in a deep breath. Her hands tightened on her clit. His grip shifted on the vibrator. She let her breath out counting slowly to ten. When she got to three she slowly dragged her nail across her clit. The searing agony of near climax took her by surprise. Her pussy convulsed, her body bucked and there was a burst of pleasure/pain in her backside followed by an unbearable feeling of fullness. The scream tore from her throat, half panic, half ecstasy.

Before the last echo faded she was on her hands and knees on the bed, Mac's big body arched over hers, his callused fingers on her clit rubbing steadily, not letting her focus on anything except the stabs of pleasure, keeping her hips grinding backwards on his cock, wanting more. More sensation. More everything.

"Mac?"

"Right here."

Mac kissed the nape of Jessie's neck, lapping at the bead of sweat there, using his grip on her clit to pull her up into him, his pelvis pressing the vibrator in, absorbing her shudders as she adjusted to his possession. He'd almost come himself when the vibrator sank home. Damn, he loved taking a woman's ass. Loved when they gave their trust. Loved to reward it with the kind of climax only anal play could give.

And Jessie. God Jessie was about perfect for him. She was going to come as soon as he moved that vibrator. Her ass was so sensitive, so primed by her years of dreaming, just the feel of that smooth plastic stroking those hidden nerves and she was going to go off like a rocket. He tested the tightness of her cunt, moving within her. It was no easier than before. When she came, she'd probably squeeze so hard he wouldn't be able to come. Oh yeah, he'd love to feel that.

He nuzzled her ear when her breaths grew easier. "You okay?"

"Uh-huh." That high-pitched little whimper stroked his desire like a loving hand. She was tense beneath him, the unfamiliar fullness making her both dread and anticipate movement.

"Fuck yourself on my cock, Jess. As hard or as soft as you want."

Her first moves were tentative. A slow pulse, a tiny withdrawal, a gradual reclaiming. He waited her out, keeping her clit between his fingers, not moving the vibrator, letting her get comfortable with taking charge. She pulled out another tiny bit. He gritted his teeth against the inevitable tugging of her internal muscles as she struggled to hold him tight, to milk him. He thought that was it, but she kept going and going until she only had the head resting against her opening. Then, with a steady push she brought him home—all the way—until she had a good three quarters of him buried in her channel. His moan ripped past his control, his grip spasmed on her tender bud, and his cry came hot on the heels of hers.

"Damn, Jess, I'm sorry."

She was shaking her head before he was done, pulling off him and ordering him to do it again, her voice breathless and airy.

He smiled against her back, and waited until she was shoving those delectable hips back, forcing his cock through the tight grip of muscle before pinching the engorged bundle of nerves, increasing the pressure with every inch she took, stopping when she did.

She glanced down between her legs and moaned. She dug her hands into the sheets, arched her back and pushed. His cock sank a fraction of an inch more. He knew then what she wanted. She wanted all of him. He kissed the curve of her spine.

"It won't work like this."

He pulled out. She whimpered, spun, and froze as her eyes went wide. He cupped her ass in his palm, catching the base of the vibrator as it slid down. "Bet that felt good."

She bit her lip and nodded. Over his palm, her ass clenched in a desperate effort not to lose the toy. He pushed up. Her head fell back and she stopped breathing altogether as it sank back into place.

"Lie on your stomach across the bed with your feet off the edge."

As soon as she was in place, he slid the vibrator all the way out. Before she could tighten up, he slid it smoothly back in. Her fingers tore at the sheets and she whimpered with every breath. He gave the base a light tap as he reached for the pillows. "From now on you keep this sweet ass lubed all the time. I want to be able to flip up your skirt and know you're ready for me."

The strength of her shudder would have taken her off the bed if he hadn't been lifting her to place the pillows.

"Is this another of your laws?"

"Yup. And one you'd better follow. Hurts like hell to have your ass messed with dry."

"You wouldn't!"

No. He wouldn't but she didn't know that. "I wouldn't suggest finding out the hard way."

He positioned her to his height, bent his knees and aligned his cock with the red pulsing entrance to her vagina.

"Are you ready for me, Jess?"

She was so wet, the question was rhetorical. Her juices were spilling over her pussy onto the pillows. Her scent rose to surround him.

"Please." She was almost weeping.

With steady pressure he pushed his cock in, feeling the hard ridge of the vibrator as he did. When he was three-quarters in, she tensed. He paused, then slowly, deliberately thrust against her, pushing at her resistance. She groaned, her hands caught in the bed sheets, as he leaned into her harder before pulling out and shoving back in. She was so tight that he didn't so much slide as forge into her, the ultra-snug grip, and incredible friction ripping at his control.

This time he got a little deeper, and brought his hand between them. Wrapping it around the base of the vibrator, he wedged one side against his groin. This time when he pulled out, the vibrator came, too. She screamed his name frantically as his cock and the vibrator stretched her simultaneously. She cried out again as they both shot back into her, driving deep, stroking hard. He did it again and again, her screams getting louder with each thrust, her body taking more of him until, finally, finally, he was seated to the hilt and his heavy balls slapped against her engorged clit. She sobbed into the comforter, her muscles tight under his hand as she tried to push back, her body begging for more.

He stroked her gently. "There you go, honey girl. All of me. Tight and deep." He pressed his cock a fraction deeper, his groin nudging the base of the toy into her ass. She whimpered a "Please."

"Do you want to come now, Jess?"

"Yes."

Her pussy flexed around him, stretched too far to hug him, but trying anyway.

"Good. So do I." He pulled out just far enough to reach the dial on the base of the toy. He turned the switch, paused at low and then turned it all the way to high. The heavy throbs were instantaneous. "Come for me, Jessie."

His hips drove back into hers. She shrieked and slammed her hands on the mattress arching back to him, her entire body convulsing on his third stroke, her pussy and ass clamping down on him like a vise as he orgasmed, stopping the flow of his seed in a painful interruption. He gritted his teeth and rode out her climax, his cries joining hers as her muscles relaxed and his come burst from his cock, flooding her channel. She came again as he pumped into her, crying and shaking before finally collapsing on the bed.

He was right behind her, catching his weight on his elbows, her pussy milking him long past dry as the vibrator kept him painfully hard. It took him three minutes to find his breath. He dragged himself out of her, wincing as his cock protested the movement. Turning off the vibrator and slipping it free, he let it drop to the floor as he hauled them both up on the bed, dragging her over him. "Go to sleep, honey girl."

He pulled the covers up and wedged his softening cock back into her eager pussy. She gasped and winced, but then wiggled down, not satisfied until she was taking more than he thought she should. He stroked her hair, tucked her head into the hollow of his shoulder and sighed.

They were really going to have to talk limits.

Chapter Nine

They were definitely going to be talking limits. Mac shoved open the door to the pickup. The late afternoon sun burned his eyes. He pulled his hat off and wiped the sweat from his brow before settling the brim low over his eyes and heading for the house. As soon as he got his hands on Jessie, he was going to flip up her skirt and paddle her bare ass. And not in a good way either. Son of a bitch, she was going to kill herself.

He didn't know where she got the energy to do the stunts she did. Lord knows he kept her up nights, working off as much of that pent-up energy as he could, to the point that he was dragging. Yet, every day for the last four, one of the hands had found a reason to come out to where he was working and fill him in on her latest antic. Every time he started swearing, they started laughing.

Today was absolutely the last straw. He should have known when he'd told her about climbing that windmill as a kid that she'd be up there first chance she got. Not a care in the world that the thing was twenty years older and in a sad state of neglect that any fool could see. She just charged forward like she had every other day since she'd been there, grabbing every experience she could, no matter how dangerous, as if she had something to prove. Well, it was stopping today. If he had to chain her to his side, she was not indulging in one more risk. His heart couldn't take the stress.

A loud whoop followed by a chorus of shouts came from down by the corrals, pulling him up short. He slowly turned in the direction of the noise, just knowing it wasn't Jessie down there. Couldn't be Jessie, because he'd told her this morning that she was not learning to "bust a bronc" as she'd put it. He'd also gone out of his way to let Will know to put a quick death to any efforts to see her try. Yet, somehow, in his gut, he knew what he was going to see when he cleared the crowd.

Slim was the first to notice his approach. He nudged Chuck and shot a nervous glance at the corral. Chuck ducked away as Slim stepped in front of Mac.

"Hi, Boss."

Mac pushed his hat back and did his best to look calm. "Who's riding?" he asked, knowing what the answer would be, not needing Slim's nervous rubbing of his hand on his jeans, or the anxious glances in Chuck's wake to understand that he was being stalled. He stepped to the left.

Slim shrugged and stepped with him, effectively blocking his progress. "Just somebody trying out old Busy Bob."

Old Busy Bob was the first horse that had ever bucked Mac off. He was twenty-two now, and the ranch's mascot. Mac couldn't name one cowboy who would consider that ornery bag of bones a challenge. He could think of one small woman who would find a trip up on him the time of her life.

He pushed Slim aside, just in time to see Jessie on top of that "old bag of bones", her body whipping around in the saddle like a sheet on the wash line riding out a hurricane.

"Someone get her off there!" Will shouted, coming onto the scene from the opposite direction. "He'll throw her."

Mac was vaulting over the corral fence before Will got the last word out. Out of the corner of his eye he saw Chuck cutting across the corral. Before either of them could get close enough to grab Busy Bob's bridle, it was too late. The big sorrel did two crow hops and then whipped his hindquarters up and around. Jessie went sailing off his back like a rag doll hurled in a tantrum. Straight into the fence. There was a sickening crack as she struck the hard wood and then a flat thud followed by a short "Uff" as she landed in the dirt. Dust puffed up around her still form.

Mac swore, and grabbed Bob's bridle as the horse continued dancing around Jessie's body, pulling him to a halt.

Even with the rider off, Bob kept prancing and side-stepping. Mac frowned and passed the reins to Chuck. Busy Bob tossed his head and rolled his eyes. Mac spared one second to order, "Check him out," and then there was nothing to do but see how badly Jessie was hurt.

It took two steps to reach her side. Two steps in which he got to relive the moment of impact when her delicate body collided with the fence. Two strides in which he got to curse himself for not seeing this coming. For underestimating her need for adventure. Two steps in which to call himself seven kinds of a fool.

He crouched down beside Jessie in the dirt. Her chest labored with the effort to breathe. Her eyes were closed, her face white. He needed to check for breaks, concussion, or worse but for the first time in his life, he couldn't just get down to doing what needed to be done. He was paralyzed. Afraid of what he would find. Afraid of what he wouldn't. This was Jessie, lying in the dirt, hurt. There was a scratch on her cheek. A strand of hair lay across her mouth. He brushed it aside, took a breath and put both hands to the sides of her neck. Her pulse was strong, her neck slender beneath his hands—so damned fragile. He gently probed. Nothing felt out of alignment, though that was indicative of nothing. Jessie's eyes were still closed, and her breathing wasn't normal.

"Ah, honey girl, what did you do to yourself?"

She didn't answer. There was a soft grunt as someone else knelt by his side.

"How's she doing?" Rafe asked, dropping the emergency kit down beside his thigh.

"She's breathing."

Rafe leaned over, forcing Mac to move further up as he put his fingers against her pulse. "Well, that's a plus."

Mac curled his fingers around the impulse to lash out. Rafe was an EMT. He was doing his job with his usual calm efficiency and easygoing manner. No reason to flatten the man. Still, Mac couldn't make his "Yeah" as light.

Rafe glanced up from where he was checking her skull. "She probably just got the wind knocked out of her."

Maybe. Or she might have broken her damned back. "What do you need me to do?" Mac asked.

"Hold her hand and sweet talk her while I get her ready for the ambulance."

"Someone called?"

"Jeremy did."

He deserved the pitying look Rafe cut him. Of course, someone had called. Just because his crew lost their heads when it came to indulging Jessie's wild side didn't mean they didn't know the drill when there was an accident. He was the only one who couldn't string two thoughts together. "Good."

He worked around to Jessie's right side. He carefully slid his hand under hers, lifting it just far enough so her palm could rest in his.

"C'mon Jessie, open your eyes," he whispered. Her lashes fluttered. She moaned and her fingers twitched in his hand. He watched her face for a second. Her fingers twitched again, and he changed his focus. Her hand looked so small in his. Defenseless. The ranch had been hell on her manicure. Her nails, which a week ago had been perfectly manicured, were bare of polish. There was a chip in the middle one and dirt under all four. He stroked his thumb over the back of her fingers.

He touched her dirt-streaked cheek with his free hand. The Circle H had been hell on her, period. His finger shook as he traced a smear over her cheekbone. Rafe nudged his hand aside as he continued his examination. Mac sat back out of the way, looking at the ring of concerned, guilty faces staring down at Jessie. He was going to kill them, he decided. Each and every one of them for ferreting out Jessie's weakness for a dare and challenging that flaw in her character.

Will was apparently of the same mind. "What in hell were you jackasses thinking of putting her up on that aging devil?" he growled.

Jute was fool enough to answer, his drawl insolent, too new to realize that Will had a temper beneath his normal calm, and the muscle to back it up. "Hell, how were we supposed to know that Busy Bob had more than a hop left in him?"

"You could have tried using that lump you call a brain," Will snapped, shoving Jute back as he stepped forward into his space, daring the younger man to give him a reason to flatten him as he said disgustedly, "Jessie's only been riding a couple days. Even that hop you expected would land her in the dirt."

"You can't pin this on me," Jute spat contemptuously.

"The Hell I can't," Will snapped, and shoved the younger man into the fence.

"I wasn't the only one standing around here while she got on that nag," Jute whined, more deference in his tone as Will towered over him.

There was a hint of puzzlement in Slim's voice as he agreed. "He's right there, Will. No one expected old Busy Bob to relive his glory days like that. Hell, we didn't even put on the bucking strap." He shook his head and looked at his companions, waving his hand helplessly at Jessie. "It was a joke. We just like to see Jess get her dander up. We figured she'd get all worked up, hop on, walk Old Busy Bob around the corral twice, and then glow all evening because of her accomplishment. Thought maybe we'd get some of those brownies out of the deal," he confessed sheepishly, running his hand through his hair.

Good God! Mac thought, staring at his men. He had a crew of idiots. He shot them all a disgusted look, watching as Rafe cupped Jessie's head in his hand and eased the neck brace under her.

"You can open your eyes now," he said to her.

Mac looked at Jessie and then at Rafe. "She's awake?"

"Yup."

"Then why isn't she responding?"

Rafe worked the buckles on the brace. "Probably terrified you're going to tear the hide off her."

"She'd be right." Mac looked down. "You open your eyes right now, honey girl, or I'll paddle your ass hard enough you won't sit for a week."

"Oh yeah, that's encouragement," Rafe injected wryly.

Jessie's fingers curled around Mac's. "Promises, promises."

"Uh-uh." He needed for her to open her eyes. Needed to see that she was okay. "Do it."

Her fingers squeezed his. "I'm okay, Mac."

"Open your eyes and prove it."

She wet her lips with her tongue. "Give me a minute."

Rafe frowned and leaned over her. "Are you feeling dizzy?"

She tried to shake her head in the brace. "Sick to my stomach."

Rafe immediately leaned back. Mac leaned in. "Don't try to move anything."

"I'll tell my stomach." Her smile was a mere shadow of its normal intensity.

Rafe laughed. "Do that. Are you hurt anywhere?"

She tried to nod. Mac cursed and cradled her chin in his palm, stilling the attempt as she answered, "My arm."

"Which one?" Rafe asked, his gaze narrowing the way it did when he focused.

"The left one. I hit the fence."

Rafe gently rolled back her sleeve. The area of the injury was immediately apparent, already beginning to bruise and swell. Skimming the area with his fingers, Rafe looked at Mac and mouthed, "Ouch."

When he attempted to move her fingers, she moaned.

Mac swore again and drew his thumb across Jessie's cheek. He'd broken a few bones, and knew what she was feeling. "It's broken, Jess," he told her as gently as possible.

She took a shaky breath and expelled it. "Damn."

Ah shit! Mac thought. He should have seen this coming. He'd had enough experience with his mother to have seen this coming. To have known he had to be more vigilant.

"Hold her while I get the inflatable splint," Rafe ordered. "She'll feel better with the arm immobilized."

"Sure."

"I need to be held?" Jessie asked.

Mac looked at her poor battered body. "Oh, yeah."

Jessie opened her eyes a crack. Mac was staring down at her, his blue gaze dark, the frown on his face belying the incredible gentleness in his voice.

"It doesn't hurt that much," she whispered, her breath just coming back to her. In truth it was beginning to hurt like hell, but it'd take more than being thrown from Busy Bob to make her admit that. Not when Mac's face was that deathly white.

His gaze left hers. She followed it as it traveled over her chest and then paused. There was a smudge across her shirt, level with her left breast. A big, wide smudge. About the width of a fence rail. A bit of anger replaced the gentleness in his voice as he said, "You shouldn't be hurt at all."

She opened her eyes a little wider. Without the filter of her lashes, he looked damned mad. And determined to do something about it. She groaned silently to herself. "You have no intention of being reasonable about this, do you?"

"Not a chance."

"Rats."

His right brow arched up, and he gently pushed a strand of hair out of her face. "I thought you promised me no more dangerous stunts?"

She shrugged without thinking. Pain halted the move halfway in. Mac's fingers against her cheek—those strong masculine capable fingers—trembled. She reached up with her right hand and caught them in hers. "I didn't consider riding that bag of bones dangerous."

The muscles in his jaws bunched. He was grinding his teeth, she knew. A habit she'd caught him at frequently since they'd become lovers. He seemed to think she needed protecting from herself. Today's accident wasn't going to convince him otherwise. *Stupid horse.* She glared at the disreputable, sway-backed source of her troubles.

"Look at him. He's ancient. Pair that with the fact that neither Chuck nor Slim would harm a hair on my head, and I knew it was safe."

Mac's eyes never left her face. "Uh-huh." As if he realized his fingers were trembling, he pulled them into a fist and tucked them against her neck. They were warm, hard and comforting. She rested her chin against them. Her arm was really beginning to let her know she'd done some damage.

"Don't start with those uh-huhs," she warned. A hard throb in her arm made her wince. His eyes narrowed on her face, studying her expression and his fingers stroked the back of her cheek.

"Being able to resist a dare is a sign of maturity."

"I'm not impulsive," she argued. "It's just that everything the men have suggested has sounded fun."

"Climbing that old windmill was fun?" He shook his head at her, obviously not understanding what drove her.

"They squealed on me about *that*?"

"Honey girl, the men delight in telling me everything you do."

"You need to give them more work." She held her arm a little tighter. The throbbing was definitely stronger now. "They've obviously got too much time on their hands."

He was not willing to be distracted. "Hell, woman! That thing is riddled with dry rot. The only thing holding it together is the determination of the termites calling it home."

"It was fun if you considered the view. I could see forever from up there."

And she'd felt connected to him up there, sharing something he had done. Something from his youth. A happy memory.

He shook his head. "I can see I'm going to have to take care of this problem myself."

She did not like the sound of that. "You're not planning anything…rash, are you?" Jessie had never had so much fun as she'd had since arriving in Round the Bend. Everyone with the exception of Jute, had welcomed her like family. The Circle H was fast becoming home. She shifted. Bone grated against bone. She couldn't help her moan.

"Shit." Mac glowered in the barn's direction. "Hurry it up, Rafe!"

"On my way," came the reply.

"Don't try to move again," he warned her, his eyes running over her as if she might have fractured something else with so slight a movement.

"I wasn't planning on it."

Though he was growling at her, his hands were incredibly gentle as they stroked her cheek and fingers. It made up for his arrogance as he said, "Good."

Jessie chewed her lip as a new, disturbing possibility occurred to her. "You're not going to send me away, are you?"

His thumb came to rest against her mouth. His expression was a mixture of regret, frustration and resignation. Not one of those emotions gave her a warm fuzzy.

"We'll discuss that later."

"Why can't we discuss it now?"

Mac glanced up pointedly as Chuck spoke up, "There's no need to be making rash decisions, boss."

Oh hell, she'd forgotten they had an audience. "Chuck's right. It's never good to make decisions when stressed," she told him. "We can talk about this later."

Mac's expression was inscrutable as he pointed out, "I think that's what I said."

"So it was." A sick feeling having nothing to do with her arm settled into her stomach. Watching the uneasy glances the men exchanged between themselves did absolutely nothing to calm her nerves.

She closed her eyes and braced herself as Rafe sat beside her. "You are not sending me away."

Above her she felt Rafe pause and then, as smooth as butter, say, "I wasn't planning on it. Just a quick trip to the hospital and then right on back here."

"Shut up, Rafe," Mac growled.

In the distance Jessie could hear the sirens howling. She opened her eyes, defiantly met Mac's, and laid down a law of her own. "I won't go."

*****

"So what exactly were you talking about when you said you had to handle this situation yourself?" Jessie asked four hours later, sitting on the bed as Mac knelt on the floor tugging at her shoes.

"What I should have done in the first place," Mac retorted, looking up the enticing stretch of her denim-covered legs. "I'm going to make the announcement that the next man who dares you in over your head will be looking for a new job immediately."

The sneaker hit the floor, the second one not far behind.

"Ordinarily, I'd argue such a high-handed interference in my life, but…"

"Since I'm about to love you until your toes curl, you're going to overlook it?" Mac interjected helpfully. The snap on her jeans was stubborn. It finally gave with a soft pop.

She shook her head. "Not hardly. I've got so many painkillers in me I can't stay awake."

"I'm crushed." He tugged the jeans and underpants out from under her hips and down her legs while she braced herself on her right arm.

"Somehow," she said with wry amusement. "I have a feeling you've got enough arrogance to overcome this small setback."

"So to what do I owe your generosity?" He dropped them on the floor, grabbing the scissors. He'd never get what was left of her sleeve over that cast.

"To the fact that from the looks I saw on the hands' faces when we headed out to the hospital, no one is going to say 'Hi' to me, let alone enter into another one of our wagers."

"Pretty grim, eh?" He cut up the sleeve of her shirt.

"Damn grim." She looked down to see how he was doing.

Mac sighed and shifted her head aside as the scissors glided over her shoulder with efficient snips. "With your track record, I shouldn't tell you this—"

"But you're going to anyway?"

He tossed the scissors on the nightstand and pulled the shirt off, leaving her in her pale blue bra, and nothing else. The bruise on her far breast made him frown. He was going to have to be very careful of her for awhile. He got rid of his own clothes before sitting on the bed beside her and admitting. "But I'm going to anyway."

Mac cupped her uninjured breast in his hand. The small, pink nipple beaded instantly. He smiled contentedly. He liked the way she responded to him. "It seems Jute slipped a metal burr under the saddle blanket."

It took her a moment to absorb what he was telling her. Probably because it was so incomprehensible. "So that's why—!" Her green eyes narrowed, the long lashes shielding their expression from view, but the tense pressure of her shoulder against his side told him she was ticked. "I'm going to bake that bastard a chocolate cake."

"The punishment hardly seems to fit the crime." He unfastened her bra, and eased it down her arms. He added it to the collection of clothes on the floor before turning her gently against him, supporting her cast on his forearm as he lay back on the bed.

"I intend to substitute a box of those chocolate-flavored laxatives for baking chocolate," she muttered into his chest.

"You've got a vindictive streak."

Her "So?" was slightly defensive.

"I like it."

Her snort could have been disgust or laughter.

"You're a sick man, Hollister."

"So I've been told." He smiled and flicked her nose. "I'm almost sorry the men took care of Jute for us. It would've been fun to see how you handled him."

"What do you mean 'took care of'?"

"Nothing serious." He grabbed a pillow and slipped it under her arm, bringing it across his stomach. "Considering Jute almost killed you with that stunt, I think taking him out to the woodshed for a lesson wasn't excessive."

"Uh-huh. Just how thorough was this lesson?" she asked.

He found he also liked the softness in her character that put that touch of worry in her voice for Jute.

"Not too bad. Will said he walked away when he finished with him."

Two steps, Mac qualified silently. The bastard had managed two steps before he'd collapsed. His brother Jeremy had to drive him to the hospital. The same hospital Jessie had just left.

As far as Mac was concerned, that was two steps too far. Jessie could have been killed. And all because that bastard Jute thought she should be sharing his bed. The thought made Mac burn. He'd shared women in the past and never given it a thought. As long as everyone was a consenting adult, why should he?

But Jessie was different. She was his and his alone. Under his protection, and that bastard had dared to hurt her simply because of that. Mac fought a killing rage. If the fool thought the beating was the end of it, he had another think coming. That was just the beginning of the bad luck that would plague Jute for as long as it took Mac to get the image of Jessie flying into that fence out of his head. He pulled her closer.

Jessie looked up, a question in her sleepy green eyes. The drugs were kicking in. He shook his head and placed his mouth over her soft, generous one. Gently. Lightly. So lightly he could feel every curve, dip and hollow. She had an amazing mouth. An amazing everything—from her sense of humor to her sense of adventure. He nipped her plump lower lip before sucking it into his mouth and soothing the slight sting with the tip of his tongue. It was going to be tough curbing her wild streak, but when a man had someone like Jessie, he'd do whatever it took to keep her safe. Even if that meant protecting her from herself. She shifted in his arms. He pulled back, and Jessie blinked at him sleepily.

"I'm sorry," she whispered, touching a fingertip to the crease in his chin. "I'm just too tired."

"No need to be sorry," he replied, pulling the sheets over her. "Considering all you've been through today, and the size of that shot the doctor gave you, I'm surprised you didn't pass out long before this."

"Are you sure you want me in here?" she asked, stifling another yawn, accidentally nudging her thigh against the rising ridge of his cock in the process. "Won't it...bother you?"

Mac looked down at the woman cuddled in his arms. His woman. Her lower lip was slightly puffy from his kiss, and her hair spilled over his arm in a shimmer of sleek honey-gold. Despite her injuries and the medication, shades of passion flickered in her deep green eyes, but what really turned him on was the smile on her lips and the acceptance overflowing her gaze. He dropped his gaze to the clunky white cast protruding from the bright red comforter, and smiled. Any lovemaking he got up to for the next six weeks was going to have to fall into the creative category.

"Oh yeah, it will, most definitely bother me."

The soft body resting against his went taut. One muscle at a time. When he looked down all he could see was the top of Jessie's head. In contrast to her body language, her tone was pure conversational as she said, "Maybe I'd better sleep in my bed tonight."

Well hell, she was hurt. He stopped her from leaving simply by curving his arm around her back. He kept her from hiding by snagging her chin on his index finger and tilting up her face. "Let's get something straight between us. I'm always bothered when I'm around you, but I would be a hell of a lot more bothered if I had to spend a night without you in my bed."

"Are you trying to make me cry?"

"Hell no!"

As Jessie grew thoughtful, he hastened to add, "And don't go thinking to get around me with tears whenever we argue."

She managed to look affronted. "I wouldn't dream of doing any such thing."

"Uh-huh."

"And what do you mean by that?"

"It means that I've seen you in action too many times to believe that you wouldn't use tears to leverage yourself out of a sticky situation."

Jessie clutched her chest with her hand. "I'm wounded."

"More likely you're frustrated with having your plans discovered," he retorted, tucking her back against him.

She laughed and turned further into his embrace, balancing her cast on his stomach. "I'll have to work on my technique if I'm that easy to read."

He hugged her, loosely absorbing the knowledge that he'd meant what he said. He couldn't imagine a night without her in his bed. "It's not your technique that needs polishing, honey girl."

"Oh?"

"Uh-uh," he said as he reached over and turned off the bedside light. "It's your expression. It gives everything away. Don't ever play poker," he advised. "At least not for money."

Her cheek pressed against his chest. "I'll keep that in mind." Silence reigned for all of two minutes before she piped up. "I don't suppose you'd be willing to give me lessons?"

"In playing poker?"

"Yes."

"We couldn't play for money," he said, keeping his tone neutral.

"Maybe we could ante up kidney beans?"

"No fun. Not interesting enough."

"Oh." One sigh of disappointment was all the warning he had before she closed the door on his plans. "As you said, I probably wouldn't be any good at it anyway."

Since when did his Jessie Girl give up?

"You'd just be bored," she added sighing again.

Not likely. Not if they played for the stakes he was working up to. "I'm sure I'd manage to enjoy myself," he countered.

"No. You're right. Someone of your experience would be bored teaching a newbie."

Her fingers stroked the side of his neck. Her breath came in slow even passes, in no way preparing him for the solution she came up with.

"I heard Rafe talking about a game the other day. Maybe he'll teach me."

"No need to bother Rafe," he interjected quickly. That's all he needed, Jessie going to the young and handsome Rafe for her lessons. One "I dare you" and she would be engaged with another in the very game he was trying to coax her into.

"Rafe seems very patient. I'm sure he won't mind."

Mac was sure he wouldn't either, but then he'd have to beat the man for poaching on his woman, and since Rafe was a friend, he really didn't want to go that route. "I've thought of a way to teach you, and to make it interesting."

"And how's that?" she asked, tilting her head back and meeting his gaze with total trust. The perfect lamb to slaughter.

He touched her lower lip where his teeth had nipped. She'd be something, all bare from paying up, and all ticked off from losing. His breath caught as his voice roughened with the effort to speak normally. "We could play strip poker."

"Well, I don't know..."

"It would be fun." He smoothed his finger over the skin under her chin, loving the way it felt against his finger. Soft, smooth. Addictively smooth. So different from his.

"For you maybe, considering you have all this experience, but I probably wouldn't win a game."

"I'm sure you'll do fine after a few practice hands."

"When do you want to do this?"

"Tomorrow's Sunday. How about we get started after church?"

She dipped her chin and caught his finger in her mouth, sucking on it before asking, "Don't you find it a little reprehensible to be planning a strip poker date for immediately following church?"

Her mouth was hot and wet around his finger. If her eyelids weren't dropping faster than her words were forming, he might have tested out his creativity, but she needed holding more than she needed loving. He slid his finger a little deeper, pressing down on her tongue, making her work just a little harder. "That depends. Does it turn you on?"

She nodded, releasing his finger. Her cheek snuggled into the hollow of his shoulder.

"Then no."

She laughed softly. Lazily. Her breath came slower and deeper. "You are a shocking man, Mac Hollister," she whispered.

"But you love me anyway."

Her answer was a quiet little mutter, so low he wasn't sure he'd heard right. He spent the night debating whether those two syllables had been an "Uh-huh" or an "Uh-uh".

Chapter Ten

She was going to hell for sure.

Jessie shifted on the pew beside Mac, overly conscious of the drone of the Reverend's voice, of the respectable members of the church listening to the sermon, but most of all she was conscious of the solid presence of the butt plug inside her ass. She wiggled back, trying to ease the pressure. The base tapped the pew through the thin material of her skirt. Even though she knew the sound wasn't audible, she froze, heat climbing her cheeks. She cut a glare at Mac. Oh God, how had she let him talk her into this!

She knew how, and it hadn't had anything to do with talking but had a lot to do with his waking her up with his big hands holding her thighs apart and his hot tongue leisurely lapping at her vagina. Nurturing the response he wanted, making his demands when she was on the verge of climaxing, holding off, not giving her what she needed until she succumbed to his dare. The pews creaked as everyone stood for the final prayer. Even though the dark floral skirt she had on was knee-length she felt exposed without underwear on.

And while she might not go to hell for showing up in church with her rear stuffed and her privates naked, she was sure to go straight to hell for liking it so much. And Mac was going right along with her if she had to arrange it herself—for standing there so cool and composed as if he didn't know her pussy was so on fire and she thought she'd come the next time she sat down. And how she was going to avoid leaving a wet spot on her skirt and the pew she had no idea. She also had no idea where they were in the service. Her whole world consisted of arousal and her efforts to hide it, which, contrarily, aroused her more.

Mac's hand on her shoulder dragged her attention away from her battle. He leaned down to whisper in her ear, "Time to leave."

"Thank God!"

His laugh was low and seductive. Knowing. People started filing out of the pews, smiling indulgently at them, speculation in their gazes as they looked at the way Mac stood, his hand on her back, his body leaning over hers. She did her best to smile. It was hard knowing what she knew. What Mac knew. Oh damn! A small shiver snaked down her spine. She felt like a tart, and she just loved it.

They stood at the edge of the pew. Under the guise of moving with the line of parishioners leaving, Mac tucked himself against her back. The difference of their heights made it easy for him to press up with his leg. The pews hid his thigh's slow slide up the inside of hers until the front of his thigh pressed up between her legs. Finding the base of the plug. Nudging it. Sensation shot outwards, wrenching the strength from her knees. His arm came around her waist as he caught her against him. She gasped. His smile slide across her hair as he asked, "Hungry, honey girl?"

"Starving."

He kissed the top of her head. "Good."

It was their turn to go. She smiled weakly at the elderly gentleman who motioned her ahead. She heard Mac call him by name, his hand on the small of her back urging her forward as the two exchanged pleasantries. The exchange passed over her head as so much background noise. She only had one focus. Getting to the pickup without embarrassing herself. To avoid waddling, she had to clench down on the plug which only invited more of that pinching pleasure that had her melting.

Across the way, she saw Zach heading toward them. "No chatting, Mac."

He had the gall to sound shocked. "Jessie, you can't just pray and run. There's a whole social network to attend to."

Zach was almost upon them, looking very Indian with the breeze from the open door blowing his black hair across his face. She just couldn't picture the man as a small-town attorney. He radiated a primitive energy that said this was a big shark who should be swimming in a very big pond. As he got closer, his dark eyes flicked over her face. He frowned, looked at Mac, and then back to her. Two seconds later, a wholly masculine smile took his face from handsome to virile as he laughed. In her current state, it was impossible not to notice the breadth of his shoulders and the sheer sexuality he oozed as he winked. She jerked her gaze away.

"Today you need to attend to me," she told Mac firmly under her breath. If he didn't, she was apparently going to jump the nearest man and have her way with him.

She felt Mac's gaze on her, but didn't look up. The fingers in the small of her back stroked lightly. "You can count on that."

He stepped to the side as Zach reached them, draping his arm across her shoulders. "Howdy, Zach."

"Hey, Mac." He nodded to Jessie. "Miss Sterns."

Jessie could have shot Mac for remembering his manners. "Jessie this is my best friend, Zach Lone Tree."

There was nothing to do but hold out her hand. "It's nice to meet you. And please call me Jessie."

His big hand swallowed hers. His fingertips slid over the inside of her wrist before he let go. The smile in his eyes deepened, making her wonder if he felt her accelerated pulse as he drawled, "The pleasure is all mine."

She blushed, though there was no way in hell he could know what Mac had gotten her into. Mac tucked her into his side, dropping a kiss on the top of her head. "You met Zach's brother the first few minutes after you hit town."

"You're Homer's brother?" The shock in her tone probably wasn't appropriate. Zach winced and shrugged resignedly.

"Yup. But I'm not exactly advertising it at the moment."

Her "I hope he finds a job soon" was heartfelt.

Zach laughed, a rich, deep masculine sound that slid across her nerves like warm honey. "You and the rest of the family. I'm sorry to hear about your arm."

"Thanks."

Zach turned his attention back to Mac, "I've got to go meet Granny Ortiz, but I just want to check on what we talked about. Still a go?"

"Definitely."

Zach nodded to Jessie. "It was nice to meet you."

"You, too." With a last nod of his head he was off. Jessie breathed a sigh of relief. Through the church door she could see the pickup across the huge, sprawling field that made up the front lawn of the church. Why in hell had she let Mac park so far away?

She tugged his arm. "Let's go now."

His smile was pure sin as he asked, "Are we in a hurry?"

"Yes!" She moved him three steps forward before the next person waylaid them. Grinding her teeth, she forced her hormones under wraps while another round of polite conversation took place. Just one more, she told herself only to realize there were a lot of one mores walking their way. She closed her eyes and prayed for strength, taking it as a good sign when a bolt of lightning didn't strike her dead for the audacity.

*****

She was in a frenzy by the time they got to the truck. Mac had stopped to chat with what seemed like every resident in the county. As a result, they were almost the last ones to leave. The only other car parked on their side of the field was another pickup truck, two car lengths down. Her pussy was gushing so much cream her thighs were soaked. Her ass was a raw ache of unfulfilled torment and she was close to tears. When Mac opened the passenger door to help her up, she almost sobbed out loud.

"Easy, Jess." When she would have climbed into the cab, he stopped her.

"What?"

In answer, his big hands came around her shoulders and his fingers made short work of unbuttoning her loose shirt and unclipping her bra. With a brush of his fingers he slid the cups to the side. The sun was warm on her exposed breasts. It only added to the feeling of wicked decadence she'd been caught up in all morning.

"Mac?"

She looked over her shoulder. He motioned her forward. "Kneel up on the seat."

"I don't understand." She just wanted to get home and get off.

His large hand on her butt gave her a boost. "Kneel on your hands and knees on the seat."

She looked over her shoulder again. "Why?"

He lifted her up so that she had no choice, supporting her left side until she got her balance. "Because I want it. Be careful of your arm."

Even thought they'd left the windows open the interior of the truck was hot. It smelled of leather and Mac. Earthy. Masculine. The sun-warmed upholstery was soothing against her palm and knees. She felt a warm breeze between her thighs and gasped. "What are you doing?"

Mac draped her skirt in the small of her back. "Seeing if you've been good." He touched the slick interior of her thighs. "Oh, yeah. You've been very good."

Yes, she had and she deserved a reward. She pushed back with her hips. Out of the corner of her eye, she saw the Reverend's car pull away from the front of the church. That only left her and Mac, and whoever owned that black pickup.

Mac palmed her ass in one of his big hands, reclaiming her focus. She wiggled back against it. His fingers dipped to the crease, sliding down until they found the base of the plug. He tugged. Shivers of delight rippled down her legs and up her spine. Her head dropped between her shoulders. She struggled to breathe. To come. Her pussy clamped down on air. Oh, she wanted to come.

His finger slid into her hungry cunt. "Almost there, Jess?"

She nodded.

"Did it get you all excited sitting there in church with the plug I put in you filling your ass, and nothing between my hand and your flesh except that wispy skirt?"

She nodded.

His hand came down on her ass. She cried out in shock, his "I can't hear you" almost drowned out by the thundering anticipation of her heart in her ears.

Surely he wasn't going to spank her here, in public?

His palm came down on the other cheek. The sting ripped through her with the ferocity of a summer storm, rich with the promise of relief, but too fast-moving to actually deliver. She closed her eyes against the torment.

"Did you get all excited in church, Jessie?" he asked again, punctuating the questions with a harder slap.

"Yes!"

The next smack came swift and sharp, covering both cheeks and the base of the plug. Her head snapped up as the impact set off titillating vibrations deep inside her channel.

"Good girl."

She thought he'd stop then, part of her relieved and part of her equally disappointed that her fantasy of a public spanking would come to a halt so soon.

She should have known better. He'd warned that he liked spanking her, and apparently he did, because he didn't stop, just settled into a soft, relentless rhythm that had her breasts swinging and had her pushing back, begging for more, pleading for those smacks that caused the plug to work inside her. His blows picked up speed, heating her ass in time with her respirations, her spanking coming in short, rapid thrums of stinging delight that held her on the edge. She arched her back, offering more. He didn't take it. Just laughed low and deep in his throat and kept to his rhythm. The muted thwack of his hand meeting her flesh filled the interior of the car, echoing in her ears, blending with her whimpers. Every sound, every delicious sensation amplified by the fact that she kept her eyes closed.

"Goddamn it, Mac," she sobbed through her clenched teeth after a particularly tormenting flurry. "If you don't let me come, I'm going to kill you."

He laughed again. "Open your eyes, Jess."

She did, ready to blast him, but froze in shock as she looked through the driver's side window. Leaning against the side of the black pickup was Zach. His pants were unzipped, and in his hand was his very large, very engorged cock.

Oh God! How long has he been standing there?

"Give him a smile, honey girl," Mac ordered.

She couldn't. Even though this was one of her fantasies come to life, it was too shocking, too embarrassing to be caught like this.

Across the distance Zach smiled, his teeth very white in his dark face. His expression a strange mix of gentle understanding and rampant lust as he cupped his wide shaft in his palm, ran his thumb across the crown, and said, "I'm not seeing a smile, Mac."

Mac's hand connected harder with her ass. She cried out, and threw her head back, absorbing the shock through her system, letting it blend with her pleasure, driving her lust higher. Increasing her need.

"Oh, that felt good, didn't it?" Zach asked, his voice pitched low and intimate. His hand on his cock, stroked firm and sure. "Let me hear that sweet little cry again." He looked over her head at Mac. "Heat that ass nice and sweet. Let me see those pretty breasts swing. Make her burn for me."

Mac did, taking him at his word, making her cry out repeatedly with the stinging pleasure.

And every time Mac's hand came down on her cheeks, Zach's hand pumped his cock. Every cry she made brought a shiny bead of come to the head. Bead after bead came to tempt her, to quiver on the tip before being swept away on another. She licked her lips.

"Oh yeah," Zach moaned, throwing his hips into his hand, spearing that shaft through his fingers, toward her, letting her see how turned on he was. How close he was to coming. "Lick those lips. Thrust those hips back," he groaned. "C'mon, sweetheart. Let me see how hot your ass is. How much you liked getting spanked."

As if she had any choice with Mac directing her passion, and her fantasy coming true before her eyes. Jessie couldn't take her gaze from Zach's cock as it jerked and swelled in his dark hand, spilling pre-come over his fingers in a steady stream as Mac filled the air with the sounds of his slaps and her pleasure. Her pussy throbbed with a relentless demand. Her anus struggled to clench around the thick plug, milking the hard base as if she had some control of anything.

She dropped her head as Mac picked up the pace to an almost blinding speed. She could no longer take a breath between the spanks. Her breasts shook and swung back and forth with her body. The line between pain and pleasure blurred until there was nothing left but an empty clawing hunger for more. More spanks. More words. More pleasure. Just…more.

"Look at Zach, honey girl," Mac ordered, his voice tight and harsh. "Look what you're doing to him."

She looked. Zach's hand pumped his cock as fast as Mac spanked her ass, his mouth set in a tight line as he braced himself against the cab, his expression hard, intent. Brutally masculine. His eyes trained on her. Her breasts. Her mouth. Her fingers digging into the seat.

"He's almost ready to come," Mac grunted behind her as he ran a series of slaps down her thighs. "Don't you want to see him come?"

She whimpered, "Oh yes."

"Then you've got to come."

"What?"

"He won't come until you do."

Panic stole some of her rush, and she glanced over her shoulder at him. "But I can't without you. You know—"

"Hurry it up Mac," Zach called roughly, his head tipping back so he was looking down the length of his aquiline nose at her.

"Trust me, honey girl, you will," Mac said, his eyes a deep blue, his expression as hard and tight as Zach's.

"Spread your legs." She did, trying to gauge where his blows were going to land as she did, giving up when she realized there was no order for her to follow.

"Watch Zach," he ordered.

She did because she had no choice. It was either follow Mac's orders or exist in this perpetual arousal forever. Her ass burned, and her pussy ached as she focused on his pleasure, trying to transfer it to her own.

She was totally unprepared for Mac's next slap. It landed high on the inside of her thigh, snatching a shriek from her throat.

"Damn, she liked that," Zach groaned through gritted teeth, his long black hair blowing across his face as his head dropped back.

And she had, the sharp sting shooting through her clit, making it throb in eager anticipation. Three more light, quick blows crept up toward her pussy. It shouldn't have shocked when the fourth landed flat on the pad of her vulva—shouldn't, but did—nothing being able to prepare her for the unique sensation. The impossible searing burn that jack knifed her body. Nor the next landing squarely on her clit, causing her back to arch and making her scream with the agony of delayed release.

"Son of a bitch!" Zach cursed, his eyes locked on her straining body.

Jessie stared at him, panting as she struggled to contain the confusing rush of demands being made on her body. As she watched, Zach's cock jerked in his hands. His hips bucked and then a thick jet of creamy come erupted from the head of his impressive penis to spill onto the deep green grass.

She almost came then, her body jerking and bucking as Mac rained quick, precise slaps on her spasming flesh. She was close, so close…

"That's it," Mac crooned. "Come for me, honey girl. Take your pleasure. Watch what you do for him, and come for me."

But she couldn't.

Zach spurted again and again. Jessie was helpless to come, helpless to look away, helpless to stop sobbing as Mac massaged her tender clit, refusing to let her come down, keeping her on that razor-sharp edge of climax, trapped between heaven and hell. Finally, she had no choice—too much for too long making the decision for her. Her strength gave out. She collapsed onto the seat, dragging long, hard breaths into her starving lungs, uncaring of the steering wheel that bruised her shoulder.

Mac eased his hand from between her thighs. It slid down the front of her leg, coating her with her juices.

"Turn around, honey girl," he ordered softly, as if knowing she was on overload. She grunted, but didn't move. His hands on her shoulders pulled her back. She went, a formless puddle of unfulfilled womanhood. He merely sat her up. She lolled against the seat and cracked her eyes. "That was hotter than I imagined."

His smile was tender as he tucked her hair behind her ear. "I'm glad, but you didn't come."

"I couldn't."

He looked through the cab and out the window, the direction in which she was making a point not to look. "I think you wiped Zach out."

"I hope you know that I have no intention of ever looking at him again," she gasped through ragged breaths.

"Now that's going to complicate things."

"Why?"

"Because I see him often."

"Oh hell." She'd forgotten about that. Which meant for sure she'd be seeing him again, which Mac had known all along. She opened her eyes a little wider. "You planned this?"

At least that explained why they'd parked way over here.

"We discussed it."

"You discussed it?"

He touched her lip before easing her down on the seat so she was lying on her uninjured side with her head by the open door. "You don't think I'd hunt up strangers, do you?"

"Well I didn't think you'd choose someone you knew!"

He smiled that bad boy grin before leaning over and kissing her mouth tenderly. "I would never risk you to a stranger, honey girl." He unzipped his suit pants and slid them down a little. Pulling his cock out, he rested its heavy weight on the seat in front of her face. He was wondrously hard. Thick.

"Open your mouth."

She did, letting the crown slide gently in, snuggling the broad head against her tongue as he worked it past her teeth.

He touched her cheek. She opened wider. He pushed deeper. She suckled him gently, eagerly, loving the salty taste that slowly spread into her mouth as his excitement increased.

The driver's side door opened. She jerked. Mac placed his hand on the side of her head, keeping her put.

"Just suck my cock, Jessie."

Her skirt was lifted. A draft of warm air caressed her skin as a broad palm slid over her buttocks.

"She didn't come?" Zach asked in his deep voice.

Oh God. Jessie wanted to sink into the floor. At the same time she wanted to press into his broad fingers when they dipped into the crease of her ass. She didn't do either.

"We're working on it," Mac grunted, his touch on her cheek steady and soothing, guiding her through the embarrassment.

Zach's fingers slid between her thighs, gliding easily through her slick folds, finding her engorged clit and pinching delicately.

"Oh, you're almost there aren't you, Jessie?" he murmured as she jumped and moaned at the light touch. "Just a little more is all you need."

Panic flared and her gaze flew to Mac's. She needed more than that. She needed Mac to come, but she'd die of humiliation if he told Zach that. And oh God, she needed to come.

Mac shook his head, and caressed the sensitive corner of her mouth. She'd never seen such a combination of lust and tenderness on a man's face before. Then, with a drift of his fingers, he closed her eyes.

Zach's hands slid back toward her vagina. She flinched.

Mac stilled and growled. Zach's low laugh filled the cab.

"Like that is it?"

The heel of Mac's hand pressed against her cheek and his hips shifted slightly as he shrugged. His thumb touched the corner of her mouth possessively.

"Looks like it."

Her skirt eased down over her legs as Zach said, "You always did have the devil's good luck."

Zach stroked her thigh. There was something akin to sadness in the touch. A hint of regret as his hand drifted down her calf and then off. The truck door closed. The unnatural stillness faded from Mac's stance as an engine roared to life. It wasn't until the truck drove away that she dared to look up.

Mac was gazing down at her, his expression serious as he pumped his cock in and out of her mouth. "There might be a hitch in knocking off the last item on that list," he told her gruffly.

She raised her eyebrows at him.

"I find I'm a little too possessive of you to share."

If she could have smiled, she would. Instead she opened her mouth wider, shifted the angle of her neck lower so she could take him deeper.

"I take it you don't mind?"

She shrugged and rolled her eyes. It was a little hard to talk at the moment.

He laughed and slid his hand behind her head, pulling her closer as he leaned forward. His thick cock forced her jaws even further apart as the bulbous head hit the back of her throat. She choked. And struggled.

He backed off, smoothing his fingers over the muscles in her throat. "Shh, honey girl." His fingers came to rest against her neck. "Just relax."

She breathed through her nose as he massaged her throat. The spasm subsided. He slipped his cock from her mouth.

It pulsed just beyond her lips. Hard. Hot. Full.

"Have you ever done this before?"

"Oh, for heaven's sake!" She rolled her eyes.

"Well?"

"Why do we always have to go through this true confession thing every time we make love?" She kissed the tip of his cock, tickling the slit with her tongue. His harshly drawn breath was music to her ears. She did it again.

He shook his head at her, the right corner of his mouth kicking up in a smile as he backed his cock out of her reach.

"Have you?"

She frowned at the distance between his cock and her mouth, then up over his broad chest to the determined expression on his handsome face. And sighed. He clearly wasn't going to give her what she wanted until she 'fessed up. "Only with you."

"Ah."

"What does 'ah' mean?"

"Ah means I understand."

She got her elbow under her side. "What's to understand?"

He tried to hold her down, but she was done being passive. She managed to rise up an inch. The smile on his face broadened.

"You haven't answered my question," she pointed out.

"I'm not intending to."

He tucked her hair behind her ear, the calluses on his fingers rasping the sensitive flesh. "I want your mouth, honey girl."

Oh God, when he said things like that to her in that slow, deep drawl that slid over her nerves like a lingering caress, she was helpless to do anything except shiver and give him what he wanted. Which right then was her mouth. On his cock. She looked at the beautiful organ sitting right before her. So tempting. Oh yes, she had no trouble giving him that.

She leaned in. He took a step forward. And they both had what they wanted.

"Ah, that's good," he moaned as she tongued the broad head, swirling around the perimeter, flirting with the slit. "Just like that, Jess. Just use your mouth. Nothing more. Just that sexy, hot little mouth. Suck it, honey girl. Let me feel you suck it, soft and sweet."

She did. Gladly. She loved the way he played with her. Shared with her. Gave her what she wanted. Let her be what she wanted. And he did it with complete ease, as if he didn't know how precious that was to her.

She held him gently in her mouth, being as tender as possible, judging from the tension in his hands and the break in his breath whether she was doing it right. He wrapped his fingers in her hair and braced one forearm against the top of the truck.

"Harder now, Jessie." His voice was rougher than normal as he began to pump gently. "Suck me harder as I pull out. Swirl your tongue over me when I come in."

She did. His big body shook. She glanced at his face. He definitely liked this. She had power over him like this. The same power he wielded when he worked his magic on her. And she knew why he liked it now. It was a heady experience gifting someone's pleasure. His hips moved faster. She struggled to keep up, finally just resorting to a steady suction which he seemed to like just as much.

"Oh yeah, honey girl." His voice was a rasp of pleasure as he added, "Harder."

She gave him harder, he gave her deeper. She wanted to give him more. She remembered what he'd told her that day in the kitchen. She pulled her lips off her teeth. As he pulled back, she scraped them gently against his shaft.

He gave a shout. There was a stinging in her scalp as he jerked his hand free of her hair and grabbed the base of his cock. His head fell back and he groaned. Out of the corner of her eye, she saw his expression. For all the world he looked like a man stretched taut on a rack. And she was his instrument of torture. How fun.

She bobbed her head on him, taking him as far as she could, all the way down to the barrier of his hand. She tilted her head back and waited. Until he looked down. She held his gaze, smiling with her eyes as she set her teeth against him. And then slowly, deliberately, dragged her teeth up his length. All the way to the crown.

"Son of a bitch, Jessie, I'm going to come if you do that."

"I thought that was the plan." His cock muffled her words, but he got her point. He swallowed twice and frowned down at her.

"You don't have to do this."

She just smiled around his shaft, and waited.

"Ah, honey girl, you don't know what you're asking for."

His hand clenched on his shaft. His cock throbbed in her mouth. And she just waited. She knew what she wanted, but she wasn't going to beg, and she wasn't going to let him get all crazy and protective on her either. He made the tiniest move forward as if against his will. It was all she needed.

She sucked him in and let him out. Using her tongue and teeth to tempt him, bring him closer to that edge he thought she couldn't handle. He pumped harder, faster, but still she could feel the hesitancy in him. She worked her hand out from under her body and slid into the vee of his fly. He cursed again, but she was getting used to that. No longer thinking the worst when he did, she kept going until she could cup the heavy weight of his balls in her hand. He bucked against her.

When she squeezed his balls, it was gentle. Her mouth on his cock was not. There she made demands. Lapping and sucking and nibbling until he had no option but to give her what they both wanted. He came with a muffled shout of her name, his cock jerking and leaping, his seed a sudden salty wash over her tongue. Filling her mouth with his pleasure. His satisfaction. Letting her give him, just this once, something he gave her all the time. Unconditional acceptance. She stroked his cock, swallowed his seed and accepted the gift.

When it was over, he leaned into the truck, his hand on her cheek trembling with the aftershocks. He eased out of her mouth, chuckling at her moue of dissatisfaction. He turned her until her legs dangled off the end of the seat. She let her head loll back on the warm leather, ripples of satisfaction arching out over her body in ebbing waves. His calloused palms slid up her calves, over her knees, across her inner thighs, spreading her legs as he went. And then his cock was pressing, nestling into the well of her vagina.

"Relax for me, honey girl."

"Again?"

"Oh yeah. Again."

He forged into her, his stroke slow and smooth, every inch of his flesh a lingering caress. Almost a cherishing. His lips at her breasts were equally tender. His fingers swirling on her clitoris, gentle. It was sweet. So hot and sweet. She never knew sex could be so sweet. The desire from before pooled in her center, rising with each slow possession until it poured over her, flowing out from her core in a molten tide of need that caught his rhythm, fed off his desire. She wrapped her arms around his ribs and pulled him closer. She needed him closer. So close there wasn't a breath of air between them. So close there was no telling where he ended and she began.

Over and over he filled her with the thick weight of his shaft, taking her to the edge again, slowly, gently holding her there with the lightest of touches. And when she couldn't stand it anymore, when the pleasure stretched her so far out on a rack of pure grinding delight that she knew she'd shatter if he didn't help her, then and only then did he come for her, freely giving her what she needed, like he'd promised he always would. His rich seed drenching her in a warm rain of pleasure, sending her flying into the bliss beyond, her muscles clenching around him over and over. And through it all she held him close, smoothing her hands over his heaving ribs, loving the way he felt in her arms, the way he gave himself to her. For her. Just plain loving him.

A few minutes later, he braced himself on his elbows above her. Cupping her face in his hands, his thumbs smoothed over the corners of her mouth, her lower lip. His face was heavy with satisfaction, his lips full, his gaze intent. Still, she never saw it coming.

"Jessie?

"What?"

"I'm keeping you."

Chapter Eleven

He was keeping her. Oh yeah, Jessie snorted in disgust. Like a butterfly in a collection. A piece of porcelain under glass, he was "keeping her". Using her good hand, Jessie grabbed a chicken wing from the huge mound on the counter and lobbed it onto the cutting board. If Mac "kept her" any longer like he'd been keeping her for the last two weeks, she was going to go borrow Will's shotgun and fill the man's sexy ass with buckshot. Keeping her. Right.

Scooping up a butcher knife, Jessie hacked the chicken wings into two parts and tossed them into a big bowl. She wished she could hack through whatever Mac's issue was with the same ease. She tossed another wing onto the cutting board. The man was driving her crazy with his hovering and worrying. He'd been driving her nuts since she'd broken her arm, but she'd been too caught up at first in their sexual games to notice.

Or maybe he hadn't been so bad at first. She wasn't sure. She just knew that with every day that passed, Mac's protective urges encroached more on her space. And she'd about had her fill. This time, she severed the joint so hard the wing went sailing across the kitchen. Damn, that was the tenth one this morning. At this rate, she wasn't going to have enough buffalo wings to feed two hands, let alone the ten she was expecting at supper tonight.

As she bent to retrieve the errant wing from the floor, a movement behind the screen door caught her attention. The scuffed tops of well-worn brown boots covered by the frayed ends of equally worn jeans showed above the jamb. As she stood, she followed the path of those jeans up over strong lean thighs, a huge belt buckle setting off lean hips, and a narrow waist that quickly veed out to a broad chest and even broader shoulders. When she reached her full height she was still a good foot shorter than the man before her so she tipped her head back and let her eyes journey the rest of the way. As she met Will's slate-gray eyes, it hit her that for all he had to be in his late forties, he was still a very masculine man.

"Hi, Will. What's up?" she asked as he took off his hat and stepped inside. "Is something wrong?"

He paused and raised his eyebrows at her. "Why would you think anything's wrong?"

Jessie checked her watch as she tossed the piece of meat into the trash can. "Because it's ten in the morning, and in all the time I've been here, no one's come knocking at the back door before lunch."

He nodded toward the clunky cast on her forearm. "I just thought I'd see how you were doing, and if you needed any help."

"Was this your idea or Mac's?"

The hat in his hand started a slow rotation. He watched it spin a second before casting a glance from under his dark brows. "A little of both. Until Suzie can get over here to help on a regular basis, someone will be checking in regularly."

Jessie wasn't buying that for a minute. Help with the two-handed stuff was going to be great, and the teen they'd hired was a nice young woman, but she was doing fine in the interim with easy-to-cook one-handed meals.

"Mac sent you to check on me, didn't he?"

Will's shrug was technically neither a "yes" nor a "no".

"What does he think is going to happen to me?"

Something flickered in Will's gaze. Something that told her he knew more than indicated by his noncommittal, "Things go wrong all the time."

"Will," Jessie asked, "how would you like a cup of coffee?"

His mouth twitched at the corners as he cocked his head to the side. "You plan on bribing me for information?"

"Is there a chance it will work?"

"Depends."

"On what?"

"You got any of those doughnuts left over from breakfast?"

"Yup."

"Then I'd say there's a fair to middlin' chance of success." With a flip of his wrist, he tossed his hat onto a hook in the wall.

The feat never ceased to amaze Jessie. "You know, one of these days, you're going to let me in on the secret of how you do that."

The smile in his eyes deepened as he strolled to the counter. "It's a gift."

"Uh-huh."

He poured two cups of coffee and sat down at the table. Taking a sip, he raised an eyebrow at her as she stood. It was a purely masculine move and she was struck anew just how attractive a man Will was. And that aura of competence he radiated just added to his appeal, backing his rugged good looks with an invite to trust.

"Just give me a second to clean up here, and I'll be right with you."

She put the chicken wings in the refrigerator. Slipping on some rubber gloves, she washed up the few utensils she'd used, and the cutting board. The gloves came off with a decisive snap as she grabbed the container of doughnuts from the cupboard. At last, she was going to get some answers. Will snatched a doughnut as soon as she put the container on the table.

"So why has Mac decided I'm suddenly incompetent?"

She had to wait until he finished the first bite for his response, and then it was an annoying evasion.

"What makes you think he feels that?"

"The fact that he won't talk to me about anything."

Will's eyebrows rose again. "Like what?"

"Like what killed that cow two days ago."

Will demolished the rest of his doughnut and took a sip of coffee. "Any one of a number of things could have killed that cow, none of them anything to get upset about."

She resisted the urge to kick his shins under the table. She added cream and sugar to her coffee in an effort to make it palatable. "But there's something about how this one died that has Mac upset."

Will's eyelids flickered, and his smile took on a tight edge as he reached for another doughnut.

"And you too, apparently," she added.

He paused and then grabbed the doughnut. "Mac said you were observant."

"So why do you all continue to treat me as if I were dumb?"

"Probably an effort not to worry you."

"What if I like to be worried?"

"Then I'd say you were the perverse sort."

She shrugged and stirred her coffee. "Or maybe just concerned?"

"Maybe."

"So what's killing the cows?"

Will shrugged. "Don't know yet."

"What does Mac think is killing the cows?"

"Why don't you ask him that?"

"Because he won't tell me."

"Why not?"

"Because he has this strange idea in his head that it isn't something I should be concerned with." The bottom of her cup hit the table with a clunk.

"And you don't agree with him?"

"No. I don't. Since he expects me to share everything with him, the reverse should hold true."

"Have you told him that?"

"Yes."

Will chuckled. "Didn't get anywhere, did you?"

"No. He keeps distracting me."

"Now, that doesn't surprise me."

It had surprised Jessie. She'd never thought she'd be the type who could be seduced off course, but apparently, she was. And the smile in Will's eyes let her know he guessed the reason behind her red cheeks.

"Well," she huffed on the defensive where before she'd been prepared to attack, "It's not my fault the man's so determined to get what he wants."

"Seems to me you could match him for stubborn. Maybe even teach him a few new inflections to put to the word."

Jessie slouched back in her chair. "It's disgusting, isn't it? Here I am, a modern woman. Intelligent, capable, and all that man has to do is whisper sweet nothings in my ear, and I put off a perfectly reasonable discussion in favor of…other things." She blew a hair off her hot face. "Single-handedly, I've probably put the woman's movement back fifty years."

"Now, that might be an exaggeration."

"Only might?"

"Well, you have been remarkably docile of late."

Jessie shuddered and reached for her cup. "Perish the thought."

Will grabbed a doughnut hole and popped it into his mouth. He chewed slowly, making Jessie wait for the advice she knew was coming. "So, you about ready to come out of your haze?"

"I'm not sure."

"Oh."

She grimaced as Will went back to his munching. "That 'I'm not sure' was rhetorical."

Will grinned. A slow, masculine "someone's in trouble" grin. Getting information out of these men was like pulling teeth. Jessie flopped back in her chair. "So, are you going to tell me what's up with these cows, or what?"

"Or what."

"Why are you all dancing around this?"

Will swallowed. "Well, for my part, since I'm not the one you should be asking, I don't think I'm the one who should be answering."

Since she didn't think a "been there, done that" comment would impress Will, she settled for the truth.

"I'm asking you because as of yet, I haven't convinced Mac that a relationship means sharing the good as well as the bad."

Will brushed off his hands. "But word is you're planning on marrying the man."

"He says he's keeping me." She ran her finger around the rim of her stoneware mug. "Not quite sure that's the same thing."

Will's grin was a quick flash of white. "Oh yeah. That's the same."

She met his gaze squarely. "Then I guess I'm going to have to change his mind about how relationships work."

"You think you can do that?"

"I have every confidence in Mac's ability to see reason."

He put his cup carefully on the table, all trace of amusement gone. "That might take a lot of convincing."

Jessie shot him a startled glance. "And here I thought I was imagining his being overprotective."

"Nope. He's all set to wrap you in a nice warm place where nothing bad can ever hurt you."

She shuddered. "God forbid!"

He cocked an eyebrow at her. "Not your style?"

"No way." She'd spent too many years losing her life doing the right thing. She didn't begrudge one moment of the time she'd spent caring for her mother, but she wasn't going to lose anymore of her life for any reason. All she said to Will, however, was, "Too boring."

"But safe," Will elaborated. "And to Mac, keeping his loved ones safe is everything."

"Well..." Jessie took a sip of her coffee, grimacing at the taste. No matter how much she diluted the stuff, it still tasted like mud. "Playing it safe isn't particularly my strong suit."

"No, it isn't." Will shrugged. "And therein lies the problem because you scare the pants off Mac."

"Because I like to have fun?"

"Because you are willing to take chances in pursuit of fun, and it's going to drive that boy crazy if he doesn't get a handle on how he feels about that."

"I'm not mindless about it."

"Doesn't matter."

Jessie ran her finger around the rim of her cup, noticed her nail polish was chipped and pointed out, "I'd bake a cheesecake for the man who can tell me why 'safe' is so all-important to him."

"With sour cream icing?"

"With sour cream icing."

"I suppose I can reveal a few secrets for that kind of bribe."

Jessie shook her head and smiled ruefully. "Especially as you were planning on it anyway?"

Will smiled back. "Does make it a lot easier."

She didn't take offense. She'd bake five cheesecakes to get the kind of answers she needed.

"Mac's childhood wasn't easy. It was pretty tough, as a matter of fact. His mom was always drifting in and out of reality on him and his dad blamed it all on the fact that she came from the city."

"From the bits Mac has revealed, it sounds like she might have suffered from depression."

"Well, nobody called it that, but I would say so. She would swing from crazy happy to soul deep sad. Never knew which way the wind was going to blow in that house." He took a drink from his cup. "Mac's father tried to stay home more, but times were tough, cattle prices were down, and he had to take on a second job just to make ends meet."

"Did she go to a doctor?"

Will snorted. "Sure she did. Jake, Mac's father insisted she go, but the damn fool quack told her to focus on her family and gave her a prescription that made sure she couldn't focus on anything."

"What happened?"

"Well, Mac was always the responsible sort. Since his brother was already off to college, he tried to step in."

Jessie could imagine that. Mac had a tendency to think he could organize the world. "It didn't help?"

Will sighed. "Nope. His helping just made it worse. Seemed like every responsibility he took over freed up more of his mother's time to either brood or celebrate."

The finality in Will's tone sent a shiver down Jessie's spine. "How did it end?"

"Mac came home from school one day and found his mom hanging from a rafter in the barn."

"Oh my God!"

Will caught her cup before it dropped from her nerveless fingers.

"That was about the reaction of the town."

Jessie took the cup from his hand. "Thank you."

In her mind, she pictured the scene. She'd lost a parent of her own under traumatic circumstances. It wasn't something a person forgot. And her mother's death had been from disease. She couldn't imagine coming home to find her mother dead by her own hand. She placed the cup on the table. It rattled with the shakiness of her grip.

"There's a reason for my telling you this," Will interrupted her thoughts.

It didn't take a genius to figure out what the reason was. "You want me to go easy on him."

"Hell no!" Will's cup thumped down on the table. She jumped, her gaze bouncing from his cup to his face. "I want you to come down on that boy like flies on—" He cleared his throat. "I want you to come down on that boy. It's time he understands that the past isn't the only way things can go."

His big hand touched hers, steadying her as he told her, "He needs to understand you're not her."

Oh yes, Mac definitely needed to understand that, but should she confront him over it or let him come to that knowledge on his own?

She took her cup to the sink. "Mac will probably figure that out for himself." Will's snort of disbelief was not encouraging.

She turned around and leaned back against the sink and confronted Will, who was leaning back in his chair looking at her with pity.

"You don't think he will? You're saying he's unreasonable?"

"I'm saying he's determined to make you happy and keep you safe which means, unless you're willing to keep stepping aside while he manages your life away to one monotonous day after another..." He paused and raised his brows.

No. She wasn't willing to do that. She shook her head.

He nodded. "Then you need to do something."

She braced her hands on the counter. "Maybe all Mac needs is a little time."

Will pursed his lips, sucked in a breath and let it out slowly before asking her, "How much time do you think you've got left to give him?"

"I can give Mac all the time he needs."

He was shaking his head before she finished the sentence. "You're fooling yourself, Jessie."

"Am I?"

"Yes."

"Well," she squeezed the counter with her hands. "I don't think so."

"Then how come you're standing in this kitchen at ten o'clock in the morning with the sun shining outside, talking to an old man?"

She rolled her eyes. Old man, her ass. On a testosterone scale from one to ten, Will would register an eleven. "Because I happen to like the 'old' man?"

"Is that it?" Will got up and headed for the back door. He paused at the threshold, grabbed his hat and settled it on his head. The brim shadowed his eyes, but nothing could hide the foreboding in his question as he looked at her and asked, "Or hasn't Mac left you any alternative?"

*****

He wasn't going to leave her an alternative. Jessie could tell the minute Mac came though the bedroom door at eight fifty-nine that evening. There was an aura of unease surrounding the man that she just couldn't ignore any longer. Unease mixed with determination. Nope. He definitely needed an attitude adjustment. As he paused in the doorway, she shifted on the bed and ran her foot up her leg, causing her silk nightgown to slide up her thighs. She had Mac's immediate attention.

He held up the small pile of chocolate kisses in his hand. "Were you afraid I'd get lost?"

She smiled, parting her thighs, giving him a glimpse of her shaved pussy and her well-greased anus. An anus that ached for his possession, but though he'd teased her with toys and plugs, he had yet to let her experience his cock. And she was dying for it. As per his instructions, she kept herself ready, but he never took her up on her constant offer.

She chuckled. "Just wanted to be sure that you got here with all possible speed."

Mac stopped dead, as that chuckle wove its way through his system, tapping into his pulse rate, kicking it up an extra three beats a minute as he moved toward the bed. Her little pussy with its mouthwateringly plump outer lips was pure temptation. Her ass cheeks below glistened with lube. As he watched, Jessie reached down with her good arm and pulled the right cheek away, letting him see the small rosy opening he coveted, shiny and eager, slightly reddened and swollen, letting him know she'd worn the plug as ordered. His cock surged to erection, stretching down his thigh, aching with want.

Oh, how he wanted. He wanted that firm little ass under his hips, hot and tingling from its spanking. He wanted to fuck that ass. Deep and hard. Make it his. He wanted the acceptance that came from a woman offering her man that ultimate trust. He wanted her cries as he took her. All of them. The uncertain ones and the joyous ones that would come as his hard cock won the battle and sank into that dark, tight channel for the first time. He wanted it like Hell on fire and he was about done waiting. He unwrapped a kiss as he reached the bed. Jessie stopped him from popping it into his mouth with a shake of her head.

"What?"

"You can either eat that kiss or trade it in on an original."

"A Jessie original?"

"Uh-hmm."

He dropped the kiss on the table. He leaned over her as she lay back and linked her arms around his neck, taking him with her.

"I love the way you smell," she murmured, burying her nose in his neck. "Pure heaven with a touch of soap."

"You don't smell so bad yourself." He levered his body over hers. "Warm, willing woman, spiced with," he sniffed and smiled, "cinnamon."

He worked two fingers into her ass as his mouth came over hers. Her cry of surprise echoed against his lips. Damn. She was still tight. He only made it to the first knuckle before he had to stop. "Relax, honey girl."

He sucked her tongue into his mouth, playing with it as she flexed around him. Then with a sigh, she eased.

"That's it," he encouraged, nibbling on her lower lip as his fingers slid deeper. "Relax and take me." He pushed hard.

"All the way," he groaned as his fingers sank to the hilt. She whimpered against his mouth. She grimaced and panted, the fingers of her right hand sank into his hair, yanking as her hips pushed up, forcing his knuckles into the soft globes. The cast on her left arm rasped across his shoulder, reminding him of her recent injury. Damn, he was an insensitive bastard.

"Easy, honey girl," he whispered regretfully, pulling his fingers free. "I'm sorry."

Her eyes popped open. Desire was replaced with a frown, and beneath her lowered brows her green eyes glittered with anger. "I'm just about as sick of this game as I am the other."

"What game?"

"This 'tease Jessie's ass but never deliver' game."

He kissed her gently, but she twisted her mouth away. It was his turn to frown. "It's not a game, Jessie. If you're not ready, you could get hurt."

"I'm ready. I don't care if it hurts. My ass is so ready I'm going to come as soon as your cock touches it. How much readier do I have to be?"

He touched the pleat between her brows. "A lot more—and I care."

Her chin tucked mutinously. "Then uncare."

Her good hand wiggled down between them, skimming his chest until coming to a halt where his hips pressed into the side of hers. He was close enough to hear her teeth grind as she realized she couldn't reach her goal.

He was not far away enough to avoid her plea.

"I want your cock, Mac. I want it deep in my ass. I want you to fuck me with that beautiful cock until I'm raw and walk bowlegged for a week. I want you to come so hard and high in me so many times that I'll be wet for days. I want to give myself to you that way. I want you to take me that way. I want it so badly I'm about to scream with frustration."

His heart slammed against his chest as he pictured it. Damn, he wanted that too. His cock jerked and begged and leaked with enthusiasm for the idea. But she was so small and tight and so recently hurt. He just couldn't risk bringing her anymore pain.

The only answer he had for her was, "When you're ready."

She screamed, a deep harsh sound, and pushed at him. He moved away, but only because it suited his needs. He unzipped his jeans and shoved them down as the cry echoed around them. Lifting his cock, he settled the head against the wet nub of her clitoris. The cry choked off to a sob as he rubbed the slick crown against her.

"There, honey girl. Can you feel how hard and hot I am? Don't think for one minute I don't want that tight little ass. I'll give you all that you want and more, but not today. Not right now."

"I mean it Mac, I'm sick of this protective crap." Even as she argued, she rubbed her hips in counterpoint to his movements, fucking her little clit on the head of his penis.

He kissed her again. "I know, honey girl." He maneuvered her so her clit rode the groove, making them both gasp. She cried out and banged her cast on his back as he asked, "How's that? Do you like that, Jessie? Can you feel my seed on you?"

"Oh yeah, baby. Just like that," he muttered as her pace became frantic. Focused. He watched her expression change. Her eyes narrowed. Her cheeks flushed, and her pupils dilated as she sought relief. Relief she only took from him. Damn, she was wildly beautiful like this.

His balls pulled up tight as he bent down to nibble on her nipple. Taking the plump bud between his teeth he sucked gently, giving her all the tenderness he felt inside until she thwacked him with her cast again, making him smile at her impatience. He sucked harder before slowly, deliberately, sinking his teeth into the resilient nubbin.

He let it go with a gasp as her hand wiggled between his legs. He drew a steadying breath and then released it on a tight sigh. Nothing had ever felt as good as Jessie's hand on his body. She faltered, misinterpreting his hesitation.

"Touch me," he encouraged as her fingers grazed his scrotum. "That's right. Work those sweet hips faster and touch me. Just like that. Come on, Jessie, take it."

Her cool hand cupped his balls. She squeezed and pressed behind them. Lights splintered beneath his eyelids as the pleasure built to an unbearable pressure. "Make me come, baby. I need you to make me come. I need you to take my seed. Make me come, Jess," he groaned. "Make us both come."

And she did. Her grip tightening to the point of pain as her hips jacked up into his. He came in a burning vocal rush, his seed rushing up his penis in an explosive flow of volcanic need. She screamed again, this time with pleasure as her orgasm convulsed her.

They both watched as jet after jet of hot, thick seed erupted over her throbbing clit, flowing over her outer lips and seeping between. He held his cock against her, letting the last drops dribble against her the way she liked. Instead of relaxing, her hips pressed against him, forcing her clit back into the fleshy protection of her pussy. He replaced his cock with his fingers.

"Do you need to come again, honey girl?" he asked against her breast, as she whimpered in response to his gentle caress. "Does all the hot come covering your pussy turn you on?"

Her chin bumped the top of his head as she nodded.

He nipped her nipple, smiling when she jumped and then pressed her chest closer. The freckle on her left breast caught his eyes. He kissed and licked it before meeting her gaze. "Then come for me, Jess. Relax into me and come for me again."

He slid his cock into her still pulsating channel. Conscious of how sensitive her little clit was post-orgasm, he rubbed delicately, sucking steadily at her nipple. Taking care that the calluses on his fingertips did little more than graze the knot of nerves, he circled the swollen tip. And she came again. Easier this time, gentler, her body turning into his, trusting him to take care of her, to know what she needed. Her cry of satisfaction was a sweet, soothing balm to his unease.

*****

Dammit! Jessie thought ten minutes later, her head on Mac's chest, her cast resting below his rib cage. He'd done it to her again. "You have to stop doing this, Mac."

"Doing what?"

Beneath her cheek his heart changed rhythm, beating faster and harder. Oh, the man was nervous. "You've got to stop seducing me whenever you don't like what I have to say."

"I have no idea what you're talking about."

"Like hell." Jessie pushed up until she could see his face. From where she lay Mac looked particularly dangerous. Dangerous and determined. She thought of her day, and grabbed tight to the resentment she found in the memory.

"I thought I'd go riding today."

"Yeah?" He picked up a strand of her hair and draped it over his fingers.

"Yeah." She mimicked his low drawl. "One of the hands told me Ladybug was sick."

"I'll check into it tomorrow."

Jessie leaned back but this expression didn't change. She had no idea if he suspected where she was heading, or if there was any reason for him to suspect anything. It really could all be coincidence. "Seems there's not another horse on this ranch available for me to ride."

"This is a working ranch, honey, not a dude ranch." He twirled the strand of hair around his finger.

"That's what I was told." In those exact words, which was what was making her so suspicious.

The next twirl was never completed, and the faint hope that Will had been wrong died an immediate death when he wouldn't meet her gaze. Mac was doing it on purpose.

"When I decided to go into town, I discovered the station wagon is still out of commission."

"I'll get someone on it immediately."

"Just how long does it take to replace a cap and rotor?"

"Apparently, more than a day."

"How about two weeks, Mac, because that's how long it's been since my fall from Billy Bob?" The satisfied smile disappeared from his face.

"Are you getting at something here?"

Jessie took a deep breath. "I was thinking you could tell me."

"Tell you what?"

"Tell me why, no matter what I want to do, it's not possible?"

He blinked. "You've lost me."

Oh she didn't think so. That slight narrowing of his eyes told her all she needed to know.

"You know what I'm talking about, Mac." Jessie sat up. "After I got this," she held up her cast, "things between us changed."

"I don't know what you're talking about."

Jessie snorted. "Yes, you do. Somehow, breaking my arm broke the equality in our relationship, and I want to know why."

The mattress dipped as Mac sat up beside her. Even sitting he was much taller than she, and despite the fact that he was fully clothed with his pants undone and that cock—that beautiful cock—lying thick and relaxed against his thigh, he did not look ridiculous. He looked exactly like what he was. A force to be reckoned with.

"Mind telling me why all this," with a sweep of his hand he indicated the bed, and her lacy peignoir, "if all you really wanted to do was rake me over the coals?"

Jessie brushed the stab of guilt aside. "I thought you ought to know what it felt like."

Mac's eyes narrowed. "Like what felt like?"

"I thought you ought to know what it felt like to be sexually manipulated."

"Uh-huh. Is that what all the screaming you were doing a few minutes ago was? Sexual manipulation?"

She ignored the heat that crept into her cheeks. "Well, that part didn't quite work out, but yeah, that was what I was aiming for."

His smile was patronizing. She ignored it as she slid off the bed. They were more eye to eye with her standing. "You've been shamelessly using my body against me ever since you found out I was brainless enough to let you."

Mac looked pointedly down to her thighs, which glistened with his seed and her juices. "But you aren't anymore?"

"No, I'm not. Moreover, I want to know why you've been working so hard to keep me trapped in this house."

"You make it sound like I've got you under lock and key."

"Close enough."

Mac ran his hand through his hair, making the chocolate-colored strands stand on end. Jessie curled her fingers into her palm to resist the urge to smooth it down for him.

"Look, Jessie, I'm sorry there wasn't a horse available for you to ride today. I'm sorry I didn't have a man to spare to finish up the work on the wagon, but," he shrugged, "that's just the way things are on a ranch." He reached forward and traced his finger down her cheek. "Things come up and plans get changed."

He was so full of crap. Now that her eyes were open she didn't need Will's words to recognize his prevarication. The way he watched his finger trail over her cheek was sexy, but it also allowed him to avoid her seeing his eyes, which kept her from seeing the truth, so when he suggested in that easy-going drawl that they both go in to town tomorrow, she merely shrugged and asked, "What if I want to go alone?"

"What if I want to go with you?"

She put her hands on her hips and asked outright. "Why would you want to?"

He tapped the end of her nose reprovingly. "Because I enjoy spending time with you and you aren't the only one who could use a break?"

Well hell, where was she supposed to go with that? She searched his eyes, his posture, looking for anything that said he had an ulterior motive, but there wasn't anything obvious. She blew a strand of hair off her forehead. There wasn't anything at all, which meant she either forced the scene or left things as they were and hoped enough had been said to get him thinking. As much as she'd just love to have this out, she was old enough to know that some things had to settle out for themselves. She grudgingly opted for the latter. "In that case, I'd love your company."

He tipped her chin up with his finger. His eyes searched her expression. Some of her dissatisfaction must have shown through because he said, "I told you life on a ranch is lonely."

Yes. He had. It was his number one fear. "I wasn't lonely, just bored."

"I want you to promise me you'll come to me when you get to feeling lonely and bored."

She put her hand over his. "I was just whining, Mac." She did her best Marilyn Monroe pout. "This damn cast has severely limited my fun."

Mac slid his hand around her neck and under her hair. Pressing the base of her skull, he tipped her face to the angle he needed for the descent of his mouth. "Not all your fun," he murmured into her mouth.

She relaxed her head into his palm. "No."

His fingers began a delicate massage of the nerve endings at the nape of her neck as he moved to the edge of the bed. "No, what?"

"No..." She swallowed hard. He brushed his lips over her eyes and slid his knee between hers. She couldn't get her lips around the words. "It hasn't limited all my fun."

His laugh wafted over her lips and down to the hollow of her throat where he paused, each breath he took, a torment of anticipation. "Did you want it to?"

She rested her hand and her cast on his broad shoulders. "No."

God, he had a wonderful mouth. She tilted her head back, shivers of delight spreading over her flesh as he lapped at the valley between her breasts. Mac slid his hands under her hips and moved her to the center of the bed before tugging her peignoir over her head.

"Good."

She watched as he scooted back and stood. He took off his clothes with calm efficiency, revealing all that hard muscle beneath. He was a beautifully put together man. Tall, with broad shoulders and enough muscle to make her mouth water, wanting to trace all those muscle cuts with her tongue, to sink her teeth into the bulges, especially his pecs. She'd really like to test his flesh there. He paused in shrugging the shirt off, his arms at his sides, the shirt draped behind his waist. She looked up. He smiled—he'd caught her eyes on him.

"See something you like?"

The heat in her cheeks let her know that she was blushing, but she didn't back down. "Yes."

His gaze flicked down to her chest, up to her cheeks and then his eyes locked on hers. "What?"

Well, she wasn't going to say it! "You just look good."

The shirt fell to the floor. "Not good enough. That was a pretty hungry look."

More heat in her cheeks, and more laughter in his gaze made her gather her courage. "I was thinking how much I'd like to bite you."

His cock jerked and lengthened in response to her defiant declaration. His smile took on a sensual cast as he shoved his pants down. "Where?"

She pulled her eyes from his swelling cock, which stretched halfway down his thigh. God, had she really taken all of that inside her? "On your chest."

He reached his hand out, and he placed her palm in his. He pulled her up until her chest rested against his. His palm slid around her back, supporting her as he ordered, "Do it."

She did, but not before teasing his nipple with her tongue and teeth. Waiting until his breath was coming in shaky gasps and his cock jerked against her thigh, she lapped her way up and in until her teeth rested against the curve of muscle beneath his collarbone. She opened her mouth. His breath caught. She let him feel her teeth, let the anticipation build, let his indrawn breath push the wedge of muscle harder into her mouth, let him wait until the last second before she bit down.

His hoarse shout rang above her head. His free hand came against her head, pulling her closer, prolonging the moment when she would have withdrawn. She indulged him, sucking at the firm muscle, trying to draw more into her mouth, and when frustrated by the tautness of his skin, laved him with her tongue. His cock stretched up. Struggling to reach her, thwarted by its sheer size. She caught it between her thighs and closed them around it. His chest jerked against her as she squeezed.

She looked up. He was staring down at her, his eyes hot blue flames of appreciation. Feeling bold and daring she released her grip. "Close your eyes."

His eyebrow kicked up, but he did as she asked.

"Keep them closed."

"Feeling bossy?" he asked, his body hard and tight, the muscles flexing with anticipation.

"Yup." She smiled as his muscles quivered and his cock jerked against her inner thighs. She hadn't known he would like to feel her teeth like that. She hadn't known he would let her take charge. Hadn't even known she would like taking charge, but now that she had, she was finding it a heady feeling. She moved to the left side of his chest and placed her mouth against his nipple. She smiled when he immediately shifted so her mouth was more centered. Again, he seemed to freeze as he waited. She didn't make him wait long. She lapped delicately and then bit sharply. He yanked back and then pressed forward, every muscle, every nuance begging for more. She gave him what he wanted, relishing her ability to do so. She smiled when a fine sheen of sweat broke out on his skin, and kept her thighs clenched, forbidding him movement.

"Witch." His drawl was a growl, low and menacing. A fine indication of how well she was pleasing him.

She let go of his chest, kissing the indentations her teeth had left in his flesh, liking her mark upon him. "Keep your eyes closed," she told him as she reached around him.

She opened the nightstand drawer. His big body pulled taut as he heard it slide.

"Honey girl..."

"Please, Mac?" She took his hands and put them behind his back. She didn't think he'd let her tie him. He was too dominant for that, but she could ask for his compliance. "Could you keep your hands here, and let me be in charge? Just for tonight?"

"Depends on what you're pulling out of that drawer."

The fact that his eyes were still closed and his hands still behind his back gave her the confidence to say, "Not good enough."

He paused and didn't answer for a long time. She could feel his internal struggle. Finally, he said, "What do you need?"

He used the word need. He'd promised to always give her what she needed. And he needed to start trusting her somewhere. "I need you to keep your eyes closed, your hands behind your back, and let me play."

"Do I get a safe word?"

"No." She smiled. "You just have to stand there and take it."

"Tough rules."

She shrugged, letting him feel her breasts rise and fall against his ribs as she did so. "You're a tough man."

His shoulders flexed and his pecs bunched and stretched as he locked his hands behind him. "Go ahead."

She kissed his chest lightly. "Thank you."

"Just remember, payback can be a bitch."

How cute. He was worried. "I'll keep it in mind."

She reached into the drawer and pulled out what she wanted. His head cocked to the side as if through hearing he could figure out which toy she'd selected.

"I think you're going to love this. I know I always do."

He frowned. "Jessie girl…"

He was worried, but he was also turned on. His cock was pumping pre-seminal fluid down her thighs in a flattering rhythm.

"I'm adding another rule. No talking."

His mouth opened and then shut. He settled his weight onto his heels. Passivity wasn't a role he was used to, so she scrambled up onto the bed before he could change his mind, placing her hand on his chest, not the least worried he'd fail to support her. She overbalanced as the mattress gave. He turned so that he caught her with his shoulder. She kissed his cheek. His whiskers tickled her lips. "Thank you."

His "You're welcome" was strained.

"I'm feeling wild tonight," she told him, stroking his shoulder and chest.

"So I noticed."

"My plan is to get you hot and hard—"

"Honey girl, I'm already there."

She nipped his lower lip. "You're not supposed to be talking."

She soothed the sting while he got past the need to respond, before continuing, "And then I want you to work that big cock all the way into my tight pussy and I want you to fuck me as hard and as fast as you can until I come." She ran her tongue over his inner lip. "You know the way I like but you're always afraid of giving to me?"

He tensed and frowned. She could hear the protest coming. "I know you're worried I'm too small, but Mac, I'm not. And since it's what I want, I'm not going to give you any choice."

His right brow kicked up arrogantly.

Her smile was just as arrogant. Behind his back she took the small bullet-shaped vibrator out of her left hand. The move wasn't as smooth as she would have liked as the cast impeded her grip, and she almost dropped it when the cord got caught around her fingers, but finally she had it securely in her right hand. She flipped the switch and the low hum commenced. He jumped when she touched it to his butt. His frown turned to a scowl.

She countered with a wider smile as she skimmed the tantalizing device up his side. She bent forward and took his left nipple into her mouth, sucking it and nibbling at it while loosening her grip on his cock with her thighs—just enough so that he could slide his huge shaft through the small hollow, stroking himself against her soft flesh. Her pussy pulsed with anticipation as he did just that, especially when she put the devilish little device against his nipple. His hips jerked mindlessly then, his cock stabbing hard and deep between her thighs, reaching only air on the other side, pulling back and trying again, stroking her clit with each pass.

She knew exactly how helpless he felt. Every time he used the little device on her, the vibrations sent spikes of delight from her nipples to her pussy, the sensation so intense she could never hold back her cries, her internal muscles grasping frantically, longing to be filled. Soothed. Which he never did immediately, preferring to torture with pleasure until she was mindless.

The same way she was doing to Mac. Mac was apparently no more immune than she because he started cursing, harsh and deep. He was mindlessly reaching for her and it was only her "uh-uh" that made him catch himself. Swearing again, he slowly put his hands behind his back. His flesh took on a salty taste as perspiration began to shimmer on his skin. She moved the little toy to his other nipple, smiling as she did so. This was going to be so much fun if he got this hot just from placing it on his nipples.

She eased down, pausing when his cock was trapped between the bed and her pussy, the throbbing shaft spreading her outer lips, cushioning her clitoris. She rubbed a little, just a little, just enough to get her clitoris hungry and aching and his muscles jumping. Then she brought the bullet down to her clit as it rested on the shelf of his cock.

"Open your eyes."

Holding his deep blue gaze with hers, she let those sinful vibrations take her toward orgasm. Clinging to his gaze, she rocked on him, sobbing his name. He caught her shoulders in his hands, holding her up when her legs gave out. When she couldn't take anymore, she leaned her forehead against his stomach. He was breathing so hard, he bounced her back and forth, those slabs of rock-hard muscles damp with his efforts to hold back, and trembling with the strength of his own need. She turned off the device, braced her knees, turned her head, and kissed his hand where it rested on her shoulder.

His cock rested on the soles of her feet, trapped beneath her. As she took a breath, she felt a pulse of come hit her skin. She smiled and looked up into his strained face. He was very close. She lay back on the bed.

He towered above her, legs slightly parted, fists clenched at his side, all those gorgeous muscles tense and gleaming with sweat, and his eyes burning with desire for her. She looked pointedly at his hands. He cursed but put them behind his back. She drew her knees up, planting her feet on the mattress and pushing up the way he liked, letting him see her swollen, aching clit, her wet thighs, the cream that pulsed in a steady stream from her throbbing pussy. Teasing him with everything. His eyes locked on her pussy like a man starved.

Hers locked on his cock, engorged and heavy with promise. It strained toward her, a drop of pre-come beading the tip, the shaft wet with her pleasure. He looked so damned delicious, she wanted to eat him from head to toe. The fact that she could if she wanted to had her smiling from the inside out. She wiggled her fingers at him in a come hither motion, but stopped him from putting his hands on the bed with a shake of her head. She brought her legs together and let them slide down until they rested between his thighs. He frowned, stopped, and then cursed, awkwardly rising to his knees. Straddling her. She had no doubt her pleasure with the situation was written all over her face. Especially when that big cock reached her face and the crown slid across her mouth.

"Oh yeah," she whispered. "Bend your knees a little and feed me that big boy."

She didn't need to repeat herself. He fed her a good three inches before he had to stop or overbalance. She suckled it gladly, loving his taste, loving—she admitted to herself—his torment, sensing how much he wanted to thrust all the way in, only his promise to her holding him back. She bobbed her head, raking him gently with her teeth on the withdrawal, swallowing quickly when a small spurt shot past his control.

Oh, this was fun.

She glanced up to find him looking down at her. Frustration, anger, and lust battled for dominance. He clearly didn't want to enjoy this as much as he was. Since she might not ever get this chance again, she went for broke, indulging her whims, turning on the little bullet and placing it against his left ball. His immediate howl had her yanking it away. The hot spurt of seed in her mouth had her placing it on the other one. This time he took it better, not howling, but shuddering above her like a man on the rack.

When she looked up all she could see was the arch of his throat as he threw his head back, the tendons extended and in sharp relief. On either side of her face, his thighs were rock-hard. In her mouth, he swelled to impossible levels. She backed the toy off, not wanting him to come just yet. While he fought for his breath, she brought the bullet to her pussy. As she coated it with her juices, she made another decision. She might be inexperienced, but she'd read enough to know there were ways she could give him pleasure, too. She turned the toy off.

His breathing was a harsh rasp above her. She took a deep breath and bobbed her head, distracting him with the scrape of her teeth. While he moaned and fought not to come, she positioned the bullet, not touching him, because she had a feeling if he knew what she was going to do, he wouldn't allow it. Once, twice more she raked him. On the third pass, she placed the bullet against his anus and popped it in before he could yank away.

"Son of a bitch!"

Damn, he sounded pissed. She wondered if it burned him as it entered the way it had her at first. She anchored him with her teeth beneath the head of his penis while he swore and glared, and she pushed it just a little deeper. He reached back, no doubt intending to yank the clever little device out. She stopped him simply by turning it on.

He froze. His blue eyes flew wide, his body jerked double, his cock springing free of her mouth for a second before he repositioned it and fell to the bed over her. He caught his weight on his hands and then his cock was pounding at her mouth, once, twice, three times he slammed it to the back of her throat, out of control for the first time since she'd known him. Almost helpless as he came, each jet of sweet come accompanied by a broken cry of pleasure too great to be borne.

His hips pumped long after his cock was dry, moaning as she stroked him, gasping as he pulled out, his big arms shaking as he struggled to find the satisfaction the little toy demanded. She flipped the switch off, holding him gently in her mouth until he found the strength to ease back. She kissed the tip of his still-hard cock. He frowned down at her. No doubt worrying if he'd been too rough. No doubt planning on lecturing her. She forestalled it all by turning on that little vibrator again. His eyes widened, his body jerked, and then his eyes narrowed.

She dropped the controller on the comforter and wiggled up until she could get her legs free, walking them up his body until she could drape them over his arms. Mac watched the process with disturbing intentness. And a certain amount of stubbornness. She fumbled for the controller. With a switch of the button she increased the power of the vibrations, Mac threw his head back and groaned. She pulled with her legs against his braced arms until she was balanced on her shoulders and her pussy teased his cock.

"Don't you want me, Mac?" she asked, her voice slightly bruised and hoarse. "Isn't your cock just dying to get into my hot pussy? To fuck me like I want? Hard and deep until there's no separating the two of us?"

"Damn, yes!"

She arched her hips higher. "Then what's stopping you?"

He looked down at her, everything he felt, everything he wanted etched into the hard lines of his face. He looked down where they almost joined and then back up at her.

"Not a damned thing," he bit off.

Bracing his weight on one hand, he aligned the wide head of his cock with her vagina. She was slick and wet and hungry. Oh Lord, so hungry. He was finally going to love her the way she wanted. As wet as she was, he should have shot right in like a torpedo, but she was also very tight and her stubborn muscles wouldn't part as easily as she wanted. He bore down. She pushed. Between the two of them they managed a slow progression. Frustration nearly made her scream. He felt so good. So damned good. She wanted all of him.

"Why is it always like this?" she groaned.

He glanced up from where he was watching his body enter hers in slow increments. "Like what?"

"So difficult?"

He walked his hands up her sides, forcing her legs higher and wider. "Honey girl," he groaned, cautiously probing deeper, "this is about perfect. Turn off that damned vibrator and let me love you right."

She bit her lip as he entered more and it pinched. "Is the vibrator making you horny?"

He kissed her cheek. "It's going to make me come too soon."

"Not if you hurry," she countered trying to throw her hips up, but he had her too stretched now—totally helpless. Once again under his control.

She kicked her feet in the air, trying to kick his face when he had the gall to laugh.

"Easy!" he grunted.

"Am I always going to be so tight that you treat me like a piece of china?"

He wiggled his hips, sinking his cock another inch. His movements were not quite as smooth as previous lovemaking sessions. The vibrator was doing its job on his control. And he was fighting it, fighting her. *Dammit!*

"I don't know," he answered, apparently not overly concerned.

Well, she knew. As long as he saw her as fragile he was never going to take her like she wanted. She chewed her lip. "But if I stay with just you it will, won't it?"

He froze. "You been thinking about trying it with someone else?"

She was so sick of his protective bullshit. His knowing more than her. Her body's limitations. So sick and tired of only dreaming about what she wanted but never getting to experience it. "I want it fast and hard, Mac. If I can't have it with you where would you suggest I get it?"

"Not from another man, that's for sure."

"That's for me to decide."

"Like hell it is!"

"Like hell it isn't." She cranked the vibrator up to high.

His reaction was primal. Instinctive. Exactly what she was looking for. His hips drove forward, spearing his thick cock through her tight muscles. His possession was as much pain as it was pleasure but she didn't care. He was finally taking her like she'd dreamed of. Like she mattered. Like he'd die if he didn't bury himself to the balls inside her tight cunt.

With every thrust, she grunted and her breasts bounced violently. The bed shook and slammed the wall. Over and over he pulled out and surged deep. Hard, fast, past her inhibitions. Past her years of being a good girl. His pubic bone ground into her engorged clit on every downstroke. His cock dragged on her resisting flesh on the outstroke. He slammed into her over and over, until he finally, finally got to that totally wild part of her that loved it. Loved every slamming, painful, pleasure-giving moment. The part of her that screamed and clawed, that took the pain with her pleasure, relished both because they meant she was woman enough to live up to his needs. Her dreams. Woman enough for both of them.

His cock jerked within her. His hoarse shout filled the room as he climaxed. She was right behind him, her forehead crashing into his chest, her teeth sinking into his biceps as she bit down in a desperate effort to hold onto something solid as the world splintered away. Her head fell back and she sobbed, the whirlwind too strong to resist.

Then he was pulling her hips up into his, his fingers bruising her thighs, his teeth biting with restrained force on her breast as if he needed to mark her even as he made her his. The dual sensations of his seed spraying into her ultra-sensitive pussy and his bite threw her into another climax. She thrashed on the bed, trying to handle the sensations taking her over. But she couldn't. It was good. So good. So good she couldn't stand it. His teeth bit harder. His cock pumped load after load of hot come into her greedy pussy and the whole world narrowed to that single moment of perfect bliss. A moment so intense, so divine, everything else just disappeared.

*****

She came back to herself with her breath rasping harshly in her lungs and a warm, damp, unstable pillow under her cheek.

"Oh God, honey girl, open your eyes."

The best she could do was crack the right one. As a result Mac's face was a little blurry but she could still make out the worry in his eyes.

"Hi." Her voice sounded as wiped out as she felt.

His hand touched her cheek. "Are you okay?"

Her smile probably looked as insubstantial as she felt. "I've never been better. Why?"

"You passed out."

Hot Damn. She hadn't even dared add that to her to-do list. "You made love to me until I passed out?"

"No. I fucked you into a stupor."

She recognized that note in this voice. She forced both eyes open. They were so not going back to the "treat Jessie like a porcelain doll" routine. "You forgot to add 'and you loved it'."

His fingers grazed her breast. "I bit you."

"Uh-huh." She let her eyes drift shut and shivered with the memory. "That was an especially nice touch at the end."

She could feel him staring at her. His hand gently cupped her breast. "You're going to have a bruise."

She wiggled her arm out from under her body to touch his cheek. "If you promise to be good and let me sleep, I'll let you bite the other one."

His frown turned into a scowl. "Damn it, Jessie. I lost control!"

By now, her smile was positively sappy. "I know. I can't wait to do it again."

"We are not doing that again," he stated emphatically.

She ignored him. Summoning all the energy she had, she half-rolled, half-tossed herself onto his chest. He sighed and worked her the rest of the way on.

"I could have hurt you, Jessie."

She shook her head. "You wouldn't."

"I already did." His fingers skimmed her thighs. She imagined he was looking at bruises there.

"Mac?"

"What?"

"Stop whining and cuddle that big cock into me so I can go to sleep."

"I do not whine." His cock, still semi-hard, nudged her vagina. She relaxed her muscles as he forced it past the tight ring of muscle. She bit her lip at the burning pressure. She was raw and bruised, and she couldn't be happier. She wanted more.

Mac pushed her hair off her face, took a look at her expression, and frowned, his hand on her hip stopping her from taking more. "Sore?"

She didn't have the strength to argue with him. "Please?"

He stared at her a minute, sighed, kissed her forehead, and let her wiggle down on him. Finally, she had him as deep as she could, and sighed in relief. Mac curved his hand around her skull and tugged her onto the pillow of his chest before pulling the covers over them both, smoothing the sheet around her shoulders, and arranging the comforter. Silence reigned for a few minutes. She was almost asleep when his lips brushed her hair.

"After this you have to marry me. No woman not my wife is having bragging rights to shoving a vibrator up my ass."

She smiled, patted one cheek of the ass in question and fell asleep.

Chapter Twelve

"If that man thinks I'm walking down the aisle next week with this thing on, he's nuts," Jessie muttered as she tried on her wedding dress for the final fitting in Granny Ortiz's front room. She looked in the mirror again, experimenting with holding her arm close to her side, but it didn't help. The dress was beautiful, Granny Ortiz's offer to let her wear it, incredibly generous, but she still looked like heck in the older woman's dress for the simple reason that the cast on her arm stuck out like a sore thumb. She fumbled with the lace on the full sleeve, but no matter how she tugged, the heavy cast drew the eye like a magnet. There was just no hiding the blasted thing. She tugged some more. "Damn!"

"What's this?" Granny Ortiz asked as she walked into the room. "The bride in tears?"

Jessie sniffed and accepted the tissue handed her. There was something about Granny that drew Jessie. A love of life and the straightforward practicality she wanted to have when she was pushing ninety.

"Not really. It's just I can't hide this thing!" She shook the cast in the air like an obnoxious rat. "Your wedding dress is so beautiful and this monstrosity is ruining the whole effect." She glared in the direction of the church across the street where Mac was. "It's all that man's fault. He couldn't wait six weeks to get married. Oh no! He had to rush to squeeze it into three."

Granny Ortiz smiled and folded her arms across her chest. "You know, you did have a say in this."

Jessie snorted and glared harder, remembering how Mac had teased and tempted the agreement out of her. "Not much."

Granny's open grin pushed her face into a mass of wrinkles. "Waited until he got you in bed to press the point, did he?"

Jessie cut her a quick glance and then shook her head. "I don't know why I'm still surprised when you say things like that."

Granny shrugged her bird-like shoulders and adjusted the skirt of Jessie's dress. "Neither am I. I may be old, but I'm not senile. I remember how things are between a man and a woman."

Jessie looked down at Granny's carefully coiffed head, touches of pink scalp peeking between the white curls. She bet the old woman had been a hellion in her day.

"I'll keep that in mind."

Granny stepped back and studied the fall of the sleeve, sparing her only the briefest of glances. "It still needs something."

"A few more weeks until this cast comes off would be good."

"Thought you said you weren't getting more time."

"I'm not," Jessie called to the other woman's back. "And for the reason you stated. The skunk seduced me into getting his way."

"Well, that's a street that goes both ways." Granny rummaged in a drawer of the antique mahogany bureau. The scent of lilacs drifted into the room.

"I'm keeping that in mind."

"See that you do."

Jessie couldn't help but grin wider at the sharp rejoinder. She hoped she had as much sass as this woman when she reached the age of eighty-eight.

"There it is," Granny cried triumphantly. Reverently, she lifted a wrapped parcel out of the trunk.

Jessie crossed the small room, as Granny carefully unwrapped the package. When she got close enough to determine, she saw the old woman held a shawl in her hands. A shawl made of lace so fine it was a mere gossamer web of incredible beauty. "It's the most beautiful thing I've ever seen in my life!" she whispered, awestruck.

"That's what you said about the dress," Granny reminded her as she draped the lace over the freshly wrapped cast.

"And it was, right up until I saw this." She ran one finger reverently across the pattern which, on close inspection, matched the lace which fell from the throat of the Victorian-style wedding dress.

Granny Ortiz patted her hand. "As I told you, my husband was of Spanish decent. This mantilla was a gift from his mother. I was going to put it over your hair, but I think it'll serve to cover that cast."

"You're being very kind to me."

"That man of yours has always had a special place in my heart," Granny said. "I'm glad to see he finally found someone able to go toe-to-toe with him."

Jessie chuckled. "You make it seem like a boxing match."

"Well, what with both your personalities, I imagine you'll be sparring both in and out of bed, but don't worry about it. All the best couples do."

She took that dubious advice in stride. "Thanks." She bit her lip. "You know I don't have any family left, at least that I'm close to."

"That I do, and a damned shame it is."

Jessie's lips twitched. "Well, I wondered if I might ask some advice."

"Don't tell me you and Mac have been living out at the ranch and he hasn't bothered to instruct you in the way of things!"

"Things?"

"Between a man and a woman." Granny Ortiz shook her head. "All the Hollister men are hot-blooded. I can't believe Mac didn't get his fair share of those genes." She grabbed Jessie by the arm. "Well, come along, honey. Must be I misunderstood you earlier." She patted her arm consolingly. "Don't worry, though. It hasn't been so long that I can't instruct you right."

It took everything Jessie had not to burst out laughing. "I think you should know that people of your generation are supposed to frown on premarital sex."

"Posh. I grew up in the roaring twenties, and you young people have got a long way to go before you catch up to us. Now, sit down and pay attention."

Jessie straightened her dress before sitting carefully beside the older woman. "Before you go any further, I think I should let you know that Mac got his fair share of the Hollister genes. And then some."

"I knew I wasn't wrong about that boy." She laughed and nudged Jessie's arm with her elbow. "And I bet you get down on your knees nightly and thank Him for that special blessing."

Jessie blushed. She actually blushed. She struggled for a witty comeback, found none, and impulsively hugged the older woman instead. The old bones felt so brittle under her hands, reminding her how fragile life was. Tears washed her vision as she drew back to whisper, "Have I ever told you how grateful I am for the way you've welcomed me with open arms?"

Granny reached up and straightened one of the white rosebuds woven into the French braid of Jessie's hair. Roses from her garden. "You made it an easy thing to do."

Jessie shook her head. "No one has welcomed me the way this town has. It's like coming home. For the first time since my mother died, I don't miss what might have been."

"Maybe you have come home," Granny said seriously. "I've always believed in the homily, 'Home is where the heart is'."

Jessie glanced in the direction of the church where she knew Mac was talking with the reverend. "And my heart most definitely belongs here."

"With Mac."

"Yes."

"Then, honey," Granny Ortiz asked, her fingers touching Jessie's, where they clenched in her lap, "why are you so nervous?"

"I don't know," she confessed, that hard knot of fear solidifying in her gut again. She frowned and her teeth sank into her lower lip. "No," she sighed. "That's not true. I do know. It's Mac."

"How so?" Granny moved to the wingback chair next to the bed. "My old bones aren't what they used to be," she explained. "Lately, they need a bit more support."

Jessie waited until she was settled. "He's changed."

"Have you talked to Mac about it?"

"I've tried but..."

"He doesn't want to hear about it," Granny Ortiz finished for her.

"No. He'd rather just pretend that everything's as it used to be before I broke my damned arm."

"That's another Hollister trait, ignoring reality in their personal lives."

"Well, it's not a particularly attractive one," Jessie said with a wry grin.

Granny choked on her laughter. "At least you're keeping your sense of humor about it all."

Jessie stood. The satin skirt rustled as she crossed to the window. "Well, it's not easy." She moved the velvet drape aside and snorted in disgust. "How long have I been here?"

"Oh, I'd say about two hours."

"Can you think of anything Mac could be discussing with Reverend Dwight for that long?"

"Nope, can't say that I can, especially since those two rub each other the wrong way more often than not. Why?"

"Because despite the fact that Mac was supposed to just drop off the procession list and then head on back to the ranch to get some paperwork done before the rehearsal dinner tonight, his car's still parked in front of the reverend's house."

"Maybe this is one of those occasions when they're getting along."

"I wouldn't say so."

Granny got out of the chair and joined Jessie at the window. She watched the two men talking on the porch for about two seconds before her hearty chuckle had the lace panels she clutched fluttering like a wave. "Nope. From the set of Mac's shoulders, I'd say he's holding on to his temper by a thread. Wonder why he just doesn't make excuses like the rest of us do, when Dwight gets into one of his tirades?"

"Because then he wouldn't have an excuse to hang around."

"Does he need one?"

Jessie sighed and admitted wearily, "Yes." She stared at Mac, sadness welling from a place deep within. "He's smothering me, Granny, and I don't know what to do about it."

"And this has been going on since you broke your arm?" She held out her hand. Jessie took it and helped her back to the chair.

"Mac has always been caring." She threw up her hands before turning around so Granny could unbutton the back of the dress. "It's his nature to be protective, but before it was a consideration. Now, it's an intrusion."

She could feel the older woman's fingers fumbling with the tiny buttons as she asked, "I'm afraid you'll have to spell it out for me."

"I can't breathe."

"Excuse me?"

"It's hard to explain. It's not a jealousy thing. He's not afraid I'm going to run off with another man. At least, I don't think so."

"Trust a Hollister not to be that easy."

"Yeah." She looked over her shoulder. "You understand I'm making assumptions here."

"Yup."

"If he applied half the determination at solving this problem as he does to protecting me from it..." Her hand slashed through the air, filling in the rest of the sentence.

"You're going to have to hold still if you want me to get these buttons undone. Nothing on me is as nimble as it used to be."

"Oh. Sorry." Jessie continued, "Anyway, if Mac would stop being so stubbornly determined that only he can handle this 'problem', it wouldn't be a problem."

"Mac tends to steamroll through trouble," Granny agreed. "Sometimes that's an admirable trait, like ten years ago when his father and brother told him to sell the ranch, that he couldn't make a go of it? That boy didn't listen to a word they said. He just took the bit between his teeth and set out to prove them wrong. Quite successfully, too."

Jessie twisted her solitaire around her finger. "Yeah, well, this time he's being successful in nothing more than ticking me off. Not only is his attitude infuriating, it's damned insulting. I am a perfectly capable adult. I can make decisions. I can even reevaluate them if they turn out to be wrong. I could wring his sexy neck for not seeing that."

"It's not me you have to be convincing," Granny pointed out as the last button came free.

"Talk about your impossible missions," Jessie muttered as she stepped out of the dress and arranged the lace train on the bed until it fell in precise folds. "Lately, I can't even pick up a knife to chop up chicken without someone appearing at my elbow to see if I need help. Twenty-four hours a day, someone from the Circle H is shadowing my steps, ready to intercede should I prove incompetent."

Just remembering had her lip curling with disgust. She had no idea what Granny Ortiz was thinking, but in the last three weeks, she'd become attached to the other woman. And, bottom line, she valued her opinion. "Do you think I should call off the wedding?"

Granny's head snapped up from where she was putting the dress on a hanger. "Are you absolutely sure this feeling isn't pure old-fashioned jitters?"

Jessie had no trouble meeting her straightforward gaze. "Positive. The shadowing has gotten more subtle since I talked to him, but it hasn't disappeared."

"Well, if your heart says marry the man, but your instincts say not like this, then rather than calling off the wedding, I'd concentrate on finding a way to convince Mac he's being a blue ribbon fool." Her faded blue eyes rested on the picture of a handsome young man dressed to the nines in a Zoot suit. "You think you have forever to work things out, but it's not always true."

Jessie followed Granny's gaze. "Your husband was a very handsome man. Kind eyes. You must have loved him very much."

"He had a temper." Granny chuckled through the nostalgia. "But he was as beautiful inside as he was outside. I thought we'd never die, that we'd simply walk into the hereafter arm and arm as we'd done in life, but then that drunken fool Elliot Chambers got behind the wheel and put paid to my dreams."

"I'm so sorry." The words seemed inadequate in the face of all that love and sorrow.

Granny blinked away her tears. The smile on her lips was forced. It trembled slightly. "I didn't say that to make you sad. I love Raoul with a kind of love that only comes once in a lifetime. Though I can't see him, I know he's here. I know he's waiting for me, and when my work here is done, we'll be together again. I just wanted you to understand that life doesn't stop moving just because you do. You and Mac have something as special as Raoul and I. It's a precious gift. Take it in both hands and cherish it. If you have to, fight tooth and nail for it, but never take it for granted. Putting off the inevitable won't stop it from coming."

Jessie stared hard at this woman that life had never managed to subdue and suddenly knew the truth. If Mac died tomorrow, she'd be still referring to him in the present tense twenty years down the road, because like Granny said, some loves were just a miracle. And she was letting hers slip away by being passive. By hoping rather than acting. By being too damned chicken to take the bull by the horns. What in hell had she been thinking? That was so not happening. "You're right," she agreed. "Mac hasn't been the only fool."

Granny smiled knowingly. "Found your feet, have you?"

"Yup." Jessie took the dress Granny was loaning her for tonight's rehearsal dinner off the hanger. As she dropped the square-necked flapper dress over her head, she said, "Ever since I met Mac, I've been aware that what we have is special. So special, I've been walking on eggshells so I won't lose it."

Granny took the hand Jessie extended and stood beside the younger woman, a tiny, wrinkled example of indomitable will. "Everyone knows the surest way to break an egg is to worry about dropping it."

"Almost everyone," Jessie corrected as she took her hair down and let it fall around her shoulders, her gaze flashing to the Reverend's house, and the two men still standing outside. "But before I'm done, we'll be adding Mac to the list."

"Do you have an idea?"

"Not yet." Jessie slid a bead-fringed headband over her forehead.

"Are you working on one?" Granny asked hopefully as she arranged a feathered headband on her sparse white curls.

"I'm definitely working on one." She looked in the mirror to straighten it.

"Promise me one thing."

"What?" She glanced up under a fringe of black beads to meet Granny's gaze in the mirror.

"When you do come up with something, make it outrageous," she answered, tweaking her feather into position. "Life has gotten pretty dull around here lately."

Jessie chuckled and linked her arm with Granny's as they prepared to head over to the grange hall where the party was being held. "I promise that if Mac absolutely refuses to see reason, I'll come up with something so out-there, tongues will be wagging for years."

*****

"How long do you think this shindig is going to last?" Mac whispered into her ear, his fingers resting on the inside of her arm. He'd never in his life seen anything as beautiful as Jessie walking down the aisle to his side during the rehearsal, her face composed, her eyes glowing with love. He wanted to take that vision to bed. Now.

A delicate flush tinted her cheeks. A trail of goose bumps sprang up beneath his fingers on the flesh of her arm as he kissed her neck behind her ear.

"Stop it," she hissed, a little shiver taking her from head to toe. "There must be three hundred people sitting out there just waiting for an opportunity to embarrass us."

"I don't care," he whispered back, taking a sip of his wine to wet his dry mouth.

Her flush deepened. "Well, I do," she hissed, nodding at Henry as he raised his glass in a silent toast, "and I am not going to disappoint these people by being rude. The whole town went to a lot of effort to make this rehearsal party special."

"And showed up for it, too," Mac grumbled despite the deep sense of belonging he got from being part of this close-knit community. The room began to resound with the tinkling demand of forks against glass. First one and then a hundred utensils picked up the request for the couple to kiss. Bowing to the inevitable, Mac slid his hand beneath Jessie's hair. He didn't have to coax her head back, it just naturally fell into his palm, just as her lips naturally parted for his, and what was supposed to be a polite kiss for the satisfaction of the onlookers exploded right out of sight as her taste, her scent flooded his senses. Loud hoots broke through the moment. Jessie's hands on his chest pressed him back. Reluctantly, he allowed her lips to part from his. He kissed the corner of her mouth, "I want you."

"Oh, God!" Jessie moaned right back, as always, her passion spiking to meet his. "I want you, too, but there isn't anything we can do about it right now."

His mouth slanted over hers in a short, hard kiss. "Like hell there isn't."

Zach tapped his glass, demanding a speech. The crowd picked up the chant until, seeing no way out of it, Mac stood. The room was slow to fall into silence. "I'd like to make a toast. Here's to Nathaniel Price of the What You Need employment agency for ignoring what I asked for, and for sending me exactly what I needed—the most contrary woman a man was ever lucky enough to take to wife."

There was both laughter and approval in response to that toast. Before Mac could sit down, Jessie caught his hand and held on tight as she rose to her feet. An elegant, laughing sprite, with eyes full of love. For him. The wonder of it never ceased to amaze him.

"I just wanted to thank you all for taking me into your hearts the way you have. By now, you all know how Mac and I got together." She chuckled ruefully. "Round the Bend's grapevine is nothing if not efficient. The man led me a merry chase, but I finally backed him into a corner he couldn't get out of." The laughter that greeted that comment drowned out her voice. She was forced to wait while jokes and one-liners bounced around the room like rubber balls gone crazy.

Mac squeezed Jessie's fingers encouragingly. He knew how much she wanted to belong. He was glad that he could offer her that.

Her smile was soft and tremulous as she continued, "When I stepped off the bus in Round the Bend, I found more than I ever expected. Here I found a husband," she reached up and touched Mac's cheek. She turned to face Granny Ortiz, "A grandmother." When that woman accepted the tribute with a regal nod, Jessie smiled. She glanced down the table to the two older versions of her husband. Men who bore the same stamp of honor. They also shared his wicked sense of humor. "I now have a father and a brother, and though she couldn't be here, a sister." She choked to a stop and tried to swallow back the tears of happiness that threatened her speech. "Cord and Jake made me feel welcome from the start. When they heard about my lack of relatives, they grabbed me up and told me I wasn't alone anymore. That I am a Hollister now. I'll never forget that as long as I live," she promised the two men. "Not ever."

"Does that mean," Cord asked, his wicked grin slashing across his dark face. "That next time I steal an apple pie you'll forgo the rap on the knuckles?"

Everyone laughed at that.

"Not hardly," she retorted. "An accountant you might be, but you're a Hollister and I've been around them long enough to know if you give them an inch, they'll take a mile."

"You've got that right!" Will called out.

Jessie accepted the response with a regal nod of her head. "Thank you." She waited for quiet before continuing. "It wasn't only the immediate Hollister family that made me welcome. You have each in your own way made me feel special, starting with and not limited to this beautiful rehearsal party." She looked at the hall, the people, and the food, "But I've got to tell y'all something…" All eyes were riveted on the podium. "You're going to have a tough time topping this party next week when the actual wedding takes place."

"Heck, Jessie. You haven't been in Texas long enough if you think this little shindig is the best a Texan can do when faced with a challenge," Rafe called out.

"In that case," she laughed, "let me say thanks and make my toast so we can get down to some serious celebrating." She raised her glass. "To the residents of Round the Bend, Texas. The best damned family a girl ever had."

Resounding cheers doubled when Mac took her tear-wet face in his hands and kissed her with all the bittersweet love in his soul. His time with her was so short, he thought. So damned short. He kissed her deeper and she melted into his embrace like butter on a hot stove. He brushed his mouth over her ear before ordering hoarsely, "Excuse yourself to repair your makeup."

Blindly, Jessie did as ordered, too caught up in passion and excitement to question why. She didn't have long to find out. Two minutes after she entered the little room set aside especially for the ladies, Mac walked through the door, his eyes glittering, his face tight, and his mouth unsmiling. Jessie put down the compact of face powder she was applying.

The lock fell into place with a gentle click.

"Mac?" she questioned, backing up. The leap in her pulse and the raggedness of her breathing made the question unnecessary. Her body knew instinctively what her mind was just grasping. He wanted her.

He stopped when his big, taut body pressed hers up against the wall. His hands cupped her cheeks holding her face still for his kiss. "I need you," he moaned.

At first, she thought he was joking, the intimation being too reckless to be real. Then she looked into his eyes, saw the agony there, saw the apology in his strained smile, and knew he was serious. Thoughts raced through her mind. People would guess. Her dress would get ruined, but she didn't care. He needed her.

She reached up and smoothed the apology from his lips. "How?"

He caught her hand in his. The kiss he pressed into her palm was hot and warm, full of emotion.

"It'll have to be quick."

She smiled, stroking his cheek with her finger as he nipped the pad of her thumb. "I have no problem with quick. You're the one always dragging things out for maximum pleasure."

He laughed. A raw sound that indicated more than words how he felt. His forehead dropped to hers. "You, honey girl, are one strange lady."

"Lucky you."

Mac rubbed his nose against hers, bringing his hips to hers, he pulled back far enough to see Jessie's face. He expected to see a little resentment under the other emotions, but all he saw was acceptance and even pleasure. She was a wild woman, his Jessie.

"Yeah," he agreed, his voice sounding tight and hard to his own ears. "Lucky me."

He put his mouth to hers, reining in his need to crush her to him, to mark her, to ensure she stayed with him, and gave her tenderness instead. He nibbled at her lips, coaxed them open with the brush of his tongue, nurtured her passion with tenderness. She didn't have to ride the wild man all the time.

She grabbed his hair in her hand and pulled him closer. "I thought you were in a hurry."

"I am." Her frown sparked his smile. That was his Jessie. Impatient, wild, demanding and giving. So damned giving he thought as her hand slipped down over his chest. He eased his tongue into her mouth, ignoring her efforts to increase the intensity. She really needed to learn to slow down. To take his lead. To let him guide her.

Her hand worked lower until she cupped his shaft, sliding down his length. But maybe just not right now, he decided as a bolt of sheer lust stabbed him in the gut. When it eased, he let out the breath he didn't remember holding on a soft groan. She glanced up at him. Her eyes flirted with his, green mischief sparkling from beneath her long lashes. The panic he felt inside leveled out as the familiar hum of desire kicked up his heart rate.

Very tenderly, she unzipped his pants, her gaze locked with his the whole time. Her soft hand worked inside his boxers until she could wrap her fingers around him. She squeezed gently as she eased her arm down his pants leg until she cupped the crown in her palm. She squeezed again. His cock surged and his balls pulled tight. He dropped his head back as he sucked in a breath through his teeth, fighting to hold back when all he wanted to do was let go.

"You poor baby," she whispered, milking the head, catching his pre-come in her palm, smoothing her movements with the silky fluid. "So hard and hurting."

The feeling of her smooth little hand on his hard flesh was divine. He closed his eyes and savored the moment. The scrape of her nails made him jump. "Oh yeah, honey girl. Do that again."

She did and then kissed his chest through his shirt. Giving his cock one last loving cuddle, she said, "Let's get you comfortable."

With the side of her cast, she pushed into his stomach.

"Easy," Mac ordered, frowning at her when she did it again, catching her cast in his hands, cradling her arm. Jessie licked her lips and sent him a quick smile. He felt the tension in her arm that signaled another push. He took the step before she could complete the gesture. He could only take baby steps because her hand was still in his pants, stroking the inside of his thigh as she urged him backwards. Two more pushes and his calves came to a halt against something firm.

"Sit," she said with a final push.

He raised his eyebrow at the order. A quick glance indicated that she wanted him to take a seat on the low hassock resting against the wall. It was a long trip for a man of his height, especially when his woman had his aching balls in her hand, massaging and squeezing them. He had to pause twice, so close to coming he wasn't sure he was going to make it, only to look up and catch her gaze on him. Happy, soft and knowing.

"You're making this as difficult as possible, aren't you?" he asked as he shifted his feet wide and settled back against the wall.

"Just keeping things humming along," Jessie countered with a smile that had his cock leaping in his pants.

She slid her hand around his hip under the waistband of his pants. "I like that you get all hot and bothered by me."

He touched her soft cheek. "I'm glad."

He was more than glad. He was amazed. He'd never expected to find a woman who could match him sexually. He'd always thought he'd have to curb his bedroom preferences when he fell in love. In Jessie he faced the opposite dilemma. She was more than his match in bed. It was outside the bedroom where he was having his doubts. That wild streak of hers went a mile wide and he just didn't know if she could be content with the lifestyle he offered.

A tug on his pants brought his attention back to what she was doing.

"Let's get these out of the way."

"God, yes." He lifted his hips so she could slide his pants clear.

The cool air in the room was almost painful on his hypersensitive cock, so he caught his length in his hand as she stepped back. She paused as he did so, one foot behind the other, balance slightly off, the way it was when caught by surprise. The beading over her bodice swayed with the suddenness of her stop. Her tongue flicked out to lick her lips as he stroked his hand along his aching cock. As he lazily cupped the crown she slowly straightened, her gaze glued to his hand. He watched her eyes as he stroked his hand down. They flared and then narrowed. The silk of her dress shimmered with her rapid breaths as he did it again. His balls throbbed. A bead of come welled over the tip as he smoothed his hand up his shaft, circling his fingers around the stalk just under the crown. He tilted the broad head with its offering toward her. She uttered a sexy little whimper that had more come leaking from his cock.

It was his turn to smile. Damn she was hot. "Come here, honey girl."

Two steps had her at his side. He caught her by the hips before she could kneel. "You'll ruin your dress."

"Who cares?" she muttered, catching his cock in her hand before it could drop.

"You will about five minutes from now," he said to the top of her head. Her eyes caressed him with the touch of a lover as she stroked gently. Her hand was much softer than his. Hotter. Infinitely more desirable. Promising so much pleasure. So much peace. Another pulse of fluid escaped his control.

On a muttered "Steady me," she bent down. If his reflexes had been slower, she would have fallen on his cock. As it was, he was just in time to control her descent as she bent at the waist. Her shoulders under his hands felt small, delicate. Her mouth on the tip of his penis, as hot and tempting as sin. She took her time taking him in, working the head past her teeth and humming in satisfaction as she snuggled him against her tongue. She sucked and lapped as he jerked beneath the whip of sensation, piling on more, humming louder with every lapse in his control. Finally, he pulled her off. "Not in your mouth," he said in answer to the question in her eyes.

She smiled that seductress smile. "Okay." She turned in his hands, her grip rotating on his cock, keeping it where she wanted it. He naturally took her weight against his palms as she swung a leg over his thighs. As delicate as a butterfly she brought her hips down. He expected to feel the barrier of her panties, was reaching to pull it aside when his cock slid into the moist valley of her vagina.

"Son of a bitch!" The curse hissed through his teeth as the knowledge that she wasn't wearing panties, hadn't been wearing panties all night long, slammed through his control.

She raised those honey-gold eyebrows on him and blinked innocently. "Problem?"

"You're not wearing underpants."

"I thought you'd figured that out already."

Hell, if he had he'd have tossed her over the dinner table and fucked her in front of the whole town. "No."

He slid his hand back along the crease of her ass. He didn't know whether to be relieved or regretful when he discovered she wasn't wearing the plug.

It was his turn to raise his brow at her as he stroked her anus.

"Even I have limits," She said in the prissiest tone he'd ever heard, even as she worked her hips on his cock. He caught her buttocks in his hands, keeping her from taking him.

"Let me make you ready, honey girl. I'm not that hungry."

"Yes, you are," she countered, her smile reflecting her satisfaction with the entire situation as she relaxed her muscles.

"And so are you," Mac uttered in surprise as the crown popped through the tight ring of muscle into the clenching heat beyond.

"Don't look so shocked," she moaned as she flexed around him. "I always want you."

Yes she did. And she held him so tightly, so perfectly, so completely, he could almost believe he could hold her with this alone.

"You do, don't you?" He cupped her head in his free hand, arching her back so she could take him more comfortably. He sank another inch. God, she was so incredibly tight. "But you are going to have to be especially hungry today, honey girl," he admitted. "One more minute and I'm gone."

He expected her to rush at being told that. To pick up the pace. He braced himself to endure, to hold on until she was ready, wanting to give her the equal of what she was giving him.

"It's okay," she answered, her eyes as soft as her voice as she cupped his jaw in her palms. Her right hand soft and sweetly giving. The left firm and supporting. Her fingers stroked his cheeks gently as her pussy rhythmically squeezed up and down on his cock. The tenderness, when he expected a passionate fury, brought him teetering to the edge. As he scrabbled for control, she whispered three little words that tore through his defenses.

"I love you."

He came then, in an agonizing rush, her hand over his mouth smothering his shout of satisfaction. His body bucked under hers, his seed pouring into her as he gave her everything he had. His heart. His soul. His fears. His hope. And as the last drop of come pulsed into her, she leaned her small body against him, as if to shelter him, her hand smothering his moans, protecting them both from detection. She kissed the hollow of his throat with equal tenderness, stroked the corner of his mouth with her thumb, held him as his body shuddered in the aftermath.

"Oh damn, honey girl, I love you, too."

Even to his own ears it was a pitiful announcement. There was more despair in the declaration than joy. Jessie didn't get upset. Instead she pulled him closer.

"Trust me, Mac." She kissed the hollow of his throat with that same protective tenderness. "We're going to be okay."

She leaned her head against his chest, and placed her palm over his heart beneath her cheek. "I guarantee it."

Chapter Thirteen

At precisely 7:30 p.m. three days later, Jessie was a nervous wreck. She'd been gnawing her lower lip all day, and now it felt hot and bruised. She watched as the last of the purloined ranch hands—the ones that were supposed to be out repairing fences—hammered the last nail into the impromptu stage. The wooden structure took up the length of an entire wall of the living room. All the furniture, except two chairs and two small trays had been either shoved against the wall or removed to various parts of the house. The lighting was muted to give the appearance of intimacy. The entry into the dining room had been curtained off. From behind that bright blue curtain came the word she'd been waiting for.

"All set, luv. You can send for the poor chap whenever." The curtains billowed outward as Coulton stepped through, his six-foot-three-inch frame shown off to perfection in his loincloth. His well-oiled muscles rippled as he let the curtain fall behind him. His face was too earthily masculine, too ruggedly handsome to ever be beautiful, but he was sexy. Even when he frowned suspiciously, like now. "You did say he wasn't the violent type, right?"

Jessie's fingers crossed on the lie. "As gentle as a lamb."

"That's all right then, isn't it?"

Jessie just loved the way the English made questions of statements. "Yes. Everything's all right." Truth be told, she hadn't the foggiest if anything was going to be all right, but she had hopes. High hopes that were pinned on the success of this plan in which Coulton figured prominently.

She ran her eyes over Coulton's legendary body. He resembled a conquering Viking from days of yore. It was hard to believe that he was actually an Earl. She forgot just exactly what his full title really was. For so long he'd just been Coulton, one of her best friends. Besides, with his drop-dead looks and that gorgeous mane of blond hair that flowed to his hips, not to mention his brawny physique, he was much too exotic to think of as a peer of the realm.

A not so subtle "Psst!" from the doorway alerted Jessie to Will's presence.

"Showtime yet?" he asked, the smile on his face letting her know he couldn't wait to see how this all turned out.

Neither could she. She wiped her sweaty palms down over the soft knit of her dress as she nodded affirmatively. This just had to work, because if it didn't, one thing was certain, Mac was never going to forgive her. By tomorrow, the story of tonight's goings-on would to be all over the state.

Jessie groaned, looking around the room and the still swaying curtain. Maybe she'd gone too far. It wouldn't be the first time she'd let anger and impulsivity lead her further down the road than she'd intended to go. She made one step in the direction of the curtains when the crunch of booted feet on gravel pulled her up short. She'd know that stride anywhere. Mac.

She should, she'd been listening to it pretty consistently for the last week. Equally recognizable was the anger in every stride. She wasn't proving as easy to manage as Mac had anticipated, and it was ticking him off royally, as evidenced by their argument last night. Over something as simple as her going out for an afternoon ride!

She shook her head. Mac was either going to loosen up after this, or they just weren't going to make it. She was never going to be happy in the soft little cocoon he wanted to wrap her in. And he wouldn't like her if she was. As much as he fought against it, the man got turned on faster than a grease fire by her wild side. And she did so appreciate that about him.

She clenched her muscles around the thick plug embedded in her rear. With any luck, after tonight's show, she'd be able to use that wild side to finally, finally tempt his gorgeous cock into deflowering her ass. Her knees went weak at the thought. She steadied herself by gripping the back of the chair as her juices gushed. Oh God, she hoped so. Four muted thumps up the steps, and then the footsteps stopped. Jessie could picture Mac standing on the porch, bracing himself for their next encounter. No doubt he was expecting either tears or more angry words. She looked around the altered downstairs. She knew he wasn't expecting anything like this.

The door opened, and Mac stood in the entryway. He immediately removed his hat upon seeing her, revealing the emotion in his eyes. Jessie sighed. Apparently, he hadn't decided to just accede to her point of view. Rats. Nothing in this relationship was turning out to be easy.

Mac let his eyes adjust to the dimness of the house after the bright sunlight. He could see Jessie standing over by the archway to the living room. He could only make out her silhouette. She wore something soft and clingy that accentuated the flare of her hips beneath her slim waist. His cock perked up and his palms itched to cradle those curves. She'd be soft and full in his palms, the muscles resilient and receptive. Damn, she had the most delightful ass. He swallowed to ease the tension in his throat before asking again, "You needed to see me?"

"Yes," she answered, her voice humming with a tension he couldn't quite put his finger on.

He squinted to get a better view and pulled up short.

"What in the blue blazes did you do to my house?" he demanded as he noticed the platform where his couch used to be. "It looks like the set of a high school play!"

Jessie winced. "Rats. It's supposed to look like a nightclub. Coulton claims that he and the boys can't perform to their best without the proper atmosphere. And please don't shout."

"I'll shout if I want to. It's my damn house." And then, lowering his voice asked, "Who the hell is Coulton?"

"Part of tonight's entertainment," she muttered, glancing at the curtain nervously as she came toward him.

"Great," Mac growled. He would have worried about that "boys", except there was something in her walk that had him paying closer attention. She had killer legs. Slim, muscular, well-shaped and in those high heels definitely wet dream material, but the heels alone wouldn't account for the slight off-ness.

He studied her more closely as she held out her hand for his.

"Who is Coulton?" he asked again as he placed his hand in her smaller one.

"A friend."

"Male?"

She led him across the room, her hips swaying side to side as she drew him along, the soft blue knit hugging her buttocks, the slightest bounce in those full curves as her stride pulled up short catching and holding his gaze.

"Yes."

"Figures." She stopped at a small table on which sat highball glasses full of ice and a whiskey bottle. She dropped his hand, turned and motioned him to his seat, shifting her stance wider as she did so and then he knew what was up. A slow smile started deep inside as she frowned at him when he didn't immediately sit.

Mac took a step forward, crowding her a little as he reached around her to pour whiskey into the glass. "I assume my money paid for this?"

Jessie nodded. This close he couldn't miss the slight start beneath her skin or the increase in her respiration. He picked up the glass and held it in his hand. The ice in the glass chimed softly as he placed his finger against the too fast pulse in her throat. "Nice of you to provide the amenities."

"I didn't." She grimaced, eyeing his smile warily. "It must have been Will."

"Remind me to give him a raise." He kept his finger on her pulse as he met her deep green gaze. "Are you wearing one of your plugs, Jessie girl?"

Her eyes widened and narrowed. She swallowed so hard he lost her pulse, but when he found it again, it was racing double-time, and the blush that started at her chest reached her cheeks in two startled blinks.

He took a step back. "Show me."

She stared at him with that "deer caught in the headlights" look and blinked again, then, with one nervous glance over her shoulder at the curtains, she slowly turned. There was another hesitation in which he thought he was going to have to repeat himself but then she bent over the low table, bracing her weight on her good arm, her back arched and hips thrust up and back. The image she presented was pure temptation.

Through the knit of her tightly stretched dress he could make out the crease in her buttocks. He traced it through the soft cloth before taking a sip of his whiskey. The liquid burned its way down his throat, the lingering taste bad enough to cut through the worst of his lust, letting him find the patience to gather the soft material up. He slid it over her hips until it pooled at her waist.

She wasn't wearing any underwear. He let that information sink in as he touched the inside of her foot with his heel. She obeyed the silent command, shifting her feet wider, but not far enough. He tapped her other foot.

"Mac..."

"Show me, Jessie."

She did. Spreading her legs wider, arching her hips higher so he had a full view of her glistening pussy, the inner lips swelling with her arousal to pass the thick outer ones. He brought the cold glass against that tempting flesh as he touched the base of the plug tucked between her cheeks. She jerked and gasped.

"Careful," he warned her. "Wouldn't want to spill my drink, would you?"

Her "No" was choked.

He slid the glass down her vulva until the smooth surface rested above her clitoris. With a couple of wiggles of his wrist, he made contact between the two. She bit off her instinctive cry. From the tilt of her head he could tell she was worried about who was behind the curtain. He kept the chilled glass against her clit as he reached up to trace the rounded rectangle of the plug base.

"Which one did you chose?"

He didn't give her time to answer, merely slipped two fingers of his other hand under the base and pulled. The resistance was substantial. Her breath came in high-pitched squeaks as her little rosette flattened and bulged. The table wobbled as she cried out again and pulled back, working against him. He leaned over, letting his chest graze her back as he put his glass on the table.

"You've been bad, honey girl," he whispered against her ear, tugging gently on the plug. "You used the biggest one, didn't you? Even after I told you that you weren't ready."

"I'm ready."

"Uh-huh." He pulled harder. "I bet it burned like hell going in."

She nodded. Out of the corner of his eye he could see she was biting her lip. He bet it was burning now as the muscles slowly stretched to open against the pressure he was exerting. "Did you wish I was there, honey girl, when you slid it home? Did you wish it was me pushing it in, giving you that pleasure?"

She whimpered and nodded again. Her muscles parted more. The table rocked and shook with her body as the widest part of the plug forced her open.

He slipped his finger down to her engorged clit and rubbed gently.

"Oh God!" she groaned.

"Shh," he soothed as he pulled back. "Just relax and let it happen, Jessie. Let me see how much you took."

The pulsing rhythms of an earthy tune filtered into the room, reminding him they weren't alone. He sighed and reseated the plug in her tight ass, stroking her clit to soothe her through the moment.

"I think your show is about to go on." He stayed where he was as she gasped and tried to stand. That gorgeous ass rubbed against his cock. He caught her hips in his hands, sinking his fingers into the soft flesh, and dragged her back and forth against him. Teasing them both with what couldn't be.

"I hope this is quick," he told her, his voice nowhere near as unaffected as he wanted.

She ducked out of his grip, shimmying her dress down as she turned around.

Her gaze dropped to his crotch. He knew what she saw. His cock was so hard, he'd break in two if he sat. Her tongue swiped at her lips. Before he could stop her she grabbed his glass off the table and took a quick drink. Her face screwed up in disgust and she wheezed for breath as she held the glass away from her with two fingertips.

"God! That stuff is awful!"

He took his glass back before she could drop it. "That's what I keep telling everyone."

Jessie wiped her mouth with the back of her hand as if she could remove the taste. With one last shudder she straightened and shook out her arms. "Before we begin, I need your solemn promise that you will remain in your chair until I say the show is over."

"Interesting rules," Mac drawled. "Why?"

"Because I asked you to."

"And that's supposed to be enough?" They both knew it was so when she rolled her eyes, he shut up, adjusted his jeans and sat.

"Do you promise me?" she asked, hands on hips.

He settled a little deeper into the seat, trying to relieve the pressure on his cock as he watched her fingers flex and straighten. She was nervous. Obviously worried about how he was going to take this. Great. He took a sip of whiskey. "I promise."

Jessie tilted up her chin and recited from rote. "What you are about to see, Mac, is a test. When it's all over, you will be questioned, so please pay attention." Spinning on her heel, she headed across the room.

"Where are you going?"

His question halted her halfway to her chair, which resided at the foot of the stairs leading off the stage. She cast an exasperated glance over her shoulder. "To my seat."

He cocked an eyebrow at her. "How come you get to sit way up there?"

"Because I rate," Jessie snapped as the lights went out and the music took off in a resounding crescendo. The first dancer leapt onto the lit stage clad only in a spandex G-string. He was a redhead, he was built, and he was very, very good.

There was evidence of ballet in his moves along with some innovative bump and grind. Jessie saw his eyes widen as he caught sight of Mac scowling in the background. When he swallowed hard, almost missing a strategic pulse of his lean hips, she tried to smile encouragingly and subtly motioned him on.

She had instructed Coulton that she wanted the men to be as seductive as possible. They were to pull out all the stops, and as they descended the stage, they were to kiss her, searching for a response. Obviously the redhead—Bob she thought his name was—had taken the instructions to heart, for the kiss he pressed onto her lips after sauntering down the stairs was a lingering one. He broke it off rather abruptly when a glass slammed down hard on the table behind them. Mouthing a silent thanks, Jessie turned and faced Mac, totally composed. The haughty lift of her brows was a reminder to keep to his promise. The redhead walked over to the far left of the stage as the next dancer came out.

There were four dancers in all and the efforts of the previous seemed to inspire the following. Their antics grew more outrageous with every new song, and the kisses got longer and hotter until only Coulton had yet to strut his stuff.

The air became full of the sound of primitive drums as Coulton leapt onto the stage, his hair a golden swirl around a body as raw and as primitive as his music. A minuscule scrap of cloth protected his modesty in front, while nothing obscured his tight, muscled buttocks from view. The wicked glint in his eyes warned Jessie just before he executed a perfect leap to land two inches in front of her. He grasped her hands, pulling her to her feet while he shimmied erotically in front of her. His fingers drifted up her arms to slide under the curtain of her hair. His leg slid between hers and his hips pulsed to the music. A chair crashed behind them. The smile in Coulton's eyes spread to his full lips.

"You're going to get killed," she mouthed as his tongue slowly appeared to moisten his lips.

Coulton's response was to bury his face in the curls by her ear while his pectorals bounced and rubbed against her breasts.

Out of the shadows rumbled a warning growl.

"As gentle as a lamb, luv?"

And Jessie knew his outrageous behavior was her punishment for the small lie.

"I'll be lucky if he doesn't feed me my butt for breakfast." The wry comment was totally at odds with his seductive dance.

Before Jessie could even form a response, Coulton's mouth was on hers. His fingers on her cheeks pried her teeth apart, and his tongue slid into her mouth in an earthy kiss that promised all kinds of pleasures, while the hips sliding against hers merely affirmed the pledge. She glared up at him. He increased the depth of the kiss. He bent her over his arm. Sliding his thigh up between her legs. One of his big hands abandoned its hold on her nape to slide down, its destination obviously her breast. Jessie began to struggle in earnest. Mac would kill him!

"You'd better tell Goldilocks here, Jessie, if that hand so much as twitches an inch, I'm going to remove it. Permanently."

There was no mistaking the deadly threat in that glacial drawl. Jessie heard it, and apparently so did Coulton, for he released her so suddenly she stumbled and would have fallen if Mac hadn't caught her arm and pulled her up.

Coulton took one look into Mac's eyes and whistled long and low before smiling, bowing and taking shelter behind the curtain. The music stopped abruptly, and Jessie felt off-balance facing Mac in the deafening silence. She didn't let that stop her though. They were settling this tonight.

"I thought I told you to stay in your seat?"

"I thought we agreed sharing wasn't my bag."

"Who said anything about sharing?"

"Honey girl, when a man kisses a woman like that there isn't anything but sex on the guy's mind."

She ignored the rumble of male laughter from the stage, looked pointedly at the erection straining his jeans and said, "You should know."

"Yeah. I should." He was stubborn and arrogant, but he was hers and she'd just have to find a way to manage him.

Stepping close, so her breasts touched his heaving chest, she slid her arms up to circle his neck, but he was too tall. She settled for linking her fingers instead. Moistening her lips, she slid her hips into the cradle of his thighs and ordered huskily, "Kiss me, Mac."

Because she was his, because he had a primal need to mark her as such in the wake of her "show", Mac did as bid. He lifted her to meet the descent of his mouth. There was nothing tentative in the caress, only a desperate, driving hunger. At the first taste of the sweetness within, some of the brittleness he felt inside dissolved beneath exquisite pleasure, but not all of it. Jessie was up to something and part of him was terrified that something was a goodbye. After several heated moments, she pushed at his shoulder. Mac set her feet back on the ground.

Hands trembling, his breath sawing in and out of his lungs as if he'd just finished running a marathon, Mac stared into Jessie's passion-smoked eyes and felt a trill of pure male satisfaction. Only he could bring that color to her cheeks, that sexy fullness to her lips. No one else. Just him. She stepped out of his arms, and pulled her composure back around her desire with a grace he envied.

"You will notice," she waved in the direction of the stage where the dancers had formed a line, "that every one of the dancers is a young, handsome male in excellent physical condition."

"I noticed." Damn, was that his voice so low and hoarse and tinged with the urge to commit mayhem? It must have been because the look Jessie sent him bordered on a reprimand.

"I don't know what you're afraid of," she continued, "but since I couldn't rule out losing me to another, I thought we'd start off with something easy."

"Easy?"

"Yes." She gave him a slight push that landed him in her chair. "We're getting to the bottom of your fears tonight, Mac."

"I don't have any fears."

"Uh-huh. You've been feeding me that bull since I got here, and I still don't buy it. I've tried being patient. I've tried raising hell. And you know what? It doesn't get me anywhere."

"Maybe because there's nowhere to go." He slouched in the chair, his attention drifting to the stage where a lot of commotion was going on. He didn't want to talk about this.

Jessie hooked her finger under his chin. "Horseshit."

His gaze snapped to hers, surprised by the obscenity.

"That's right, Mac. I can swear like a trooper if I choose to."

Something crashed behind the curtain on the stage. "Hadn't you better go see what's going on back there?"

"No. I'm more interested in what's going on out here."

Jessie didn't flinch at the sound of breaking glass, but he did.

"Am I going to have a house left when this is done?"

"I'm sure Zach has everything under control."

"Zach?"

"Yes, Zach. You see Mac, I've decided I'm not willing to give you up."

"I wasn't aware that you were considering it." The very thought wrapped his gut into a tight knot of pain.

"I wasn't, but I can see it turning into an eventuality."

"You can?"

"Yup." She actually patted him on the head. "But don't worry. I'm not going to let it happen."

"And how do you intend to stop it?" A man flitted out from behind the curtain before disappearing again. Mac couldn't make out the face, but the long blond hair was a dead giveaway. "By having a bunch of half-naked men kiss you?"

"Well, I had to know if jealousy was one of your motivators."

"And?"

She sighed. "And you have a normal amount, but that's not *it*."

"It?"

"Yes, *it*. The *it* that keeps you up nights. The *it* that makes you forget I'm a perfectly capable adult. The *it* that makes you..." Her hand waved in the air encompassing everything, clarifying nothing. "The *it* that makes you the way you are now. Overprotective and fearful." Her gaze collided with his in perfect conjunction with her finger driving into his chest. "That's the *it* I'm going to fight."

Mac folded his arms across his chest. They were back to this again. "There's nothing wrong with a man taking care of his woman."

"Could you rephrase that?"

He set his chin stubbornly. "Why?"

"Because it makes you sound like a Neanderthal who's misplaced his century."

Despite his simmering anger, Mac grinned. "Want something more modern, huh?"

"Even something from the eighties would be an improvement."

"I can't remember the eighties."

"Try."

All joking fled. Mac caught her hand in his. It felt tiny, fragile, arousing all the protective instincts she wanted him to will away.

"I can't, Jessie." She stared at him. He didn't look away. He owed her this much of the truth. "What I feel for you isn't neat and tidy. Hell," he laughed. "I'm not even sure it's civilized."

"Then what is it?"

"It's primitive, all consuming. It's tenderness combined with lust. Admiration partnered with dismay. Joy mingled with fear." His fingers tightened around hers. He wanted to pull her close, the urge to make her understand that she was his stronger than ever before. "It's a mess is what it is," he admitted wearily.

"But a loving one?"

"Yeah. Definitely a loving one."

She squeezed his fingers gently before slipping free. It felt like an apology. "I've got to go."

"Go where?"

"Back on stage."

He ran his finger down her spine, a little confidence reasserting itself when she shivered helplessly and leaned back into his touch. "I gotta warn you Jess, my 'normal amount of jealousy' isn't going let me just sit here while another one of those steroid gods gets his jollies feeling you up."

"I don't think that's going to be your problem," she said obliquely over her shoulder as she hurried away and disappeared behind the curtain.

"Did you know," a voice at his shoulder announced in a disgustingly proper English accent, one Mac was sure drove women wild, "that steroids can utterly ruin a man's abilities?"

Mac looked into the amused blue eyes of the blond dancer. He looked at the man's hands which held two glasses and the whiskey bottle from his table. The same hands that had been on Jessie a few minutes ago. "Did you know that putting your hands, not to mention your lips, on Jessie in the future will make that causality a moot point?"

Instead of leaving, the male bimbo pulled up a chair. "Ah, but they were there by invitation only."

Mac poured himself more whiskey. As the amber liquid filled the glass, he set his teeth in a polite imitation of a smile. "If I were you, I'd consider that invite closed."

The man laughed outright. "It was never really open and you know it. Otherwise you wouldn't be sitting here talking to me."

"You're every perceptive for an...Englishman?"

"And you're very amusing for an American." He pointed to the whiskey bottle. "Mind if I have a bit of that?"

Mac noticed Jessie sending glances their way. "No shirt, no service."

The man laughed. "Relax, man. I couldn't turn that woman on with a blowtorch."

Mac raised an eyebrow, wondering if he was going to have to spoil that perfect smile after all. "That sounds like the voice of experience."

"She's something, our J. C."

"Considering you just had your hands all over her, I'd advise you to refrain from referring to her in any possessive sense."

"Can't help it." The blond looked unconcerned as he slouched back in his chair. "I asked her to marry me once."

Now, that was a surprise. "She turned you down, I take it?"

"Without a bit of tact, too."

Mac's smile was genuine this time. "She does have a way of just blurting out the truth without regard to self-preservation."

"Discovered that for yourself, have you?"

"Among other things." Mac held out his hand. "Mac Hollister."

"Coulton Westcott," he said, shaking hands before taking a sip of his drink. "So, what did you do to make all this necessary?"

"I'm not sure."

A drum roll interrupted the rest of what Mac was about to say. As the makeshift curtain slid open, Coulton stated the obvious. "Well, I'm sure by the end of tonight, there won't be much doubt."

"Damn! That'd better not be my lucky saddle."

But it was. Mac knew it in the pit of his stomach. The saddle that had taken him to three rodeo championships was now sitting in the middle of a huge bull's-eye.

"It doesn't look good, chap."

No. It didn't. Mac took a fortifying sip of whiskey as Zach came out on stage, dressed only in moccasins and breechclout, brandishing a set of throwing knives.

"Nice build," Coulton remarked before pointing to the saddle. "Wonder if he's supposed to hit or miss?"

"It'd better be miss."

"Either way, looks like you'll need this," Coulton said as he topped off Mac's already half-full glass.

"Thanks." Mac glared at the stage, at Jessie, and especially at Zach.

"Don't worry Mac," Zach called with a grin. "I'm feeling 'on' tonight."

Before Mac could respond, Zach let loose with three knives, so fast it looked as if only one flew toward the target.

Mac released a sigh of relief just as fast as they found their place. And chugged two swallows of whiskey.

"Looks like he was supposed to miss."

"Yeah," Mac wheezed as the liquor burned its way to his stomach. "God, I hate this stuff."

"Then why are you drinking it?"

"Because it's the only thing anyone ever shoves at me when I'm in need of support."

"Oh." Coulton lifted his glass toward the stage. "In that case, you might want to state a preference for whatever it is you do like pretty quickly."

Mac had a sneaking suspicion of what he was going to see before he looked up. Bracing himself didn't diminish the impact of Jessie standing where Zach had been, two knives on the table beside her, one in her good hand, and her eyes glued to the target.

Her "Pay attention, Mac," coincided with his chair toppling over as he jumped to his feet.

"Dammit, Jessie," he hollered. "That's my lucky saddle!"

Coulton grabbed his arm, halting his flight to the stage.

"Trust me, Mac," Jessie called over her shoulder. She dropped one of the knives. Muttering an "Oh, damn" that clearly carried to the men at the table, she bent over and picked it up. The knit dress hugged her curves every inch of the way.

Coulton whistled appreciatively through his teeth and rocked his chair back on two legs. "That woman always did have a body that could stop traffic."

Mac freed his arm. With a well-placed shove to the middle of Coulton's chest, he sent him the rest of the way to the floor. "Jessie…do you know how hard it is to break a saddle in? How attached a man gets to one once it's proven itself?"

Jessie spun around and placed her hands on her hips. Mac caught his breath as one of the knives came close to pricking the underside of her breast. "I'm well aware of your attachment to that saddle. I've even been meaning to discuss it with you." She frowned disapprovingly. "It borders on the unnatural."

"Just because you're jealous of my saddle, there's no need to throw knives at it."

"I'm not jealous of that hunk of leather," she retorted, "And I happen to think it's entirely necessary."

She turned around. Her arm drew back.

"Can I ask how long you've been doing this?" he called out desperately.

She halted mid-throw and turned back slowly. Coulton straightened his chair and resumed his seat. Mac didn't even spare him a glance. There was a certain light in Jessie's eyes that didn't bode well for his stalling tactics.

"Three days."

"Holy shit!"

"She's the best student I've ever had," Zach called out.

"She's the only student you've ever had," Mac corrected.

"You're ruining my concentration," Jessie informed him, facing the target. "So please, just hush up and trust me."

Mac opened his mouth to argue, but Coulton's hand on his arm distracted him long enough for the other man to point out, "As she's determined to do this, you might want to contemplate increasing the odds in your favor by closing your mouth."

He had a point. Mac shut up, and as her arm drew back, prayed. The first knife missed the saddle by a good four feet. It damned near missed the target altogether. He closed his eyes and didn't breathe as she released the next two. When the last thud indicated she was out of knives, he opened his eyes. Not a single knife was embedded in his saddle. Two were in the target. One was nowhere in sight. He raised an inquiring eyebrow at his companion.

"I think you've got sheetrock work to do."

Mac slowly unclenched his fists. "That's easier than breaking in a saddle."

Coulton grinned and started clapping. "That's one way of looking at it."

Jessie, her face glowing with success, took a bow. The front of her dress gaped far enough for Mac to ascertain she wasn't wearing a bra. He shot a glare at Coulton. "Don't even say it."

The other man laughed but switched to swearing so fast, Mac was left blinking. "Even Jess wouldn't dare…"

Mac swung around to face the stage and the blood drained from his face. Zach was tossing knives in the air and catching them. One of the dancers was carrying off the saddle, and standing in the middle of the round target was Jessie. Her arms were above her head, her hands sliding into straps on the outer circle of the target. With her feet, she searched out the stirrups at the bottom.

"Son of a bitch."

"Ordinarily, I'm not one for interfering," Coulton began, his voice more of a hiss from between his teeth, "but if you don't step in here and stop this lunacy, I will."

"Don't worry," Mac countered, already in motion, "This has gone far enough."

Jessie stepped into the stirrups and rocked the target experimentally. "I think it's fine, Zach. What do you think?"

"Looks good from here."

"It looks like hell," Mac countered, stepping onto the stage. Zach caught his knife and put it with the others in his right hand. He looked entirely too happy for a man on the verge of death, Mac thought.

"Hey, Mac. How are you enjoying the show?"

"It's been interesting." He walked past Zach and stopped directly in front of Jessie. "I'm not going to let you do this."

"You don't have any choice."

"Yes. I do."

She shook her head emphatically. "No, you don't. You promised you'd stay in your seat and that's where I want you to go now." She rocked the target again.

"Tough." He slid his hand behind her waist and pulled. She anchored her good hand in the strap, and held on.

"I asked you to trust me, Mac."

"No." He pulled again. Harder. The target slid forward a couple inches, then stubbornly caught. Jessie was equally stubborn. She trapped his gaze with hers.

"I'm only asking you to trust me, Mac. Is that so very much?"

He looked over his shoulder at Zach who was arranging his knives. He looked down at Jessie as she arched over his arm, her head thrown back as she strained against his grip. The whiteness of her throat, the thrust of her collarbone all conspired to enhance her appearance of vulnerability. "Yes, it's a lot to ask of me when all it would take is a twitch on Zach's part for one of those knives to…" He traced the vee-neck of her low-cut dress with his finger. "I don't want to lose you Jessie," he finished hoarsely.

She raised her broken arm, awkwardly touching his cheek with her fingers. "And I don't want to lose you, so why don't you just trust in my judgment and go take your seat?"

He caught her cast in his hand, kissing her fingers. "I can't."

She pulled her hand free. "You're going to have to if you don't want me to walk out that door."

Astonishment relaxed his grip. She slowly subsided against the target as he asked, "You'd leave me over this?"

"No. I'd leave you over your lack of faith in my judgment."

"Ah, Jessie."

"Go back to your seat, Mac."

He stood there, waiting for her to understand, waiting for...hell, he didn't know what he was standing there for. He just knew going back to that table was more than any man could be expected to do.

Zach touched his arm. "Go back to your table, Mac."

"If you throw even one of those knives—"

Zach raised his eyebrows and looked down the length of his big nose. "Now who's being a fool?" He pointed a knife in Jessie's direction. "You willing to lose that woman over a few measly steps?"

Mac's hands bunched into fists at his side. "It isn't a few measly steps and you know it."

"Trust me, Mac," Jessie interrupted quietly.

She wanted him to trust her when she was going to let a man throw knives at her? Was she crazy? He opened his mouth and then shut it just as quickly.

"Please?"

God! How was he supposed to resist when she turned those eyes on him? Begged him in just that tone of voice? He spun on his heel and stormed back to his seat. Coulton's frown was the last thing he wanted to see. "Don't look at me like that."

"Like you've lost your mind? Now why would I do that?"

Mac grabbed his forearm as he made to get up. "No."

"I'm not going to let her—"

"We're going to let her do whatever the hell she wants."

"Why?"

"Because if we don't, she'll only do something more stupid."

"It would be pretty hard to top this." Coulton slowly resumed his seat.

"Trust me. The woman is as inventive as all get-out. She'd find a way to top it."

"And that's the only reason you're letting her do this?"

"No." Mac shook his head, scanning the room all the while for where they'd hidden the phone, just in case he had to dial 911. "She asked me to trust her."

"And that's it? You're going to let that big guy throw knives at her because she asked you to trust her?"

Mac shook his head. It did indeed sound crazy when put like that. Asinine even. He folded his arms across his chest. "Apparently so."

Chapter Fourteen

He changed his mind almost immediately.

"Do you want it spinning or stationary?" Jessie asked Zach as she stood inside that target, fiddling with one of the straps.

"I'm feeling lucky tonight. Why don't we let her rip?"

Mac considered that a poor choice of words. Coulton echoed his sentiments. "Couldn't he have chosen a different adjective?"

Mac clenched his fists so hard, he lost feeling in his fingers. "Zach was never overly concerned with what other people think."

"Really?" The speculative glance Coulton cast toward the stage gave Mac pause. "Can he dance?"

"Well, I can't say I've ever had the pleasure of him as a partner," Mac answered dryly, "but he never seems at a loss for the beat."

"Hmm."

"Move away, Jessie," Zach called, shifting the knives, "I want to take a couple practice shots."

The first one he threw hit the target high.

"Damn," Zach muttered.

Mac echoed that damn along with a few stronger epithets. He stared at that knife as it quivered in the target. In his mind he measured the distance from the foot straps to the knife. If his calculations were on, the only bull's-eye Zach was likely to find tonight would be the one between Jessie's eyes. It would be a cold day in hell before he would allow that. If Jessie chose to label his decision *interference,* so be it. He'd rather see her walk away than leave in a body bag.

Jessie's laugh filled the room. "Good thing we're using this dummy rather than myself."

A dummy? Mac paused halfway to his feet. Feeling like a total fool, he saw Jessie crossing the impromptu stage dragging a straw dummy as big as she was along with her. *Trust me, Mac.*

Hell. He sat down, rubbing his eyes and pinching the bridge of his nose between his fingers. He didn't need to feel like a fool. He really was one.

"That should do it, Jessie."

"Good luck, Zach."

"Thanks."

Mac heard the voices, but since he didn't care what was happening on stage, he didn't look up. He had some major fence-mending to do, and he wasn't quite sure where to start.

Native American music filled the air. A chant backed by flutes and drums.

"Hi, Coulton," Jessie whispered as she came up beside their table.

"You really had us going for a minute there."

From the corner of his eye, Mac saw Coulton's smile flash brightly. *Damned handsome bastard.*

"Really, Coulton, you should know me better."

"Apparently so."

Mac winced at hearing his words parroted so mockingly.

"I assume this part of the show is for my benefit?" Coulton asked.

"Yup. Zach thinks exotic dancing might be his niche, too."

"Isn't he a lawyer?"

She shrugged. "He said he could use a paid vacation."

"This business is good for that."

"Is he having trouble?" Mac asked with a frown.

Jessie didn't know. "He said it was personal when I asked." She turned to Coulton. "Will you let him audition?"

"He's got the body to make money, and that 'fuck the world' attitude of his will have the ladies swooning for sure, if his dancing holds up better than his knife throwing, I'd be a fool not to take him on."

"Good." She leaned forward and kissed his cheek. "Could you excuse Mac and me for a moment?"

"No problem."

* * * * *

There might be, Jessie thought looking over to where Mac sat hunched over. He had yet to look at her. She wondered if he ever would again. Some people had problems with getting the beejeezus scared out of them. And she knew she'd done that to him by giving the impression she was going to stand and let Zach throw knives at her. Foolish man. "Mac?"

He didn't look up. "What?"

"I'd like to talk."

"Could you manage it without me?"

"Not likely."

"Damn."

When he didn't show any signs of moving on his own, she grabbed his arm and tugged. "C'mon, Mac. No one's died of embarrassment yet."

"Uh-huh." He sounded anything but sure, but he got to his feet. Once there, he held tight to her hand and gathered momentum. He didn't stop in the hall, on the porch, or on the front lawn. He kept going until they came up against the corral.

Jessie reached down and took off her remaining heel. She'd lost the other somewhere between the porch and here. The summer grass tickled her feet as she waited for him to speak. When he did, it was an accusation. "You deliberately made me think you were going to let Zach throw knives at you."

"I know."

"Anyone might have thought you meant it."

"Probably. Until a natural sense of disbelief kicked in. That's the difference, Mac. When it comes to me, you have no common sense."

He ran his fingers through his hair. To his credit, he didn't argue, just curled his hand into a fist on top of the corral fence and admitted, "I owe you an apology."

"You'll get no argument from me."

He looked down, the light from the setting sun striking across his eyes making him flinch.

"I don't know where to start."

"Someone once mentioned the beginning was a good place."

His chuckle was weak, but there. Jessie viewed that as a good sign.

"Want some help getting started?"

"Yeah."

"What are you afraid of, Mac?"

"I'm afraid of losing you, Jessie."

"To another man?"

"No."

"To what, then?"

With a sweeping gesture of his hand, he indicated the barn, the corrals, and the vast emptiness beyond. "I'm afraid of losing you to the land."

"You think I'm so in love with scrub brush that I'll just wander off into it one day and not come back?"

"Damn you, why are you making me laugh when I should be crying or down on my knees apologizing?"

She stepped up onto the first rail of the fence. One step closer to Mac. "Maybe because I'm not interested in tears or apologies."

He turned to face her, his arm resting along the top rail. "So what are you interested in?"

"I'm interested in getting to the bottom of whatever it is that's driving us apart." She slid her arms around his waist, loving the solid warmth that immediately encompassed her. "I don't want to go anywhere, Mac."

His hand came up to cradle her head. "You want me to give you a reason to stay?"

"That would be a start. Along with an explanation."

He stared at her, his eyes dark with turbulence. She waited, knowing from the way his muscles tensed that he was ready.

"My mom never adjusted to life out here. She liked parties and people. She loved knowing she only had to step out the door in order to feel civilization surround her."

"And she loved your father."

Mac sighed. "Yes, she loved my father." He stroked her hair. "Dad said everything was fine at first. He met Mom at college in Dallas. They got married and lived their first two years in the city while Dad finished up his Bachelor's in Range Science."

"So what changed things?"

"Dad finished his degree. They moved to the ranch, and Mom got pregnant with my older brother Cord."

"A triple whammy."

"Yeah." He paused, lost in the memories. He resumed stroking her hair, his words picking up the careful rhythm. "Mom never recovered from it."

"And you think this is what's going to happen to me?"

"Not exactly."

"So what? Exactly."

"You don't know what it's like, Jessie," he burst out, his low drawl replaced by the staccato reverberations of memories, "watching someone you love sit day after day staring at a wall, slowly wasting away because they can't see the point in eating, or drinking. And they can't tell you why, because they can't hold the thought long enough to form an answer—"

"I've heard depression can be devastating to the entire family," she cut in, not able to hear that much pain in his voice without doing something, even something as mundane as interrupting, to alleviate it.

"It's hell."

"I've also heard people can be genetically predisposed."

"I'm not like my mother."

Jessie reached up and touched his cheek, knowing another fear had just found its way to the light. "I suspect you're a lot like your father, but Mac..."

"What?"

"I'm not like your mother, either."

He sighed and dropped his arms until both surrounded her waist. Then he hugged tight, rocking them back and forth. "It can be lonely and boring here, honey."

"I don't find it lonely and I'm only bored when you curtail my fun."

He slid his arm around until he could tap her cast. "You take too many chances."

"Bull. The only chances I take are calculated risks. I never would have broken my arm if Jute hadn't slipped that burr under the saddle."

"You have a wild streak in you, Jessie; that scares the hell out of me."

"I like to have fun, Mac, but I don't do anything without consulting my brain first."

"You made that point very effectively this evening."

"I'm glad." Jessie took two steps back, feeling his arms slip regretfully away from her. "I hope you'll remember that in the days to come."

"I'll try."

"Good, because, Mac?"

"Yes?"

"I'm moving into town."

"What?" He snapped up straight, all nostalgia gone.

Jessie had expected just such a reaction. That's why she'd moved away, but it was still hard to say this.

"What in hell for?"

"I'm leaving because while I think tonight might have opened your eyes to the problem, I'm not fool enough to believe it's a cure."

"So you're running out?"

"No. I'm giving you space."

"I think you're going overboard."

"Uh-huh. Look me in the eye, Mac."

"I'm looking." Technically, that wasn't true. He was doing an in-depth study of the general area, but she wouldn't call it direct contact.

"Now," she said, letting the discrepancy pass. "I want you to think how much you love me and tell me you don't see an image of your mom as you last saw her."

He was a long time answering, reinforcing her conviction that she was doing the right thing despite his next words.

"I can get a hold on it Jessie, now that I know what's driving me."

She folded her arms around her waist, needing an anchor, knowing it couldn't be him right now. "I'm counting on it. That's why I'm leaving."

"I hope you understand that doesn't make a bit of sense."

"It makes perfect sense to me."

He leaned his shoulder against the fence and crossed his arms over his chest. "Would you be in the mood to explain it to me?"

"I might." She wished she could maintain the same confident pose while confessing this, but she couldn't, so she concentrated on her cast, her finger tracing the signatures there. "I have my weaknesses, too. And you're one." She risked a quick glance up and caught a slight smile tilting his lips. "I have a tendency to think I can fix anything if I try hard enough." She shrugged, feeling the helplessness, burying the doubts. "I can't fix this for you, Mac. This battle is yours alone. If I stayed here, I'd make excuses for you, allow you to seduce me away from reality, and just," she shrugged, "generally screw things up trying to make things easier for you."

His finger under her chin forced her gaze to his. There was a world of love and compassion in his eyes. "But you'd still be unhappy?"

"Yes."

"You'd still feel trapped?"

"Yes."

He sighed wiping a tear from her cheek with a brush of his thumb. "Then I guess maybe you're doing the right thing."

"I hope so."

He laughed, a hoarse sound that combined humor with love, misery with hope. "Don't go shilly-shallying with determination now, honey girl. Not unless you want me to succumb to my instincts and kiss you until you can't imagine any life but one with me."

"I can't."

He hugged her tight. "But not the way things are now?"

"No."

"Then pack your bags."

She looked up into his eyes, loving him so much for his understanding. "I already did."

He flicked the end of her nose with his finger. "Not taking any chances, huh?"

"Plain mush when it comes to you." She swallowed. Hard. Fresh tears burned her eyes. "Thanks for making it easy for me."

He wiped a tear off her cheek. The tenderness in the gesture almost undermined her resolve. "Just keep in mind I'll be making it just as easy for you to come back."

"As I said, I'm counting on it."

"What are you going to do?"

She wanted to ask him the same question but she bit her tongue. Whatever Mac did, he had to do it himself. "Bull has offered me a job running the Bar and Grill. He said he and his wife have always wanted to take a second honeymoon. If I want a job, I've got one covering for them."

"And after that?"

She bit her lip, but replied honestly. "I don't know. I'll just wait and see what happens."

Between them lay the unspoken hope that she would be back at the ranch. Jessie never appreciated anything more than she appreciated the fact that Mac didn't throw out promises they both knew he might not be able to keep.

"When are you leaving?"

"Tonight."

"So soon?"

They'd already gone over the reasons why, so she didn't drag them out again. Damn, it was so hard to walk away when he stood before her, tall and strong, looking capable of winning any battle, but she had to, because if she hung around, he'd never work up to the fight. She wiped at the tears seeping down her cheeks, forgetting about her cast and scraping her cheek in the process.

"Ah, honey, don't cry. I'll get this thing under control in no time. Heck, after tonight, it's probably just a formality."

"It'd better be," she warned half jokingly. The kiss she aimed at his mouth landed on his chin. "I love you, Mac Hollister." Dropping to the ground, she dashed for the house, a deep, yawning void opening up inside, growing wider with every step.

* * * * *

For a mere formality, it was taking a long time, Jessie thought, six weeks later, as she stood in front of the grill at Bull's Bar and Grill. She sighed and flipped the burgers she was frying. Reaching into the bowl beside the cook surface, she pinched up a bit of her special spice and sprinkled it over the top of two of the burgers.

"Hey Jess, why don't you put a bit of that seasoning on mine, too?"

"You got it, Henry," she called over her shoulder as she zapped the last burger, waited a minute, placed a slice of cheese on one and then removed all three from the grill to the waiting, prepped plates.

"Did you want a pickle with that today, Henry?"

"Nah, I'll pass." She turned and slid the plates down the counter. Henry and his cronies each stuck out a hand at the appropriate moment, stopping their lunch before it could pass on by. It seemed she'd done this enough in the last weeks that it was a well-orchestrated play. A sad smile mustered its way from deep inside. She was going to miss this town.

"Mac will come around."

Jessie forced more cheer into her smile. "I know, Henry." She wiped her hands on her apron. "It's just that he's going to have to go a bit further after this week."

Henry sighed as if her problems were his own. "Bull can't afford to pay you anymore?"

"This isn't the busiest time of year."

"Maybe you could find a job somewhere else…?"

She shook her head.

Henry shoved a French fry into his barbecued beans. "Nah. I guess you couldn't."

He looked so woebegone, Jessie found herself in the position of having to cheer him up. "Hey, I can always come visit."

He lifted his eyes from his plate and the sadness in their depths was based on understanding. "But you won't, will you?"

She sighed. It seemed everyone in the restaurant stopped chewing in order to hear her answer. "No."

"Because it will hurt too much."

"Yes."

Henry thumped the ketchup bottle on the bottom so hard the contents gushed all over his plate. "Damn."

"Let me fix you another."

He pushed his plate out of her reach. "No thanks. I'm not hungry anyway."

Henry was always hungry. Jessie was touched that he'd forgo a meal in honor of her misery, but not enough to let a slight to Mac go unremarked. "Don't you give up on him."

"Why not? It isn't as if he's kept in touch. You could be dead for all the attention he's paid."

Jessie laughed at the absurdity of that. "C'mon, Henry. This is Round the Bend. I bet Mac is as aware of my movements as I am of his." She shot him a reproachful glance. "Or did you think I assumed your reports only went one-way?"

The older man had the grace to look uncomfortable. "I was kind of hoping you wouldn't think too hard on it either way."

"So…?"

"So what?"

"So why is getting information suddenly like pulling teeth?" she asked as she grabbed a soapy cloth and started wiping down the counter. "Is Mac back from wherever it is he disappeared to?"

Henry picked up a French fry and started drawing faces in the mess in his plate. "No."

She scrubbed harder at the counter as if through that alone she could release the frustration inside. "Damn."

"Maybe it is time you got out of here."

"What?" Jessie looked up at Henry's friend Cole, not understanding his reference.

He nodded in the direction of the towel in her hand. "The way you're rubbing at that counter brings Bull to mind."

Jessie tossed the towel in the sink and threw her hands up in surrender. "Heaven forbid!" She turned as a commotion in the street caught her attention. And held it.

Two horses raced up the street, a dust storm kicking up in their wake. On top of the horses two men perched, wild whoops heralding their approach. One of those riders looked familiar. There was no mistaking the long black hair flowing out behind him. She squinted to be sure. "Is that Zach?"

"Sure looks like him," Bull said, coming out of the back where he'd been doing books. "You don't suppose he finally came to his senses and quit that damned dancing, do you?"

Jessie frowned, concentrating on the second man. "I don't think that's likely. Coulton said he's the hit of the show." She held her breath, because the second man looked familiar too. Dearly so, and she was afraid of hoping after six weeks of disappointment.

"Is that Mac riding with that crazy fool?" Cole asked. "What the hell is he dressed up like an Indian for? And what's that stuff on his face?"

Jessie caught the edge of the counter for support. Speculation ran rampant around the bar, but she didn't participate. Couldn't even care less, because it was Mac. He was finally here and those were laugh lines peeking through the crazy blue makeup surrounding his eyes. Zach dismounted and opened the double doors of the bar.

"You don't suppose he plans on…" Henry stopped to hoot with laughter and slap his thigh. "Hot damn! Clear a path, folks. That boy's coming on in!"

And he was. Horse and all plunged up the steps and into the restaurant. People scattered right and left, dragging tables and chairs with them, alternately laughing and shouting encouragement. Mac knocked his head on the top of the door. He swore, rubbed the spot, but he kept on coming. Straight to the counter behind which Jessie was standing. And with every step, the lines around his eyes deepened.

An answering laughter blossomed deep inside Jessie. "Hi, Mac."

"Nice woman."

She smiled, recognizing her cue. "Thank you."

"Me great warrior."

"I can tell that from your coup feathers attached to…" She peered around the horse's neck, "…your arm."

He ran his eyes from the top of her head on down. He took so long with his perusal, goose bumps sprang up along Jessie's arm and the bystanders started catcalling advice. "Damned nice woman."

She reached behind her and untied her apron. "If this is some sort of Western pickup, I've got to tell you, I'm…" Her eyes did just as thorough a perusal of his bare shoulders and chest as she tossed the apron on the counter, "definitely interested."

Mac's teeth were very white against the black makeup he'd smeared around his mouth. He scooted back on the horse's hindquarters and held out a hand, "Come, woman."

Jessie debated the barricade of the counter for a moment, but then Bull's hands around her waist took care of the matter. "Up you go."

Her "Thank you" went unnoticed as the grill's patrons and the small crowd outside cheered when her hand met Mac's and he pulled her sideways onto the saddle in front of him. She immediately wrapped her hands around his waist and snuggled close to his chest. He reeked of greasepaint and horse. She didn't think she'd ever smelled anything as welcome in her entire life.

As he backed the horse around, he dropped a kiss onto her head and stated clearly, "You my woman now."

She was, but there was something she wanted to know before she admitted it. She looked up into his laughing blue eyes and demanded, "What in hell took you so long?"

The cheer that had been dying down took off on wings of laughter as those closest to the door heard what she'd said and passed it down the line.

Chapter Fifteen

"What in hell took me so long?" Mac asked as he stood in the master bath of his house, scrubbing the last of the greasepaint off with cold cream. "Your man does his romantic best to sweep you off your feet, and that's how you respond?" His right eyebrow kicked up in the manner she loved, bringing a smile to her lips. "Not 'I love you', not even 'at last'. Just, 'what in hell took you so long'?"

Jessie leaned her shoulder against the doorjamb and smiled up at him. He wasn't angry. Tired, yes. Relieved, yes. Anxious, yes. Her gaze dipped to his groin where his cock bulged—and maybe a bit horny. But he wasn't angry. "It was what I most wanted to know."

Mac tossed the towel he'd been using on the toilet lid and peered into the mirror while asking, "Did I get all that gunk off?"

"Mostly." She took the step necessary to touch a finger to the corner of his mouth. "You don't look so fierce anymore."

He slid his arms around her waist and leaned back, bringing her hips into his. Her braid fell over his arm, as he wrapped it around his wrist, tugging her head back further. "I don't, huh?"

A tiny frisson of anticipation skittered along her nerves. He had that look in his eye—the one that said he knew something she didn't. The one he always had when he took over and gave her the hottest times. She snuggled the ridge of his cock into the crease of her thighs. "Nope."

The laughter took Mac by surprise. Almost as much as the overwhelming surge of tenderness that accompanied it. "You've been sorely missed around here, Jessie girl."

Her response of "Good" sounded off, and her gaze avoided his. He tipped her chin up. Shadows flitted in her eyes. Kissing each lid closed, he dropped another kiss, just for the hell of it, on her nose, and then backed her out of the bathroom. She kept her eyes closed, probably thinking she hid her uncertainty from him, yet trusting him to steer her safely. He pulled her chest a little tighter to his. Damn, he loved her. Her eyes popped open as soon as the back of her knees hit the bed.

"You weren't thinking of sidetracking me, were you?"

He placed his fingers on her shoulders and gave her an easy push, toppling her onto the mattress. She lay there, a smile on her face and a question in her big green eyes. Hopeful.

"Nope. When I get serious about that bed, you'll know, and it won't be anything as trivial as a side trip." He sat beside her, running his fingers along the soft curve of her cheek. "I was just planning on getting more comfortable."

She shifted up onto her elbows, and narrowed her eyes. "This talk isn't going to be a formality, is it?" There was a wealth of suspicion in her voice as she pointed out, "'Cause your definition of formality stretches into forever."

Mac laughed and braced himself on his elbow beside her, cupping her chin in his hand. "I'm humbly sorry for taking so long to get my head screwed on straight." He shifted. When she lost her balance, he pulled her into his arms, snuggling her cheek into his shoulder. "That's better."

She didn't move, just lay there, soft and trusting against him. When he looked down her eyes were closed and her face had an expression of intense concentration. She opened her eyes and lifted her left hand to touch his jaw.

"I missed you." The aching sadness in her voice tore at him. Catching her hand in his, he pressed it hard against his cheek. "I missed you too, honey girl. Every damned minute of every damned day."

He ran his thumb over her fingers and frowned. Something was definitely missing.

"Where's your ring?"

She touched the hollow between her breasts with her fingers. Beneath the material of her T-shirt, he noticed a bump. "That is not where it belongs."

Her eyes darkened with that uncertainty he wasn't used to seeing, and did not want to see.

"I wanted to wear it, but when I went to switch it over to my left hand after the cast came off, it just didn't seem right." She shrugged, her teeth going to work on her lip, a sure sign she wasn't comfortable. "Not with things still up in the air between us."

Hell. He touched her cheek, the faint shadows under her eyes. "I told you I was keeping you, honey girl. Nothing was ever up in the air between us after that." Her teeth were at her lip again. He couldn't ignore her question anymore. He'd go through any level of embarrassment to put the confidence back into her gaze.

"I'm sorry you thought differently." He pulled her lip from between her teeth. "After you left, it took me a while to figure out where I should start."

"Where did you start?"

He grinned ruefully. "At the bottom of a whiskey bottle."

"Oh, Mac."

"Don't go looking at me like that." He kissed the disappointment from her lips, lingering to tease himself with her response. Only after her mouth opened beneath his, her breath mingled with his, her tongue yielded to his, did he pull back. "It wasn't as if I went on a bender. I can't stand the stuff."

"Then why did you drink it?"

"Because I didn't want to go on a bender."

"Oh."

"It was rough, Jessie. Real rough."

She propped herself on his chest. He knew the memories were in his eyes, the remembered helplessness. It was all he could do not to look away. "I got halfway through the bottle before I could bring myself to remember that day."

"The day you…found your mother?"

"Yeah."

"What'd you do then?"

He laughed, a short, bitter sound that had little to do with humor and everything to do with pain. "I chugged the rest of the bottle so I could forget the little bit I'd brought forth."

The expression on Jessie's face said more than words. "I know, not exactly productive. It took me another week to work up my courage to call a doctor in Dallas. They were willing to meet with me, but I had to wait six days for an appointment, and I only got that because someone cancelled."

"I'm assuming you're talking about a psychologist?"

"Yup. The first appointment was a breeze. All he had me do was outline the situation. He didn't ask me how I felt or anything."

"I'm assuming they all didn't go that way?"

"Heck, no. At the end of the first appointment, he gave me a list of books to buy, all dealing with depression. There was even one that talked about the history of treatment."

She held her breath as she asked the next question. "How did your second appointment go?"

"Like I got my foot caught in the stirrup and got dragged a good mile."

"That sounds pretty nasty."

He opened his eyes. "I never knew I could feel such rage, Jessie. It was like a stranger leapt into me and started using my mouth to make conversation." He grimaced. "And it wasn't exactly polite."

"But it helped?"

"Not at first. At first, I was too shocked by the things I said to really understand. I could understand being mad at that doctor who gave her the Valium even though it was common practice in his day. I could understand being mad at my dad for always working, but how could I be mad at my mother? She was sick, scared, and eventually, dead."

He could tell she didn't know what to say, but the kiss she pressed against his chest said all she really needed.

He curved his hand over her skull, weaving his fingers into her hair, holding her mouth against him, the heat teasing him through his shirt. They had way too many clothes on. "You don't have to say anything. I've been meeting with that psychologist twice a week for the last month. I've talked and read until I'm blue in the face and blind in both eyes."

He lowered his head until he could feel her breath on his lips, soft and hesitant.

"I wish I could have been there for you," she whispered.

"This is better. Me with you. Whole." He brushed her lips with his. She smelled of burgers, pickles, and dearly beloved woman. His woman, and he was never going to let her go again. Because it felt so good, he rubbed his lips over hers again. When the tip of her tongue snuck out to moisten the flesh he was playing with, his good intentions went straight down the tube. "Ah woman, I've missed you."

In answer, her arms came around his neck, and her lips parted under his. She tasted like heaven. Like the other half of his soul. He kissed her hard and deep, trying to express how much she meant to him with every brush of his tongue, every nibble of his lips. She leaned into him as if she too needed to imprint him into her being with the same intensity. When they drew apart for air, he asked hoarsely, "Want to know where I've been this weekend?"

"Not at this particular moment," she announced, her eyes on his lips.

He laughed, bouncing her around on his chest as he did so. He curved his fingers through the hair at the base of her neck to stabilize her. "We'll get to what you're thinking in just a minute, but first I want to say this."

"And then you'll kiss the socks off me?"

He rubbed his bare feet over her equally bare ones. "Since I've already done that, why don't I make a more interesting promise?"

She arched her hips against his and chuckled, and then chuckled some more when her laughter produced the inevitable surge of his cock.

"How about I promise to spank that sweet ass of yours?"

"For what?"

He raised an eyebrow at her. "Does it matter?"

The blush crept out of the open neck of her shirt to spread over her cheeks. Against his chest, her nipples hardened. He caught one between his fingers, squeezing it until she moaned and arched into his hand, keeping the pressure there as she sighed a "Yes."

"How about for doubting I was coming back?" He twisted the plump nipple slightly, watching her face. Her breath came in little hitches and her thighs shifted on his. "You're going to come like a firecracker when we get serious, aren't you, honey girl?"

She bit her lip, but didn't avoid his gaze as she nodded. "It's been so long."

The way she said it—her body tight with anticipation, her muscles quivering, almost desperate—made him pause. "You didn't get yourself off while we were apart?"

She shook her head. "It didn't seem right."

He sensed the "Without you" that she left unsaid, but he wanted to hear it aloud. Needed to hear it. Releasing her nipple, he slid his hand down her belly, smiling when she stopped breathing altogether as he reached the snap of her jeans.

"Why?"

Her expression turned mutinous as the zipper on her jeans slid down, and he slipped his fingers just under the flap. "Tell me, Jessie." He tugged the curls at the top of her pubic bone while nibbling at her neck. "Why didn't it seem right?"

His finger slipped into the crease of her labia. The hard nub of her engorged clit bumped his finger.

"Because you weren't there," she gasped, arching her hips up to increase the contact. The tightness of her jeans frustrated her efforts.

"Good. I don't want you ever coming without me."

"Did you come without me?"

"Only when I was so lonely for you I couldn't bear it."

She frowned at him. "How often was that?"

He kissed the belligerence from her lips. "At least three or four times a day I'd picture you in my mind, and remember how it was between us. How you make that sexy little whimper when I please you just right..."

"And you came for me?"

"Oh yeah."

"And it was enough?"

He rested his forehead against hers and rocked his head in a small negative movement. Words would never be able to convey how empty he had felt without her. "Not nearly enough."

"Good."

He smiled at the satisfaction in her tone. He acceded to her body's demands and stretched his finger to touch her clit again. This time he didn't pull back, just let it rest against the swollen, slick nub, noting the acceleration of her breathing, the narrowing of her gaze, and the rising of her desire. Oh yeah, she liked that.

"Can I finish my explanation now?" he asked.

"Are you insisting on it?" she countered distractedly, her focus clearly lower.

"Yes." He made the tiniest of circles with his finger. She whimpered the way he liked, the way that made his cock throb and his balls threaten to burst. "But first let me hear that sweet little whimper again."

He pressed a little harder, a little longer. Her nails sank into his shoulders as she tried to tug him closer. Jessie cried out, her body jerking against him.

Maybe further explanations could wait. "Are you going to come for me, Jessie?"

Her eyes slightly desperate, she shook her head, her gaze flying to his groin, her expression hungry. "I can't."

He really was going to have to do something about that hang-up.

He stilled his touch and very tenderly kissed her mouth. "Yes, you can, honey girl. Just let go. You don't have to worry about me; I'll come for you whenever you want."

"Now," she panted rocking on his finger, her lips nipping at his. "I want you to come now." He stroked her firmly and she screamed, "Oh God! I need you to come now."

He shook his head, pulling back. "No, you don't."

She arched her back off the bed, her face a mask of frustration. He withdrew his hand.

"Damn you!" she cursed, swinging at him. He caught her hand and brought it to his mouth, pressing a kiss into the palm.

"Shh, Jessie. We'll get there but right now I need you to undress for me."

Her fingers curled until her nails pressed into his cheek. He met her gaze steadily. She groaned again and pushed off to stand by the bed, shoving her jeans down. Her thong caught on her thighs. He smiled as she kicked off her jeans and tore off the thong. She reached for her shirt and he stopped her. "Just the bra."

She frowned at him. "You want me to leave the shirt on?"

The white knit top skimmed the juncture of her thighs, teasing him with a glimpse of her swollen eager pussy, and the long, endless expanse of her legs. "Definitely."

Her gaze followed his. Her lips quirked and she flicked the hem, giving him full view of her delectable pussy. Then she turned, looking over her shoulder at him, flashing her ass, as she reached up under her shirt to unclasp her bra. He smiled at her antics, letting her play for the moment. She wiggled out of the bra, held it out to the side, tossed him a grin and let it drop to the floor. His smile broadened as he twirled his finger. She turned. The cotton lovingly hugged her curves, making them seem fuller, softer, more lush. He sat up on the bed and crooked his finger. She came, hips swishing, breasts bouncing, nipples perking. One step, two steps until those incredible breasts bobbed in front of his face. While he watched, she cupped them through the T-shirt, squeezing at the base, dragging her hands forward until it was the nipples she was squeezing and drawing out, holding for his pleasure. And hers.

He leaned forward, taking the right one in his mouth, sucking it through the shirt as she held it and gasped, the scent of her arousal softly wafting up to surround him. His cock throbbed and ached. He fought back his impatience and lightly scraped the engorged nubbin with his teeth, catching her hips in his hands as she whimpered and stumbled. Then he moved to the left one and treated it to the same pleasure. When he nibbled it, she fell into his grip, needing him to support her. He took her weight easily, pulling her into the cradle of his thighs. He put a couple of inches between them. Just enough that he could enjoy the sight of the wet cotton clinging to her breasts, delineating their proud thrust.

He touched her nipples. "These are definitely worthy of ornamentation."

She sucked in a breath. "If you think I'm getting pierced..."

He covered the tips with his fingers. "Hell no." He stroked them softly, protectively. "I was thinking some danglers might be nice, though. Maybe something with stones to match your eyes."

She relaxed into his hands, her back arching slightly as she reached and brought her braid around. "How do they stay on?"

"A little noose."

She looked down as she undid the braid. "A noose?"

He smiled at the skepticism in her tone. "First I get your nipples all hard."

She smiled. "That sounds fun."

"Oh, it is." He tugged her nipples out, twisting them delicately, tempting them to reach for him, for more, and then harder as she stirred against him. "Yeah. Just like that."

Both peaks thrust out from dark centers under the wet cotton. "Then I slip the noose on and tighten it up."

She fluffed her long, honey-blonde hair around her shoulders. Tossing the band onto the nightstand, she asked, "Will it hurt?"

Bracketing her rib cage between his hands, he fanned his fingers over the surprisingly narrow expanse. Sometimes he forgot how much smaller than him she was.

"Does this?" He cushioned his teeth behind his lips, caught the base of her engorged nipple in his teeth, and bit down—gradually, deliberately—feeling the resilient flesh compress.

"No."

He bit harder. Under his hands, her ribs expanded on her harshly indrawn breath. He paused. Her fingers sank into his hair. More of her weight fell against him.

"Don't stop!" she moaned.

He added a little more pressure. She ground her pussy against his stomach, her movements short and awkward at first, becoming smooth and flowing as her juices slicked his skin. Damn, she was hot. He held her there on that edge, not giving her more, not letting her take less. She stroked against him, frustration making her whimper as she struggled for the relief she needed.

He released her nipple. "It'll feel just like that."

She yanked on his hair, her head falling back when she realized the demo was over. "Oh no..."

"Easy, honey girl."

She bucked against him as he stretched his thumbs in and down until he reached the top of her wet slit. He pressed. She jerked. Her head fell forward to rest on his shoulder. A quick check revealed she was watching his hands on her, her lower lip locked in her teeth. Hoping. Anticipating. He turned his head and kissed the corner of her mouth.

"I'm going to touch your clit now," he whispered against her cheek, his voice hoarse with need. "I'm going to stroke it and rub it, and you are going to come for me."

She cut him a panicked glance, her lip sliding free as she gasped, "But I can't. I need—"

He held her gaze, and slid his thumbs down. His "All you need is me" coincided with his callused fingertip tenderly scraping her aching bud. She blinked, bit her lip, and groaned.

"Doesn't that feel good?" he asked as he circled the nub, his fingers moving smoothly with the aid of her juices.

She nodded. He stopped. "I want the words. No holding back."

"Yes."

"Yes what?"

"Yes. It feels good."

"Then let's do it some more." He did, over and over, widening the circles, deepening the pressure, tipping her hips forward, forcing her to rely on him more and more for her balance. Her pleasure.

Her body was taut, quivering with tension. He could feel the fine tremors racing under her skin as her breathing became more and more labored.

"Come for me, honey girl."

She shook her head, her long hair swishing across his skin like silken fire. "I can't."

"Yes. You can." He caught her clit between his thumb and forefinger. She was very hard, very swollen. Very sensitive. "Just let it happen, Jessie."

He tugged gently. She screamed, her fingers locked on his shoulders. He did it again. Her knees buckled. He stroked back to her vagina, keeping his touch featherlight. Circling the small opening, he teased the ring of muscle with the threat of penetration, smiling in satisfaction when it spasmed and clutched at him. He caught the sweet spill of juices as they flooded his hand, carrying them back to the tight rosette just behind, spreading them over that tempting opening as he whispered in her ear, "If you come for me, Jessie, I'll fuck your ass." He probed the dark channel, giving her just the tip of his finger. "Don't you want that? My cock in this tight butt? Parting you? Taking you? Making you mine in every way?"

"Yes." It was more of a sob than a word.

He eased his finger in all the way. The smooth muscle clenched at his finger, making penetration difficult.

"Oh God! Oh God! Oh God!"

She was tight, very tight. Sweat dripped off her belly onto his hand.

"Have you been using your plugs, Jessie?"

"I did."

He pulled his finger out, letting it hover against her anus as he asked. "Did?"

"I stopped—" She moaned when he slid his finger back in, bearing down. She gathered her breath while every muscle stretched and searched for a deeper invasion. "I stopped when you didn't come," she confessed.

"Why?"

The word hung between them—he didn't know if she was gong to answer. Didn't know if he wanted to hear the answer, but knowing he needed to. "Why Jessie?"

He slid his finger back out, and then in again. She worked her hips on him, her movements frantic. Out of the corner of his eye he could see her biting back her answer, her teeth white against the red of her lip. He slid his other hand around until he could center his thumb on her clit, rubbing it in time with his fucking of her ass, and repeated himself, raising his voice to be heard above the whimpering screams. "Why?

"Because it was too damned pathetic." More sweat dripped on his arm. Her shirt was drenched and still she wouldn't let herself come.

He fucked her faster with his fingers, driving her toward the edge, watching her expression. "What was?"

She sucked more of her lip into her mouth and bit hard enough to leave dents as he added a second finger to the one seducing her ass, but she was still pushing back, begging for more.

She turned her head to look at him, the anger in her expression doing nothing to hide the agony in her eyes, the vulnerability. "A twenty-nine-year-old, screwed-up, near virgin fucking her own ass with a plug in the hope that a guy who's probably already moved on might think she's worth coming back for."

He froze, taken off guard, shocked that she could see herself that way. He certainly wasn't prepared for what she did next. She yanked free of his hands, yelping when his fingers pulled at her ass. Crossing her arms across her chest, she backed away, her green eyes moist.

"Not that I can blame you. Christ!" She bent down and grabbed her thong and pants, the tears she wouldn't let fall dripped in her voice. "I can't even orgasm normally."

She stood in front of him, her clothes clutched to her chest and had the gall to apologize to him.

"I'm sorry. I know you want me to, but I can't."

He'd never been more pissed in his life.

"Come here."

She took a step toward the door. "I'm—"

"Goddamn it, Jessie. If you apologize to me one more time I'm going to beat your ass black and blue and it won't be the sexy kind of beating you enjoy."

Chapter Sixteen

Jessie stared at him. Who did he think he was kidding? There's no way Mac would ever harm a hair on her head. Still, she'd never seen Mac like this. Wild. Primitive. Like he meant exactly what he said. It was scary, and it was thrilling if the way her womb clenched was to be believed.

"I said come here."

She did, albeit reluctantly.

"Put the clothes down."

Again she did, goose bumps chasing over her skin at the tightness of his expression.

His hand cupped her cheek, the tenderness in the gesture at odds with the harsh scrape of his drawl. "Take off your shirt."

She reached for the hem, but then paused, part of her afraid to break eye contact with him, not sure what he intended. He grabbed the bottom of the shirt and ripped it over her head. The shirt fell to the floor. He levered her chin up with his thumb. With the other hand, he lifted his ring from where it dangled between her breasts. When she had the guts to meet his gaze, it was hard and unyielding. "You're mine."

The mewling whimper that slipped past her control was pathetic. So was the way her juices spilled onto her thighs at the order, the scent of her arousal once more heavy around them. Heat crept into her cheeks, but it didn't matter if it wasn't right or if this was the new millennium. She loved him like this. Her body loved him like this.

The tips of his fingers grazed the side of her neck as he unfastened the necklace. The ring fell into his palm. She looked at it sparkling there, and then up into his hard expression. He took her left hand in his.

"You're mine," he repeated. He slid the warm metal over her finger. "Always have been, and always will be."

She stopped him before he could push the small circle over her knuckle. This was so not going to be a one-way relationship. "And you're mine."

The smile started in his eyes. "Always have been. Always will be."

The ring slid home, and the stubborn knot of cold uncertainty deep in her abdomen began to dissolve.

A tug on her hand and she tumbled onto the bed beside him. He leaned over, one hand stroking over her buttocks and down her thighs, easing them toward the floor, his hard chest pressing against her shoulder as he whispered in her ear, "Show me."

"Oh God." Lust spiraled up and out from her pussy, all the arousal of before coming back tenfold as she got her feet under her and braced her upper body on her forearms.

"Good."

The mattress shifted as he stood.

"Spread your legs."

She did, moving them a little further when he touched the inside of her left foot with his boot. He didn't do anything more. She could feel him behind her. Hear his even breathing, so different from her own choppy breath. He was waiting. For a desperate moment she couldn't think why. Then she remembered. Feeling awkward, embarrassed and somewhat silly, she reached behind with both hands and spread her cheeks.

His finger slid into the opening. There was a soft double thud. She looked over her shoulder. He was kneeling behind her, his face just inches from her ass. She buried her face in the comforter. She was so never going to be used to this. He stroked her ass soothingly. "Easy, Jessie. I just need to see if you hurt yourself."

"Couldn't you just ask?"

He laughed, his breath brushing across her sensitive flesh, causing the muscles to clench in delight. "It wouldn't be as much fun, and I can't chance you lying."

She rubbed her head back and forth, knowing she was going to regret asking. "Why not?"

His fingers probed gently. "Because I have plans for this sweet ass tonight. Big plans."

She dug her fingers into her cheeks. "Oh God, you're not going to torture me again, are you?" She couldn't take it if he did.

His fingers covered hers. "Gentle." She relaxed her grip. "Hold still now."

She did, not knowing what to expect. But even if she had known, nothing could have prepared her for the sensation of his lips on her ass or the charge that shot through her as he kissed her anus, his tongue coming out on the end of the caress to rim her sensitive rosette in long leisurely swirls.

"Oh God, you are."

She felt his smile spread across her crack. "Just a little here and there."

"Damn it, Mac!"

"Wider, baby."

"What?"

"Spread your cheeks wider."

"I don't want to."

"Why not?"

"Because you're mad and this is punishment and I'm so damned hungry for you I want to die."

He took her hands and slid them up her sides, his body following so he covered her like a blanket, his jeans rough against the backs of her thighs as he kissed his way up to her ear. "I would never touch you in anger." He placed her right hand by her head. "I was only mad because you don't know how precious you are to me." He placed her left hand on the other side of her head, "and the whole point of tonight is so that you never, ever, doubt it again."

The words wafted against her ear and shivered down her spine. Still she wanted one thing clear. "If convincing me means you tease my ass but never deliver, I'm not interested."

He set his teeth to the curve of her neck. She shivered helplessly, arching back into him as he snuggled the bulge of his cock into her buttocks. "You'll be interested in whatever I dish out."

"Said the big he-man."

"Said the man who loves you and knows what you want."

"And what's that?" she challenged, wiggling despite herself to seat him more firmly.

"My tongue in your ass."

Oh God! Did he ever know what she wanted. It was decadent and wicked and she was whimpering before he'd halfway reached his goal.

"Oh, I like that little sound. Let's see if I can make you give it to me again."

He did. Easily. All it took was his rough hands on her soft flesh, parting her, exposing her for the lash of his tongue. And she was whimpering, bucking, relaxing when he told her to, pushing back as he ordered her to, taking everything he gave her, helpless to do anything but seek the hot, decadent pleasure he offered so generously. Mercilessly. When she was sobbing into the comforter, he pulled back far enough to ask, "What do you need, honey girl?"

The need was relentless. Demanding. Consuming. She needed him. His scent. His taste. "Your cock. I need your cock."

He stood. The air was cool on her saliva-slick flesh. She shuddered. He reached into the drawer. A hand in the middle of her shoulders kept her still when she would have looked. Then he was beside the bed, his huge cock in his hand, the fat crown just inches from her cheek.

His hand slid up her spine, riding the bumps until he got to her nape. With gentle pressure he turned her head so her cheek rested on the comforter. He held her there while he brought his cock closer. She could smell his seed, earthy and sweet, see it glistening on the tip.

His fingers brushed a strand of hair off her face. "Take what you need, honey girl. Open your mouth. Let me see that little tongue that's going to make us both feel so good."

She did. When his cock rested on the hot wet cushion of her tongue, they both groaned.

"Suck my cock, Jessie. Any way you want. Any way you need."

His fingers on the back of her neck pulled her closer. She opened her mouth wide, working him past her teeth. His flavor melted through her mouth, salty and male. Uniquely Mac, reaching beyond the small space to the empty parts of her that had hungered for him for so long.

She moaned. He shuddered. She suckled him gently, content for the moment just to have him again.

"Damn, that's good," he sighed, reaching over her.

Yes. It was. She loved pleasuring him like this. Feeling him shake from the stroke of her tongue. Feeling the tension in his muscles, the fine tremors he couldn't stop. Tremors that she controlled. His pleasure hers to give or withhold. She could come from that alone.

He shifted his stance. His cock slid deeper. She sucked harder, lashing the tip with the whip of her tongue. A heavy weight settled on her back just above her waist. His hand, dry and warm, slightly rough. She paused.

"Ease up, honey girl," he ordered. "Keep me hard, but don't make me come. Not yet."

She arched her brow at him. After six weeks and the last half hour, she was more than ready to come. And for that she needed his cooperation. She cupped his balls in her palm. They were hard, drawn tight against his body. He was as eager as she was to come. If she could have smiled, she would have. Instead, she pulled her lips back from her teeth and raked him delicately in time with the squeeze of her hand.

His reaction was not what she expected. Instead of fucking her mouth hard in a prelude to coming, the hand on her back pulled her onto his cock. His thick shaft forced her jaws wider as he surged to her throat. She gagged. He pulled back. Just slightly, but he stayed deep enough that she couldn't do anything but hold him.

When she met his gaze, his was tolerantly amused. "I told you *not* to make me come."

Something thumped on the bed and then his hand came down on her ass in a sharp stinging blow that had her whimpering in pleasure. He added another to the first, and then a third, pacing the blows so she knew when to expect each one, letting her adjust to the sting, giving her time to feel the warmth spread out from her ass. The fourth blow had her whimpering again as it sent vibrations of heat ricocheting through her pussy that reached all the way to her womb. The fifth caught her by surprise, coming out of rhythm as it did, adding a driving edge to her desire that had her shifting in his grip.

Oh God! She wanted more. She tried to pull off his cock to tell him, but the hand on her back kept her firmly gagged. She could only communicate with the arch of her back, the twist of her spine, the presentation of her buttocks. It was enough.

He spanked her faster, then slower. Hard and then soft. Never predictably. Never exactly how she wanted, missing her clues so frequently he had to be doing it on purpose. The uncertainty only made her focus harder, experience each tantalizing connection deeper, until she was almost crazy with desire. Her pussy ached and cramped with emptiness, craving his touch, his cock. She needed to move. To be filled. To be fucked. She needed to participate. She needed him. Needed him.

She reached back, grabbed his wrist and tugged. He laughed at her ineffectual effort, a low seductive sound that became just one more aspect of the assault on her senses. She tried a different angle, working forward, taking his cock deeper, struggling with the urge to gag in an effort to drive him past his control to what she wanted. He laughed again, his swat on her ass too hard to be pleasurable. A warning.

She froze as the truth washed over her in a rolling wave of lust unlike anything she'd ever experienced before. She had no control here. Would not have any control here. She was totally and completely at his mercy. Exactly the way she'd always fantasized. As much as she'd fantasized, though, nothing could have prepared her for how intense the experience would be. How arousing.

She subsided back onto the burgundy comforter with a smothered sob, understanding what he'd known all along. Breathing carefully though her nose, acknowledging with her body's relaxation what she'd just accepted with her mind. She was his to do with as he saw fit.

Mac watched as Jessie relaxed, no longer fighting him for control. He gently stroked her hair as he eased her onto her side. He was going to make this so good for her. Better than what she'd sketched in her to-do list.

He pulled back until just the crown of his cock was in her mouth and repeated, "Keep me hard, honey girl, but don't make me come."

She did, sucking softly, working him with her tongue, her mouth gentle and accepting, but her body quivered with the feelings racing through her. Feelings he intended to take to the max. His hand shook as he held her head against him, battling his own need to fuck her mouth hard, to dominate. Her tongue toyed with the slit in the mushroom head. A light flick followed by a deep probe. He sucked in a hard breath. A bolt of desire tore up from his cock. Come leaked past his control. She eagerly sucked it down, and then, with a knowing glance at him, opened her mouth, letting him watch as her pink tongue swiped over the huge head of his cock. Jesus, she was always challenging him.

He grabbed up the inflatable butt plug and lube he'd tossed on the bed. In an efficient move he had it greased, and at the entrance to her rectum. Her eyes flew wide and locked with his.

He pressed. She jumped and then wiggled back, her soft moan of appreciation vibrating straight down his shaft to his balls. "I'm going to put this in your ass now, honey girl. Slow and steady."

Her eyes closed in satisfaction. He smiled. "There's just one catch…"

Her eyes opened. "I'm going to pump it up as it goes in, and I'm going to keep pumping until you suck the last drop of come from my cock."

Her expression was a combination of excitement and intrigue. He'd had a feeling she'd like this game. He nudged the tip in, watching her expression dissolve into bliss as her body stretched that first tiny bit. "Which of course means, how big this gets before it gets inside is totally up to you."

Her eyes flew wide as he gave the first pump. Her lips clamped down on him, her hands reached for his shaft. He shook his head. "I'm afraid not. You'll have to get me off with just your mouth. I need those hands back here, holding your cheeks clear."

She blushed and shook from head to toe. Her nipples beaded so tight and hard they looked ready to burst. Nevertheless, her hands went to her ass, and slowly, carefully spread her cheeks. He rewarded her with a deeper penetration of her rectum, taking the opportunity to gauge the tightness of her muscles. She had the first quarter inch. Damn, she was a snug fit!

She worked her head up and down the tip of his shaft, sucking hard on the withdrawal, easy while taking him in.

"Oh that's it, Jessie. Work that mouth on me. Come on, baby, suck me harder, let me feel your tongue."

She did. He made a big production of pumping the bulb. Not actually squeezing hard enough to inflate, just making enough noise that she thought he was. He pushed the plug in further, meeting her resistance. "Push back, honey girl. Push back and take it, baby."

He brought his hand around to her swollen clit. He stroked it in time with her sucking. "I'm going to make you feel so good tonight, but you've got to hurry and get me off. If you get too sore taking this too early, we won't get to do half of what I want."

He squeezed the bulb again. Her body jerked. He pressed hard on her anus. She sucked his cock with painful intensity. He stroked her clit with the same urgency with which her tongue lashed his shaft. Her muscles began to part, to let him in.

"That's it. Take it. All of it. Imagine it's my cock. Wouldn't you like that Jessie? Wouldn't you like it if this were my cock taking you? Coming into you that first inch?" He kept a steady pressure, forcing more into her as his balls drew up tight and pleasure radiated out from the base of his spine. "This is the thickest part, baby. I can't come until you take this. Relax for me. Show me how much you want me to come. Come on, baby. Show me."

He took her clit in his fingers, milking it in small strokes as she thrashed beneath the dual penetration of his cock and the plug. "Ah baby, I'm so close. Are you close? Your little clit is hard and throbbing. Are you ready, Jess? Can you come for me, honey girl?"

She squirmed and fought. Her fingers dug into her buttocks. Her teeth raked him once, then twice, letting him know in the only way he'd allowed her the answer to his question. Oh yeah, she was ready, and none too soon as he wasn't going to last much longer. She was too hot, too sweet, and he'd needed her for too long.

He pinched her clit hard as his come burst from his balls with a pleasure so intense he cried out. His cock jerked and throbbed in the compact heat of her mouth. He seated the plug in her ass as the first splash hit her tongue. She jerked forward on his cock, screaming as she convulsed. Against his hand her pussy clenched rhythmically as her juices gushed. He cradled her head against him as she moaned and sucked, stroking her clit lightly, prolonging her climax as she lapped and swallowed, taking all he had to offer, demanding more. Somewhere, from deep inside, he found just that little bit more of himself that she wanted. And handed it into her keeping.

*****

He waited until she calmed, smoothing the wild mane of her hair off her face, wiping a stray tear from her cheek, before kissing her temple. Her arms were wrapped around his hips, her lips around his cock. And though she'd just come, her legs moved restlessly on the comforter. While powerful, what they'd just shared wasn't enough for either of them. As witnessed by the way his cock was still hard, still straining in her mouth, rising to her needs. Needs he was eager to fill.

He slid his hands down her forearm. "Let me go, honey girl."

She shook her head. His cock bobbed against her cheeks. The sensation was unique. He paused, letting it flow over him before forcibly removing her hands and flipping her onto her back.

"Enough."

"But I like the way you taste."

"Good."

He held her down while he reached behind the headboard and flipped up the restraints tucked there. Before she could register what hit the bed, he had her right wrist in the cuff.

"Hey."

He knew the protest wasn't real. She had too many fantasies on that to-do list that involved being tied up to really protest. And her battle to keep the left one free was half-hearted at best. As he sealed the Velcro on her wrist, he smiled down into her anxious green eyes.

"This is going to be fun."

"It is?"

"Oh yeah."

He let his body drag along hers as he knelt between her thighs. His mouth stopped at her pussy while his hands skimmed the insides of both thighs until he could grasp each ankle. Her clit peeked out at him from between her red, swollen pussy lips as he brought each ankle up to rest beside his shoulders. He lapped it delicately as he grabbed the ankle cuffs attached to the wrist restraints. As she pressed her clit into his tongue he tied off her right ankle. The left wasn't as easy as she panicked. He held her as she struggled, using his torso to keep her flat, kissing her lips between soft murmurs. "It's okay. Jessie. Settle down, honey girl. We're just going to work on the last two things on that to-do list."

Jessie heard that. She lay very, very still, mentally going over what was on the list. Anal sex. And if she remembered correctly, being fucked by two men at once while being restrained. As the soft cuff fastened on her right ankle, another bubble of panic popped up right beside an incredible surge of lust.

"Mac?"

"What?" he asked as he pushed a button on the cell phone he dragged from his jeans.

"Are we still crossing that one item off the list?"

She had her answer before he turned to her, his softly voiced "Come on up," telling her what she wanted before he actually answered with a "No."

She tested her bonds. The straps were just long enough to rest her hands by her shoulders as long as she kept her feet tucked up tight against her, and unless she developed more muscle in the next five minutes—unbreakable.

The doorknob rattled.

"Mac, I'm not sure..." she whispered as she watched it turn.

He cupped her pussy where her juices continued to spill, her body's excitement far outweighing belated second thoughts. His dark blue eyes met hers. "I am."

He stepped back. The door opened. Zach stood in the entryway. He'd obviously availed himself of the downstairs shower because his face was scrubbed clean and his hair hung in long damp strands around his wide shoulders. Jessie blushed to the roots of her hair as his dark gaze went straight to her pussy and his fingers went to the buttons on his black shirt.

"Show him, Jessie."

The order caught her by surprise. Her gaze bounced between Mac's stern face and Zach's serious one. Part of her wanted to obey and part of her wanted to curl up into a ball of embarrassment. Mac leaned over her, his big body offering her some protection. His hands cupped her cheeks between his palms. "If you don't want this, honey girl, we can stop right now. Nothing happens that you don't want, but if you're only having second thoughts because you're worried that I'll think you other than perfect afterwards, think again. I've waited a long time for someone I could love, and who could match me sexually."

She bit her lip, measuring his expression for a lie. As far as she could tell, he was telling the truth.

"And I do?"

"And then some." He kissed her softly, sweetly. "I want to give you this pleasure, honey girl. Ever since I read how you wanted to be taken anally the first time, I've been on fire wanting it, too."

"You won't be jealous?"

"Pleasure doesn't have anything to do with possession."

"Everything okay, Mac?" Zach asked in his deep, easygoing voice.

Mac stood, keeping his gaze on hers, his body still sheltering her in an illusion of privacy, his fingers lingering on her cheek as he stood back and said, "Show him."

Jessie bit her lip. It was now or never. Either she had the courage to see her fantasy through or she didn't. A glance at Zach revealed he was standing at the foot of the bed. His shirt was unbuttoned, revealing his broad muscular chest, the dark hair that started just above his unsnapped jeans accented the gleam of his red-brown skin. He looked all male. More than capable of pleasing any woman. Mac came to stand beside him, equally masculine, equally strong. Definitely capable of pleasing her. In his eyes was a question she didn't have an answer for yet.

Her gaze skittered back to Zach. For the first time she dared look at his face. She expected to see anticipation and lust. She didn't expect to see the understanding or the gentleness. Not in a man this big or this tough. She bit her lip, and made her decision. Clinging to Mac's gaze, drawing her strength from him, she lifted her hips, watching the flare of satisfaction blaze in his blue eyes, not letting herself think of anything else beyond the pleasure she was giving him.

Her hips hit the mattress on a high squeak as she felt a hand cup her pussy. She wasn't used to anyone but Mac touching her.

As if they understood, Mac and Zach both stepped closer, Mac slid his thighs under her shoulders, sitting crossed-legged so he created a cradle for her shoulders, his touch comforting and supportive. "Hold your position, Jess."

She did, but it was hard with Zach's hands on her thighs, smoothing over the quivering flesh, working his way back up to her pussy. She curved her fingers into the hollows behind Mac's knees and held on as Zach stroked her thighs, pressing them further apart as he wedged his shoulders beneath.

"A very pretty pussy, Jessie."

His broad fingertip stroked from her swollen clit to her vagina, tracing lazy patterns she couldn't recognize. His fingers slid lower, encountered the base of the butt plug. He tapped it and looked over her belly at Mac.

"Your cock going in here?"

Mac stroked her shoulders. Against her cheek, his penis jerked. "Oh, yeah."

"She prepared?"

"I was just working on it when you came in."

"Mind if I do the honors?"

"Go ahead."

Hearing her lover give another permission to prepare her for him did strange things to Jessie's insides. Quivery, lustful, primitive things. Things that had her lifting her hips higher.

Jessie felt Zach's hand fish beneath her and then there was the sound of the bulb being squeezed followed by a sensation of fullness in her rectum. Mac slid the tips of his fingers down over her shoulder, over the bump of her collarbone and then up the gentle rise of her breasts until he reached her nipples. The sense of fullness increased as Mac asked, "How's that feel?"

"Good." And it did feel good. Both Mac's hands on her nipples squeezing and pulling, and the plug stretching her ass, adding a bite of uncertainty to the calm. And then there was the threat of Zach himself. Big, wild Zach. She couldn't exactly see him as a passive participant. Which just had her nerve endings hopping with excitement as the bed sagged under his weight.

"Damned by faint praise," Zach muttered, shifting his muscular body. Out of the corner of her eye she saw his shirt fall to the floor. And then all that heavy bone and muscle was between her legs again. "Let's see if this makes you feel better than just good."

That was his mouth on her cunt, his tongue lapping leisurely at the outer lips, working toward the center of her passion with deliberate skill. Above her Mac played with her breasts, his rough fingers sure and strong as he milked the turgid tips, timing the pressure with the flick of Zach's tongue. Between her thighs, Zach sucked and nibbled. Slowly, slowly the tension left her until her hips settled into the support of Zach's broad palms and her shoulder relaxed into the security of Mac's powerful thighs.

This was her fantasy. And it was all for her to enjoy. Two strong powerful men devoted to her pleasure, giving her what she wanted. Needed. What in hell was she nervous about? The floodgates opened with her acceptance and all the sensations she'd been suppressing stormed over her, wrenching a gasp from her throat. Oh God, this was going to be great.

She felt Zach's smile as he nuzzled deep within her folds, seeking her nectar. His hair brushed the side of her thighs in a silken caress, his thumbs parted her further, making room for the hot thrust of his tongue.

"Oh God!"

Mac bent close to her ear. "Can you feel his tongue, honey girl? All hot and wet, stroking your pussy, lapping up your sweet juices?"

"She is sweet, Mac," Zach groaned in his deep voice. "A sweet, juicy peach. Damn I'm going to eat her alive."

Against his thighs, Jessie jerked and whimpered, her hands struggling in the restraints, forgetting that she had them on, groaning again when she realized anew that she was helpless.

"Such a sexy little sound," Mac whispered in her ear. He picked up the bulb Zach had discarded. Jessie gasped and arched higher as the plug stretched her further, whimpering when it didn't stop, her breath catching on a sob as it expanded.

Zach looked up, his face wet with her juices, his smile knowing. "She liked that, Mac."

"Yeah." Mac pinched her nipples harder, drawing them out, holding them as she arched, watching her eyes close and her face twist with the pleasure they were giving her. He was giving her. He kissed her mouth, feeling her soft lips cling to his.

"Damn, you're beautiful, honey girl."

"Mac..." Her eyes opened, desire warring with confusion.

He could tell Zach had homed in on her clit, the muscles in his shoulders flexing as he fucked her with his thumb.

"It's okay, Jess. Just go with it."

"It's too much. He's too good. It feels too good."

Her hips rose and fell with Zach's mouth. Her skin shone with perspiration as she twisted on his thighs.

"No, it's just right."

Her fingers dug into his thighs. "I can't stand it."

"Yes, you can."

"I can't."

Against his thighs her back tightened.

"Just relax and let it happen. Feel my hands, his tongue. Squeeze down on the plug, baby."

She did as he ordered and grimaced again as he flipped the release and pumped more air into the toy.

"Hurts," she grunted. "It's too big."

"It's going to be my cock in your ass next, Jess. Just think on that and relax. Let it stretch you. I've been dreaming of taking that tight ass of yours for so long, I don't know if I'll be able to hold back once I get in."

Her eyes narrowed, her lips pulled back from her teeth as the plug reached its maximum inflation.

"Do you want to come, Jessie?"

"Yes."

"Then come."

"I can't."

She suddenly arched against him and cried out. Between her thighs, Zach's head bobbed in quick short jabs.

"Mac!" It was a high-pitched, desperate, agonized scream.

He caught her head in his hands, holding her steady, keeping her teeth away from his flesh.

Between her thighs, Zach froze. His hands backed off. His fingers gently stroked her labia as he shifted back. Over Jessie's heaving belly, his dark gaze met Mac's. "She's so hot to come, it hurts her to be touched. What's going on?"

"I was hoping..." Mac sighed, kissed the sob from her lips and stroked her hair off her face, before explaining, "She can't come unless I do."

Zach's dark eyes flared with heat and longing. "Hell!"

"I'm sorry," Jessie whispered, trying to turn her head. "I'm sorry. I'm so sorry."

The mattress dipped as Zach knelt between her thighs. He stroked a tear from her cheek. His touch was very gentle. Mac would have killed him if it had been any different. Jessie was very fragile right now.

"Look at me," Zach ordered.

She did, reluctantly, checking with Mac first, every muscle in her back braced for the censure she expected.

"That's about the sexiest thing I've ever heard," Zach said.

Mac smiled. "And I thought I was just a selfish bastard for feeling that way."

Zach laughed and flashed him a look of pure envy. "You are one lucky son of a bitch." Then he sobered. "So what do you want to do?"

"Let's turn her over and give her what she needs."

Chapter Seventeen

They had her on her hands and knees on the bed, the restraints keeping her legs tucked under her body, her hands under her chest. There was enough play between the cuffs that she could support herself comfortably, but not much else. They'd added another strap that went behind her thighs and attached to the one binding her hands. Her ass was thrust out high behind her, leaving her vulnerable to whatever Mac had in mind to do. The only movement she could manage was to fall to her side or rock back and forth on her knees. It wasn't a surprise why the latter was allowed. They'd adjusted the straps so that she was higher on the bed, up near the head. The agonizing, too sharp arousal had dulled to a steady throb as they got her ready, but it didn't go away. It hummed just under her skin, ready at a moment's notice to flare into life again.

"Got a blindfold, Mac?" Zach asked.

"In the drawer to the left."

"Blindfold?"

"Thanks."

"Lift your head, Jessie."

She did, but only to shake it. "No. I don't want to be blindfolded." There was something very scary about not being able to see.

Zach's smile was gentle, but he didn't take the black piece of silk away. "You need it."

She jerked her head away. "No."

Zach cupped his hand behind her neck and pulled her forward, looking over her head at Mac as he did so. "Is she always like this?"

"She has a tendency to challenge authority."

"She needs a good spanking."

"She just had one."

Zach brought his face close to hers. His eyes were very dark and hot as they met hers. "Maybe she needs another."

"Maybe I just need to be able to see," she pointed out, a little breathlessly as her entire body jerked at the possibility.

Zach's smile was knowing. "Oh, you're hot to have that little ass tanned, but good."

He slipped the blindfold over the back of her head. "Pull back again, and I'll do it for you."

She didn't know if that was a threat or an invitation, but she didn't want to risk it either way. Zach simmered with an intensity that scared her. She held herself perfectly still as he pulled the blindfold over her eyes and the world went dark. She didn't so much as breathe when his fingers touched her face as he adjusted the blindfold. His chuckle was low and deep as his fingers skimmed her cheek. "Good girl."

There was no sound in the room for a moment. She strained to hear where the men were. What they planned. Then there was the rasp of a zipper. The rustle of clothing. The jingle of change shifting in pockets. The drawer slid on its hinges. Plastic crinkled as it separated from cardboard. There was a click as something fell into place and then Mac's ominous low drawl of "All set?"

And Zach's equally serious. "Yup."

A hand touched high on the inside of her thigh. Her breath squeaked in as she jumped. The palm opened over the curve, squeezing it firmly before sliding around, the rough calluses telling her immediately who touched her. Mac. She relaxed. He drew a strap around her left thigh and fastened it. He did the same to her right. Then he pulled something hard and smooth against her vulva giving it a tug so it pressed into her engorged clitoris. She could only kneel and shudder as he fastened the strap around her waist. The sense of helplessness amplified every sensation. It was thrilling, and it was as scary as hell.

"There you go." The light slap on her buttock caught her by surprise. Her senses were so overloaded, she yanked away from the stinging pleasure.

"I don't think so," Mac countered.

The bed shifted and hands at her waist dragged her back. They lacked calluses.

Zach. She strained against him. Another slap came down on her ass, and another. Zach pulled her into each one, holding her there, offering her ass up to the waves of concentrated pleasure that crashed into her pussy, gathering at her clit before exploding throughout her body. Those mind-bending, thrilling, scary waves that stole her strength and her control. Another slap, another explosion. Another unraveling of her tenuous control.

It was too much. Too much. She fought, bucked. To no avail. The more she wiggled the harder and faster the slaps came and the more the unrelenting arousal increased. She took a shuddering breath, dropped her head and forced herself to hold still. The grip on her waist loosened. The spanking stopped. Hands caressed her butt cheeks, soothing and yet still arousing, but not so intensely. Not so much that she couldn't endure.

"Good girl."

Zach again. Where was Mac? She needed Mac.

And then he was there. She felt a callused palm on her skin. "Now, honey girl, I'm going to have Zach warm this ass for me. And when Zach starts spanking you, I want you to thrust that sexy butt back at him. Let him know how much you're enjoying it." His fingers drifted across her skin, bringing goose bumps up in their wake until he slid into the crack and found the base of the plug. He pulled steadily on the massive toy as he said, "Keep him coming back for more until you think you'll scream from the need to come."

"And then what?" she asked breathlessly, the erotic pressure of the plug only adding to the throbbing anticipation. "I can't come without—"

His hand cupped her sex. His finger thrusting within. Tiny muscles clamped down on him. Needing him desperately. "Oh, honey girl, we'll come for you," he drawled roughly. "You just need to tell us when and we'll come."

He tugged hard enough to have her womb clench while thrusting another finger inside her greedy cunt. Her arms collapsed. "Where?" she moaned.

He pressed a tender kiss to the hollow of her back. "Wherever we want."

She shuddered, and bit the comforter. She was almost tempted to say now. She needed them to come now, but if she did that she would miss out.

He pulled his fingers out of her. The plastic over her vulva shifted as he took hold of it. He slid it back and fourth across the peak beneath. Her womb clenched again in unfulfilled ecstasy. She squealed and pressed harder into his hand. He laughed low and deep, the sound skittering along her nerves before lodging in the hard knot of desire swelling to consume her lower body. He kissed the corner of her mouth, his breath teasing the sensitive nerves there as he said, "Oh yeah, we're going to have fun." With a last caress to her buttock, he stepped away.

She expected Zach to start immediately. He didn't. She waited, her muscles tense. Braced. And waited some more. Her breaths grew shorter. Her pussy clenched. Her fingers dug into the quilt. She thought she heard someone move. Nothing happened. Oh God, was the plan to torture her? Her whimper broke the silence. It was followed by a soft male chuckle.

The first blow was light. Just a tap. The second was no harder. She hadn't expected such delicacy from Zach. This time her moan was of disappointment. Again that male chuckle, and another butterfly tap. Remembering Mac's orders, she pushed back into the next tap. And the next. And the next.

Zach worked the soft blows over her entire ass and down her thighs, sensitizing her skin. By the time he got to her inner thighs, they were drenched with her cream. That deep, knowing male chuckle came again just as he rapped the end of the plug, sending the merest glimmer of potential vibrating up her spine.

And then he was working his way back up to her buttocks. She didn't need to remember Mac's order to push back, her body was doing it instinctively, doing its best to force Zach into making firmer contact.

Instead, he started all over again, with just the barest hint of more.

"Stop teasing me, damn it!"

Mac, who'd been silent up until now spoke, "Unless you need to come, Jessie, no talking."

"Mac, I need more," she implored, turning in the direction of his voice.

A ghost of a touch whispered by her mouth.

"Zach knows exactly what you need. Relax and let him give it to you."

She didn't have a lot of choice. With the exception of hoping to entice with the swing of her hips she had no choice but to endure the erotic torture. He was back at the inside of her thighs now. She held her breath as he got to the plug, the tap was harder, but nothing like what she needed.

She groaned as he started over. Her body quivered with the sensations he was giving. Light shivery promises of what she needed. Her pussy ached and flowered, reaching out, wanting him to connect there. Anywhere she could really feel it. Her ass clenched down on the plug, welcoming the sting. Her whole body was alive with a breathless anticipation. A shimmering excitement.

A new sensation entered the game. The device strapped to her vulva began to vibrate. Jessie jumped, strained.

"Don't fight it, Jessie," Mac ordered in a rough drawl, his voice seeming to come from across the room. "Relax into it. Let it take you higher."

Higher? She'd never survive higher.

"Do it, Jess." He was closer now.

She did, as Zach kept up his own personal torment of her poor overcharged body. For the briefest of moments, the toy offered a respite, at last delivering sensation to where she needed it, but then it too just became another tease of not enough. Promising everything, delivering nothing. She dug her fingers into the comforter and moaned.

"Are you ready?" Mac whispered darkly in her ear. "Are you ready for Zach to spank you like I want?"

"Yes." *Oh God yes. Anything but this!*

"Hard Jessie? Hard enough to make those cheeks shake and shiver? Hard enough to turn them nice and red. And hot. Hot enough when I take your ass, I'll feel their heat on my thighs?"

Her arms collapsed again. Her thoughts, the ones she meant to keep secret spilled from her mouth. "Oh God, yes. Spank me like that," she mumbled into the comforter.

Mac pulled her up with a hand under her chest, his fingers lingering to play with her engorged nipples. Her body reacted to the stimuli with pathetic enthusiasm. Mac wrapped his free hand in her hair, pulled her head back and kissed her mouth hard. "Damn, I love you."

She felt the disturbance of his nod, and then Zach's spanks picked up in intensity. Not one circuit to the next, but from one blow to the next. Harder and harder they came. More and more. Faster and faster. The one that landed on the plug sent shock waves through her pussy. The vibrator also picked up its tempo.

Where before she wanted more, now she wanted time. Time to breathe. Time to figure out how to control the sensations coiling deep inside, but she didn't get it. The vibrator continued to buzz its tormenting song, Mac continued to whisper hot words of encouragement into her ear as he milked an equally hot response from her nipples, and Zach… Zach just continued his relentless herding of her arousal toward a peak she'd never, ever dreamed existed. A peak so high, it terrified her. And suddenly she was there, hanging on the edge, too far over to go back, too scared to go on alone.

"Mac!" she screamed.

"Right here, honey girl," he whispered against her ear. "I've got you. No need to be afraid."

But she was. She couldn't fight this. Couldn't control this. The bed dipped as he knelt beside her. Her left shoulder sank with the mattress as his hand settled beside hers. She dug her nails into the back of his hand, holding on to him for dear life as the wild desire inside roared and twisted for freedom, threatening to push her over into that bottomless pit she could sense on the other side.

"Help me!" she sobbed. "Help me, Mac."

"Shhh!" His big hands stroked her back from shoulder to waist. "I'll help you, honey girl. Just hold on."

His hands on her body should have been soothing. They weren't. It was just one more sensation piled onto too many already. Behind her, Zach rained a series of slaps onto her inner thighs that had her whimpering. The last landed square on the vibrator. Her whole body arched and jerked as heat flooded up her spine and out over her arms, uncontrollable shaking coming in its wake. Mac's arm came around her waist, holding her tightly. Her only security in this sensation-charged world.

"Now, Mac. I need you *now*!"

The bed dipped in front of her. The vibrations stopped. The restraints let go. She fell forward. Another pair of strong male hands caught her, brought her cuffed hands up and over his head, catching in his long hair. Zach held her with ease as she untangled herself and her hands dropped behind his back. And then he was lowering her down his chest, the sweat on both their bodies making it a smooth slide, the muscles slabbing his torso teasing her hypersensitive nipples unmercifully. She bit his right pectoral in retaliation. He laughed deep in his throat as he slipped his arms free of hers.

"She likes to bite," Zach observed, holding her mouth against his chest with both hands, the well-honed muscles flexing beneath her teeth.

"Yeah," Mac grunted as he tilted her hips toward him. "Forgot to warn you about that." There was a hiss of air being released and then the tremendous fullness in her rectum abated. "She's a bit of a wildcat."

"Oh, I don't mind." Zach stroked her cheek, pulling her close when she would have let go, prolonging the contact. She lapped at the indents left by her teeth. He groaned—or growled—as he lifted into her mouth. His muscles bulged beneath her lips. His skin was hot and salty against her tongue. "She can sink those pretty teeth into me any time."

He tipped her chin up, and brushed her lips with his. "But if you forget and bite my cock," he warned her in a quiet drawl, "I won't come for you."

Jessie shuddered as the warning wafted over her lips at the same time Mac's cock wafted over her clit and the tide of lust rose again to torment her. As the plug drew clear, Zach took her cry into his mouth.

"Sweet," he whispered, before kissing her deeply, his tongue expertly exploring hers, his hands tilting her face the way he wanted. The way she needed.

A finger touched her sensitive anus. It was cool and slippery.

"Mac...?"

"Right here, honey girl."

He slid a second finger in, scissoring them, testing, stretching. It felt so good.

"Don't tease me anymore," she whispered to both of them as Zach's hands dipped to her breasts.

"No teasing, honey girl," Mac answered, his big cock snuggling against her anus.

The shock of pure lust that hit her at the darkly erotic connection would have toppled her if Zach hadn't been holding her.

"We're going to make you feel so good," he promised in his deep voice as he steadied her.

Mac felt impossibly huge like this. Powerful as he pulsed against the small, hungry opening, his hair-roughened thighs brushing the inside of hers as big hands touched the small of her back. Steady pressure forced her forward. The heel of his hand smoothed up the ladder of her ribs as he urged her down. Zach's hands guided her descent.

"Open your mouth, Jess," Mac ordered as she doubled over, her chest resting against the warmth of what felt like Zach's calves.

She parted her lips, knowing what was coming, wanting it.

She remembered vividly how Zach's cock looked. Darker than his skin. Thick. Impressive. Simmering with the same energy that would have scared her if Mac weren't here. She wondered if he tasted as wild as he looked. As pleasing and as earthy as he smelled.

She leaned forward, following Zach's lead. The hair on his legs scraped her nipples. She whimpered, and moved on him again.

Zach laughed the deep way he always did when she found pleasure. "I aim to please."

She couldn't see, and she was off balance. She felt awkward with her arms locked around Zach, searching for a cock with her open mouth. Helpless to do anything but trust in Mac's lead.

Zach's cock brushed her lips. Just a soft butterfly touch, but she felt it all the way to her toes, especially when Mac ordered, "Take him in your mouth, Jessie. Let him give you what you need. For me."

Mac jerked against her as Zach's fingers touched the corner of her mouth. *Was he watching?*

"Open for me, Jessie," Zach ordered.

She did.

"Wider."

She stretched her jaw. The heavy weight of his shaft rested against the shelf of her teeth. Behind her, Mac pressed. Both men were poised to fill her. Fulfill her. Oh God she'd been dreaming of this for so long. And she was so empty and hungry.

"You won't stop?" She meant it to be a clear statement. It came out a tense whisper, the words caressing the tip of Zach's eager penis.

Mac's cock jerked against her again, the wide head sliding across her sensitive rosette in a red-hot caress. His response was just as tense. "No, honey girl."

She needed this reassurance. Needed to know for sure this time. "No matter what, you'll fuck my ass hard and deep like I want?"

"Jesus!" Zach swore. His cock jumped against the shelf of her lips.

The broad head of Mac's cock centered on her anus. "No matter what."

She closed her eyes briefly at the divine pressure. "And you'll come for me?"

"God yes!"

"If he stops, Jessie," Zach muttered, his voice sliding across her awareness like warm velvet, "I'll shoot him myself."

She didn't know what else to say except, "Thank you."

Mac's cock at her back entrance was a big tease. She tried to push onto him to encourage him. Zach held her still.

"You trust Mac?" he asked her as she groaned in frustration.

She nodded as best she could.

"Then you let him take charge here. Trust him to give you what you need."

Shit, he needed her to trust him, Mac thought as he pushed against her, watching her take Zach in her mouth, hearing her moan as her anus began to part. He met Zach's gaze over Jessie's back.

Zach shook his head. He wasn't hurting her. Zach's hand came over Jessie's head, very dark and big against the shimmering blonde of her hair, guiding her movement.

"Get me nice and hard, Jessie," Zach told her as he stroked her hair back from her face, "because the moment Mac buries that cock in your ass, I'm going to come for you, long and hard."

Zach's breath hissed through his teeth as Jessie redoubled her efforts. Mac knew how Zach felt. How hot and tight her little mouth was. How good she could make a man feel. Almost as good as being in her pussy. Almost as good as he was going to feel when he got into her ass. He worked his cock against her, timing his thrusts with the bobbing of Jessie's head, making sure she was filled at both ends, knowing how that would turn her on. Needing her to be turned on.

He reached for the control of the Venus butterfly, flipping the switch to low. He wanted this to be as good as possible for Jessie. He met Zach's dark gaze over her back. The tightness in his friend's face told him he was close to coming. The shudders racking Jessie's spine told him she was almost there, too. He caught her hips in his hands, steadying her as he pressed forward.

"Can you feel me, Jessie?" he asked, his voice a parody of itself as he watched his cock force that tight muscle to thin and widen. "Can you feel how hard I am? How eager? You need to relax, Jessie. Let me in. My balls are so full they ache, honey girl. They ache for you."

She whimpered, and bobbed her head faster. Zach stroked her cheek, his face tight with the effort of holding back. "So are mine, Jessie," he moaned. "You can have it all. All that you want. Just relax that sweet ass and let him in."

Mac felt her muscles flex against him. A delicate kiss on the head of his cock. "That's right. Push back. C'mon baby, push back."

He leaned into her, watching as her body opened for him, knowing he just needed a little more and they'd be at the point of no return. The point where her muscles surrendered the battle and her ass would be his. She would be his. Only his. In every way that mattered.

She whimpered again, and then moaned. Her body arched, she twisted as if to get away. Her head pulled back, but Zach brought her relentlessly back onto his cock, filling her mouth to the point that she gagged, but unlike Mac, he didn't back off, just held himself there while she struggled to adjust, his head falling back as her rapid swallowing brought him to the point of orgasm.

Mac flipped the switch on the vibrator to high, Jessie's smothered scream reaching him even around the muffling of Zach's cock. Zach jerked against her, driving deeper. Jessie screamed again, a high, thin plea for satisfaction. Against his cock, her anus contracted and relaxed in time with her pussy as she swallowed and fought the way she always did when she was ready to come.

It was all he'd been waiting for. With a hard lunge, Mac drove in. The tight ring of muscle resisted at first, before finally giving way with a popping sensation, and then he was inside the incredibly smooth heat of her ass. Jessie's scream crescendoed into a new octave. He pulled his thrust up short.

"Jesus," Zach cursed brokenly at him, as he held Jessie to him, his body jerking as his balls pumped into her mouth. "Don't stop now."

Shit, he knew better than to stop now. He thrust in short, deep jabs until she had half of him. He spread his hand over her belly, holding her to him as he waited for her body to adjust, absorbing her shudders into his bigger frame, whispering nonsense to her as she swallowed the last of Zach's come.

Zach eased her mouth off his cock, and pulled her head up against his chest. "Can you feel Mac's cock in your ass, Jess?"

Jessie nodded weakly. Her breath came in pants as she battled for control. The muscles in her stomach pressed against the restraint of Mac's hand with each hard-won jerk. "Yes."

Zach's expression was knowing as he pushed the hair away from her face. "Hurts like a son of a bitch doesn't it?"

She bit her lip and nodded.

"But it feels good, too, doesn't it?"

"Yes, but I don't know if I can take it..."

"But you want to take it, don't you? Because this isn't enough, is it?" Zach asked her in a deep, dark drawl. "You want more. You want it so badly, you're ready to come from the idea alone. But you've got more than the idea now, Jessie. You've got the real thing. Don't be afraid of it, reach for it. And when you're done, all you have to do is present that sweet butt to me, and you can have it all over again. I'll fuck you until neither of us can stand it anymore, and then I'll pump you full all over again."

The mewling cry slipped past her control, past the pain because deep down inside, he was right. This wasn't enough. She wanted more. Needed more. Her ass clenched. This time it was Mac who laughed that sexy laugh.

"And you're going to come for both of us, aren't you, honey girl? You're going to give us your trust and those sexy little screams and you're going to come so hard, feel so good."

"Oh God, yes."

"Kiss me," Zach ordered. "Kiss me hot and deep while Mac fucks that sexy butt the way you want."

She did, her high-pitched cry as Mac pulled out getting lost in the heat of Zach's incredible kiss. And then Mac was back, harder, deeper. And Zach was kissing her harder, deeper, his hands working between her thighs. The toy fell free. She didn't know if her scream was from the disappointment of that or Mac's strong thrusts. And then she was screaming into Zach's mouth for a different reason as he slapped her pussy, driving her buttocks back into Mac's thrusts as vibrations raced through her, dropping back down for another, ricocheting back when she got it, sensation building on sensation, pain turning to pleasure, the pleasure to erotic pressure, the pressure spiking over and over again until she couldn't contain the explosion.

"Come for me, Jessie," Mac ordered. "Now!" On a last violent thrust that sent her crashing into Zach, Mac came, her name a hoarse shout in her ear as he jerked within her, filling her dark channel with his hot seed. Zach's last slap snapped against her clitoris, the sting catapulting her into orgasm.

She splintered into a thousand pieces, her body jerking convulsively, spots dancing before her eyes as the piercing pleasure seared her from the inside out, her ass clamping down on his thick cock, as she struggled to hold him inside her. To her. Forever.

She didn't realize she'd screamed it out loud until minutes later when her breathing had settled to sporadic hiccoughs and she was sprawled on Mac's chest, her thighs on either side of his hips, his penis resting between them. Removing the blindfold, he tipped her chin up. His blue eyes were serious, tender. In his expression, there was love and pride. In his words a promise.

"Forever, honey girl."

Oh, she liked the sound of that. One of his big hands moved down her spine. Nerve endings that should have been exhausted perked right up, twitching wildly when he palmed her buttock. He gently pinched her chin between his fingers and pulled. She went into his kiss willingly, eagerly. His hand cupped her skull, holding her still for his tongue as the kiss turned from tender to dominant. She went from exhausted to hot to trot in a heartbeat, setting a new record in the arousal book, she was sure.

The bed dipped. Mac growled in his throat. Jessie popped her eyes open. A shadow stretched beside Mac's head. Strong hands circled her calves, gliding up to the backs of her knees.

Pausing to tease. Her breath caught on the sensation. Her hips twitched.

Zach. Round two.

Oh God! Round two. She looked down at Mac. He smiled as he pressed her hips against him. Her pussy clenched as he caught her nipple between his thumb and forefinger. Behind her Zach's hands moved up her thighs, pausing here and there to probe places that stole her breath and made her ache with desire. How did he do that?

When he reached her buttocks, his hands became magic, pressing, tormenting, until she was twisting on Mac. She closed her eyes, straining back, wanting, needing to be filled again. Behind her Zach laughed. Below her, Mac growled. And inside, her, a niggling something came to life. She squashed it, wanting to enjoy this moment, her fantasy. Her gift.

The heat of Zach's flesh reached her first as he covered her back with his big body. His cock, equally hot, fell into the crack of her ass. He was pulsing and hard, as big as Mac and hungry. Oh, so hungry, if the way he throbbed was any indication.

"Are you ready for me, Jess?" he asked, his thick finger sliding under his cock, painting her anus with the slippery lube. "Are you ready to come again?"

She nodded, her fingers digging into Mac's shoulders as Zach pushed two fingers into her rectum.

"Easy, honey girl," Mac murmured in a tight voice. "Zach knows what he's doing."

"I know you're tender," Zach soothed, kissing her shoulder. "Don't worry. I know how to work it in nice and easy, okay?"

She didn't know how anything could be nice and easy with an organ that large, but she'd experienced enough of Zach's skill to know if anyone could, it would be him. She bit her lip, tamped down on that protesting little voice, and nodded.

"Good girl."

He moved his fingers inside her, angling them to a certain spot and pressed. Fire shot through her body. Her clitoris engorged in a burning surge and her pussy and ass clamped down hard. One on air and one on broad male fingers. Beneath her Mac swore. Above her Zach laughed and murmured, "You are so sweet."

His fingers withdrew. His penis slid down her natural crevice in a smooth caress before he aligned the fat crown.

"Bear down now, Jessie," Mac murmured in that same tight voice, his grip on her nipple as relentlessly tight. "Bear down and let him make you feel that good with his cock."

The little voice stopped talking and started screaming as Zach pressed against her. Her body cringed away, down into Mac's arms. Mac's embrace.

"Easy, Jess."

"Wait." she moaned while desire fought with something even more elemental. More instinctual.

"What's wrong?" Zach asked against her ear, almost like he knew.

She didn't know, but something was wrong. Zach pressed against her. Despite the aching, empty gnawing hunger that surged through her at his touch, something was wrong. Zach pushed harder. Her muscles closed in upon themselves and she knew. She knew.

"I don't want this."

Below her, Mac froze. Above her, unbelievably, Zach laughed. His voice, darkly seductive, whispered against her ear, making her shudder, "Are you sure? I'm very good at pleasuring a woman's ass." He kissed the curve of her neck before repeating. "Very, very good."

She couldn't help shuddering again. She believed every single word, but she also knew no matter how good Zach was, he wasn't Mac. She shook her head. "I think some things are meant to stay fantasies."

She couldn't bear to open her eyes and see Mac's disappointment. "I'm sorry," she whispered. She meant the apology for both men. "I just want Mac."

"I wouldn't be sorry," Zach said, laughter and passion in his voice as he kissed her cheek. "If you open your eyes, I think you'll see you've just brought Christmas early."

She did. Mac's eyes blazed up at her with blue fire. Passion, possession, jealousy and love burned in their depths. His hand cupped her skull as he wiped Zach's kiss from her cheek with his thumb. "Get your goddamned cock away from her ass."

Zach laughed and leaned back. He swatted Jessie's right cheek, bringing another growl from Mac as she jumped against him, soothing it immediately with a gentle caress.

Jessie glared at him over her shoulder. Zach's hair swung about his muscular shoulders in a thick, wild tangle that suited him far more than clothes. His cock, as impressive as Mac's, hung thick and hard between his thighs. Unfulfilled. She expected to see resentment in his eyes. Instead she saw only an incredible sadness and loss as he looked at his hand on her buttock and then at Mac.

"Take very good care of her, Mac. You won't like life much if you lose her."

Chapter Eighteen

The door closed softly behind Zach as he left.

Jessie stared down at Mac, unbelieving. "You didn't want this?"

He dragged her mouth to his, kissing her hard, deep, all the possessiveness he'd been withholding pouring over her in waves. He kissed her until she didn't have air left in her lungs or doubt left in her mind. "Hell no."

"Then why?" she asked as he rolled them over so she was beneath him.

He touched her cheek gently. "You waited forever to have a lover. Never had anyone but me."

He paused, the flare of pride in his eyes telling her how much he liked that fact. "I didn't want to be one more person you loved who needed you to make a sacrifice for them."

"So you were willing to let another man take me?"

His jaw clenched. She wondered how she'd ever believed sharing her with another man was all right with him as he forced the truth past his gut instinct. "It was something you needed."

And he'd promised to give her whatever she needed. She stroked that hard muscle in his jaw. "The to-do list was a compilation of lustful moments. Things I thought might bear exploring."

"I know."

"I never expected to enjoy them all."

"But you do," he said, and search as she might, she couldn't find a bit of censure in his voice or his expression.

"Except for the last," she agreed. "I don't want anyone else in me but you, Mac."

"Good."

"Mac?"

"Yeah?" His response was distracted.

"Where'd you go last weekend?"

He slid his hand down to her leg. "I flew to my mother's grave in New Jersey."

"Why?" She had a good idea, but she wanted to be sure. His fingers closed around her ankle.

"I needed to tell her goodbye." He kissed her softly as he brought her right knee up to her chest. "It helped more than I thought it would"

"I'm so glad."

"Me, too."

And that should be the end of the questions, but there was something else she had to know. Something she was probably better off not knowing, but she couldn't stand it. He'd fooled her on the ménage. She just had to be sure he wasn't fooling her on the other. Jessie bit her lip, debated and then asked as her left knee joined her right. "Was there anything else on the list that you were humoring me on?"

He placed both his big hands on her knees and rocked her back. His expression was hard and tight as he flicked a glance at her face, "Like what?"

Oh God, this verged on humiliating. "Well, I was thinking since it took you so long to get around to it. I mean, maybe you're not that enthusiastic about…"

He pulled her knees together and held them back with one hand. "What?"

It was hard to talk with her chest so compressed. She settled for just blurting it out. "Anal sex!"

He pushed two fingers into her ass, forcing them past the initial resistance. The burn took her by surprise. She groaned.

"Relax, honey girl."

"I'm sore."

"It won't matter in a minute."

"Easy for you to say."

"Trust me."

His expression didn't change as he rotated his fingers inside her, and then he was pressing on that special spot. Her body snapped to attention. Unlike Zach who had only stroked it once, Mac stroked it over and over until she was sobbing his name and twisting under his hands. She was empty. So agonizingly empty.

"Do you want to come like this or with me in you?" he asked in that same intense, deep drawl.

"You. I want you."

"Where?"

"In my ass. Please, Mac. Fuck my ass."

"My pleasure."

He moved up the bed, his chest braced against her knees holding her in position while his cock lined up with her spasming anus. At the first touch, she cried out. The pleasure too intense to be borne, but he kept coming and she arched her head back and wailed as he slowly, slowly worked his big cock past her body's resistance and into the eager, grateful channel beyond.

"God damn, you're going to burn me alive," he muttered over her cries. His strokes were gentle. Tentative. Restrained She grabbed his face in her hand and threatened him.

"If you don't make love to me—hard—right now, I'm going to burn dinner for a week."

He laughed, actually laughed, and then leaned back so he could put each of her legs over his shoulders. "We can't have that."

Mac leaned forward, bringing her buttocks into better alignment before powering into her like she wanted, holding her gaze as he did so, smiling as the shock of his possession tore through her as her muscles parted under the relentless assault. He held himself there, deep within her, letting her adjust to the depth of his possession, stroking the swollen bud of her clit as he waited.

"Just relax, honey girl. Get used to it."

She held him so tight and hot, he didn't know if he'd ever get used to it. All he wanted to do was pound into her until the image of Zach's hand in her ass was obliterated by the power of his release. She whimpered and flinched as he flexed his cock. He soothed her with a soft kiss and a circling caress on her clitoris.

"In answer to your question, honey girl. With the exception of maybe eating or fucking your sweet pussy, there's nothing—nothing—I love more than fucking your ass."

He flexed again, this time she whimpered, but didn't flinch. "I only held back because I worried you couldn't take me, but now that we know that's not true..."

He pulled out, keeping his gaze locked to hers, letting her see in his eyes and his face the extreme pleasure the feel of her gave him. "You'd best be prepared to have my cock up this sweet butt on a regular basis."

Her ankles hooked on his shoulders, and she tilted her hips up as he tunneled back in. "Oh yes."

She took almost all of him that time before she winced. He held himself there again, petting her pussy, dipping his fingers into the river of juice spilling over them, spreading it over the base of his cock, massaging it into the drum-tight skin surrounding his possession. "I'm going to keep you so full of my seed you won't need lubricant."

This time her whimper wasn't due to discomfort. "Promise?"

He kissed her, tenderness welling from within. "Oh, yeah."

"Mac?"

She was going to chide him again for taking it too slow. That was just tough. "What?"

"I'm sorry about Zach."

He froze. He didn't want her sorry about anything. "Did you enjoy it?"

Her gaze darted from his. He removed his hand from her pussy to bring it back. His fingers were slick with her juices. He spread her essence across her lips before leaning down to lick it off.

"Did you enjoy it?" he repeated.

Her "Yes" was shy. Uncertain.

"Then I'm glad." He flexed. She didn't wince. Good.

She caught his hand as he would have pulled away. She took his fingers into her mouth, lapping her juices off, making love to them the way she made love to his cock. Thoroughly, completely.

"He wasn't as good as you."

"Shit!" he arched his head back, fighting for control.

"Having him in my mouth just made me hungrier for you..." she continued. Each softly seductive word nibbled more and more at his restraint. "Wishing you had two cocks so I could have you in my mouth as you came in my pussy, or," she tilted her buttocks, "my ass."

He looked down to find her smiling at him knowingly. She was doing it on purpose.

"Goddamn it, Jessie."

"I want you to make wild passionate love to me, Mac. So hard I'll feel you long after you've stopped, and for so long, I can't remember anyone's touch but yours."

God, he'd hurt her if he let go and gave into the wildness tearing at him. "You don't know what you're asking for, honey girl."

She kissed the palm of his hand, her lips soft on the hard flesh. "I'm asking for you, Mac. All of you. No holding back. Just my own personal wild man loving me with all he's got."

Oh yeah, he could go for that.

"Can you love me like that?" she asked, her voice as soft and as tempting as her body.

He closed his eyes. He'd kill to love her like that. His "yes" was hoarse.

She brought her hand down beside her head, still holding his, so he pinned her there, the love in her eyes big enough for a man to drown in. "That's all I've ever wanted Mac. No one else. Nothing else. Just a man willing to love me with everything he has, nothing held back."

"I can give you that," he managed to say past the emotion clogging his throat.

Her smile grew even softer. "You already have.

"But?"

She wiggled her ass on his cock. "My heart's sold, but my body still needs convincing."

"I don't want to hurt you."

"I hurt now. Look at me

He did, seeing the flush on her chest, the tight bead of her nipples. Against his groin, her clit throbbed. Around his cock, her ass clenched. She was a woman hot to be loved. His woman. And she was waiting for him to realize that with a wild hunger in her eyes that matched, pulse for pulse, the hunger that thrummed in his blood.

"You want me."

She parroted his favorite expression back at him. "Oh yeah, so why don't you make me yours—"

"Like you always have been…"

"And I always will be."

He could do that.

He pulled out and surged back hard, the way he wanted to, not stopping until his groin sank into her buttocks, claiming her with his body and soul, taking her scream for what it was; a tiny culmination of what they both wanted. He didn't give her time to adjust, just gave in to his body's demands and loved her hard and deep, tunneling again and again into her hot ass, not giving her a chance to breathe or think, just driving her ahead of him, higher and higher toward the waiting peak, forcing her past her hesitation, ignoring her pleas for him to come. He just kept giving her what she said she wanted. All of him, no holding back, until finally, when he thought he couldn't contain his release any longer, when his balls were on fire and his cock ached with the agony, she threw her head back and screamed his name. She continued to scream as he drove high, holding himself deep inside her as she spasmed around him, gritting his teeth against the need to join her, wanting to enjoy this moment, the first time she'd trusted him enough to let go and fly solo.

She came back to him in soft quivers, her eyes closed, chanting his name, all the love in the world locked in that one syllable.

"You've got me, honey girl," he whispered against the side of her neck.

Her hands curved around his shoulders, her smile dreamy as she whispered back, "Forever."

He smoothed the hair off her beloved face. The last of his worries slipped away at the acceptance there. "And then some."

"I came for you."

He touched the corner of her smile as it tinged with satisfaction, letting her see the pride he felt at her trust. "Yes. You did. Like a firecracker."

She stroked his cheeks and worked her buttocks tighter against him. "Now, it's your turn."

"I can wait." It might kill him, but he could wait an eternity for her.

Her laugh flowed over his control in a sultry caress, stroking his desire so his cock jerked and danced within the snug confines of her body. "What if I don't want you to?"

"Then I'd say you are one strange lady," he said as she shivered under him, around him.

Her muscles clenched up and down his shaft, milking him. Her eyes closed and her expression dissolved to bliss as he groaned and pushed deeper.

"Damn!"

"Maybe I'm just a very hungry lady." She ran her tongue over her lips leaving a glistening invitation in its wake. "I need you, Mac."

"Dammit Jessie!" He bent and nibbled at her lips. She was tearing his control to shreds. He wiped a bead of sweat from his face with his shoulder, and bit his cheek against the driving need for release raging through his being.

Her lids lifted slowly, her attention focused inward. "What?"

"I don't want to come without you," he groaned through clenched teeth

Her full lips parted in a smile. "Oh, you won't. I'm so close, Mac. So very close. And my ass is so sensitive, I know I'll feel every little drop as you come. I need to feel you come. Can you do that? Can you come for me, Mac?"

"Hell yes!" He would move mountains for her if that would make her happy. Coming when he was so on fire that he felt he would explode was no biggie. He eased his cock out until just the tip stretched her, holding the position for two heartbeats before sliding back in with deliberate gentleness, savoring every caress, letting the fire of desire out of his control, letting it burn over him, over her as he reseated himself to the hilt, rubbing his pelvis against her clit as he pressed deep. She moaned and begged for more. He gave it to her, taking his cue from the shift of her hips, her broken breath when he hit just the right spot.

Two short jabs were all he needed to go hurtling over the edge. His release tore up from his balls in a searing rush. Knowing what she wanted, wanting to give it to her, he pulled back until just the thick head stretched the clasp of her anus and let go, letting her feel the powerful jets bathing her dark channel, groaning her name as she whispered "Oh God" in rhythm with each hard spurt, each time her voice pitching higher until with a shriek, she exploded around him.

He held her gaze as the climax took her, watching anticipation turn to wonder and then to shock as the pleasure tore her away from herself. She took everything from him, every emotion, every demand, and gave it all back tenfold. She was the lover he'd always dreamed of. The one he'd never expected to find and she was here, in his arms. His. He dropped his forehead to hers and kissed her cheek.

Her shudders mellowed to shivers. He eased her legs from his shoulders, being careful, knowing they would be stiff. He would have pulled from her body, but she moued a protest.

He brushed her hair from her cheek and kissed her swollen lips tenderly. "You're sore, honey girl. Let me ease you."

She sighed against his mouth. "I need you just a—" Her voice caught as another shiver came over her. "A little longer. Can you live with that?"

"Oh yeah." He kissed her again, taking her broken breath into his mouth. His lips slid over her cheek. When he reached her ear, he asked, "Do you need me deeper?"

Her lips brushed his jaw as she nodded and drew up her knees. "Yes."

He very carefully worked his cock in. not missing her wince as her flesh parted, nor her sigh of satisfaction as he seated himself to the hilt. He held himself still within her ass, stroking her right breast, fondling her tightly-beaded nipple as the last remnants of her orgasm worked pleasurably over his cock.

With a final shiver and sigh, she dropped her knees to the bed, and relaxed back into the covers.

"All done?" he asked gently, loving the way satisfaction and love lit her face from within.

She nodded. He turned them both onto their sides before pulling out, massaging the base of her spine as the raw muscles protested the friction. She pressed her face into his chest and moaned as the head popped free.

"Ok?" He slid his fingers over the sensitive opening, taking a visceral pleasure in trapping part of him inside her, prolonging their connection.

She nodded and took two deep breaths before sprawling on her back and beaming up at him.

"I'm afraid I'm going to be a very greedy wife," she confessed with an unrepentant smile as she closed her eyes.

He dropped onto the bed beside her and tucked her sated, limp body into his side, his smile matching hers for satisfaction.

He could live with that.

Enjoy this excerpt from

Promises Keep *Promises*

"I'm not going to hurt you, Miss Kincaid."

Thrown off balance, she could only ask, "Why?"

The fingers on the back of her head threaded through the shambles of her bun and massaged small circles on her scalp. "Because it's not my way."

Two hairpins hit the floor with little pings of protest. Mara closed her eyes against the urge to melt into the first kindness she'd experienced in a long, long time. "It's been my experience that men and women define hurt differently."

"I wouldn't base the opinions of a lifetime on the last few months if I were you."

It was probably a trick caused by the way his chest muffled his voice, but somehow his tone sounded kinder and gentler than she'd remembered from their previous encounters. She tried to pull back, but he wouldn't allow it and that fueled her anger more than a slap ever could. "Well, you're not me, and until you've been drugged, torn apart by a man's lust, and then ostracized because of it, you've no right to think anything."

Was that her imagination, or did the man just wince?

"I'm sorry that happened to you."

So was she, but that didn't change anything. "Let me go, Mr. McKinnely."

"I can't do that."

"Yes. You can. All you have to do is drop your hands to your sides and keep them there."

His response to her snapping was a laugh that rumbled up from deep within. "If I do that," he pointed out in a reasonable voice, "you'll fall."

He was right. For all her belligerence, her body was resting against his as if he was the sole support in a world gone awry. Her face flooded with heat. She pushed herself away. Mara ducked her head in the hopes that her hair would hide her embarrassment.

It was a vain hope.

Cougar chuckled and steadied her with a hand to her shoulder. "Doc's back at his place," he said. "We're going to have to get you out there."

She slowly straightened and flicked at his hand with her fingers. "You may go anywhere you like," she snapped. "I'm staying here."

"You are going with me." He slid his hands around her body, lifting her up.

The ease with which he sidestepped her wishes struck a raw nerve. The gentleness with which he accomplished it was even more galling. She didn't understand him, nor did she want to. She just wanted him to go away. Wrapping her fingers in the chest hair peeking between the dangling buttons on his shirt, she twisted viciously, wanting to hurt him the way he was hurting her with his casual arrogance. "Let me down, you, you—"

"Bastard?" he supplied with a lift of his brow. "Son of a bitch?"

"Yes." She twisted harder. She knew it had to hurt, yet he gave no sign. Unless the broadening of his smile could be considered one. Leaning forward, she bit him in the hard muscle of his chest. Let him ignore her now.

He swore and stopped moving. Mara bit down harder, bracing her body for the blow to come.

A thumb and finger surrounded her face and then applied force to her jaw. There came a point when she had to admit his greater strength and unlock her teeth. The body beneath hers was tense, the muscles corded. She could feel him staring at her as he tilted her face up. Finally, she couldn't stand the tension any longer and she opened her eyes. To her surprise, his hand wasn't raised to strike.

She searched his dark face for anger and found none. There was only a strange sorrow and something else. Something so disgusting, she wanted to kill him.

"Don't," she hissed. "Don't you dare pity me!"

He took the bandana from around his neck with his right hand and dabbed at the blood on her mouth.

"Why not?" he asked, transferring the bandana to his chest where he scrubbed with a lot less gentleness. "Nothing much more pathetic than attacking someone who's trying to help."

"I don't want your help," she growled.

"Well, that's neither here nor there, seeing as how I was raised that a man doesn't desert a lady in distress."

"I am not a lady, and I am not in distress."

"Uh-huh."

She was tempted to point out that the only distress she was in was caused by him, but her brief stint with lunacy was apparently over. Angering him while he had her in his arms was no longer desirable. The man was a keg of dynamite. She could tell that from the energy pulsing beneath his skin. She just couldn't figure out what would set him off. An unknown enemy was a dangerous one. She forced the anger out of her tone.

"Mr. McKinnely, I appreciate all you've done for me, but I'm truly all right now. If you'll put me down, I'll be on my way."

If she wasn't mistaken, the look he shot her was reproachful.

"I'll put you down as soon as Doc says it's all right. That was a hell of a shot you took." His eyes ran the length of her body. "And there's not much of you to go around."

Not much to go around? Where on Earth did he plan on...spreading her? She lifted her chin, put on her most off-putting expression, and stated with cool implacability, "I assure you, Mr. McKinnely, I am perfectly fine. Bruised at the most."

A muscle along the side of his jaw snapped tight. "That's something we'll let Doc decide."

"Where do you get this 'we' from? I should know how I feel."

He ignored that. He shot a glare out the window as he hitched her up in his arms. "It shouldn't have happened at all."

"At last we agree on something. Now, if you could just see your way to being reasonable." She pushed tentatively at his chest. Nothing happened.

"I'm always reasonable," he said as he shifted her weight in his arms.

That was debatable. Mara took a calming breath. She could see that he was taking special care not to jostle her more than necessary. Still, it hurt. The minute she gasped, she had his full attention and an apology. She wanted neither.

"Mr. McKinnely, I can see that you are a true gentleman. I'm grateful you stepped in and put an end to that cowboy's insult."

"Sweet talking me isn't going to get you anywhere."

"Excuse me?"

"You're right fond of that expression, aren't you?" He grabbed a black shawl that was hanging on a peg and draped it over her, before continuing, "I'm not putting you down until Doc says it's okay. And leave that on."

Mara kept on pushing at the shawl. "It's hot enough to fry an egg out there."

"You might be in shock."

"For the last time, Mr. McKinnely, I am perfectly fine."

He snagged the edge of the shawl with his fingers, stopping its tumble. "I'm not taking any chances."

"Nobody is asking you to."

"I made you a promise, Miss Kincaid. I intend to keep it."

All this hassle was because of some promise she didn't remember? Lord help her! "What promise?"

He paused in reaching for the door. This close, Mara could see the wrinkles fanning out from his eyes above the sharp plane of his cheekbones. His Indian ancestry was evident in the darkness of his skin and the blue-black sheen of his long hair as it fell on either side of his face in a thick curtain, framing his rugged features. She followed the flow of his hair from his wide forehead to the sharp edge of his cheekbones, down the flat planes of his cheeks to his full, purely masculine lips. And there she paused, her attention caught by the way his mouth lifted slightly at the corners as if in anticipation of a smile. It just seemed so at odds with what she'd heard about him. What her fear said about him. What she knew about him. This was a very, very dangerous man.

She looked at his mouth again and then back at his eyes. At the lines that she knew in her gut were caused by laughter rather than long hours spent in the sun. And adjusted her assessment. Cougar McKinnely was a very dangerous man, but apparently, he was also a dangerous man who liked to laugh.

He dipped his head until his nose tapped hers, bringing her attention back to here and now. She forced herself not to look away from the intensity of his gaze as he uttered with the utmost sincerity, something impossible to believe.

"I promised you everything is going to be all right from here on out."

About the author:

Sarah has traveled extensively throughout her life, living in other cultures, sometimes in areas where electricity was a concept awaiting fruition and a book was an extreme luxury. While she could easily adjust to the lack of electricity, living without the comfort of a good book was intolerable. To fill the void, she bought pencil and paper and sketched out her own story, and in the process, discovered the joy of writing. She's been at it ever since. http://www.sarahmccarty.com

Sarah welcomes mail from readers. You can write to her c/o Ellora's Cave Publishing at 1056 Home Avenue, Akron OH 44310-3502.

Why an electronic book?

We live in the Information Age—an exciting time in the history of human civilization in which technology rules supreme and continues to progress in leaps and bounds every minute of every hour of every day. For a multitude of reasons, more and more avid literary fans are opting to purchase e-books instead of paperbacks. The question to those not yet initiated to the world of electronic reading is simply: *why?*

1. *Price.* An electronic title at Ellora's Cave Publishing and Cerridwen Press runs anywhere from 40-75% less than the cover price of the exact same title in paperback format. Why? Cold mathematics. It is less expensive to publish an e-book than it is to publish a paperback, so the savings are passed along to the consumer.
2. *Space.* Running out of room to house your paperback books? That is one worry you will never have with electronic novels. For a low one-time cost, you can purchase a handheld computer designed specifically for e-reading purposes. Many e-readers are larger than the average handheld, giving you plenty of screen room. Better yet, hundreds of titles can be stored within your new library—a single microchip. (Please note that Ellora's Cave and Cerridwen Press does not endorse any specific brands. You can check our website at www.ellorascave.com or

www.cerridwenpress.com for customer recommendations we make available to new consumers.)

3. *Mobility.* Because your new library now consists of only a microchip, your entire cache of books can be taken with you wherever you go.
4. *Personal preferences are accounted for.* Are the words you are currently reading too small? Too large? Too... **ANNOYING**? Paperback books cannot be modified according to personal preferences, but e-books can.
5. *Instant gratification.* Is it the middle of the night and all the bookstores are closed? Are you tired of waiting days—sometimes weeks—for online and offline bookstores to ship the novels you bought? Ellora's Cave Publishing sells instantaneous downloads 24 hours a day, 7 days a week, 365 days a year. Our e-book delivery system is 100% automated, meaning your order is filled as soon as you pay for it.

Those are a few of the top reasons why electronic novels are displacing paperbacks for many an avid reader. As always, Ellora's Cave and Cerridwen Press welcomes your questions and comments. We invite you to email us at service@ellorascave.com, service@cerridwenpress.com or write to us directly at: 1056 Home Ave. Akron OH 44310-3502.

ELLORA'S CAVE
ROMANTICA PUBLISHING

Printed in the United States
40438LVS00001B/28-51

9 781419 951701